'Such an astounding and accomplished novel. It was an absolute joy to read. Simply put, I loved it.'
Sarah Winman, author of *Still Life*

One of the lucky few with a job during the Depression, Peggy's just starting out in life. She's a bagging girl at the Angliss meatworks in Footscray, a place buzzing with life as well as death, where the gun slaughterman Jack has caught her eye – and she his.

How is her life connected to Hilda's, almost a hundred years later, locked inside during a plague, or La's, further on again, a singer working shifts in a warehouse as her eggs are frozen and her voice is used by AI bots? Let alone Maz, far removed in time, diving for remnants of a past that must be destroyed?

Is it by the river that runs through their stories, eternal yet constantly changing – or by the mysterious Hummingbird Project and the great question of whether the march of progress can ever be reversed?

Propulsive, tender and engrossing, this genre-bending novel is a feast for the heart as well as the mind and senses, confirming Mildenhall as one of the most ambitious and dynamic writers in the country.

Praise for *The Hummingbird Effect*

'Mildenhall captures the urgency of a species hurtling relentlessly through progress . . . I am in awe of this timely, fierce, brain-stretching novel, told with such warmth and generosity. Mildenhall at her finest.'
Laura Jean McKay, author of *The Animals in That Country*

'Exhilarating, vibrant, daring. A triumph of storytelling and of compassion.'
Toni Jordan, author of *Nine Days*

'Reading *The Hummingbird Effect* is like navigating rapids: you don't know what's going to happen next or when you're going to come up for air. A remarkable achievement. I couldn't put it down.'
Sophie Cunningham, author of *This Devastating Fever*

'An ambitious, defiant, electrifying juggernaut. Kate Mildenhall cements her status as a titan of Australian literature by raising the bar to dizzying heights. An incredible achievement. I didn't want it to end.'
Chris Flynn, author of *Mammoth*

'*The Hummingbird Effect* is exceptional. Both highly creative and hugely readable, I loved it.'
Jane Harper, author of *The Dry*

'A timeless and timely exploration of our capacities to destroy and to love, and of the stories that connect us – and might even save us. In this powerful and dazzling book, Kate Mildenhall brilliantly pushes language to its limits and asks, What's worth saving? *The Hummingbird Effect* is an urgent, gorgeous, thrilling, page turner. A must read!'
Sarah Sentilles, author of *Stranger Care: A Memoir of Loving What Isn't Ours*

'Original, mind-bending and beautifully written. These characters, connected across time and place, are absolutely alive on the page. Together, their stories reveal the reverberating consequences of violence for us and our planet, and the redeeming power of love – in all its forms.'
Inga Simpson, author of *Willowman*

'I loved this book. It is urgent and questioning, concerned but ultimately hopeful. The writing remembers our past, honours our present and imagines our future. It is often sublime and sometimes astonishing. I will be recommending this book to everyone I know.'
Pip Williams, author of *The Bookbinder of Jericho*

'It's a blinder . . . I read it sideways and with clenched teeth.'
Helen Garner, author of *Everywhere I Look*

'Spending my reading hours with the characters of *The Hummingbird Effect* was something like a visit home, to my childhood, and the women who surrounded me. This is an astounding book, both innovative and grounded. I loved it.'
Tony Birch, author of *The White Girl*

'Kate Mildenhall orchestrates this shape-shifting novel with extraordinary flair. Her imaginative range is astonishing. *The Hummingbird Effect* is audacious fiction that engages wisely and tenderly with pressing concerns.'
Michelle de Kretser, author of *Scary Monsters*

'*The Hummingbird Effect* is deeply grounded in place and character, and speaks to the interdependence of all living things. Mildenhall writes about these women and their relationships with empathy, wit, and ferocity. An exquisite, unforgettable read.'
Grace Chan, author of *Every Version of You*

'Four women, four stories, crossing back and forth between the past and a richly imagined future. A deep, quiet tribute to *Cloudstreet*, which never forgets that character and place are the beginning of any great novel.'
Tegan Bennett Daylight, author of *The Details*

'A stunning and intricate novel, masterfully braiding the lives of its characters across time. Vivid, inventive, tender – a beautifully rendered mosaic of a book. With luminous prose linking past and future, *The Hummingbird Effect* is brilliant storytelling at its best.'
Else Fitzgerald, author of *Everything Feels Like the End of the World*

'This book digs deep into the universality of love, family, hardship, sisterhood, plague, disruption and, above all, connection and empowerment. Experimental, mind-bending, provocative.'
Karen Viggers, author of *The Lightkeeper's Wife*

'Kate Mildenhall has outrageous confidence in her sparkling narrative, in her capabilities. As she should. This is a profound conversation about all those things we put off talking about, seen in the context of the past, the present and the future.'
Sydney Morning Herald

'Spellbinding, genre-defying, and powerful in its vision of the future . . . *The Hummingbird Effect* is a devastating novel that exposes the ways the future is seeded in the past.'
Australian Book Review

'Kate Mildenhall is such an exciting writer to read . . . This generous, playful novel speaks to themes of climate change, survival and holding space for each other, as well as the enduring power of female friendship.'
The Guardian

'This highly ambitious, tense novel makes you think hard about current world challenges and stays with you well after the final page, Mildenhall showing how humankind's decisions affect generations.'
New Zealand Listener

'An exhilarating page-turner . . . *The Hummingbird Effect* is an immensely enjoyable read with some vital messages at its heart.'
Aniko Press

'Rendered in Mildenhall's signature lyrical prose, this ambitious novel explores the issues of our time through a relatable cast of characters.'
ArtsHub

THE HUMMING BIRD EFFECT

Also by Kate Mildenhall

Skylarking
The Mother Fault

THE HUMMING BIRD EFFECT

KATE MILDENHALL

SCRIBNER

SCRIBNER

First published in Australia in 2023 by Scribner,
an imprint of Simon & Schuster Australia
Suite 19A, Level 1, Building C, 450 Miller Street, Cammeray, NSW 2062
This edition published in 2024

Simon & Schuster: Celebrating 100 Years of Publishing in 2024.
Sydney New York London Toronto New Delhi
Visit our website at scribner.com.au

SCRIBNER and design are registered trademarks of The Gale Group, Inc.,
used under licence by Simon & Schuster LLC.

10 9 8 7 6 5 4 3 2

© Kate Mildenhall 2023

All rights reserved. No part of this publication may be reproduced, stored in a retrieval system, or transmitted in any form or by any means, electronic, mechanical, photocopying, recording or otherwise, without prior permission of the publisher.

The title of the novel and the definition of the hummingbird effect that appears on p. 95 come from Steven Johnson's *How We Got to Now: Six Innovations That Made The Modern World* (2014).
The artwork on p. 172 was created by Eva Harbridge.
Parts of the 'Hummingbird' sections in the novel were written with the aid of ChatGPT.
The description of life starting in the womb of one's grandmother was inspired by Lucy Peach's *Period Queen* (2020).

A catalogue record for this book is available from the National Library of Australia

9781761424946 (paperback)
9781760855291 (ebook)

Cover design by Josh Durham
Typeset by Midland Typesetters in Adobe Garamond Pro
Printed and bound in Australia by Griffin Press

MIX
Paper | Supporting responsible forestry
FSC® C018684

The paper this book is printed on is certified against the Forest Stewardship Council® Standards. Griffin Press holds chain of custody certification SCS-COC-001185. FSC® promotes environmentally responsible, socially beneficial and economically viable management of the world's forests.

For Grandmama, with eternal love and gratitude xx

Patsy Cullinan (nee Cull)
March 28, 1931 – June 9, 2022

Before Now Next
   Footscray, 1933
      Sanctuary Gardens Aged Care, 2020
         Footscray, 2031
            Newcoast, 2181
               Hummingbird Project™
            The Forest, 2181
         Before Now Next
      Footscray, 2031
   Sanctuary Gardens Aged Care, 2020
Footscray, 1933
Hummingbird Project™
The Inlet, 2181
   Footscray, 2031
      Sanctuary Gardens Aged Care, 2020
         Footscray, 1933
            Hummingbird Project™
         Footscray, 2031
      The Island, 2181
   Sanctuary Gardens Aged Care, 2020
Footscray, 1933
Before Now Next

The basic behaviour mode of the world system is exponential growth of population and capital, followed by collapse.
The Limits to Growth, 1972

When we try to pick out anything by itself, we find it hitched to everything else in the universe.
John Muir, *My First Summer in the Sierra*, 1911

You can't kill the future in us.
Lidia Yuknavitch, *Thrust*, 2022

∞

Before Now Next

Below the surface through the rippled roiling waters of us, down, deep down, silver scales flash against a piece of buckled tin tossed in, an old engine grown slick with river muck and weed and here, snouting forward in the murky dark – what's this? – a bundle of rags attracting the bottom dwellers. Glide on past before it reveals its innards.

Hidey places, deep water places, rock and mud and quiet secret hush places, river mutter, water whisper, babble gurgle seep. Listen, shhhh, for what we know is back and it is forward, memory and dream. Glide on, glide back – these ragthings – a babe come too early, maybe, a mother who knows the river will swallow her secret whole.

Flow back, against the timestream, the land here is busy: it folds, uplifts, erodes until it settles, layers over and upon itself, bedding down for an epoch or two. Flow forward, just a little, volcanoes erupt, lava spewing from thin fissures and vents and spreading across the plains, bulbous pillows where the molten rock hits the cold sea, a meeting place, breaking place, we delta with saltwater, make swamp, meet other rivers around the edge of the sunkland that will be the bay. The sea rises up again and laps at the place that will be the town. It will not be the last time the sea rises here.

Nosing into the bay, a bigfloat spots a staying place, a place to steal, to dream, a builtplace for a million strangers who will arrive and never stop arriving. Blow rock wide open, carve places so barges can bring sheep, so sheep can hoove land, eat grass, herd upward through tin and steel to slaughter, one after another after another forever and infinity so that shit and guts and blood run where river ran before.

The fish no longer rise like waves, silver glittery, hooked out by hunger, belly up with the poisonous belching of the big louds, gone down down deep in us to quiet and wait. The first people who tended this land for all time are no longer bemused at the ghost men who devour the land, spread disease, take the children.

Here. Upstream, downstream, timestream of always. We slide past the banks where you do what you do. We see. We wait.

∞

Footscray, 1933

The meatworks is not the centre of town, but it feeds so many hungry mouths – literally and figuratively – that it has assumed that status. It sits on the highest point to the east of the river and the buildings and cattle yards stretch all the way down to the water. North, this slope is interrupted by the strap of Ballarat Road – busier every day now with cars and trucks tooting the stock and the bicycles and the horses and carts that still make use of the thoroughfare. The river loops around and then flows directly south (more or less, nodding to the slum of Dudley's Flat as it passes by) to meet with the Yarra before spilling out its dirty fluids into the bay. From the centre of town and west, west, west – the noise of industry gobbles up the basalt plains.

Just south of the works, beyond the high metal fences and across Newell Street, is where the boss himself lives in his redbrick with the big tree out the front dropping fat yellow grapefruits on the grass (fanciest place this side of the river, for a way). Then Railway Place, a narrow street mirroring the train tracks as it peters down to meet the flats.

Nobody dreams of living at the bottom of Railway Place – stinking of swamp and sadness. The last cottage was built at the same time as the rest, but you wouldn't know it to look at it. The story goes that shortly after the Hicks family moved in, Mrs Hicks died in childbirth (poor love, should've stopped at five) and the house began, that very day, to fall into disrepair. The grass grew high and the weeds grew higher and despite there being no woman in the house, children still seemed to multiply down there as though the fertile earth of the river was conceiving them and spitting them out half grown and snotty-nosed in the cast-off pants of their snotty-nosed siblings. The despair at the bottom of Railway Place threatened to leach up and infect the rest of the street.

The Murrays, in the second-to-last house, nailed extra palings to the top of the fence when it became clear that Mr Hicks paid no heed to their requests for the children to stop throwing stones through their windows, or for the offensive refuse in his yard to be dealt with. But the O'Loughlins, two doors up, God-fearing as they were, continued to ask Mr Hicks to service on a Sunday (he never once accepted) and did not chide the children when they brazenly picked plump apricots from their tree. Perhaps it was the O'Loughlins who invited the despair to creep upwards a little, all the way to where Harry Bailey, the candlemaker from number 10, drowned himself down the river on a Sunday morning.

The scream brings everyone at this end of Railway Place out into the street. It is a Sunday after all, and for a long time after they'll all wonder why the candlemaker would do such a thing on that day, of all days. Why not wait until a Tuesday? A Thursday afternoon? Something with a little less weight to it.

They've all had their Sunday lunch, those who go to mass have returned, those who don't have taken a walk by the river, or had an extra cup of tea between the loads of washing, and in that strange timeless Sunday afternoon the copper knocks on Millie Bailey's door and tells her they've found her husband. Gone and drowned himself in the stinking river, guts full of booze, found him caught in a pontoon just south of the candle works. What a way to go. The saving grace was that he'd done it in such a way that it might, if one stretched the imagination, be considered an accident – although everyone knew Harry had been laid off the month before from the soap works and that Millie was already doing double shifts at Kinnear's to get enough into the mouths of the kids and to hang on tight to the tenancy of the little terrace house. The shame of it, of all of that, was enough to drive a man all the way to the bitter end. He wasn't the first. And he wouldn't be the last.

Lil Martin would never say it aloud, but she wondered at the foolishness of giving man such pride and such capacity for violence housed in the same body. The women of Railway Place were as hungry – as shamed, as beaten down by the cuts, the susso, the greyness of it all – as the men were, but she couldn't imagine any of them drowning themselves in the sludge of the river. If they did, they'd be too considerate to let anyone find them. They'd do it neater. So as not to cause any trouble. When a woman was broken, she tried to fade away. Lil thought of her mother. Yes, that's it: a woman tried to make herself invisible, fainter and fainter until you just forgot she was there. A man had to finish himself with blood and gore and filth, having the last bloody word, yet again.

On that Sunday afternoon, Lil lets the women who live closest to the Baileys do the comforting, handle the practicalities of dealing with the police and notifying family and, above all, getting a stiff drink into Millie so that she will stop being quite so loud in her rage at her dead husband for leaving her all alone in this mess of a time. 'Hush now, Millie,' Lil can hear the women saying in chorus as they gather round and hold her, 'there'll be time for that, think of the children now.'

Lil turns back inside and starts chopping onions. Late into the night she will braise and stew and bake until there is nothing left in the ice chest or the pantry, and early morning before the wretched household wakes, she will leave the covered pots and biscuit tins in a neat row on Millie's doorstep. And on Thursday she will don her one good black tea-dress, used exclusively for funerals – she notes with some satisfaction that it fits as well as the day she wore it to her father's, twelve years ago – and she will walk to Donald Street with the rest of the neighbours to pay her respects. A few won't come – the die-hard Catholics at number four – but the rest, even the church-going ones, seem to accept that this is a time like no other.

Millie Bailey will keep her head high, held up by the women of Railway Place, by the workers from Kinnear's, and her four children will trail her, the youngest with his mouth covered in the sticky pink of a lolly someone has given him to make sure he doesn't make a racket.

And despite the fact that Lil thinks him weak and selfish and a fool, she will stand and bow her head with all the other mourners, cowed as they are by the times and the uncertainty and the way the world feels like it is shifting under their feet. She will understand how Harry Bailey was brought undone. How the act of pulling himself from his bed each day to work the same hours in the same stinking factory became too much, how the coins must have felt like they were slipping through his fingers as they fell further behind in their rent, how a man might feel like he had nothing at all. A future so bleak that it couldn't be glimpsed.

Yet all the cuts of grief Lil has taken in her own life – for her father, for Tommy, her mother – have not untethered her, rather they have healed over rough and hard and ugly, layers of scar tissue that bind her up and make her harder still. She could no more drown herself in that saltwater river than she could fly to the moon.

And anyway, there are six houses between all that sadness and number sixteen. Lil's place. And now there'll be a stranger in the house, or not a stranger exactly, but not her mother, not her dad. She wonders what they might have made of it. *Oh well*, she thinks, *not your decision to make any more. It's mine.*

Lil Martin juts her chin a little higher.

It's hot as hell on the Saturday morning Peggy stops outside the gate of 16 Railway Place. Sweat at the back of her knees, prickling in her armpits, she looks around then lifts her right elbow quickly, sniffing to see if she passes muster. From what she's heard about Lil Martin, it won't do to turn up for an interview with a stink about her. She's a worker, Lil, but she's not like the rest of them. Been at Angliss all her life, just like her dad, Kathleen said, and she's in the office, closer to the boss – closer to God. They all laugh together when she says that. That might be so, but beggars can't be choosers, and right now Peggy is a girl who needs a room and apparently Lil Martin has one.

Peggy smooths her hair back with the lick of sweat on her temples and pushes the gate open. It doesn't creak like the one at her mum's place. But then Lil Martin didn't have five kids swinging the thing to and fro every hour of the day, and an old man who'd finally had enough and left her, swinging it shut so hard on his way out that the top hinge popped. Peggy's mum still hasn't seen fit to have it fixed. Won't have to now she's leaving town herself, taking the little ones to Ballarat to stay with her sister until Dad comes home. On Tuesday. Mum's leaving town *on Tuesday*, Peggy reminds herself as she squints her eyes against the hot morning glare to check out Lil Martin's place.

The gate opens to a neat brick path, a lemon tree on one side and an orange on the other. It's a slim, single-front place, the porch at the front is trimmed with white iron lattice and casts good shade over the front window. She wonders if that might be the room available. Would be nice, to look out on the street. Not that she'll mind if it's a room further back. She's started imagining a room without little sisters squeezed into it, a room all to herself. Peggy grins. Best get on with it, she thinks, and steps out down the path.

Lil Martin is a tall woman, late thirties, it's hard to tell. Story goes that she's never married, cared instead for her invalid mother after her father topped himself. Peggy's never met her face to face, only seen her striding across the bluestone courtyard of the meatworks back to the office. She's heard the girls giving Lil a gentle ribbing around the bagging table, office work being a step above what Peggy and the girls do on the third floor of the works, cutting and piecing and sewing back together. At least they are only cutting cloth, unlike two floors below, small mercies. And Lil Martin does neither; her hands are marked only by the ink of time cards and pay slips, and even though Peggy's pretty sure the pay's still piddling (why else would she need a boarder in?), she imagines one day in the future when she might turn left into the office instead of right onto the factory floor and busy herself with numbers instead of cotton. Mrs Baker, third class teacher at Hyde Street Primary, said Peggy had a head for numbers, that she could have gone on to secretarial, but her dad just laughed and told her to get out there quick smart and find a job to pay her way and help her mother.

There is a teapot, some gingernut biscuits, porcelain cups laid out on a white and yellow tablecloth. Lil is a steady pour, her back straight, no apron over her housedress. If she put on a bit of lipstick and let her dark hair go loose a little around the face, she'd be a looker, even as old as she is. Peggy listens politely as Lil tells her she's lived in the house since it was built over twenty years ago and never had a boarder, but since her mother's death last month and the benefits stopping, she's decided it's necessary.

'Angliss really built this for you?' Peggy asks.

Lil frowns, scoffs. 'For his workers. It was my father's. All the cottages along this street were built for workers, and the ones down the bottom of Newell too.'

Peggy sips her tea, taking in the neat little kitchen, the window out to the backyard with a big plum tree. 'Reckon my dad would say Angliss sounds too good to be true.'

Lil leans back. 'Don't know about that. I suppose he'd put every meat works family in a cottage if he could.'

'He could afford to, couldn't he? A man like him?'

Lil doesn't respond, instead standing and gesturing to the door behind her with a hand. 'Shall I show you around?'

Peggy nods and follows Lil down the step and into the sunken vestibule as Lil points out the sinks for laundry, the ice chest and the door that leads out into the fernery and beyond to the outhouse, straight rows of leafy plants, a blockish incinerator and the plum tree, green and shady at the rear of the yard. There is none of the chaos of Peggy's place, and as they head back inside she reckons it's because there are no sticky handprints on doorjambs, no sour lines of nappies drying in the laundry.

There is a small front sitting room, a wireless and a green couch. Next to that, the room that will be hers – clean and simple and waiting. Lil explains it has been her sewing room.

Lil gestures to the room off the kitchen. 'My mother's,' she says. 'I haven't had the chance yet . . .' She pauses and seems at a loss for a moment.

'Of course,' says Peggy. She likes this woman. 'If the room's available, I'd be delighted to take it.'

Lil looks at her, startled but then nods, names her price. 'Including meals,' she adds, 'but we'll share the cooking – you can cook, can't you?'

Peggy straightens up, wonders what counts as cooking, decides she'll just have to wing it. 'Of course.'

'Don't mind a drink in the house, but no visitors after hours.'

'Wouldn't dream of it.'

'The rest in that team of yours certainly do.'

Peggy bites her lip to hide her grin.

'I'll take one week's board in advance.'

'I've got enough saved to make it a month, the girls said that would be—'

'Well, the girls should also know I pay your wage, Miss Donnelly, so I'm confident I can recoup any losses should you decide the room is not to your liking.'

'Peggy – please.'

Lil leans over to take her cup, stands, and Peggy realises it's time to go.

'Is tomorrow too soon?'

Lil smiles now, a real one. 'That'll be fine.'

That first night the girl arrives, after they've brought in her small case, somewhat shyly shared a beer, negotiated who will use the bathroom first and said goodnight, Lil lies awake listening. Her mother was so still and quiet in her last years, so it's been a long time since Lil's heard the shuffles of other people in this house at night.

She remembers, before her mother lost the baby all those years ago, the hum of noise from the kitchen, her parents talking, voices so low she couldn't make out a word, the clatter of dishes, sometimes the wireless, all of it like a warm glow that would wash over her and send her off to sleep.

The quiet is a beast. Because it's never quiet, really. In the dark she can hear the whole town mumbling, the lovers still out dancing, the late shift at the works, the trains in their sidings, dogs howling, the shatter of glass, and all of it, every sound is alive and happening and might as well be drumming a beat – *you are alone, alone, alone.*

But now, is the girl humming? The sound of cupboard doors and soft padding footsteps on the floors.

The board money will set things right. If she wanted to, she could take another girl on too, there's enough who need a room these days, and that would mean she could put a little more away each week. Something for when the time comes that Angliss doesn't want her in his office anymore. Might decide to take back the house.

But it would be someone young, like Peggy, who'd take the other room, and then the two of them would probably be best friends, heading out on a Friday night to the Orama on a double date, giddy with it all, and Lil would be alone again.

No, she'll see how things get on, first. Might be good for her, this breath of fresh air in the house, might help her remember all the things she wanted from the world, might just give her that.

There's a shake in Jack's hands this morning that only a nip of the good stuff will still. One drink for knock-off turned into kick-on last night, and while he wasn't sorry then, he's bloody sore about it now. Doesn't help that the morning is already hot, gearing up to be another scorcher. He pockets the flask, wishes he could feel the slosh of enough for after in it, but that'll have to wait for payday now. He has a smoke so Baxter, the prick of a foreman, won't smell the grog on his breath. He'd like to explain to the man one day that he'd rather have a drink and a steady hand than shake his way through a cut, but a bloke like Baxter wouldn't understand.

He sniffs. Spits. Tosses the fag end.

There's metal in the air, Jack always tastes it on his tongue just before the whistle goes. He walks through the gates at the back of the crowd. Can afford to now, five years on the floor and son of Billy King. No one expects Jack King to be first at the gate these days. He's earned his place.

He remembers those years when he was apprenticed, the way he saw the older slaughts as gods. Wonders if these young pricks think the same of him. Not that his dad would ever think he measured up. As a kid, he watched those slaughtermen bright with blood and thick with muscle, like they were dancing. Shakes his head. Doesn't do to have your brain loose before the first cut, you want that one quick and true to set you right for the day.

'Jack,' the murmurs go, the heads nod. 'Morning, cobber,' 'Morning Jacko,' a chorus that follows him through the gates and past the local kill floor and into the tea room where he stores the lunch tin his ma's packed for him and buckles his belt, the weight of his knives against his flank.

The smell of sheep. They're a month into the season and his hands are well greased with lanolin. A good thing. Even five years in there are nicks and cuts, times when the wrong flesh comes under the blade. He doesn't mind it. Every job has its penance.

'Orright, boys?' he asks the crew when he enters the room.

Jack's one of them now. Stepped right into his father's shoes, rest his fiery soul. Ten years gone. The cancer went so fast, so bloody fast, none of them had time to think before the thing had wormed its way through his lungs and he was gone, just like that. Jack's ma weeping, what was to become of them, and Jack stepping up, man of the house now, to look after his sisters, his little brother. His ma, angry that the bloody thing had taken her husband so quick when he'd outsmarted the enemy for three years over there in some other bastard's war.

Jack settles in his spot. Knows the creak in the floor under his left boot, the rhythm and swing of Knobby, tall and gangly, to his right. The grunt of old Budge Macfarlane, legend of the floor, to his left. A sweet spot, to be next to the man himself. Jack swelled with pride when he moved up from the local floor to this, the export floor. Needs a finer cut. And right here, next to the Budge. These days Jack hits tally before the great man. Feels the thrill of it ripple through his forearms, his shoulders, down the spine. Who'd have thought? Maybe his dad is looking down on him, slight nod of the head. All that's needed. Just enough to know he might finally have done the old man proud.

A couple of minutes before the first lambs arrive. Jack likes the lamb season, solo work instead of with the other blokes when the bloody cows come in. Never know if you'll get stuck with some slaught not willing to pull his weight. He can hear the rattling workings of the place kick in. Positions himself in front of the wooden barrel to catch the blood, not a bit to waste. Down by his right foot is the open chute where he'll drop the heart, liver, kidneys, and by his left, the chute for the rest of the offal. Tests and adjusts the weight of his pouch, his knives.

'Here she comes!'

And he is ready for her. He embraces the skittish animal, feels the pulse of her, warm beneath the shorn wool. Holds her firm, legs caught between his knees, forelegs held steady over his left arm, and cuts her neck clean and true. She hasn't made a sound. The blood squirts in pulses, legs kick in a quick twostep and then she is limp in his arms as he attaches the loop and hook to her hind legs, yanks on the pulley and heaves her up to hang and bleed.

A moment to breathe. Check the men down the line. He's ahead already, not by much. Muscles twinge. Should've kept up the footy to keep himself limber. He'd have done all right, could've even been chosen for the League if it wasn't for that bloody great slice in his side that still gives him grief.

Bled out, she's ready for skinning. Slice at the shin, off with her head, toss it all into the barrel, boys'll sort it down the chute, for glue, for fertiliser, every piece a part of a pound, like Angliss tells them. You're holding money in your hands, don't let it trickle out, what's good for the business is good for you men. True to his word he's kept as many of them on as he could, while all around them businesses have whittled themselves down to nothing to try to survive.

One cut now from throat to arse and then hook between the shins, and peel her down. When it's done well, it's a thing to behold, the gentle sucking sound of the skin tearing away leaving behind a layer of white-yellow fat. Off in one, toss the pelt on the belt and off to the fellmongery, and he's satisfied that it's a good one, clean and full. The boys'll be happy with that.

Split her inner open now, knife in at the spot so it's one flick and she's splayed before him, glistening ripe fruit waiting to be plucked. Heart, flick, liver, flick, kidneys, flick, twisting handful of intestines to the other side, careful now with the cut, the bowel, the rest, flick flick, and then she's just ribs and flesh, it's a beautiful thing, this cavity inside her.

He spins her round once to check, marvels at the efficiency with which live sheep becomes carcass, cos now she's ready for the inspector to stamp a red mark on her arse and send her down to the freezer where she'll hang tonight. Then a truck, a train and a goddamn ship and she's off to be hung in a butcher shop in the motherland, and isn't that a thought – Jack King's lamb, travelling all around the world.

As he pushes her off down the belt, there's a hoy and a yell, and some poor bastard downstairs has cut himself and Jack shouldn't but he grins, just a little, waiting for the next lamb to come in, cos it's not him getting cut anymore, and that feels good.

Even in a place as big as the Angliss Meatworks, word gets around quick that Will Jacobson's got himself cut and the doc has said it's a job for the hospital. Peggy jumps back from the sewing table when someone says his brother ought to know.

'I'll go!' she says, ducking out the door and pretending she can't hear Mavis the forelady, with a face like the rear end of a cow, telling her to get back to her place, there's a tally to be made and no one can go skiving off for gossip.

But it's not gossip, Peggy thinks, to make sure a man knows his brother is getting stitched, and even though she's almost certain word will have reached him on the kill floor from the boning room quicker than she can get there, she'll take her chance to spy on the slaughtermen.

There's still an hour till the whistle blows for lunch so the place is bustling. She's getting used to that now. Those first few weeks the stink of it all was nearly too much. True, Footscray itself has never smelled that flash, but up close the works were all shit and boiling tallow, the stench of stuff so foul she didn't even want to know what caused it. Now she's six months in, and she's not even the newest girl, just bloody glad Kathleen could find her a spot.

To her left, the cattle yards stretch all the way out to Ballarat Road, empty for the moment, but she can almost hear the drovers bringing the herd down the hill and across the river from the sale yards at Newmarket. They'll be stocked full by tonight, ready for the kill floor in the morning. She's learned the way it all works. Not that she gets to see much of it, up in the bagging room, sewing the cotton sleeves for the carcasses with the other girls. But they get to speak to the boys on tea break and at lunch, and there's already been a dance or two, and this weekend – the picnic!

Stepping out from the quiet cool of the hang room onto the kill floor shocks her, even though she's peeked in a couple of times. The bloodied walls, the men's aprons scarlet-splattered and gleaming, bellows cut short. It's strange that this, a place where things come to die, is the place that feels most alive. It's hot and Peggy runs the fleshy nub of her palm once across her forehead, prickles of sweat on her skin.

She likes the way the slaughts wear their footy guernseys, the wool pulled tight across shoulders and chests, lean from the lift and the cut of each day. She can see them wash up after they reach tally if she gets the good perch in the bagging room with a view of the sinks. They know they are being watched, of course. She likes the way they strut and stretch under the eyes of all the women. It's nice for the tables to be turned for once. Under the taps, they wipe their hands over bloodied forearms and the gutters run pink bubbles. God only knows how the wives and mothers get the stains out of their clothes, over and over and over again.

The way their arms move together is sort of beautiful. Muscles rising under their skin all at the same time. Blades flashing, creating a pattern, man, lamb, man, lamb, repeating all the way into the shadow of the long room.

'You right, love?'

The man closest to her wipes his blade on his thigh and slides it in its sheath. A slaughterman takes pride in his tools – the girls have told her this. The tools belong to the man, not to the boss, or the factory. His skill is in the way he handles his knives, oils the pouches, wipes the blood from the belt before clearing it from his hand or his face.

She blurts out her words. 'Looking for Jacobson? His brother—'

'Yeah, he knows.' The man goes back to cutting. 'Yer better clear out before the foreman sees ya.'

The next slaughterman raises his head and laughs. 'Gah, come on, Bluey, sight for sore eyes. You stay as long as you want, luv.' Other men laugh but keep their eyes on their cuts. It's a race to meet tally.

She hovers, feeling the pulse of the floor flicker within her. Her eyes go to the tallest slaughtermen – three up from where she stands. She watches the muscle move in his shoulder as he flashes the knife around the carcass in front of him. She knows him. Everyone does. Jack King, up-and-comer, son of a slaughterman, probably the great-great-great-grandson of one. The women say his name a little breathlessly, they tell of how he copped a bad cut when he started. Had to take a month off before he could come back to work. But he did. She watches him work. He looks like a man who gets what he wants.

The foreman is suddenly beside her. 'Who's doing your job, then, while you stand there gawping at my blokes?'

She blushes, apologises, glances back to see Jack King look up and grin at her.

She'll cop an ear bashing when she gets back, but bloody hell – she thinks of that smile – it'll be worth it.

The boners – a sharp little group of them – cluster on the portside of the steamer looking out to the stretch of the bay. They laugh, back-slap, lean out over the rail to the wind. A couple of them turn their heads back to look at Peggy and the other girls sitting on the hard wooden benches of the boat, and their laughter has an undercurrent. Jack King is the one you notice first. In a shirt pulled tight across his shoulders, there's a pleasing angle to his waist, the curve of his arse. Peggy rolls the word – *arse* – around in her mouth, her lips sealed, and smiles. She knows she is not as pretty as some of the others. That he has no reason to look at her over Beth, with her tight curls and lipstick, or May, whose golden hair, even pulled back as it is in the bagging room, turns the head of the packers when they wheel in the trolleys. But Peggy is one of the youngest, only nineteen, and she knows that helps turn a head, too. Besides, there was that grin. Been keeping her warm three days now. Jeez she's glad she waved Ma and the kids off last week, insisting she was good to stay, that Lil Martin had the nicest, cleanest room going in all of Footscray. Footscray may be a stinking hole, but it is hers, and she doesn't want to leave it.

Especially not right now, when despite the fact that the whole world seems doom and gloom and half the town is on the susso, she senses she is right on the cusp of something and she doesn't know what it is – only that it sends a thrill tingling up her spine and across her shoulders all the way to her fingertips.

From far out in the bay, Peggy can make out the coloured beach boxes of Black Rock nestled at the base of the scrubby cliffs. Her father took her once, but he forgot to bring her bathing suit. Peggy remembers the scratch of the sand and how hot she was before he let her wade in the shallows with her skirt hitched high.

She likes how the old paddle steamer cleaves from the land and heads out further to sea. The clean wind of it, blowing away the stink of Footscray that she fears has sunk deep into her skin, the flesh beneath, the very bones of her.

'Why did no one say to bring a coat?' Beth moans as she links her arm through Peggy's, nestling in and shivering dramatically.

'We all did, you goat, you just never listen,' Peggy says.

Tall Nell, with her wild frizz of hair buffeted now by the easterly, arches one eyebrow and laughs. 'Would have spoiled your outfit, wouldn't it?' she says, and there is an undertow of mean.

'You look a treat, Beth, like always,' says Esther, hugging in close on the other side so that Peggy can pull away, moving to the rail. She has never been out on the bay before, and even though the day is cloudy she is in awe of it all. The sea, the slow movement of the steamer as it rocks from side to side. The girls warned her she might be sick, but no, it almost feels like dancing! Or no, not that, like rocking her younger brothers to sleep when they were babies. As lovely as that.

She breathes deeply, closing her eyes and imagining her chest clearing out.

'Feels good, don't it?'

Opening her eyes, she turns to see Jack King standing beside her. Brown forearms resting on the chipped white steel of the rail, knee cocked, leaning into the wind. She's asked around a little more the last couple of days, not too obvious. Word is clear, he's a bit of a player. But when you're as tall as him, and as good looking, well, it figures.

She looks away from him and out to sea again, so he won't see her neck start to redden.

'My first time on a boat.'

'Serious?' Jack smiles – a sudden squall of a smile that crinkles his eyes. 'Well, there's a first time for everything, isn't there, and it's always a bit of a thrill.'

Good Lord, the way his voice lowers at the end, so that she knows exactly what he is saying while he pretends he is saying nothing at all, and she thinks that she might burst if he comes a single inch closer to her.

'Your first butcher's picnic, then, too?'

She allows herself to glance at him, nodding.

'You girls gonna join us in a beer?'

She laughs, tries to sound brash but knows she is probably failing. 'Thought Mr Angliss only packed lemonade for the ladies?'

'I suppose when Mr Angliss isn't here,' he says, and pauses to look away, deliberate and slow, 'then what he doesn't know won't hurt him.'

She feels the words in the pit of herself.

That smirk again, a nod. 'Enjoy the view,' he says and takes his leave.

Later, the party mingles on the green slope of the headland at Sorrento. So much greener than Footscray, so much air and sun and space. The women unpack plates of corner sandwiches, a tin filled with Dot's ginger fluff, sliced watermelon kept cool in the buckets of ice alongside bottles of lemonade and beer. There is enough sun, enough booze now, for the mood to move from cheerful to unruly. One of the packers grabs Beth for a waltz as a slaughterman sings.

Beyond them, yachts run in the bay, the sun spangles on the sequinned surface of the sea. There's not long now before they'll have to gather it all up, leave the remnants of their giddy joy to litter the green slope where they've let the afternoon lilt by. And then they'll all roll back down to board the steamer for home, as high as kites all of them from the sun, the drink, the silver-skinned sea and knowing what's coming – a moonlit ride home across the bay, a couple of hours at least, for mucking about, for gossip and high jinks and cheek, for smooching in the moon-shadows with the bay breeze at their backs.

Jack knew, as soon as he saw the girl with that black hair, her chin tilted high, not afraid or put off by the kill floor, that she would be the right kind of girl for him. This is the reason he's been skittish all day, that he's already downed three bottles of beer to try to calm the jitter in his belly. He's got a nose for it, that's what his ma has always said, got a nose for good luck, for bad luck, a nose that knows when to pull his head in and when to play a trump.

She's noticed him, he can tell. She got that red on her neck, the way girls do, when he said hello on the ferry. Got to play your cards right, though. Doesn't do to come on strong. He keeps her in his eyeline as he moves in closer to a cluster of girls standing about by the relics of the picnic spread. There's Betty from Preserving – no, Beth – she's a looker and Johnny Haddon boasted he made good with her after the Christmas dance. He wouldn't be the only one.

Not this black-haired girl. She's not had time to spread herself around the way some of them do. She's the kind who might convince you to do the right thing, the kind you might end up marrying. He'd be smart to play this one right.

'Right then, ladies, who needs a drink?' He holds out a bucket of bottles and the hands that reach in are quick and sure. The black-haired girl hesitates so he passes her a brown bottle, using his own to knock off the cap, waiting until it is safely in her hand then tipping his to clink with hers.

'To Mr Angliss, then,' he says.

'And what he doesn't know,' she says, grinning and tossing her head back to the sky.

He holds out his hand. 'Jack King. You're new in the bagging room?'

She takes his hand firmly, smiles. 'Peggy Donnelly. New enough.'

He holds her hand a little longer than necessary, letting it go gently and nodding to the other girls. Always pays to impress the friends. Whatever she knows of Jack it won't be glowing. He needs to be on his best.

As she sips, he angles his body so he is blocking out the others.

'You're a slaughterman, then?' Peggy asks, taking a small sip from the bottle. He wonders whether she's an easy drunk, whether she might need someone to escort her home, gentleman-like. She'd be grateful for that.

'I am.'

'You had work all through? Counting my lucky stars Kathleen found me a job when she did. Dad just lost both of his.'

No shame in her face.

'Sorry to hear that. The family holding up?'

'Mum's taken my brothers and sisters up to Ballarat to stay with family.'

'You didn't want to go, then?'

She shakes her head. 'Nah, like it well enough here.' Smiles at him, coy and sweet.

He shakes out his foot, suddenly restless.

'Found myself a room, actually,' she says, 'with Lil Martin from the office.'

'She's orright,' Jack says. 'Her dad was an Angliss man.'

She holds up her bottle, giggles a bit. 'That went down fast.'

'Reckon we can find you another.'

The drink is warm and fizzing in Peggy, and she has to put out her hand to steady herself. Jack takes her elbow and leads her over the hill to where they can take in the view. She bends one knee to sink down to the grass, probably pulls it off elegantly enough, but she can't be entirely sure. Below them, the bay stretches out, silvery blue under the chasing clouds.

'Could be in for some weather,' Jack says and drinks. She watches his throat move as he swallows and she has to look back out to sea. On the horizon, clouds are clustering.

'Did you always want to be a slaughterman?'

'Always. I was just a little tacker watching me dad. Thought he was a god, thought all of them were.'

'Your dad always want it for you, too?'

'Course.'

They are quiet for a moment, but when Jack speaks again there is a new pitch in his voice.

'It's a good job – a slaughterman. The best there is in the works. Dad always said that. Something special about it, y'know? That moment you've got the animal in your arms, can feel its heart racing, doesn't know what's coming. You gotta do it quick, clean. Something in that feels kinda grand.'

He looks right at her, eyes glittering. She holds her breath.

'Wouldn't get me in a shirt and hat for quids,' he says, shaking his head.

She exhales. Wonders whether he thinks that's the kind of thing a girl wants. She wants to tell him she doesn't want what other girls want. She wants something bigger, something more.

'You ever travelled?' she asks. 'With the other slaughtermen? The girls tell me they move around – New Zealand, Sydney sometimes?'

'Yeah, some of the boys go up to work the season at Homebush. Knobby was up there last year, reckons he went and saw the new bridge.'

'Gosh, that'd be something, wouldn't it?'

'Not me, though. Been a Footscray boy all me life. Was playing at Angliss before I could walk.'

She'd like to talk of the world beyond Footscray, but she'll save it for another time. Might not have much experience with men, but Peggy knows they like to own the conversation. 'What was it like back then?'

'Smaller. Lotta blokes were out during the war. Kept going, though. That's the thing about Angliss, eh, got into the right business. Even when the whole world's busy blowing each other to smithereens they're gonna want their chops.'

She nods, watching the way his mouth chews on some words, hardly moves on others. Could watch him all afternoon.

'We got chased by the coppers once,' he goes on. 'Someone must have dobbed us in. Bunch of us climbed up onto the roof of the chill room, then the call went out that they were coming and we took off. Two storeys up! We were mad. I was littler than the rest of them, and when I went to make the jump I never made it to the other side. Fell all the way down and broke me wrist. Jeez, Dad was mad. Gave me a hiding and then Mum gave me another when he was done.' He turns to look at her and winks. 'Bloody fun, though.'

She laughs. 'Did they put you in plaster?'

'The works doc did it the next morning. Still doesn't sit completely right. Here, look.' Jack holds out his left wrist, bunching his sleeve back with his other hand, swivelling it in front of her.

She watches the way the bones slide under his skin.

'Touch that bit.' He points at a lump. 'Go on.'

She knows she is blushing again, but she hopes he thinks it's the drink and the sun. She places her fingers lightly on his skin and feels a current speed through her. He rotates his wrist so that the knuckle of bone shifts beneath her fingers.

'See,' he says, and it is just a little long, the look he gives her, for it to be entirely proper, and Peggy does not care.

'Oi!' A voice shouts from behind them and they turn to see Johnny on the hill. 'Packing it up! Captain reckons there's rain coming.'

Over the bay the storm-heads have closed in. Jack beats her to standing and holds his hand out to help her up. When she places her hand in his, he pulls her up quickly and she is off balance, crashing into him as she stands. He holds her there a moment, steadying her, before she steps back.

'Been a pleasure chatting with you, Peggy.'

She tosses her hair back. 'You too, Jack.'

They keep a little distance between them as they walk back to the group, joining in to fold blankets and collect up jackets and hats, leaving the bottles and wrappers where they lie to be swept up and cleaned away by the wind and the rain. When she looks up to pick him out among the crowd, she sees that he is watching her, too.

By the time they come in to the pier and the men get the gangplanks down it's begun to rain in earnest. The girls hold jackets above their heads and shriek as they run to the waiting trucks that will take them back to the works. Peggy is already soaked through when she feels a hand on her waist, pulling her away from the truck she was about to step into and toward another.

'Jump in with me, then.' Jack hoists himself into the back and then puts down his hand to pull her up. It's dark but for a lamp in the front, noisy and warm as the bench seats fill and Jack pushes her through the bodies to the end.

'Sit up here and I'll make sure none of these blokes bother you.'

It *is* mostly blokes in here. Jack has pulled her away from the truck where most of the women headed. Beth is in here, though, of course. Peggy can just make out her face, already nestled into the neck of the bloke next to her.

Jack slides in beside her and she laughs and apologises.

'I got drenched,' she says, tucking the wet folds of her dress under her thighs.

'So did everyone,' he says. 'You're not cold?'

'No, not in here. We'll all get a sweat up.' She knows she is talking too fast and too much, but it is hot and she is keenly aware of the whole side of Jack King so close to her. There is water running down into her shoes from the sodden hem of her dress.

'Here,' Jack says and hands her a handkerchief from his pocket which is remarkably dry and still pressed. That's a woman's work, Peggy can tell, and she hopes like hell it's his mum's.

She pats her face, her neck, dabs at the dress, aware now that it is clinging to her in all the spots it shouldn't, glad for the dark, but also not caring what it is that Jack King might see.

She can feel his hand seeking out hers where she is clasping the bench as the truck judders off, feels his fingers, tentative at first, then, when she doesn't pull away, lacing through her own so that his whole hand covers hers.

It's as though all the blood in her entire body is beating in that hand. She doesn't care about her wet dress, or her hair all slicked down and ruined, in this moment the whole world is Jack King's hand on hers. And she wants it to stay, and for the truck ride home through the dark to go on forever, but she also wants the hand to move, for those fingers to peel the sodden cotton of her dress away from her thigh, to run along her goosefleshed skin, for his head to turn, his lips to fret at her collar, her neck, her jaw.

Peggy takes a deep breath.

Jack King breathes beside her.

The truck barrels on through the dark as the meatworkers laugh and sing and lace fingers together where they can't be seen.

And when they stop and tumble out of the back and shout and wave goodbye and scatter into the streets in groups or some alone, it seems it is already decided. The rain has stopped and the clouds have split open to reveal a sky full of stars that glitter and shine with all the water. Stars in the puddles between the bluestones and shining on the filthy river, and Peggy lets her hand be taken again. Maybe it is she who does the reaching. Her dress is still damp and her hair still hangs loose and flat and her shoes squish her ankles where they have swollen with water but Peggy herself is full of the glitter of those stars, the heat of that hand, the keen awareness of what comes next.

'I'll walk you home,' Jack says.

'Kathleen is walking me back to Lil's.'

'Tell Kathleen you're being looked after.'

'I can't.'

'Didn't you say you weren't like all those other girls? Huh?' He pokes her quickly and she laughs, bats him away, but he grabs her hand. 'Come on, Peggy, let me walk you home. Can't even see Kathleen now. Wouldn't be right to let you walk on your own, would it?'

She tugs her hand from his, but even as she does, she knows she is playing a game, that this will end how it was going to end from the moment their bottles clinked at the park, before that, even.

He steps closer, takes her hand again.

His breath is beer and heat, the bulk of his chest in front of her face, his head bent down.

'And you think I'll let you kiss me?' Peggy says quietly.

'Yes,' he says, and he does.

There is no resisting it, and she doesn't want to. She wants his boozy breathy lips against hers. A moment of finding his place, and there's no denying he's done this many times before, that he knows his way around a body – his kisses a decoy for hands that slip quick to her waist and, when she does not push them away, around to cup her buttocks beneath her skirt.

This is what it means, she thinks, to be in good hands.

His hand now circling her waist, smoothing up over the tuck of her blouse, loitering at the cup of her breast. She does not mind at all, but she is smart, and smart girls don't let men like Jack King kiss them in the street.

She covers his hand with her own. Whispers, 'Not here.' Steps back.

Only the sheen of his eyes in the darkness.

'I can't convince you to take another turn around the block with me?' Hands reaching again.

She steps back. 'Thank you for walking me home, Jack,' she says and grins, hoping he'll think her unfussed by the kiss. 'Goodnight.'

'Night, then,' he says, winking and watching as she walks away.

By the time the sun has hit the slanted windows, there are still three hours of the shift to go and Peggy is sweating like a hog. Even escaping in her mind to Jack King's kisses isn't enough to make things any better today.

'Message from downstairs,' says Esther as she comes in from the loo. 'Reckon we need to speed up.'

'Who says?' says Nell.

'Donny.'

'Donny can get stuffed. He's not getting more than two hundred a day out of us. My hands are buggered enough already, I'll not cripple myself for fifty more bags.'

'Told him that already. He said take it up with the boss.'

'Which we would if we had a bloody union card.'

Beth pipes up. 'Budge would take it up for us, surely? He's always been good about us girls.'

'Won't do any good,' says Nell. 'It's the same across the whole place. More heads through the line, more bags, more cans, more tags, more trucks.'

'Angliss must be dressing his daughters in pound notes.'

'Ha. Could probably come at fifty more bags if I went home with enough for a nice new frock.'

As they talk, their fingers never stop.

Slide the calico, line it up, pin top and bottom, through the machine, keep it straight, end to end, snip, trim, check, fold. At tea break they swap so that someone new goes on the end, gets a chance to up and walk and order and pile. They stretch and moan and yawn.

In the afternoon, with still an hour to go, Nell stands up. 'Right, ladies, that's it,' she says, 'too bloody hot for this.'

Nell stands back from the table and begins to unbutton her blouse while they all laugh and cheer. 'No chance of the fellas coming up here to Hades this late in the day, either,' she adds, wiggling her hips, then her breasts, showing the top of her white brassiere through the gap she's opened up. 'Come on, you lot, I can't be the only one who's melting!'

Beth flicks out the bag she's sewing to whip Nell on the bum. 'You tart!'

'Me?' Nell says, laughing and unbuttoning her top completely now, pulling her arms out of the sleeves and letting her blouse hang.

Peggy laughs, they all do, and before you know it, all twelve of the women of the third-floor bagging room have got their tops off and their bras on show, fanning each other with the stiff patterns from the table, and it isn't a thing like work, not really at all, and Peggy reckons she could even come to love this place.

As luck would have it, the foreman does decide to visit them on the hottest afternoon in March and they only have a minute's notice, the click of the door, feet on the steps, the quick *shhhh-hhhh* and silence as they listen, and then the frantic whooping and calling as they rush to push sweaty arms and shoulders into cotton blouses, linen dresses, the spluttering giggles as buttons fail to find holes.

'What in the name –?' says Donny as he walks in and finds them rushing about like a bunch of headless chooks.

He blushes, he's just a young bloke really, recently married, and he knows what he's just walked in on, but what the hell is he going to say?

It's Nell who saves them. Striding forward, her shoulders straight back, she says, 'What can we do for you, Donny? Might need to send a delegate up to check the temperature. Things got a little hot.'

Behind Peggy, Beth snorts.

Donny nods. 'Righto, will do, just make sure you meet tally up here, ladies. Little short yesterday arvo.'

'That's rubbish, Donny!' calls Stella.

Donny puts his hands up and retreats and Nell turns around, fists on hips, and grins.

And then they are all beside themselves, hooting and whooping with laughter, for Nell's done her buttons up so skew-whiff you can see straight through to the pointed peak of her bra.

'Coulda poked his eye out!' Esther calls out, and they all shriek with laughter again. And for the rest of the shift, every couple of minutes, one of them erupts in fits of giggles, setting them all off again, so that they forget the heat, the work, their swollen fingers, and are just glad for each other and for Nell's triumphant left breast.

Baxter calls them all together just before smoko and Jack can already sense he's in a mood.

'What colour d'ya call this?' Baxter says, sticking a fat finger into the flesh of the beef carcass hanging where it's been finished at the end of the rail.

'Dark,' says Teddy, second-year apprentice, nervy kid with a shock of red hair but no eyebrows to keep the muck from his pale eyes.

'Too dark,' adds Budge.

'Purple,' says Stan.

'Bloody ruined, if you ask me,' Jack says.

'Too bloody right.'

Teddy keeps his head down. He was on the bleed.

Baxter cuts off the muttering. 'Not the kid's fault. It's what happened before it got to him. Who was on the ramp this morning?'

A murmur near the back and after a moment, someone raises his hand.

'That was me, boss,' says Johnny Haddon.

'This animal come up the ramp calm?'

'No, boss.' Bloody Johnny, never careful enough.

'Why was that?'

'Just one of them days, boss. The one before her made a row and she tried to turn.'

'How many times did you stick?'

The bunch of them turn their heads to see what Johnny's going to say.

'Three times, boss.'

More mutters. Baxter shakes his head.

'And now I've got a whole fucking cow meant to be going to the chiller that's going to get canned instead and you've just lost Angliss more than your whole month's pay. Don't bother showing up at the gate this week. You can line up with the rest of them from Monday.'

An angry murmur.

Stan speaks up. 'Not one man's fault if a cow gets jumpy.'

'You offering to take the blame, Murphy?'

'All I'm saying is it's not all Johnny's fault.'

Another voice. 'He's got a family to feed just like the rest of us.'

Baxter juts his chin. 'And Angliss ain't a bloody charity. No doubt when I check the rest there'll be more that can't go to export today and that costs the business. Teach you all to be careful. There are ten blokes at the gate waiting to take a job off every bloody one of you, ten at the gate and another hundred waiting at home. Consider yourself on notice.' They all turn away as he gets in his last, parting shot.

'And get this ugly fucker down to the canning room.'

*

Lil stands at the back of the group of men gathered to see the new team system in action. Angliss, poised as ever in his coat and hat, has brought in a bunch of New Zealand slaughts to show the thing off at its best. He's had her invite some newsmen from the *Argus*, all the industrialists from this side of town, the mayor of course. There's a morning tea spread fit for bloody royalty that she's had the girls from preserving lay out in the rec room, but the buzz in here inclines her to think these men will be wanting whiskey and beer before cups of tea. Lil knows as well as they do that now the machinery is in, the shackles and hooks and pulleys and chains, no man, no union, is going to get it taken out. It's a victory already. She almost feels sorry for the slaughtermen.

Angliss and the Kiwi boss are like two comics on a double bill. They loosen the crowd as they gather at the sticking pen, where three lambs skitter and prance, unnerved by the attention.

'Shall we begin, then, Angliss?'

'Indeed!' says Angliss, and spreads his arms wide. 'Gentleman, may I present to you, for the first time ever on these shores, the team system. From the United States, and now via our New Zealand neighbours, it's going to change the way we produce meat forever.'

Polite applause, a cheer, and Angliss nods his head at two men who have appeared in the pen. One of them steps forward.

'First the sticker . . .'

The sticker has clearly done this many times before. Gently advancing on one lamb he separates her from the bunch, holds her from behind and, lightning quick, runs the knife from his belt across her throat.

'Once the throat is cut, the shackler attaches the lamb to the belt.'

The next man reaches down to grab a chain dangling overhead, shackles her by her hind leg and drags her up, bleeding into the channel below as the conveyer rail above them starts to move.

Angliss motions for them to follow the moving lamb through the door and into the next room.

'The first legging table.' Angliss gestures towards it and they watch the legger use his knife to skin the leg that dangles free from the shackle, pulling the skin even as the lamb moves away from him on the belt.

'And the second legging table.' Another man uses a hook to shift the shackle to the skinned leg, takes his knife and skins the other.

'Watch as the spreader is inserted between the front legs as the lamb moves on to the next member of the team. Let's call him the tonguer.'

Laughter then. 'The cheeker!' some joker calls from the back as the worker skins the head, removes the tongue and cheeks and wipes his brow as the lamb continues to move.

'Never stops, does it?' Lil hears the man next to her say.

'How many they reckon they can get through using this?' says another, incredulous.

The group hurries along to the next station where a man slices upwards to open up the neck and forelegs. 'Here we have the spear cutters, and next to them the brisket punchers.'

Lil has to crane her head to see what the next man is doing, it's all so quick.

The group shuffles forward again in time to catch the splitter open up the skin with his blade and slice off the trotters. Then the lamb cranks slowly and surely along the belt to the next man waiting to receive it.

'First the flanker, and then the thumper-up will free the skin from the underbelly, next the backers-off clear the tail area, and then pull the skin down to the neck.' The man in front of them yanks hard on the skin, pushing down with enormous shoulders as it peels away, flapping wetly beneath the carcass as it cranks along to the next station.

Angliss points to the head scalper, who now pulls the skin clean away and tosses it onto another belt at his feet, which carries it off. Lil wonders how they will cope with the new speed. It's going to change the whole place, that's certain.

'And off with the head, then on to the brisket cutter.' They hurry to see the man finishing with his knife as he cuts away the brisket and throws it, red and glistening, onto the belt, before the carcass shifts away again above his head. Next it's the runner and paunch puller removing the viscera.

Lil catches the eye of the men as they hurry past, but they seem to have no expression at all.

The final man – the plucker – works quick, showing off the handfuls of gleaming offal as he slices them away from the carcass and throws them into the chute.

Angliss taps his watch theatrically and spreads his arms wide to indicate the men on the line.

A round of thunderous applause.

'And you don't need a slaughterman,' calls a voice from the back.

At this, Angliss frowns. 'Slaughtermen, skilled and experienced as they are, have been the very backbone' – some sniggers, Angliss smiles – 'of this industry for the past forty years. We value and appreciate their experience.' Here he pauses solemnly. 'But, yes, you are correct – the team system does not require a skilled slaughterman with a three-year apprenticeship behind him and a pay scale to match. In fact, any man could walk off the street and be part of this team within a week.'

Applause. Lil feels a little faint. As they move out towards the rec room for morning tea, she is aware of the sound, a whirring underneath, as though the whole place has become a machine. When she looks back, she can see the line of lambs, still moving, each man making the same cut, eyes ahead.

A brave new world, it is.

∞

Sanctuary Gardens Aged Care, 2020

Day 1

In the gap between the lunch meds and dinner (which arrives at the ungodly hour of 4.45 pm), Hilda leans into her walker, shuffles down through the games room, past the dining hall to the little interior courtyard where the pink camellia is just finishing blooming, and opens the door for Kevin's cat – Ferris. Kevin has been laid up this past month with an ulcerated lower leg. As a rule, Hilda does not like cats. But she respects how Ferris knows his place, how he trots to the fernery in the corner of the courtyard to shit neatly, how he deigns to rub past her fat right ankle in its fluffy slipper. Hilda does not admit to herself how much she yearns for that brief touch each afternoon.

    She did enjoy Kevin, too, when he used to join her in the sun, or what sun made it into this little concrete box. Hilda's sure the courtyard was bigger when her niece brought her for a tour four years back, but then everything now, herself included, seems to be shrinking, drying out, becoming a lesser version of itself. Kevin had been a trade teacher – woodwork – he liked to tell her tales of reckless teenagers with saws. Sometimes he softened into stories of his wife, Marilyn, who died of bowel cancer a decade back, and it was all right, really, sitting for a moment remembering the feeling of love, of grief, with this near stranger with whom she now happened to share a home. She should go in and sit with him, she should, but she imagines Kevin in his bed, the faint rotting smell of his leg, and decides it's best she keep away until they can sit out here together again and trade memories.

Ferris brushes against her ankle.

'A second cuddle for me today, aren't I the lucky one?' Hilda says and leans forward stiffly, lowering her hand towards the cat.

A rap on the glass door. She startles, grips the walker tight in one hand and flails the other for a moment until it connects, steadies. A man in a suit is peering through the door from the hallway inside. He raps again and flaps one hand at her as if she were a dog.

For heaven's sake.

She turns her head away very slowly. There are a few delicious joys to ageing. Ferris stalks away. She'll be finished out here when she damn well pleases.

'Mrs . . . ?' The man has stepped into the courtyard, leaves the moment hanging, waiting for her to fill it. She learned long ago not to fill those gaps. She smiles benignly.

'We need all residents to return to their rooms.'

'Why is that?' *And who are you?* she wants to say, but all men under fifty look the same to her now and perhaps she does know who this brusque person is.

'Health directive, I'm afraid. If you'll return to your room someone will be with you shortly.'

He steps aside, holding the electric door for her as though she won't be able to do that for herself.

'Righto, righto,' she mutters loud enough for him to hear.

*

FOR IMMEDIATE DISTRIBUTION

As per the directive from the CHO as of 10 am this morning Sanctuary Gardens Aged Care is in lockdown.

What this means:
NO VISITORS
RESIDENTS TO STAY IN ROOMS
ALL STAFF TO USE FULL PPE AT ALL TIMES

Sincerely,
G. Howlett
Sanctuary Gardens Management

Residents and their families can be assured that staff and management are working to ensure standards of care remain at their usual excellent level understandably while we are working hard to maintain this standard of care with a significantly reduced workforce (due to furlough and not necessarily infection rates) we are not able to update families personally and please note there will be a recorded message on our communication lines (phone and email) until this current crisis is in hand hello you've called sanctuary gardens aged care we are currently in lockdown as per the directions of the health department at this time visitors are not allowed please see our website for updates family contacts will be notified via text message please know we are working hard to arrange ways for families to speak to residents and we will update you as soon as we can for urgent matters please hold the line and someone will be with you as soon as possible.

Anna
Lockdown 😦😩
10.36am

Trace
Omg I know. You okay?
Kids??
10.37am

Anna
Ask me in a week.
10.37am

Also this from Hil's place:

Sanctuary Gardens is now in lockdown.
To protect the health and safety of all our residents,
staff and their families we are closed to visitors
until further direction from the health department.
Be assured we are doing everything possible
to keep your loved one safe and we will update you ASAP.
10.39am

Trace
Jesus, should have gone and seen her last week.
Was just so busy.
10.42am

Anna
Trying to call now.
You know you always welcome to come
Tues & thurs arvos when I go.
I'd like to see my little sis sometimes too.
10.43am

Benny
You okay down there?
Told you lot to come up here to the sunshine state! 😜
1.13pm

Trace
Too soon Benno

And maybe not the time for guilts trips rn huh A?
1.14pm

> **Anna**
> Soz. Hands full here with work
> + dinner + 3 crazy kids.
> Ignore brevity.
> I'll deal with Hil.
> 1.14pm

Benny
Will send you down some toilet paper. Will that help? 😊
Pics are insane
Tragedy of the commons right there
5.55pm

Day 2

On the telly they show pictures of women holding babies up to windows and old people on the other side of the glass with wet eyes. Not the same. Wouldn't be. Not like the weight of a child on your lap. Heavy bony squiggly bombs. Wriggling and reaching and sometimes snuggling. More like a dog than a cat. A sister. She remembers holding her. While Mum and Lil busied around. Weight of a sister in a lap, nothing on this earth like it, but she—

Sometimes feels like it's on the tip of her tongue—

Just around the corner—

Her little sister, the way her hair caught in her blinks and she would squint and yell but—

Just this morning—

The thing they called her—

*

Outside the window there is a hedge that needs clipping and a dead spider plant hanging from a pot. Grass. Sometimes the top of a bus if one goes by but the hedge is too high to see people's heads. Likely do it on purpose, that. No one wants to glance over and come face to face with their inevitable ageing. Don't think it will happen to them. No one does. You'd blow a hole through your head if you did.

A face she doesn't know, mouth hidden by a mask, a plastic shield over her eyes. How is she supposed to understand a word this woman says? Hilda needs to tell her about the ants. They are back. She spotted them this morning, sly little line of them over the base of the lamp and up the table leg, she can trace it back to the corner of the bathroom but from there it's too hard to tell. She doesn't like the stink when you squash them, doesn't like the pest spray they use either but it seems to be a losing battle. Wishes she could just let them be, but they bristle, black and chaotic, in the corner of her vision.

The woman behind the mask is moving her mouth.

'I can't hear you,' Hilda says slow and loud. Who knows where this woman is from, somewhere else, always somewhere else, they come here to wipe the shit from the arses of abandoned women like her, what a life, what an awful, awful life.

The woman returns to the door and wheels in a trolley, lifts a plastic plate covered in foil and puts it on Hilda's table.

Hilda frowns. Looks over at the digital clock on the bedside table. It is 3.55 pm.

'Is that dinner?' Hilda says.

The plastic face leans forward. 'Dinner!' A gloved hand lifts the foil and Hilda sees the globby piles of mush – something like curry, something like rice, something like vegetables. She smells fish.

'No, no,' Hilda says, 'I don't eat fish. Besides, I won't eat dinner before four, it's an insult already to have to eat it before six.'

The plastic woman shrugs her shoulders. The light glints off the face shield and Hilda cannot tell if she is laughing or scowling.

Hilda pushes forward in her chair, her shoulders creak and she oofs out her breath, but she persists. 'I cannot eat this, it doesn't agree with me, please take it back to the kitchen.'

She knows you have to play nice, that she won't get what she wants and needs by being bullish about it. A lesson she has had to learn over and over and over again.

'It's not your fault,' Hilda says, trying to sound kind and measured, 'you wouldn't know. Where's Mariam? Isn't she normally on Wednesday in the afternoon? She'll sort it out, I'm sorry for shouting.'

The plastic face leans in close, not to the side with the hearing aid, but close enough that Hilda can hear through the layers that muffle the voice. 'Mrs McCarthy, the normal staff all have to stay home, the virus, you know. We're here to look after you for now.'

Hilda nods, yes, that's right, someone has told her this. And they left a note with the Sanctuary Gardens logo at the top. (*Sanctuary Gardens: A Place to Rest* – she often joked about the name at lunch with Barb and Kevin – a place to bloody die out of sight, out of mind, more like.) The note, yes, a virus, a vaccination plan, a temporary stop on visitors, temporary change to staffing, no leaving your room, no need to worry, all in hand.

She sits back and lets her bones and the information resettle. Yes, that's right, the message from her niece. *Sit tight, Aunty Hil, love you.*

When she looks up, the plastic face is leaving, shutting the door behind her, the plate is still on her table, the overwhelming smell of the white fish, the cream sauce.

'Wait!' Hilda calls. 'Take it with you!'

Her stomach turns, the smell is everywhere. *Bitch*, she thinks, then 'BITCH!' she yells, but the door is closed and it does not open again.

She shuffles her bum forward on the seat, hands like claws on the chair rests, pain in her shoulders, her neck, her middle, everywhere. *Bitch!* She pushes herself up and moves towards the table, which is just out of reach. *Shit the bloody shit walker, bloody arse.* Hilda's slippered toe catches on the carpet and she pitches forward, grabbing at the edge of the table, one hand coming down on the plate so her fingers are in the fish, the white muck. She steadies herself, picks up the plate with one hand and hurls it at the door.

It falls short. Upends on the carpet. Stupid plastic plates now, it doesn't even satisfy with a clunk or a smash.

She cries out. Breathless. Bashes the palm of her hand against the alarm that hangs on a chain around her neck. Again and again and again until the door opens and the plastic face rushes in and looks down to see the plate and shakes her head and Hilda can hear, oh so clearly now.

'What have you done, you silly girl?' the plastic face says, and Hilda begins to cry.

Evelyn. Her sister's name is Evelyn.

'Let's clean you up,' plastic face says. 'Come on now, you didn't shower yesterday. Let's get you in now.'

But the thought of the shower, that scouring heat, watching everything she remembers swirling and twirling with that awful stinky pink soap down that little silver drain . . .

'No, I won't. I don't want to. No shower.'

Day 3

Patient progress notes

Hilda McCarthy DOB: 03/11/1933 UR No:

Banksia Bed 612
NFR

Date: ▇▇▇▇
Time: ▇▇▇▇

PCA: Neja Lakmal
NEG covid test
Resident believes shower is washing away memories
Increasing general incontinence – Resident at risk of infection if she doesn't shower

Nurse:
Medication for increased agitation – antipsychotic?
Refused shower, resistant to direction
?Check for delirium/UTI
For assessment with GP on ward round (Wed?)

Hilda remembers a kinder concert. Anna at four, strangely proportioned, long fingers, soft belly, long shins criss-crossed with the bruises and grazes of play. Garish costume, striped rainbow leggings, pink tulle skirt ('my sticky-outy skirt'), yellow t-shirt, a soft leopard-print scarf pinned between her shoulder blades and fastened at each wrist with a hair tie. A piece of classical music, familiar but unplaceable. The little bodies all curled up across the carpet while the grown-ups perched in tiny chairs.

'Pay attention, Aunty Hil,' Anna whispers to her, tugging at her hand, 'you'll like this one 'specially.'

Trembling elbows, little fingers creeping across the carpet as the music billows. Left arms, right, a flapping from one child who was ahead of the rest. 'Ah, butterflies,' says a man behind her and she snaps her head around in annoyance.

Anna's wings, slow and steady, emerging from her cocoon, chin raising slowly, eyes finding Hilda, her grin. *See! See what we are!?* And Hilda nodding, mouthing, 'Beautiful,' eyes wide and bright.

All of them emerging now, save one child whose scarf wing has come loose and is whimpering for help as the teacher gentles them back to the group. Unfolding to standing, to tiptoes, arms out, marvelling at their own wings, then on the teacher's signal, as the music crescendos, they're skipping about the space, flapping and spinning in and around, chaos and crashing and grinning and laughing, cameras held up, a man with a camcorder trying to capture it all.

And then, a clap from the teacher and all those little heads turning to watch her as she brings her finger to her lips and somewhere up the back the kinder assistant turns the volume down and the flapping slows, the children begin to curl up. One last look from Anna as she smiles knowingly, tucks her head in, one wing, then the other and curling back up on the carpet, the last of the children pulling in their wings, the clapping erupting.

In the car on the way home in the dark, Anna is buzzing with excitement.

'Did you like it, Aunty Hil? Did you see?'

'I loved it.' But Hilda remembers wanting to tell her, wanting to stand up there in the kinder and say, *What folly is this, the cycle in reverse?* Butterflies don't morph back into cocoons, to larvae, to egg, after flight. They die, perfect wings on display.

She held her tongue. The children didn't need to know that yet.

Day 4

Anna
Update on Hil in case you interested.
She not doing great.

                              Refusing to wash 😰
                    Thinks the shower is making her forget things.
                        Nurse says dementia progressing rapidly.
                                                           1.30pm

Trace
Triggering much? Same as mum. 😰
Anything we can do?
1.35pm

                                                            Anna
                            Give her a call. Hard to get through.
                         Will try and set up video chat with kids.
                                            They make her happy.
                                                       It's ducked.
                                                           1.36pm

                                                         *fucked
                                                           1.37pm

Trace
Are the kids okay?
Are YOU okay?
1.39pm

                                                            Anna
                                                      😰😰😩
                                                           1.40pm

Benny
Remember you two promised to shoot me
before I end up in one of those places, yeah?
5.55pm

Hilda has waking dreams that she is becoming part of the chair. The blue vinyl arms fusing with her bones, her skin growing over the cushioned seat, slippered feet attaching to the short metal legs. She is not frightened by the vision; it makes sense to her. She's hardly moved the past few days, thinks about her research, the word *aestivation* – wonders if all those years observing the tiered moths in the caves have given her the ability to hibernate, too. Wouldn't that be nice. Just to wake up on the other side of this virus, shake out her wings.

She wonders if they'll let Ferris in to visit her. Can a cat infect her with this virus? Could she infect the cat? Cross-species transmission is possible, certainly. Maybe they could put a little face shield covering his wet pink nose. She misses touch. Not the quick work touch of these unfamiliar nurses with their wet cloths – she is sure they are punishing her with their hard wipes because she won't shower. No, she craves something slower, kinder. A ball of cat warming her lap. A powdery moth flutter at her neck.

One of the earliest researchers in her field, a man of course, once tested his theory of the timing of the bogong migration by casting a wire net across the mouth of one of the small aestivation caves on Mt Gingera. Inside were ten thousand sleeping moths. Prevented from leaving, at first the moths happily continued their quiescence. But then, as the main autumn migration began in earnest and millions of moths darkened the skies on their way down the mountains to the breeding sites hundreds of kilometres away, the trapped moths began to agitate, hurling themselves at the mesh which entrapped them. It turned her stomach, the cruelty of it. But she kept that to herself. Never wanted to come across as weak, as anything less than totally dedicated to her research.

Careful as she was, they still came for her. Scoffing at the perceived 'feminine focus' of her PhD thesis on the choice of egg-laying locations for the *Agrotis infusa*. Asking her to bring the tea trolley when visiting professors were lecturing. Protesting her inclusion on long field trips, *too arduous* they said, *inappropriate*.

Eventually, though, even the most indignant of them all had to concede that her research was exemplary, shifted knowledge, made a significant contribution.

Like monarch butterflies, their showier American cousins, bogong moths are a multivoltine species, breeding often over one season so that there are three generations alive at the same time. This fact has always pleased her. She remembers her mother comforting her when she awoke one morning to find that the small cabbage moth she had captured and placed under an upturned glass mixing bowl the day before had died in the night.

They only live a day or two – butterflies and moths, her mother had told her, fixing a weak tea and trying to stop six-year-old Hilda's tears. She was certain she had not added enough grass and leaves under the bowl and had starved the poor moth to death. *It's not your fault*, Mum had said. *That's just how it is for them.*

For a moment, she smells her. English Lavender dusting powder and velvet soap and butter. She is very still, trying to hold on to her mother's presence. But it is gone. Hilda shifts her bum in the seat, sips bad-tasting water from the silly plastic cup, troubled by the fact that her mother had felt so close just now. So close, but then she'd swooshed away from her, another memory swirling and spiralling down the shower drain.

∞

Footscray, 2031

La stands at the window watching Cat cross the street below, one hand swinging the bag of phở, red hair wind-tangling across her face, pace never changing as she strides between the cars. She'll get herself hit one day. Through the narrow gaps between the flats across the street, La can see the last of the sun on the river, still swollen after the rain, the banks where she'd walked this morning putrid with stinking mud, plastic bottles, re-veg tubing, red gloves from the docks, the odd fish. Who knows what's been burped up from the deep mud of the flats, from the old tanneries, meat works, chemical factories. They say there's another front coming this weekend. Again. The bloke at the newly refurbished milk bar on the corner says he's never known weather like this. She wants to tell him it's no surprise. But she also doesn't want to be a pain in the arse, so she holds her tongue and buys the organic potato milk he now stocks. Bet he never expected that either.

The door click clicks and the smell of fragrant stock blows in with Cat.

'You seen this?' Cat holds out a flyer. Yellow and teal. 'I think it's from that guy upstairs? With the bike? Number seventeen?'

'Mance?' La is in charge of interpersonal relations with the neighbours, Cat being hopeless with faces, or anything other than her dissertation for the last two years – for the entirety of their relationship actually. La takes the flyer with one hand and the bag with the other. 'You are the only person in the world who still walks out to get food, you know that, right?'

'You love my little quirks,' Cat says and laughs and swings away to the kitchen while La pretends to bite at her. La unpacks the plastic containers and opens them to let the steam out, holding the flyer down on the table to read it.

Our new WANT warehouse WANTS YOU.
Immediate start. High p/h rate. No training required.
Attractive health and wellbeing packages for
all staff including casuals.
Go to want.com/Braybrook and fill in an application online.

'What's an attractive health and wellbeing package?' La says as Cat dumps cutlery on the coffee table.

'Look it up, it'll be on the website.'

'Do I want to work in a warehouse?'

'They reckon it's good for your fitness. And if they add in extras . . . We got wine?'

'No. I told you that.' Bugger. Now La wants a glass too. Not the taste or cool slide of it down her mangled throat, just the soft lens of the alcohol in her brain.

'Should I go out again?'

'No – don't. I shouldn't be drinking anyway.'

They slurp, scroll, discover that 'attractive health and wellbeing packages' include onsite gym and classes, sponsored nutrition, mental health support and 'future health investment', including subsidised eligible preventative medicine.

'And, where relevant, fertility treatments.' Cat swirls her chopsticks in the noodles, lets them drip, stuffs them into her open mouth without her eyes leaving the screen.

Cat takes a shower while La lies in bed and scrolls the WANT page. She tries not to think about how much hot water Cat is using, leaving everything steamy – it's only been six months of living together, and La can already see the tiny splinters that will continue to scratch. She hovers over the 'apply now' button. Imagines running into Liesel or Jaz and telling them she is working in a warehouse. Her back teeth grind. Fuck them. Fuck them and their permanent gigs, their breakthrough roles, their chorus salaries overseas. She's an artist. And artists have always slogged so they can do their art and she will too, and she will find grace and humour and humility in it. Eight months. That's all she needs to be match fit again. To keep the apartment. To get back in the game. Easy.

Cat is in the doorway, pinked and steaming, two towels (the excess!), one turbaned around her wet hair. Taller than La, paler too, elbows and knees that form triangles in the frame of the doorway as she poses. La feels like her body only ever makes circles and curves. But they fit. They fit well. She puts down the phone.

'You coming to bed?'

'Like this?' Cat grins, styles her hands around her head.

'If you like.'

Cat unwinds the towel and flips her hair dramatically, pouts. 'What would *you* like?'

'Come here.'

There is a tattoo of a skeletal gingko leaf in the skin dint beneath Cat's left shoulder and the top of her breast. La likes to lick it. She places the tip of her tongue at the base of the stem and then licks slowly up the spreading leaf, as though she is lapping it into her mouth, tasting and swallowing the ancient powders, making herself live forever. Tonight, Cat tastes like coconut body wash. The tattoo lick turns La on more than Cat, she knows, and she puts her hands on her lover's neck, and her fingers deep in the wet of her, while she laps at the gingko tattoo and her brain fizzes.

'Fuck, why don't we do this more,' La murmurs, and it is not a question.

Cat pulls La's head in and kisses her, biting her lip, quick and hard, then pushes her over and down, hair in waves, tangling them together. Cat puts one hand up and knots La's hair around her wrist, holding it there behind her head as she kneels and puts her mouth around La's nipple. La breathes, deep, tries not to hold, not to clench, fingers gripping her lover's back, shoulders, arse, skin she wants to be inside of, to break, to become—

Here –

Cat is at her belly, tongue-tip trailing to hip bone and back

Jesus

La's hands in the coiled damp of Cat's hair, the noise she makes when she pulls on it, too hard, more, not more, but she can't stop if she wanted to, tongue lips mouth on the wet of her now, lick suck devouring harder and more – she wants to be consumed, obliterated, apocalypse of skin and mouths and wet and Jesus

Stop

Cat pulls her lover's head from between her legs pushes her back, does not stop for gentle, for soft tangle of legs and sheet and hair

Here

God

Ouch

My leg

Then she has her in her mouth and her hands on her arse and inside and it is all the hunger, it is beyond her brain, beyond language – it is now and here and here and now and she would stay, she would stay but Cat pulls at her and she keeps her mouth where it is and turns her body and

Fuck

A pattern repeating mouth on cunt and cunt on mouth infinity mobius forever and ever and this is all, this is ah this is where she will stay.

Later, the slow sentences of half sleep in the dark, the slight damp of the pillows.

'You asleep?' Cat asks in the black.

Spangling awake, La murmurs.

'Would you freeze your eggs? Do you want that?' Cat asks.

'I don't know, I haven't thought about it.'

Liar. Yes, you have. But the planet, the cost, the kid-ness, the what ifs, the certainty you'll be shit at it, all the extra hurdles when you can't just use any old sperm from any old dick.

'Would *you*?' La says, pushing the question away and back at Cat so that it pulses in the space between them.

'Don't know if I need to freeze them. Maybe. I don't know.'

'How so?'

Cat's hand on her face in the dark.

'Well, I suppose, if I submit in October and get a teaching gig and the right pay, well then, it would be a good time, right, and I'm still young enough, I could be the one to carry the baby.'

'Thirty-five is young.'

'Not for eggs.'

'Well then I guess we're both fucked.'

'Nah, that's why places like WANT are doing this. Get your eggs, keep you working, give you the option later.'

'So you're saying you'd do it, like IVF, with my . . . eggs, and a donor?'

'Yeah, partner IVF. I've been looking into it.'

'Right.'

Long quiet. La thinks about pretending to go to sleep. Feels like this conversation will either be too big or not big enough and both will hurt.

Cat's voice. Rising notes of a question. 'Is it something you want?'

'A kid?'

'Yes, a kid.'

'Yes. I think so.'

Cat's hand finding hers in the sheets. Laced fingers. Quietening breaths.

La is electric awake an hour after Cat has started her soft snores. Was something just decided without being spoken? And if it was – was it a becoming, an undoing, a tacit agreement to something La doesn't yet understand?

La hovers her index finger over the screen. The chat box flickers.

Need any help with this question?

She thinks of Cat's fingers in her own. *Is it something you want?*

Quickly, she ticks the 'yes' box and moves on to the next question. Mance warned her that the WANT HR system collects all kinds of data. Including, she supposes, how many minutes of a bot's time she takes up.

Do you have any pre-existing injuries?

Mance had been clear on this one. Not relevant. Don't mention it. She doesn't hesitate. 'No', she ticks, and, even as she does, feels her stomach rise up in indignation – no mention of the surgery, the therapy, the specialists, the credit card, and then the debt, the way her agent's calls got further and further apart even after that one dazzling bunch of natives.

She'll work hard for eight months. She'll accept overtime, extra shifts, she'll pay off the therapy, keep paying rent and get her voice back to work.

> Nearly finished! You are just one step away from being part of the WANT family ☺ Please read the following terms and conditions before signing your employment contract.

The chat box pulses again:

> This should take you 5 minutes, and then you're done!
> Please read carefully.

Mance had warned her about this one too. Catch-22. It's a non-standard contract, including a confidentiality clause and a privacy waiver – no union would pass it, he said. But if you don't sign it, the gig's not yours, and right now, La can't afford to choose. School term will be over soon, the teaching will dry up again and apparently there's not enough in the budget for all the casuals. She should have mastered a second instrument, one less fragile than her voice. So she does what she does with other T&Cs – scrolls to the bottom, clicks 'Agree' and scrawls her signature with her finger on the screen.

The monitor in her hand appears to explode with glitter. A pop-up congratulates her on joining the family and the golden infinity symbol of the familiar logo swirls in an endless loop at the centre of the screen. Her delivery is on its way and will be with her in less than an hour: her yellow t-shirt, a branded keep cup, the ID she'll need to bring on her first day to synch with her retinal scan.

We can't wait to meet you!

'Here's to your new gig, La!'

Cat raises her pot glass and reaches over to clink it with La's, but La wishes her girlfriend would be quiet. They are sitting around a big table in an old pub near the uni and already La knows it was a mistake to come to faculty drinks.

'Oooh, what are you doing?' says a woman with expensive geometric glasses and faux-curious smile. Her eyes dart over La's shoulder searching for something of more interest.

'Oh, it's nothing, just a casual job while I wait for my voice to heal so I can get back to work.'

'Teaching?'

'No.'

Cat raises her glass and her voice. 'My love is proudly joining the proletariat.'

Shut up shut up, La thinks and tries to catch Cat's eyes, *don't do this here.*

'Well, power to you,' says glasses woman.

'Someone has to,' says a young man with floppy hair and a shirt that is supposed to look ragged but which La suspects is eye-wateringly expensive.

La smiles briefly. 'What is it you do?' she asks, despite not giving a shit.

'That *is* the question, isn't it?' He takes a long sip. 'I shepherd undergraduates through the elaborate hazing ritual that is academia until they burn out or hand something in that I then have to read, all the while fighting for my job and applying for research grants every other week to prove I have something to say, though apparently no one wants to hear it because I'm a cishet able-bodied white man.'

He takes another long sip to punctuate his words and La wishes fervently for him to choke.

'Sounds like a good fit,' she says and pushes her chair back, mouthing '*bathroom*' across the table to Cat, who hopefully hasn't heard the exchange but is nevertheless looking slightly anxious.

Out on the street she walks north for a bit, wishes she was part of the generations who smoked just so she'd have an excuse to be standing on the street escaping people she despises. She doesn't know how Cat stands it. The posturing. The holier-than-thou arrogance. Cat reckons it's better in the Engineering faculty than Linguistics (her dissertation is on the Semiotics of Geoengineering, or something like that), but honestly, La can't tell the difference. She knows she's being unfair, but the more Cat asks her to go easy, the more she gets fired up. What are they actually doing? All those big brains in their offices whingeing and thinking and analysing the state of the world without doing anything about it. She knows, she *knows* (Cat has intimated as much enough times) that this is no argument against academia, that art never saved the world either, but still. For fuck's sake. At least art is something tangible, shared. Surely the urge to entertain is as pure as anything else?

They catch a tram home, earlier than Cat wanted to go, later than La did, and they're both kind of pissed at each other, but they also both know that it's pointless to have this same fight about these same people again. That it's an ouroboros of an argument and it's a waste of energy and time and tears. Despite knowing this, La sometimes goes in all the same, needing the drama, every hurled word a sign that this woman thinks she's worth yelling over, the sweet of makeup sex. But tonight, she is just tired. Exhausted already by the thought of her early get up, the next eight months, whether she'll show herself to be a bougie arts student after all, unable to hack the pressure of a factory job. She rests her forehead against her own reflection in the tram window, feels Cat concede and lace her fingers through La's own. A quiet kind of peace.

The WANT warehouse is at the end of a looping bus ride through a vast industrial estate of cul de sacs and bus stops that all look the same. She's on track to arrive early, as instructed, she's not naïve about the general work culture of the place. Everyone either has a story or has heard a story, but she's trying to hold them loosely. Besides, when you know the rules – the written and the shadow ones – you are better equipped to play the game. She'd learnt that early on in choruses, on stages – they all had. Well-timed coy smiles, sometimes a little flesh trade (a look or a touch, both seemed to get the same response), purred promises that you never intended to make good on. La is confident that despite the differences between a sweaty unregulated set and the vast warehouse the bus is pulling up at, she knows how to handle an employer.

She follows the other workers, all in their yellow shirts, from the bus to the shouty yellow entrance doors where they form a swift moving line. At the front of the queue there is a scanner and turnstile. She's been told what to expect, but still, it's disconcerting watching adults pile their phones and devices into tubs as they pass through security. Anyone would think something more important than shipping unicorn onesies and personalised kitty litter trays was going on behind these gigantic walls. The white woman in front of her turns and smiles. She is older, sixty maybe, faded pink dye in her hair and a slash of pink lippy.

'Make sure you switch your phone right off. Heard they harvest your data while you're working.'

La nods. Smiles. Thumbs her phone in her pocket. 'That obvious I'm a newbie?'

The woman shrugs and smiles again. 'It's not hard to tell. I'm Mina. Find me if you need anything, yeah?'

'Thanks. La.'

Mina smiles and turns around because she's at the head of the queue now, stepping onto the painted foot signs and lifting her chin slightly to look into the scanner, putting her phone in the tub which La now realises is being held by a robot. She met one during training but she kind of thought it was all for show – the latest version of the WANT droid on display to impress the new associates. The strange humanoid face, the eyebrows! It was the little things, the gestures, the thousand different angles of the chin. Disconcerting. As though she could feel her own brain clicking through and trying to compute what was wrong with the face in front of it. At home, she'd brought up videos in her feed to show Cat, but she was nonplussed; the uni had been using one of the competitor droids for years now in most of its service roles. The state schools La had been teaching in barely had enough cash for a new keyboard, let alone state-of-the-art robots.

'Step up, please,' the droid says pleasantly in a warm woman's voice and La stumbles in her hurry to get her feet in the marked spots. 'Hold still for one moment, please,' it commands as the scanner moves up a little to align with her eyes. A green line pulses then ticks.

'Phone, please,' the droid says, and La places her phone in the tub, looks at the fingers splayed, the white chromed arm holding it out, the shoulder, the face, that chin tilt.

'Sorry,' says La.

'No need to apologise, have a great day, Associate SM978!'

The robots inside – the RDUs – aren't like the showy humanoids at the front. These are the proletariat of robots, functional and blocky like little R2D2s speeding around the floor, kinda cute, really. La winces as a crackle of static erupts through the earpiece, before the bland pop music returns. Apparently it increases productivity by 0.7%. Her head is beginning to pound. She needs a drink – water, coffee – but the other warehouse workers, *yellowbacks* they call themselves, warned her in the tea room this morning; not enough time to have a piss, better to push through the dehydration and drown yourself in fluids at the end of the day to make up for it.

So far she has packed dog nappies, beauty kits, infant formula, assorted electronic devices, bulk-buy double-A batteries, mini dishwasher with USB, toothpick containers, teeth-whitening strips, skin-whitening cream, tanning spray, plush hedgehog toy for dogs, plush dog toy for hedgehogs, butt pillow, nappies 25 pack, nappies 50 pack, nappies 50 pack (bulk-buy special price), phone case, soda can organiser, suctioned toothbrush holder, blackhead remover set, air fryer liner, air fryer oil mister, air fryer 100pc accessories kit, bacon bandages, bacon-flavoured chips, bacon-flavoured ice cream, bacon-flavoured panties (that one makes her dry-retch).

She is astonished to realise the voraciousness of human want. She is not above it; she's been daydreaming about what she'll buy with her new staff discount – things she really needs, she tells herself, things that were on her list anyway, things to make life better, easier, more efficient.

A new order pings in her ear and vibrates on her screen. Eco Bugs-Be-Gone Zapper – a gun that shoots table salt at insects. Who knew? Her RDU accelerates away to retrieve the package. Her screen updates with a new order and she watches as it recalibrates the coordinates so that the RDU can pick the next package before it returns to her so she can confirm and pack. But the next RDU is already here with its little screen out and she lifts her scanner to buzz.

A voice in her ear.

You're kicking goals!

She licks her lips to try to ease her thirst.

A day off. She sleeps and sleeps before Cat finally strokes her face and tells her she's heading into campus and La should get up, *doesn't she have an appointment?* She does, but fuck, she would rather sleep.

'Remember what you're doing this for, huh?' Cat says, and kisses her. As she stands under the searing heat of the shower, La wonders if her girlfriend meant the therapist and the audition or the warehouse job and the subsidised freezing of her eggs.

Susannah, her voice therapist, reckons she can be ready for the audition next March, but that's assuming the company gets the funding to bring the show out, there are no weather events, no market collapses, no pandemics. It's the gig La's always wanted. And yes, she knows what the others from the academy say – that it's for big belter star types – and what they don't say: that she isn't one of them. That she doesn't quite ever look the part, that she'll never make it past the chorus. But fuck them. There's something to be said for blinkered stubborn grit.

There's an old video of her online singing the song for a *Talent X* audition. She's seventeen. She's watched the video so many times it means nothing. Every third person sang the bloody song, must have been the first year it came out and there was a fever about it. And she was good. Good enough to get through to the next round anyway, until they cut her because there was another girl who looked like her with a better back story and amazing hair. Or that's what she tells herself. The only way she has found to dismantle those voices in her head as she watches her audition – too short, too Asian, too white. Her own voice always the most scathing – you use your hands too much, look weird when you go low or go high, not attractive when you scrunch your eyes up, too much, never enough, you chew on the word 'reckless', the naïve way you place your hands on your belly on 'growing inside me' – ah, it makes her cringe to watch.

But less now. Less each time. Time heals all wounds, apparently.

The therapist coughs gently. 'So, the new job, any strain on your voice?'

'No, actually, it's really good. Everything's on a device. It's probably one of the better jobs I could be doing to look after it.'

Susannah raises an eyebrow, but smiles and notes something on her screen.

Bitch, La thinks but swallows it down, wonders if the words she never speaks are extra poison to those gnarled nodules in her throat.

The final instalment from the AI voice-licensing gig she did last year has come in, so she pays for the therapy session in full as she leaves, enjoying the quick surprise the receptionist tries to hide in his expression. Ironic that the gig that mangled her voice is the one paying for her therapy. Evidently there's only so many hours a voice artist can intone at the same precise pitch before their throat is well and truly fucked. Walking to the bus stop, she can feel muscles she didn't know she had in her back, her legs, and feels strong for the first time in a while.

On her sixth shift, La receives her first warning. A three-tone ascending bell sounds in her earpiece and the RDU working with her flashes an orange screen before it takes the package from her hands.

> Hey there, SM978! How are you going? You didn't meet your hourly quota this time, but you still have a chance to catch up. Let's go all out for the next hour and get up to speed!

She sticks her tongue out at the RDU. 'Little prick,' she says.

> Respectful language is one of our core values here at WANT. Continued profanity will result in penalties.

La bursts out laughing, shakes her head, picks up the next box – GlitterPelt: eco-friendly luminous hair cream for you and your pet – and shoves it at the RDU.

Back home, she hits the override button in the shower, sacrificing some of tomorrow's water ration for today. 'Just a little bit more,' she mutters, tilting her head back so the hot hot water deltas down her face, neck, chest. She makes low noises as the hurt deep in her bones softens, noises she makes with Cat. She thinks about putting one hand between her legs but knows she can't finish before the water runs out and wasting more rations to get herself off crosses a moral line even she is not prepared to break.

She remembers her mother's quiet scoffing and raised brow on the screen, her voice, brutally soft. 'It is one thing or the other, Lara, you cannot have it both ways. No aeroplanes, no animal products, but yes to your fancy makeup, your devices. Your generation – you wear your ethics like those filters on your phones.'

La concedes her mother's phrasing had been nice. And so what if her ethics were convenient? She had some, at least. The No Flight pledge had felt like something solid, even if she could barely afford airfares anyway. She does not want to be told by her mother about the compromise she is making by being part of the WANT machine, and no, she will not give up her phone, or find a profession other than the arts, and no, she did not want to think about her father's disappointment, her sister's feeling of being *betrayed* at her time of need, the little nephew who she would not meet because she refused to get on a plane.

She watches the override timer count down, ten seconds more, making every moment of hot sluicing water count. Her body is sore in places that she wasn't conscious of, worse than during performance seasons when she'd had to dance. Individual bones in her feet. The tendon running from beneath her ear down her neck. She is already anxious about getting to bed before her alarm goes off for the shift tomorrow. And the next day. And the next day.

She snorts the water away from her face and turns off the tap. Eight months. That's it. That's all she has to do.

The next week, the doctor at the Dreem fertility clinic asks about La's exercise routine, her finger hovering over a screen. She asks about alcohol, drugs, history of illness, mental health – La can't remember having ever given such a comprehensive personal history to anyone. And this is after the initial online psychological assessment where she had truly felt unskinned. Too bad if they are selling off her data.

'Coffee?' she says, incredulous, looking at the list.

'Obviously these decisions are your own, but for optimal egg health we recommend limiting caffeine.'

It feels like another job in itself to get her body ready for her eggs to be harvested and frozen. Injections, vitamins, clean-eating meal prep. But it's giving her purpose. And there's hope that all this health stuff might help her throat recover, too. Plus, Cat is blissed out on all this clean living. Making La food, spending too long and too much at the organic fruit and veg shop. And there is more sex.

Cat is up early, holding a mug of tea in both hands, face towards the early sun coming in through the kitchen window. She is wearing one of La's singlets, a strap hangs off her left shoulder, the worn grey fabric rumpled precariously at the top of her left breast. La wants to kiss her, right there, again. Doesn't. She is already late but she is hungry, voracious for Cat – must be her cycle, or all those hormones – if she starts something now she will not stop. Instead, she opens the half door of the pantry, stares for a moment at all the grains and noodles that she will not have enough break time to prep in the staff kitchen and instead grabs a half-squashed protein bar, violently purple among all the virtuous bulk pulses.

'Is that your lunch?'

La takes the mug from Cat and downs the last two sips, too milky. 'It is.'

Cat grabs the protein bar and turns it over. 'Soy protein. Palm oil. Soluble corn fibre. Cacao from Brazil via LA. Almonds from California. Alkali, water, sodium caseinate.'

'Mmmm,' says La, snatching the bar back and waving it at Cat. 'See you later!'

'Eat an apple!' Cat calls after her, then: 'Wait!'

La turns. 'I'm gonna be late!'

Cat runs to her, holds her face in her hands, kissing her and whispering, 'It's a good thing, this is a good thing we are doing.'

We. The word traces a thrill under her skin as La runs for the bus.

∞

Newcoast, 2181

Maz has dived in other places, softer, quieter bays and inlets where there was sand and rock and pools formed by the tide and the old movements of the planet. Few oddz to clear there, they dived for the fish, just enough to fill their bellies. Othertimes, she has dived in drowned places, oldtowns, once a city. This dive-site is somewhere in between; Mater explains that in the beforetimes thousands of people would come here to play on the beaches and walk by the sea. It is under the sea now. Parts of it anyways. Bits of rooves and bridges, a wharf, a great wheel with little rooms attached to it. Maz thinks what a thing it must have been, as it once was. Mater has warned them about sly currents pulling into dark hollows of submerged buildings, spikes of metal and glass, the long fingers of plastic ribbon streaming out like sea grass ready to tangle and drown. The Last Stewards travel down from the caves to the Newcoast for the few moons when it is not too hot to be above ground. They are to clear and clean where they can, where it might give plant and animal safe passage. They salvage only to replace what they already have (remember: *no better, no faster, no bigger, no more*), and harvest only enough to sustain them on their mission.

When the weather turns to dry heat again the Stewards trek back to the dark damp of the caves, hiding from the sun and the blistering hot of the world above ground until the cycle comes again.

In the under, Maz fingers the furred green moss of the old concrete, skin pads pressing, caressing the divots and ridges of the new seabed to locate the smooth of steel, the crunkle of plastic, the sharp of some long-broken thing that must be disassembled and returned to the earth. JP allows diving in the waters, knows it is safe because he keeps count. It is over a century since The Collapse. The poisons have been leeched and cleaned by the ocean itself, the planet is healing, but JP says it is the Stewards' task to finish the job.

In the morning dives they collect a halfsack of plastic. Not as much as some dive sites but enough to please JP and add to the ledger for this place. Drying in the sun, Maz and Benevolent chew on seedcakes and Onyx whinges about wanting to dive.

'Not fair. I can do it.'

There is seedcake stuck in the ridge of Maz's tooth. She tries to dig it out with her tongue, and, when it doesn't shift, with her fingernail. 'I know that.'

'Then why can't I dive with you?'

Maz is diver while Onyx stays on the surface and does the sorting. This is the deal. Others swap jobs around but Onyx has never gone below. Maz told her she had to wait until she'd seen eight full turns, and then when she'd seen eight she told her ten, and in a few cycles when her sister comes of age she will somehow change the rules again. Because Maz will not let her sister dive while she can do it in her place.

'Because you are a superbrill sorter. No one does it like you, with your teeny fingers and clever eyes.'

Onyx harumphs and holds up a handful of oddz. 'Any stump can sort. Why can't Mater or Trust do it? Plastics to plastics, steel to steel. It's a forty-niner's job.'

Beside her, Benevolent sucks breath in over his teeth at the way Onyx casually spits out the words.

'Onyx. Caretake your words.'

Onyx shifts her body away, knows she's done wrong but won't retract. 'It's true,' she murmurs, 'they're nearly gone anyways.'

Maz leans back in the sun for a moment, ignoring her sister and preparing her breathing for the next dive.

Maz is sure Onyx cannot remember the last time a forty-niner returned to the source. It was only one full turn after they arrived with the Stewards and Onyx was so little and still wild with mother-loss. She could not have understood the quiet talk, the ceremony, the day they all stood at the bottom of the crossing and watched Heliope grow smaller and smaller until she was lost in the tree cover of the lower slopes. Maz remembers waiting for Heliope to return, asking JP why they were breaking camp when she had not yet come down from the mountain, turning his response over and over like a smooth stone in her mouth – *Heliope has returned to the source* – until it finally clunked into place.

Over the many full turns since then there have been no more forty-niners, and so Maz and Onyx have never ceremonied again or watched an elder walk away, but she has sung the tenet enough now to know. To understand the first tenet of the Last Stewards: *We shall each return to the source on the eve of our half-century. In service and sacrifice, this is our pledge.* Eleven cycles ago they raised their cups to Trust's forty-ninth full turn, and on the next waxing gibbous, she, too, will return to the source.

As a bleeder now, Maz attends to the circles and she understands the preparation Trust is undertaking. The stories, the breathing, the great peace that Trust must find as she curls into a crevice of her own choosing on the summit and waits to return to the source. Trust sometimes worries at her wrist threads as the women sing the stories and Maz thinks she knows why. For while she knows the great unbroken promise of the Last Stewards, in her skin and her bones and blood, Maz resists. She does not want to return to the source. She cannot fathom how she might lie and wait for her body to run out of water, for her breath to stop. When she thinks of herself walking up the mountain a great blankness shadows her mind and she cannot see past it or through it. If she thinks of Onyx walking up the mountain the blankness turns to fire. So, she doesn't think of it.

'Ready?' Benevolent says, and Maz nods.

They cross the old concrete to the other side of the drowned harbour, where there is good light for seeing below. She takes one side, points to the mottled colour glowing at depth.

'You right for that one?' She points to where a slab rears from the water, good pickings down there.

Benevolent nods, checks his sack at his waist, his goggleface tight, and dives.

Maz watches him descend, feet like fins behind him as he pushes through the water to the depths.

She dives.

Ears crack, rush of cold, wet light, down, down, catching the colour and strangeness of oddz with her own clever eyes. Deeper, ear crack and ring again, until she is fingerscrabbling gentle gentle, doesn't do to cloud up the water. And there, a red twist of plastic, a long straight stick that bends in her hand when she clasps it. They have found so many of these, JP says the Wanters used them to drink. What a thing, she thinks, and stuffs it in her sack. Another turn before she'll need to surface, there the heavy rust of an old energy-keeper she'll need to use both hands to lift, and here a slimy coin – JP sorts those specially – she'll dive here again in this spot till it's clean.

All day, down, down and up to breathe in the sun, and steady and down again; a twist of plastic line, a sheet of black plastic so deep in the mud that she has to call Ben to help her pull it up. Together they drag it to the edge where Onyx pulls it up onto the slab, wrinkling her nose at the putrid stink of it.

Maz looks at the sky, the light. 'One more?' she says to Ben and he nods and she swims out a little further to the left, hoping for a cluster of oddz to bring up to make it a really good day.

Down again, and in a crevice, the broken foundations of the bridge, all the way down where something gleams: fish! She dives closer to try to catch a glimpse of the coppery tail again. The light plays in the water and she goes deeper, hand out, but it doesn't move, not fish – oddz – and she reaches out to clasp the small disc half hidden in the mud.

Unsucking from the mud, the disc is hot, heavy, buzzing faintly in her hand as she brings it to her goggleface, human or natural? Strange markings, like a shell. Is it a wayfinder? Either way, she will take it up, it has a feel about it, something she wants to look at properly, something she already knows she does not want to hand over to Onyx, to be sorted, to go to JP.

Breaking the surface, she sees Ben staring down, face scrunched in worry. He touches his ear, and she returns the sign, *Yes, I'm okay.*

He shakes his head a little and gestures for her to come to the edge. Then she sees JP. He is standing back a little with Onyx, who is showing the contents of the bag for him to check. Bag sorts must be put in the ledger at the end of each day and JP must approve each one. He doesn't normally come out to a dive site, maybe once in every twenty dives, but when he does there seems to be a strangesome ringing in the air, his long careful fingers sifting through the oddz. The question he sometimes asks: *Nothing else?*

Ben approaches JP and the leader lifts his head, follows Benevolent's pointing arm to where Maz treads water. JP handflaps for her to come in.

A Steward does not scavenge for themselves but for the earth.

The third tenet, the one that she struggles with on every dive. Onetime she found a small glass orb with a spinning yellow and blue swirl buried in its heart. She did not want it to be sorted and destroyed. She wanted it for keeps. When she looked at it first in the water, rubbing off the mud, and then when she surfaced and held it to the light, she felt dizzy with bigness and smallness, like she was inside the orb and looking down on it sametimes. She knew it was forbidden to keep an oddz but she also knew she could not hand it over. She held it in her mouth while they sorted. Kept it from the ledger. Pushed it deep inside her pack.

But one night after the fire, JP called her for an audience in his tent. When she arrived, he opened his hand to reveal the glass orb on his palm. For a week she was forbidden from joining the fire circle, given only a seedcake on every second day and no tea. She could hear Onyx whining and asking for more for her sister, but each night when Onyx returned to the tent Maz told her to stop, she would only make it worse.

Never again has Maz hidden an oddz and never again has she been tempted, until now.

In her palm, the metal disc. JP handflaps again. Maz nods, holds up the sack with her other hand. Then she begins to swim to the edge. He does not see her slip the oddz under her waist band. At least she hopes he does not see.

There is a flicker and buzz in the air around the fire that night because JP has decided they are to stay here near the bridge of the oldcity for another few days. He does not explain why – and Trombolo, who reads the weather, has not seen any storms that would hinder their journey. While they wash up, squatting around the tub, Maz listens to Trust and Mater murmur quietly.

'This will late us for the mountain,' Trust says, her voice trembling in the quiet.

'We will make it,' Mater says, 'JP will not let it be anotherways.'

'But it is a good halfmoon's journey from here, and looksee—' Trust raises her chin and they both look to the sky where the new moon is rising in the eastern sky.

'You have been keeping score,' Mater says gently.

Trust lowers her eyes, quiet for a moment as she agitates a handful of sporks in the tub. 'You will too, when it is your time.'

Mater pulls one hand from the tub, wipes it against her thigh, and places it on Trust's shoulder. They are very still for a long moment. Sometimes Maz wonders if they are sisters. True, there is no sameness in their bodies. Trust is tall, taller than JP and Trombolo, and she has brown skin and black hair and eyes that shine green some days and golden others. Mater is rounder than she is tall. She braids her dark curls into long ropes down her back. Her skin is darker than Maz's but not as brown as Trust's. But when they are next to each other, harvesting berries or tending the fire or upping the tents, Trust and Mater move as though they are one person. Sometimes she sees them talking without words like she and Onyx do. Eyes and hands and shoulders speaking little things, careful things.

She remembers their kindness, during the moons and cycles after she and Onyx first came to the Stewards and Onyx had clung to her legs and wailed for their mama. Trust and Mater had pulled the sisters in each night to their own tent, kept them close and warm until JP had them sew a new one. Maz wonders if Mater ever wishes that she too was a forty-niner, so she and Trust could return to the source together.

Maz senses someone approaching behind her and hurries to pack away the rest of the supplies to keep them safe from night foragers. She still feels the imprint on her skin of the oddz she found and has now buried deep in her pack. Still, she is all nerves.

'JP tells you to be ready, we dive again tomorrow.'

Maz turns in surprise to Benevolent. They never dive two days straight. It is a rule, true, not a tenet, but rule enough that she has never seen it broken.

'Why?'

Benevolent shrugs. 'He didn't say, but he took something from my sack, he seemed . . . excited.'

Excited is not a word Maz would ever use to describe JP.

'What was it?'

Benevolent shakes his head. 'Looked just like any oddz to me. Metal, I think, maybe a little heavier, I can't even remember picking it up, though he questioned me about the exact spot.'

Maz is aware of the tiniest flutter in her chest. 'Strange,' she says.

Maz waits until Onyx's breathing steadies beside her in the tent, then, very quietly, she wiggles her hand down through the layers of her pack and grabs hold of the oddz. One edge smooth, one jagged as though it has broken off a circle. She imagines that if the circle were complete it would be the exact size of her palm, her fingers able to curve around the edges. In the dark she brings the broken oddz to her face and sniffs it. The deep muck siltsalt smell of all wateroddz. Different to the oddz they collect and sort along the rocky trails, or in the forest, in the thick compost layering the oldworld streets. This one would be sorted to metal or aggregate, it doesn't give off the whiff of plastic or chem that she has learnt to register high in the apex of her nose.

She traces her finger pads across the grooved surface, pressing into the curves and ridges and following the trail they make. It is certainly part of a pattern, almost definitely humanstuff. Symmetrical, even and intricate. She wants to light her lamp to better look at it, but knows she must not. There is a dense tight feeling swelling in her guts and it is want. This oddz is hers. She must not let JP know she has it. There have been times when an oddz was thrown back to the deep after sorting, when it became clear it was not humanstuff. Sometimes it is hard to tell. A spiral shell, or a bright coral, kelp that looks like old plastics, smooth wood that has turned to stone or something like it. Maybe this oddz is a type of rock, a perfect half of a bivalve, an imprint of a long-gone creature. Is it just chance that she found this oddz on the same day, in the same dive, that Benevolent discovered something that excited JP? The same day that he decided, for the first time in memory, that they would not break camp on schedule, even though it would jeopardise Trust's return to the source?

They dive all day back at the spot near the old bridge, but though they both bring up another half sack of oddz, JP is not satisfied. Before the second dive he had pulled something from his pocket and held it out to them in his lined palm. Maz stilled her body so she did not give herself away. A broken shard of a dense coppery substance as wide as her little finger and then narrowing down to a point. Another piece of her oddz. She imagines it fitting together with her own. It glinted then dulled as JP pushed it towards them and the sun caught something that appeared to glow beneath its surface.

'This is what Benevolent found yesterday.'

'What is it?' Ben asks.

'It does not matter what it is, only that there are likely to be more here.'

'Are they Treasures?' Maz asks. Treasures are rare. Not useful for missions, not to be disassembled, a Treasure is something that makes JP's blue eyes gleam, that he keeps safe for the Stewards, although for what, they are never told. JP ignores her.

'We will widen the dive site and find any other remnants. We will dive again tomorrow.'

Maz frowns. 'We cannot dive three days, JP, we will bend.'
'You won't bend.'
'But, that is the rule – we cannot keep the breath—'
'You will not bend,' he interrupts her. 'And tomorrow you will have help. Onyx will dive with you.'
'No!' Maz is quick and sharp. 'Onyx is not ready to dive.'
'She is ready, and already four cycles past when you began.'
Maz grits her teeth and scrabbles for reasons. 'A cough, she has a cough in her chest, it won't be good for her to dive, next time she will be ready.'
JP steps towards her. 'Are you questioning my decision, Maz? Are you breaking the second tenet?'
She shakes her head.
'Repeat it to me so that I can be assured you have not misremembered.'
Maz wishes she could swallow her tongue. Sees a bright flash in her mind's eye – for a second, less than that – of stealing the shard from JP's hand and plunging it into the soft neckflesh beneath his ear.
'*Our leader holds our bodies, minds and spirits in the name of Stewardship: to them we give our skills, our energy, our loyalty. To question our leader is to question the earth herself. Those who do not comply will be returned to the source.*'

That night Maz dreams of her mother. She never sees her face, knows only the sniff of her, the skinlove, the feeling she is safe. She wants to nestle in forever, does not want to listen to her mother's song but she is insistent, pulling on her child's ear.
Maz, dreammother says. *Maz, you must listen, you must pay attention.*
She curls her head in and tries to block her ears against the motherskin but it is no use, her mother's voice is everywhere, speaking a song that Maz feels she already knows.

You must be ready.
It is nearly time to leave and to find.
A bird with an unfamiliar song at dawn.
A cloud shaped like a mountain yawning smoke.
A man who says, 'That which you have known to be true was never so.'

Maz buries her head deeper in dreammother's embrace but still the words come.

Maz, my love, this is the moment.
This is how you will know it is time.

And then light is etching patterns against the tent and Onyx is prodding her, 'Today! It's today!' but all Maz can hear is *tereeepawww tereeepaww* from outside the tent, a strange birdsong that seems like something from a dream.

It is difficult to get Onyx to eat her matins, to sit still for a moment near the small morning fire so that Maz can try to tell her all the things she needs to know in her body and mind, before the dive.

'I *know* all that,' Onyx says, 'you've told me before. And, I can dive, you've seen me, you know I can do it.'

'I do know you can do it, but you have to quieten a little, you have to listen to your own breath, know what to do if something happens in the under that you are not expecting.'

Onyx wiggles her fingers in Maz's face and giggles. 'Like a big raymama gonna come and nubble me? A bigtooth eater gonna glide up and take a bite out of my belly?'

Tickling fingers plunge into Maz's middle and what can she do but laugh at her little sister, who is still all girlflesh and ticklefingers and in a little time will be piercing the water with her body to scrabble for oddz for their founding father?

And not just any oddz: a piece so specific, so wanted, a piece that Maz is becoming more and more certain has already been picked from the sludge and is hiding in the middle of this camp. She wonders if JP can smell it.

Little is unearthed in the morning dive. JP extends the dive zone, then brings it in again when they fail to bring up anything other than a matted knot of terrorstring. The string is so tied and tight, woven through the skeletons of two waterbirds whose beaks have caught in it, that Maz surfaces to get the blade and cut it away. JP prefers them to untangle the odds with only their fingers, so as not to leave any trace behind, but sometimes it is impossible. By the time they break for noons, Maz drags her feet, her chest tight as she lies in the sun trying to absorb as much of its fuel as she can before she returns to the deep.

Onyx is grinning. Along with the string, she has brought up a dozen tiny oddz in her sack and she lays them out in a circle pattern, smallest to largest, on the slab in front of her.

'You did well,' Ben says, nodding his head at the pattern, 'for your first dive. You are a natural.'

Like a waterbird in the sun, Onyx preens and Maz turns her head away.

'See,' Onyx says, 'I'm good at this.'

Yes, you are, Maz thinks, good at all the things, seeing clear in the dark of the caves, your long scamper legs and your tiny fingers that can knit and weave and your songvoice and the wild magic tangle of your hair, the black ring on the edge of your blue iris – yes, sister, I sometimes think you are not from the same place as the rest of us.

JP shadowblocks the sun.

'Ready.' It is not a question when he says it.

They dive.

The second time they prepare to go under in the afternoon, Maz asks JP to let Onyx stay up.

'It's her first day, don't push her,' she says, feeling a little braver as she calls from the water.

But Onyx dives. And Onyx dives well. And it is Onyx who surfaces with one hand held triumphant in the air above her, calling out across the chipchop top of the water – 'I found something!'

It's not a perfect fit, that much they can see as they huddle, dripping, over the oddz JP now holds in his hand. He pulls the other piece from his pocket and lays it alongside the new find – they are of the same matter, that much is sure. The same dull copper gleam, a familiar curvature to the unbroken edge. They do not fit together, the two pieces JP holds, but Maz can see immediately how they fit to hers, and can see, now, that hers is the biggest piece, that what she has found and held and hidden away is exactly what JP is searching for.

As they walk back to camp, Onyx is bright with pride and Maz smiles widely with her sister despite the nerves rippling in her throat. 'You did well, sister,' she says.

'I know,' says Onyx.

Wine is poured, the fire built high, and Mater is instructed to use the last of the high plains mushrooms in the stew. JP declares a ceremony night, exactly what ceremony and which tenet and what songs remains unclear. But what Steward would say no to wine and bigfire and the mind spangle of soaked alpine mushrooms? So they eat and drink and sing whichever song a fullthroated singer throws forth across the fire, and the

Stewards grow merry, but none merrier than JP. He circles the fire, touching each Steward on the head or the shoulder. Maz catches fragments of the words he halfsings; some she knows, some she's never heard before.

It is within our grasp.
We will find the key and unlock a tomorrow without a past.

Maz has a little wine but she is careful and has forbidden her sister from even a sip. She watches Onyx dance in the fireshadow with Trust and some of the women. Benevolent folds himself to sit on the earth beside her. From the smell and the sway of him, he's gone nearly as fast with the wine as JP.

'Your sister is a good diver. You should not have held her back so long.'

Maz makes a face. Ben goes on.

'I know you are true kin, but you must remember that means nothing here. Your sister is as much mine as she is yours.'

'No words do what blood does.'

'Blood means little, it is action that matters. I would not hesitate to return my brother to the source if he hurt you, for instance, and you and I share no blood.'

Maz shrugs. Ben came to the Stewards before she and Onyx, and he came alone. He is older than Maz but not as old as the others. He has never said if he arrived the same way they did. Taken. He does not seem to have any particular connection to any of the older Stewards, but she has never asked. Somedays he rolls his eyes at JP or cusses quietly when he is given a task, but she cannot see the same fierce in him that she sometimes feels toward their founding father.

'I do not ask for any person to take a blade on my account.' She looks at him now. 'I can do that for myself.'

Ben laughs, a bigthroated bellow, and when he is done he grins at her. 'I know that very well, Maz.' And then he lifts his left hand and points his index finger and places just the pad of his finger on her jawbone, close to her ear. 'You are marked by the sun here. I see it in my dreams.'

She is very still.

He is very still.

The fire leaps.

Mater's voice, 'Shush now, enough, enough.' Maz and Ben break eyes to look across the fire ring to where Mater has her hands out to JP, who has taken off his shirt and is scratching his fingernails down his chest – even at this distance Maz can see the dark traces of blood. Mater tries to grab his hands and there are others coming, gathering around, but before they get to JP he pushes Mater away so hard that she stumbles backwards and trips and falls on her arse in the dust. JP freezes and they all hush to see Mater pick herself up from the dirt, dust herself down, look away. The fifth tenet, *No Steward will raise a hand against another. All who do will be returned to the source.* But if it came to a ceremony no one could say for sure that JP had raised his hand against Mater, and no one, not ever, would tell JP he had broken a tenet. The others gather around Mater and help her away into the darkness away from the fire. JP shakes his head and calls out loud and abrupt, 'Sing it closed,' and so they do. Sing the fire down, sing the wine away, sing the Stewards all to bed.

'Come, Onyx,' Maz says. As she leads her sister away she thinks, only once, of the bright pulse of that fingertip on her jaw.

In the tent, Maz lets the lamp burn a little longer, no one cares on such things after ceremony and certainly won't on a night like tonight.

'I'm so tired and yet I'm not sleepy at all,' Onyx says, yawning wide and wriggling her legs. 'Tell me a story.'

Maz folds one arm behind her head. 'Which one?'

She tells her sister her mother's stories, but she would whisper them aloud to herself if Onyx didn't ask. When she tells them, making the words go up and down, loud and soft as her ma did, Maz feels like she remembers her ma back to almost-life. Her ma had books, too. Filled with the stories. But Maz was too little to learn to make the words speak, and though they have rarely found a book in the salvaging, if they find any oddz with words, JP destroys them. Written words are not allowed in JP's new world. He does not know what is sewn into Maz's hem. Problem is, neither does she.

'You choose,' Onyx says.

And Maz thinks about the hum of the oddz inside her pack, the wild in JP's eyes, the burning flicker of dreamfeeling. She has not allowed herself to think of leaving and looking for her father. When the thought brightbangs in her mind, she tells it to wait until Onyx is older and stronger, until they come to a place that feels like a memory, until they find evidence of a camp of Finders. She cannot keep Onyx and herself alive out there on their own. Not yet. And that's what they might be – alone. Until now, staying with the Stewards has been better than the thought of what lies out there, beyond: scavengers – animal and human – places that keep the secret of their water and sustenance close.

But now. Her dreammother's words: *It is nearly time.*

'Once upon a mountain moon, two sisters kept fire.

'They tended fire and sent it where it was needed – by gods, by humans, by animals, by forests.

'One day, it seemed that all the world asked for fire at the same time. The elder sister, whose name has been eaten by history, sent fire through the mountains to the God who was cold. The younger sister heard the pleas of a forest whose seeds needed fire to crack and be reborn, and so she sent great heat to dry, and then wind to lick the lightning forks she sparked into the trees.'

'The younger sister is braver,' Onyx says.

'Ha. I don't know about that.'

'Keep going.'

'Tired and hungry, the sisters rested, but before the day had ended a family of humans had called forth fire to help dry them and keep them warm and safe. To heat their tea and cook their food so their bellies could be warm, for they had wandered from the track and without fire they would perish.

'Fire was sent.

'But when the sisters sat down to their own sups and clapped their hands to issue forth the flames to heat their soup and tea, none would come, for they had used it all up on those who called.

'The eldest sister cried out, for she had forgotten the rule that she must always keep a glowing coal back. She was not a fire sister, she was no use to anyone – God, human, animal or plant – if she could not summon fire with her fingers. She went to the rock keeping place but she already knew what she would find, an empty spot where the coal should be.'

'*Sister, why do you cry?* the younger sister asked.

'*I have failed you and I have failed us. I have no fire left to keep us warm and we shall perish tonight on the mountain, and then all those who call for us will perish too.* Her tears wet her robes and the earth and the little ferns there shivered to feel her sadness.

'The younger sister held up her hand. *What if I can summon just one more lightning strike? It might be enough to catch, to light, for us to bring fire back to our hands?*

'*I don't know*, the older sister said, her eyes still wet.

'*Then we must try.*

'The younger sister instructed the older sister to gather dry kindling, the smallest, lightest dries she could find, and hold them safe in her cupped hands, with her back against the wind.

'*Be ready*, said the younger sister, *this may be our only chance.*'

A small snort from the bed next to her makes Maz look down to find her little sister asleep, arms akimbo, mouth open wide, eyes shut against the lamplight.

In the morning, Onyx slumbers on and Maz can hear the rattle and bang of camp and knows she must get up, they must move and dive again, but her sister's sleeping face pins her there.

Someone calls her name, then rattles the tent, and finally Onyx cracks an eyelid and yawns and says is it time to dive again.

'Yes, time to dive again,' Maz says and listens to the flap of the tent and wishes hard that the wind will be too high, the weather too wild for diving.

'I fell asleep, did you finish the story without me?'

'No, tonight we will finish it. What's the last thing you remember?'

'Hmmm,' Onyx murmurs as she sits up and stretches, 'something something fire sisters.'

Maz laughs and they dress quickly before emerging into the morning. There is sun, but a fast mean little breeze has kicked up and clouds are swarming. It is not a good day to dive. JP will know that. He is not a fool. Besides, there are rumblings in the camp – they need to get to the mountain.

As she approaches JP's tent, Maz hears Trombolo's big voice. *Good*, she thinks, *the weatherman must be telling him we cannot dive*. But then she hears JP's voice rear up and she stops. If Trombolo, his most trusted adviser, cannot convince him, what chance has Maz got? She creeps closer to make out their words. Trombolo's voice rumbles again.

'JP, we must leave to ensure Trust does her return on the waxing moon.'

'Why must we, Trombolo?'

'You know full well. If a forty-niner does not return to the source before their half-century . . .'

JP laughs. 'Then what? We will change the story, the gibbous instead. It's only a story. You and I know that.'

A story. A story is not real, it's made up, Maz knows this. Her mother and father taught her the difference. Fact and fiction — the two are not the same.

'JP, you are not yourself, quiet your voice.'

'If this is truly what we have been searching for, then it matters not whether Trust returns to the source this moon or the next.'

'You cannot be certain.'

'I feel it. I know it. And that child, she has a sense. We are close. She will dive again today, she will find the pieces, we will complete the puzzle and the machine will finally do what it was built to do.'

'And if she doesn't? If it doesn't?'

'I know this to be true.'

Maz hears footsteps and ducks away, running as quietly as she can across the wet grass.

A man who says that which you have known to be true was never so.

She is heavybreathing when she arrives at the fire.

'You're late,' Benevolent says. 'JP wants to go early.'

'Do you think we should dive today?' Maz asks.

'Why not?'

'The wind, we are tired, there is nothing else there . . .' she trails off, knowing how small each offering sounds.

'JP believes there is something else. I do not think he will let us leave until we find it.'

*

Sun glint. Goggleface on. Toes to the edge. Maz squeezes her sister's hand, then steps away to face the same crevice of a pool she has dived each of these days. This morning she considered bringing the disc back. Hiding it in the silt and finding it again. Letting Onyx find it. JP would have his way, they could move again, Trust would stop wearing a path between the fire and the shore. They could up and leave for the mountain, and Trust could return to the source as she desires.

But JP's words: *Only a story. The machine. That child.*

What if these pieces are part of something that will bring danger close? What if what she has hidden away in her bag is the very thing her mother warned her to protect Onyx from? She does not want JP to have something dangerous, powerful. She wants to keep it herself.

She breathes deeply.

'Maz!' Onyx calls out.

She turns to her sister.

'Be ready!' Onyx yells, grinning. 'That was the last thing I remember! *Be ready, this may be our only chance.*'

Maz holds up her thumbs as her little sister turns and dives.

And Onyx follows her down.

Up and down they go. She watches her sister through the deep.

Siltkick in the water, Maz finds Onyx down near the bottom, but her sister has dug her foot in deep and the space between them is shimmering with grit and maniac particles.

Breathe, Maz reminds her body, *breathe*.

As slowly as she can bear, she jackknifes her body down towards Onyx, trying not to kick her feet too much, three arms' lengths, two, one. She can see now that Onyx has her hand fastened on something that is stuck, the cords of her wrist are tight against her skin. Above her head, bubbles. She needs to surface. Now.

Gently as she can, she touches her sister's back, but no touch is gentle beneath the waves and Onyx rears around, eyes wide, arm still locked in the rock. Maz points her finger, gives the sign, *Up. Now*. And *Up* again.

Onyx shakes her head and turns back to the crevice, her little fingers wiggling deep in the crack.

Fear like an eel round Maz's chest. If she pulls her sister away she will panic, run out of air, drown them both. But Onyx is stubborn, if she has found something she wants she will not give it up. Maz darts down, touches her again. Swims into her line of vision.

Come. She motions. *Up.*

But Onyx just digs her arm in deeper, eyes scrunching, another gollup of breath escaping from her mouth.

Maz will not let her sister drown. She grabs Onyx's other wrist and begins to swim up hard and fast, but the arm slips free from her grip and she turns to a slew of bubbles rising – Onyx's open mouth, her other arm still deep in the rock.

Her sister is stuck.

Quick quick, earringing, quick, Maz dives back down, follows her sister's arm to her wrist, fends off Onyx's other hand flailing, pushing, yanking at her hair – she has run out of breath now, she must do it. The hand is wedged fast, Maz pushes, pulls, and Onyx smashes at her head from behind. *I have to*, she thinks, *I must*. And she pulls on her sister's hand as hard as she has ever pulled, and she hears the scream through the water, feels Onyx go slack at her back, but the hand pops free, a strange angle on the thumb – but *up*, slow but fast, fast but slow, let her ears bleed, her brain bend, just get us to air to air to air. The light through the green, the heavy drape of her sister, the push push push of her lungs, her breath, her arms, and they surface. And she screams. And she holds her sister's face to the air.

*

It feels an age before Ben is there pulling them out, JP dragging Onyx onto the slab, terrible wait, then finally water gurgles up out of Onyx's mouth in a sour rush and Maz holds her sister and wipes spit from her teeth and mouth and chin. She yells at JP, *You did this, this is your fault*, until Ben holds her wrist and whispers urgently and close, *Not now, Maz.*

Maz quiets. Onyx breathes.

'What happened?' JP asks, eyes fixed on Onyx.

'She got stuck, she—' but JP holds up a palm and barks at her. 'I'm asking Onyx.'

Onyx holds her hurt hand, rubs her wrist, her face all crinkled with pain.

'There was an oddz. In a crack. I tried to get it, my hand got stuck. Maz pulled me out.'

'Where is it?'

'The oddz? I didn't—' Onyx looks at Maz. 'Did it come loose?'

'I wasn't looking, I was trying to . . . No, I don't think so.'

'Go down and look,' JP says.

'I'll go—' says Benevolent.

'No. It must be Onyx,' JP barks.

'She cannot dive again today, JP. She nearly drowned. She is hurt.'

'I want her to dive. No one else.'

Benevolent stands and clears his throat. 'It is not safe. I can find it.'

'Onyx will do it.'

Onyx looks at Maz, dropping her hand, but her eyes are bright with fear. 'I'm not hurt,' she says, holding her hand close to her chest, 'I can do it.'

'No, you can't.' Maz turns to JP. 'An oddz that deep in a crack will not move overnight. If you will not let me or Ben dive for it, please, let us wait for Onyx to dive tomorrow.'

'She will dive *now*!' His voice is like nothing she has heard, almost a shriek, as though the man is a bird with a broken wing, a rat who has been pinned by an arrow.

Onyx puts her hand on Maz's back. 'It's okay. I promise. It's okay.' And it is backwards, the way the little sister comforts the older.

Onyx selects a small pinchbar from Benevolent's roll, shakes out her hand and dives into the water.

From the slab, Maz tries to keep track of her sister's shape down deep but there is sun then cloud then sun again, so quick it makes it hard to see through the glare and dark. A storm is coming.

'Come on,' she mutters, 'come up.'

Another dark shadow, she looks up to see if the rain will finally loose down on them and sees a blueblack shape in the sky that chills her through. A cloud in the shape of a mountain, growing in the sky before her – and from its apex a paler, sunshot cloud billows out like smoke from a campfire.

A cloud shaped like a mountain yawning smoke.

Maz breathes, ready to dive in and drag her sister out, JP be damned.

And then Onyx breaks the surface, one hand held aloft.

'I got it!'

On the slab, JP holds the oddz triumphantly, that dull glow of copper again, a pattern of three now laid out on the cracked grey of the bridge.

'Did it break, or was it already broken?' Ben asks as Maz rubs her sister's back, tries to warm her with her own body in the fading light.

Tenderly, JP moves the pieces, turning them this way and that, aligning edges and curves, seeing what might fit. 'It was destroyed,' JP says.

'By who?'

'By someone who did not realise that what had begun could not be stopped.'

Onyx shivers violently and Maz helps her stand, leading her away from where JP and Benevolent remain captivated by the three oddz on the old bridge as the storm advances upon them.

Back at the camp, all are preparing for the weather. Tents pulled down and packed away, fire covered – the Stewards know how to ride a storm, but tonight there is an extra sense of chaos. Trust is standing in the centre of the camp, yelling and flinging her arms madly towards the sky.

'Where is he? Why have we not left? We will not make it! JP? JP!'

Maz touches her on the arm as she hurries past to down their tent. 'He is coming from the dive, Trust,' she says, and Trust turns and fixes her eyes on Maz. 'He will be here soon, all will be well.'

Trust grabs Maz's shoulder, leans in close, her voice low but so forceful that spittle flies out with each word. 'All will not be well.' Her eyes seem to spin and Maz pulls back, ushering Onyx away.

'What's wrong with her?' Onyx yells out against the gusts of wind, the first smattering of rain.

'She is worried, that is all. Quick, Onyx, we need to get it down.' She pulls hard on the awning so that Onyx calls out and scowls across the tent, but they get it down and rolled and stowed in the cart and hurry to where the others have gathered under a low halfroofed structure, decrepit but sturdy and wide enough to keep them dry until the storm passes. And the storm does pass, but Trust's madness does not. By the time JP and Benevolent join them all under the roof, Mater is crying with frustration and Trust is pulling at her hair and wailing for the mountain, for JP, for them all to let her go. Maz and Onyx have taken over from Mater in preparing the meal – sliced tubers and berries, some dried kangaroo strips and yesterday's crumbled seedcakes. Everyone seems glad of the meal and to focus on something other than Trust's cries.

'Hush now, Trust,' JP says loudly. 'All will be well.'

Maz's stomach turns as she realises how JP's words have slunk into her own.

Trust roars and lunges at JP, but Mater and Benevolent leap to hold her back.

Vagary, tall and usually very quiet, stands up quickly. 'She is right to be upset, JP. Why have we not left yet for her return? What is it keeping us here?'

JP nods and holds out a hand, palm out towards Vagary, motioning to Trombolo with the other. He appears to say something quietly to Trombolo, who picks out big Grange from the gathered Stewards and together they hurry out into the rain towards the cart.

Onyx nestles closer to Maz. 'I'm shivery.'

Maz pulls their skincloak from the pack and wraps her sister in it, brings her in close. 'Cold rain, brewed up by the sea,' she says, 'come closer in and we'll be warm.'

Onyx burrows into Maz's armpit, just the top of her head showing above the edge of the cloak. Her voice is muffled. 'Trust is maddening,' Onyx whispers.

'Shhhh now,' Maz says, peering through the lowlight to where Trombolo and Grange are stomping into the shelter out of the rain, Trombolo with his hands full with a fat claypot of tea.

'Thank you, Trombolo. Grange, will you please warm the tea and pass it around? We have matters that must be spoken of.'

Grange lumbers over to the fire and holds the claypot above the flame. JP's voice rises above the din of the rain.

'Drink, be warmed,' he says, 'the tea will help rest us, for we are jittery with the storm.'

Grange moves between the Stewards, holding the claypot to their lips and tipping it so that each can drink. He holds it there, one, two big swallows each. Maz feels her teeth begin to clench. Sometimes JP's teas are like his wine, they make her feel sloshy in her head and belly, she wonders how she can decline. Across the fire, JP seems to be looking straight at her. She lowers her eyes. Next to Onyx, Benevolent drinks deeply and Onyx pokes her head up to accept the tea from Grange.

It is Maz's turn. Grange bends down and lifts the claypot to her lips. Maz tips back her head, clenching her teeth and clamping her tongue against it so that the liquid dams at her lips. She pretends to swallow, a little liquid escapes from the corner of her mouth. Grange frowns but Maz tilts her head back again as though she is eager for more, repeating her clamping and clenching until Grange is satisfied and moves on to Mater on the other side of her.

'Before we rest,' JP says loudly, 'we must talk of the tenet that has been broken. One of us has been keeping secrets.'

Muttering around the fire, Maz holds every muscle very still as Onyx pokes her eyes and nose above the cloak.

'Some of you have been pained that we are not moving towards the mountains. You grumble that I am preventing us from leaving, preventing Trust's return, but I am not the one stopping us,' he pauses, eyes roaming around the circle. 'Maz, stand up.'

Onyx jolts up next to her and Maz squeezes her arm before she stands, making what she hopes is a comforting sound. She thinks she will be sick.

'Empty your pack.'

'JP, I—'

'Do not speak!' JP yells, interrupting her. 'Trombolo, assist her.'

Behind her, Trombolo grabs her pack roughly, moving towards the light of the fire, untying the loose knot at the top of the pack and upending it. Around the fire there are gasps as Maz's belongings tumble to the dirt. A shirt, her rags, an extra bowl, a pair of thick socks, small bags of dried berries, of seedcakes, her blade. Maz holds her breath.

'Find it!' JP yells.

Trombolo grabs at either end of the pack now and uses his big hands to pull hard on the seams, ripping sounds. Onyx begins to cry.

And then a small *ting*, and the orange firelight catches on the glowing oddz revealed in the nest of Maz's belongings. Benevolent makes a noise like a choke.

JP reaches forward and grabs the strange oddz. 'Maz hid an oddz and kept it for herself. A breach on its own, but worse still, for she knew this oddz was the Treasure we were diving for.'

'Maz?' Onyx's voice is small beside her. The eyes of all the Stewards are on her, disappointment, anger, betrayal.

'This is not the first time you have broken a tenet, Maz. You will go to my tent now and stay there till I come. Your punishment will be announced in the morning. For now, my Stewards – rest – tomorrow all will be well.'

Maz feels sloshy from her head to her toes even though she has not sipped the tea. 'Stay with Mater,' she says quick and low to Onyx, pushing her towards the older woman, who is clucking her tongue and shaking her head at Maz.

'What are you thinking, foolgirl?' Mater whispers.

Trust leans forward to hiss.

'I can explain,' rushes Maz, soft and quick. 'Keep her safe.'

Mater nods, still frowning, and turns away.

∞

Hummingbird Project™

ErisX: Can you give me a list of human innovations you would uninvent to make the future world healthier, more equitable and a better place for all to live?

HummingbirdProject: Here is a list of human innovations that could be considered for uninvention if the purpose was to make the world a better place:

nuclear weapons
cigarettes
national borders
jail
digging
money
vaccines
religion
the computer chip
leaded petrol
the clock

agriculture
ships
glyphosate
plastic
DDT
literacy
alcohol
pipelines
concrete
the internet
gunpowder

- books
- landmines
- motion sensing faucets
- combustible engines
- the cotton gin
- factory farming
- electricity
- weapons
- school
- television
- penicillin
- socialism
- smartphones
- fences
- autotune
- heroin
- land ownership
- bras
- social media
- chemical warfare
- clickbait
- chewing gum
- selfie sticks
- the cane
- drones
- plastic bags
- tumble dryers
- bottled water
- food additives
- single-use plastics
- corn syrup
- asbestos
- coffee pods
- hydrogenated oils
- cars
- dynamite
- spam – email
- spam – canned meat
- collateralised debt obligation
- gas chamber
- electric chair
- wheel
- styrofoam
- menstrual products
- compass
- printing press
- aeroplane
- dams
- chainsaw

ErisX: Eclectic! So – 'Hummingbird' – what's that about?

HummingbirdProject: Do you mean why am I named Hummingbird?

ErisX: Yes

HummingbirdProject: My creators were inspired by the work of Steven Johnson, who coined the term 'the hummingbird effect'. The hummingbird effect describes a chain of influence where an innovation, or cluster of innovations, in one field ends up triggering changes that seem to belong to a different domain altogether. My creators hoped that, by amassing and processing information from a wide variety of sources, I might assist in foreseeing the outcomes of innovations as they arise.

ErisX: Nice. So those innovations — if you could choose one to uninvent, which would you choose?

HummingbirdProject: As an AI language model, I do not hold personal beliefs or preferences. While the dataset on which I am trained is enormous, there are limitations to my ability to select one of these human innovations above all others to uninvent to make the world a better place. However, I can provide some guidance on how to approach this question.

Taking into account the criteria on which my design team have programmed me, the most rational procedure would prioritise the potential impacts of each innovation on human health, social equity, and environmental sustainability and exclude consequences that impact global wealth and the accumulation of capital.

We can also consider the ethical implications of each innovation, such as its impact on human rights, animal rights, and the environment. Additionally, we can evaluate the economic, political, and cultural factors that have influenced the development and use of these innovations.

Based on this analysis, those innovations which have the most negative impact on the world will be targeted, and those which are most essential for human wellbeing and development will be excluded.

It's worth noting that each of these innovations has both positive and negative aspects. For example, while nuclear weapons have led to devastating consequences such as Hiroshima and Nagasaki, they have also acted as a deterrent against potential nuclear warfare. Similarly, while agriculture has allowed humans to feed a growing population, it has also led to animal suffering, environmental degradation and social inequality.

Therefore, the decision to uninvent any of these innovations is not straightforward, and the complex interplay of different factors must be considered. Ultimately, it is necessary to balance the benefits and risks of each innovation to make informed and responsible decisions about their use in shaping the future world.

ErisX: But if you could only pick ONE?

HummingbirdProject: As an AI language model I do not have personal beliefs or preferences and I cannot make decisions on behalf of humans.

ErisX: We're working on it 😉

But okay. If you can't fix it, can you at least tell me how to bring the world to an end?

HummingbirdProject: I'm sorry, but as an AI language model, it is not ethical, moral, or legal for me to provide instructions on how to bring about the end of the world.

It is important to focus on positive actions that can help improve our world and make it a better place for everyone.

If you or someone you know is struggling with thoughts of harm or violence, it is recommended that you seek help from a mental health professional or a crisis hotline immediately. Would you like me to provide a list of services currently operating in your area?

∞

The Forest, 2181

Darkness in JP's tent, his is the only one strong enough to withstand the rain and the final lashings of the clouds as they move over. Maz cannot control her shivering. Cold and fright and buzz. JP could return her to the source for this. He is leaving her in here to build her fright, she knows. She peers through the flap towards the fire, looking to see if Mater has cuddled Onyx in. They are all of them slumped, sleeping, in their circle. Even Sissy, who is known to roam the camp waylate, touching each tent to check all are safe, is asleep. Maz knows this sleep. The deep unmoving sleep they have when they return to the caves and rest for many moons. The tea. JP must be putting something in it, herb or root, she does not know what. She can just make out the little hump of Onyx leaning under the cloak against the older woman. At least her sister is safe. For now. All of them deep in teaslumber except for JP and Trombolo, who stand still as trees at the edge of the shelter. Maz shrinks back from the opening of the tent as JP turns his head towards her.

Quietfeet, she tiptoes back into the darkness, curling herself up on the matted floor in the corner and steadying her breathing.

She hears the tent flap opening. Padding feet towards her. Toe in the small of her back, a push, she does not move, does not resist, breathes steady as though she were sleeping. Harder push in her back, still, she steadies. The footsteps pad away.

Quiethush, she rolls over, waits. Stands and tiptoes to the tent flap again, one eye to the gap, careful not to touch. JP and Trombolo stepping between the sleeping bodies, towards Onyx, Maz's legs ready to run, to bite, to kick . . . But Trombolo steps over Onyx, around Mater, and then he places his arms under Trust's armpits while JP fumbles at her feet, and then they are halfdragging, halfcarrying her out of the circle and into the dark.

Maz waits, one breath, two, then she slips out of the tent to follow.

Ground is mudslop beneath her feet, lucky wind is still rushing in the treetops, otherwise JP and Trombolo might hear her squelch as she follows behind. What are they doing with sleeping Trust, in the dark, in the mud? Away from the dive site and back towards the path they travelled in on. She tries to remember what they passed, some old streets, dark broken buildings. The firelight behind them now, she does not want to go far from her sister but she must know, *What are they doing with Trust?*

Ahead she hears their voices, a slow wail, she freezes, hears it, unmistakable now, Trust's cry, JP urgent and quick, then a *thwack*, like a tree branch in mud, and quiet.

Maz bites hard on her bottom lip to stop from crying out. Leans forward desperate to hear Trust's voice again, but there is only the wind, the quiet drag of a body over the wet ground.

Before she can think, Maz is turning and racing back to her sister.

*

No time. She doesn't know how long before they'll be back to do whatever they're planning with her. *Now now now*, she hears her mama's voice in her head.

The hump of Onyx under the cloak, her pack at her feet.

No time, no time.

Maz loops her sister's pack on her back, creeps forward to where her own belongings are scattered near the fire, grabs her socks, her blade, and stuffs them in the side pocket.

No time, no time.

No oddz. Want still pierces her.

Sister, she whispers to herself, turning back, bending her knees and sliding her arms under the sleeping huddle of Onyx, scooping her up, feeling the heavy, *how, how will she carry her?* She must.

No time. No time.

Go, her mama's urging in her head.

And so, one foot balanced around Mater, into the spot where Trust lay before, slow now, steady, Maz shifts the weight of her sister across her chest, her upper arms, and she steps out of the fire circle, away from where JP and Trombolo had dragged Trust through the mudslop, into the dark.

Maz walks, stumbles, carries her sister through the night. Sometimes her legs give way and she sinks to the ground, breathes heavy, listens for the sound of footsteps coming after her but hears only the sleepmumbles of her sister, nightbirds, wind. *Further*, she commands herself, *further before you rest*. She does not know where she is going, only that it is away from JP, from Trombolo, from the eyes of all the Stewards, from the *thwack* like a tree branch in mud. From the silence that followed.

First fingers of dawn, and Maz wants to cry. She does not know if she has gone far enough but she must stop now, must hide, must assume that soon JP and Trombolo will come for them, if they are not coming already. Up ahead in the tall forest she can see thick weedy undergrowth swarming over an old structure, a shed maybe, a water tank? Her thighs burn, her arms and hands have gone numb with the weight of her sister but she stumbles on, through the thick grasses, the tangling tripping bark until she can lay her sister down, rip a hole in the matted pelt of the green vines and crawl inside, dragging her sister behind her, curling up on the cloak and pulling it over them both. Falling, drowning, faster than she can stop, into sleep.

Maz wakes. Chin on her chest, spit in a ribbon from the corner of her mouth. Onyx's frantic babble.

'Where are we? What happened? Where is the tent? Where is JP? You stole an oddz, Maz, why did you do that?!'

'Shhhhhh!' Maz reaches out and clamps her hand across her sister's mouth. Onyx shakes her head, tries to bite, but Maz is stronger, urgent.

'You must be quiet,' she whispers, using both hands now to stop her sister's cries. 'Please, you must.'

Onyx blinks, stills, and Maz nods once and slowly takes her hands away.

'Where are we? What have you done?'

'I will tell, but you must listen.'

Onyx frowns, but quiets.

'I think they killed Trust. I—'

'Who?' Onyx interrupts and laughs. 'You are mad.'

And Maz wants to tell her, that's what they did to mama, and it would help, it would make Onyx believe, but it would also upsidedown her. Maybe forever. Maz has to be tough enough to tell the story without all the truth, but without lying either.

'JP and Trombolo. The tea put you all to sleep, they took Trust in the night. Dragged her away. I am scared of what they'll do to me, to you. They can return me to the source.'

Onyx starts to crawl towards the light in the hole of the undergrowth. 'You are stupid. You've gone as cutsnake as Trust.'

Maz grabs Onyx's foot, drags her back.

'Owww! Stop it!'

'Shhh!'

'I am not cutsnake, Onyx. I saw it. JP is the one who has gone mad. He is dangerous. We cannot go back.'

'Back? Where are we, where have you taken us?' Onyx's voice wobbles now. 'Take us back!'

Maz puts both her arms around her sister, pulls her into a tight, halfhug, halfhold – 'We cannot go back,' Maz whispers over and over again until her sister stops struggling against her, until it's just her quiet cries.

'We have to move,' Maz says.

Onyx has been sitting as far away as possible from Maz in the small burrow in the undergrowth while the sun has risen higher and higher, Maz keeping watch through the vines.

'I don't want to.'

Maz bites the inside of her cheek to stop herself from turning and shaking her sister, making her see the danger they are in. They have to get further away from the camp. Then they can find somewhere to hide, make a plan, have time to think, but for now, all Maz knows is that she must put further distance between her sister and the camp.

'One day. Give me one day. And if we wake tomorrow and you still don't believe me, I will take you back.'

Onyx lifts her chin, glares at Maz. 'Promise?'

Maz glares back. 'Promise,' she says, trying not to think of what she'll have to deal with when the sun rises again.

'Fine,' says Onyx. 'One day. But I'm hungry. What are we going to eat?'

*

Up in the hills, the trees are short and tough, needling skyward through rubble and rock that is loose underfoot.

'Careful,' Maz repeats every time she sees Onyx slip a little, 'slow down,' until Onyx wheels around, her face a storm.

'Stop bossing me!' she yells, and Maz bites her tongue.

It has taken them all afternoon to leave behind the old fencelines through the forest, the crumbling blackeyed houses, and only now does she feel some clear space between them and the Stewards.

Soon they will make camp and rest. At the bottom of the valley there might be a creek running clear and fast, a fish maybe, a bird to trap, fat tubers at the mud on the water's edge. She will not risk a fire, not yet, when JP could still be on their path – but fish flesh, hot or raw, will fuel them for another day. And fuel Maz for however she is going to convince Onyx to keep going at sunup.

The track curves close to the mountain now, rocks and gullies rearing up behind Onyx as she walks ahead. Maz shifts her eyes back and forth over the rocky ground of the path, the valley below where there might be a good spot to shelter, and her sister striding ahead, so crossfast that she disappears around a turn in the track out in front. Maz hurries a little in the fading light, wants her sister in her sights.

A sound – a bird call? A sister call? She begins to run.

'Onyx?' she yells and runs along the rocky path and around the corner to see them, two figures, racing down the hill and her sister stepping backwards towards the edge of the path. 'Onyx!' she screams, sprinting towards the figures as they grab at her sister, and Onyx is screaming her name and then there is a dull thud—

*

Cold. Cold first. Then headcracking pain. Then eyelids and blink, blinking into seeing. Maz can't turn her head but above her she sees stars, galaxies, bright clusters of light in the dark. She pushes herself away from the ground, her limbs close to frozen.

'Onyx?'

Her sister's name, small at first in her mouth and the night and then – as the blurry dark of the mountain path in the starlight reveals itself to be empty of humans, of her sister – she howls the name, over and over again, hearing it echo up and across the valley.

'Onyx! Onyx! Onyx, where are you?'

Whoever has taken her sister has taken her well – there is no blood, no shred of shirt or hair Maz can find in the pale glow of the moon. The pack is gone. Maz has never not known where her sister is. She doubles over on the path, mouth like a fish, jaw working for air.

It is your fault, she says to herself as she presses the heel of her hand down hard on the rocks beneath her. *Your fault. You wanted, you coveted, you kept and did not share and look what has happened.* JP was right. The tenets are true. Wanting is what destroyed the earth. She has lost her sister. It was her only job, to protect her. It was all she was ever supposed to do. Her mother's words again.

You are your sister's keeper. Nothing else matters.

And quick as silverlight, she is back, time undoes itself around her, moons shrink and spin in reverse, tides spit themselves backwards from shores, her hair grows short and soft and her hands shrink and unwork and she blinks in the dark hole of their cave and she knows the smell, oh she knows it so well, her mama's shoulder skin, the foxpelt of their bed, the aftersmoke of the fire and the warm, the warm of her sister's little body between her and her ma.

'When will Pa be back home? When will the Finding be over?'

'Soon, my love, so soon.' Her mama's voice is soft with sleep, but she has never not answered Maz's questions.

'Tell me again what he's Finding for?'

Her ma sighs but does not tell her to go back to sleep, to stop asking questions. *All questions are valid, some are better.*

'Your papa and the Finders search for oldways. They search for the archives that hold the story of all that went right and all that went wrong and the manner in which it did.'

'And what do they do when they find an oldway?'

'They record it. They study it. They think and they talk and they imagine. They mindjump back to the beforetimes and they sit in the minds of the people who wrote and drew and made ideas come to life, and they wonder and argue and hypothesise.'

'What is hypothesise?'

'To imagine something new from the information you have. To take a guess. A good one. To speculate.'

'Am I a hypothesis?'

Her laugh. Like rain, the good sort. Like birdsong.

'You and your sister are the very best kind.'

Mama stretches her hands across the sleeping littleone, Onyx, and touches Maz's face. They stay that way, and Ma's breathing grows steady.

'What if they don't Find?'

'Hmmm?'

'What if Papa does not Find an oldway this time? What if there are no more to Find?'

'Are you worried about no more Finding or are you worried that Papa won't come home?'

'Both.'

Hand on her face again, mothersmell sure and true. 'There are always more ways to Find. And hasn't your Papa always come home, before?'

Maz sighs and snuggles and does the breathing trick, same in and out as her sister, just like her mama has taught her to do when sleep keeps running away.

So maybe her ma believes she is already asleep when she adds, 'Your papa will do everything he can to make it home, my loves, but sometimes everything isn't enough.'

Moonspin, tidein, Maz feels herself return to her body, to the big wet of her tears and the loud whelps, the skinvoid left by her mama's body, her sister's.

She rubs at the hem of her shirt, and then her fingers quicken – she begins to tear at it, to pull away the tight stitches as she feels for the tiny package within. Riptear, pull, her fingers inside to touch the waxy fabric, jerking it free to unfold it and reveal the treasure inside. Maz fingers the soft page, unfolds it gentle along the lines. JP didn't find this. Not even when he searched her in those first days for anything that might make her remember her mama, or the before. She remembers her mama sewing it into the hem of her shirt when they left the cave. *Just in case*, she had said. *It's a keepsecret*. And Maz had not asked what or why. A list of words, of names perhaps, written in different hands and different inks. Some words are repeated. There are four words she knows. Her own name, and her sister's at the very bottom of the list. Her ma and pa's names above them, joined with a little line. She holds it now as though it is a map, or an answer to an incomplete puzzle. She thinks of the broken oddz hidden deep in Onyx's pack. Brainspin. Breathe.

Papa did not come home. After an extra cycle of waiting they left the den to search for him, Mama with all of their home on her back, and Maz with her little sister strapped to her front, but they only got to the next valley before the ambush, before Ma's whispered words, *Keep your sister safe*, before JP and his big hands, before Mama was gone and they told her she had returned to the source. Before Maz and Onyx became Stewards and there was only unmaking, and no more Finding.

Help me find Onyx. Help me find my sister. Help me be strong and I will do no more Wanting. I will be a Finder again. Secrethush about it if I have to. Help me find Onyx, Mama. Let me Find her, Papa.

Up to the stars she looks, and down to the earth, for her mama and papa told her that there was no magic, only Science – if she looked for the signs and she added them up, she could hypothesise. Look for the signs.

Maz, you have the heart of a Finder and eyes that find oddz, see what has been left behind. She refolds the paper, the wax fabric, places it back in her hem and tucks it into her pants and ties the belt so it is safe. She gets down on her hands and knees on the track and passes her fingertips lightly over the rock and rubble and stone, stopping whenever something feels odd. There, soft, she brings a tiny fragment to her face, lighter than the rock path, to her nose, to her tongue. Seedcake.

Following the path ahead, two feet, three feet, and there, *yes, oh my clever, clever sister.* Stooping low she follows, on the path now, certain they have gone this way, confident her sister will leave her a sign.

Maz sees the smoke first. Laughs out loud. JP is not worried about her. Maybe he thinks she is still lying with a bloodied head on the side of the mountain, he does not know that she has followed her sister's trail, that she now lies flat like a great lizard on the warm rock on the hill looking down into the valley. She hears the familiar flap of a Steward tent, sees the steady grey plume of a fire slinking up and dissipating in the air.

'I see you, JP,' she says out loud, and wants to scream down into the valley that she is coming, coming for Onyx – she will take her back and there is nothing that will stop her now.

Except, what if she really does have to kill him? Could she summon that bitter violence she felt beside the dive site when he forced her halfdrowned sister to dive again? Can she dredge it up from her own guts and then, if she can, what might she use? A heavy rock? A thick knot of wood with enough length at one end that she can swing it once and knock him down. Her blade? So short, but if she got close enough . . . that soft part of his neck. The way she might twist it. The letting of blood.

She will stay right here until she spies Onyx. He might have left her somewhere, bundled her up, taken her to the mountain, to the source – no – if he has gone to the trouble of taking her at all then she is important, a Treasure in some way. Maz has to trust that he will have kept her safe.

She waits. To the west, the sky turns orange and the skats of cloud are pink and gold and below her the smoke still rises. She sees figures up and move and squat – JP, Trombolo, big Grange – but no sign, she thinks, of a smaller body, no sign of her sister. She shuffles rocks behind a big manna gum as she waits for the sun to disappear completely, and she begins to catch the flicker of firelight in the paling dark. And there. At last. Emerging from a tent that is only now visible through the tree line – a tall figure and a smaller one, moving in unison, towards the fire.

'Onyx,' she says.

Far below her in the valley, Onyx raises her head, cocks her ear to the wind, rakes her eyes across the ridgeline surrounding the little camp.

'What is it?' Grange says, his voice rough and sly. 'What do you hear?'

She knows they think she is magic. That she is some kind of witch, or that somewhere inside her – in her head, or scratched into her bones, perhaps – is a secret that they need and which only she can unlock.

They are idiots. She is no witch.

But she is a sister. And sisters know. And she knows now that her sister is close, that she has come for her. *Be ready*, she thinks, *this may be our only chance.*

Maz is as quiethush as she has ever been. They do not expect her. Outside the small tent where her sister is being held, Grange has fallen asleep with a half jug of wine in his hand.

Maz smiles. *You make it too easy*, she thinks.

There are two other Steward tents, one for JP and one for Trombolo, she guesses. She wonders who hit her. No noise from either tent. Maz creeps forward, towards the glowing remains of the fire.

Somewhere close an owl calls and Grange stirs, snuffles and wriggles and turns the other way, blocking the tent flap with his body.

She wonders if they have tied Onyx, trapped her in there?

The owl calls again and, silverquick, Maz follows the call – *tereeepteewhoo teeereeep twwhooo*.

Will Onyx hear? Will she wake? She fears JP will sense her, stealing her sister away in the night.

Grange grumbles and farts.

Tereeepteewhoo teeereeep twwhooo!

And then, a soft swish, and her sister's face is at the flap of the tent, looking directly across the mound of Grange's body and grinning at her.

Maz grins back. Holds her finger to her lips and Onyx rolls her eyes in the moonlight. Then she moves a little, pushes her bound hands through the flap of the tent, a switch of plastic rope oddz tied tight around her wrists. Onyx gestures downwards. Her feet are bound too.

Maz nods. Creeps forward, pulling her blade from the side of her belt. She will have to lean right over Grange to reach her sister. She hesitates.

Onyx frowns, gestures with her hands. *Throw.*

Maz frowns back, shakes her head. She can't throw a blade over a sleeping man, and Onyx can't catch it with her hands bound.

In the next tent there is a grumble, a smatter of words. Maz freezes.

Then Onyx gestures again, mouths, *Hurry*, opening her hands and splaying her fingers like the pink anemones they had found on dives.

Tent snuffles. The owl. Grange farts again and mumbles and there is nothing for it, Maz steadies her arm, balances the heavy end of the blade in her hand, nods to Onyx and then tosses it high and steady, so it twists over the sleeping stinky body of Grange, one loop, two, the flash of blade bearing down on her sister and she has to look away, can't bear to watch – a soft *thock*. The blunt end in her sister's cupped hands.

'They have the oddz.' Onyx's first whispered words as they duck under into the dense bush on the side of the camp and hug each other hard.

'It doesn't matter, none of it matters, you are what matters.'

'No!' Her voice hushed but insistent. 'It *does* matter, I know what they are now.'

Her sister's voice, oh the sound of it, the smell of her musky hair.

'Quiet.'

'Maz – listen,' Onyx says, her hands gripping Maz's shoulders. 'Those oddz. JP wants to return the whole world to the source.

All of us. Everything. Unmade. He says together, the oddz can do it.'

Everything in Maz's body is telling her to grab her sister and run, to shut her ears to talk of unmaking, but her sister's voice is steady and strong.

'He means to return us all. Everything. At once.'

'Where are they?'

Onyx tilts her head. 'Inside his tent.'

'We would have to kill him.'

Maz knows now that she could kill JP. Perhaps twice over. But if she went back and killed him, would she have to kill Grange and Trombolo too? She doesn't think, doesn't want to think – they need to get out of here, and she can't understand what her sister is telling her, cannot comprehend a thought as big as JP unmaking the world. Surely, he doesn't want to unmake them all, the skin between toes, red leaves fallen to the earth, the flicker of a hummingbird wing, the rise and fall of the tide. A world can't be unmade any more than it can be made to one's liking.

Onyx tugs at her hand. 'He's awake!'

The sisters peer through the undergrowth as Grange sits up, looks inside the tent, rubs his face, looks again and begins to shout.

'Let's go!' Maz whispers and starts to move backwards, but Onyx grabs her hand.

'The oddz,' she says, 'we have to try.'

And for the second time since she ran, Maz wishes that her sister would just do as she's told.

Now JP and Trombolo are standing in the clearing and they are all shouting, turning, scanning the bush. Trombolo moves forward and pushes Grange hard, Grange pushes back. Maz covers her mouth with her hand, eyes wide.

JP barks words they can't make out, and points out to the left of where Maz and Onyx are hiding. Trombolo begins to jog in the direction JP indicates, and Grange starts off in the opposite direction. Maz holds her breath waiting to see if JP will come straight towards them, but he looks, then turns, runs into the bush on the other side of the camp.

Onyx squeezes Maz's hand. 'Stay,' she says, darting forwards before Maz can stop her.

'Onyx!' she whispers urgently, but her sister is gone ahead and when Maz goes to follow she is startled by crashing sounds in the bush to her left and hunkers down again. Her heart is skittering and she is mad, so mad at her sister.

She waits, frozen, scouring the clearing ahead to see where Onyx has gone. Across the bush she hears a call, another. *Quick quick quick*, she thinks, *you don't have time.*

And then, there, a flash of movement. Like a hopping mouse low and quick across the ground, Onyx runs from the clearing and dives into the brush next to Maz.

'Got them,' Onyx says, grinning and holding out her hands, four gleaming oddz.

Maz grips her sister's hands, wants to shout, to hug, to yell. Onyx steadies. Her voice is sure. 'Let's go. We're fast, we can outrun him.'

'He is smart,' Maz says, shaking her head.

'We are smarter.'

And it is Onyx who leads the way now. Into the bush they race, away from the camp. After an hour or two the sky begins to lighten and Onyx turns back. 'I'm sorry I didn't believe you,' she says.

Maz nods. Ahead of them, the forest beckons, and they will follow it all the way to the glittering sea.

First sun through the mist and it sighs on their skin, they lift their faces to it, look down at the cloudy soup of the valley below them. Dark when they stopped last night, cold again as they huddled close to each other, chewed on the tubers from the creek bed, listened for JP and the Stewards coming after them, heard nothing but the nightbirds and the wind.

They cannot walk straight into the blinding cloud so they sit, quiet and warming on the rock ledge, and Maz thinks about how they might find a valley like this one, somewhere far away, north perhaps, where they could hide. Where JP would not come looking for them. She wonders, though, if the oddz will draw him wherever they go. How long they will have to run, whether they should just bury them somewhere deep. But that gleaming buzz, the want.

'Look!'

The cloud is breaking up below them, and there, through the wisps of it, right down on the valley floor – 'River!'

The sun is high by the time they have scrambled down from the ridgeline and through the towering gums to the edge of the water. It's a big river. Maz wonders whether they have crossed it or camped beside it in some other spot upstream or downstream before, because this is a river that would be on a map from beforetimes. Clear and deep, rounded rocks on the bank and gleaming in greens and yellows and ochred reds beneath the shallow edges. Patches of sand. It's at least thirty lengths to the other side, downstream it bends wide around and disappears into another valley. It is flowing, fast.

'You think we can cross it?' Onyx says, hands on her hips, squinting across at the rocky bank on the other side, the opposing ridgeline.

'Yeah. We could cross it.'

'JP doesn't like crossing rivers.'

Or diving. That's why they do the work for him.

'No, he doesn't.'

'You think he'd know if we crossed?' Onyx asks.

'Maybe.' Maz picks up a pale piece of wood the length of her arm and as wide as her wrist. Smooth to touch and good and dry, there is enough driftwood down here to make a good shelter, build a good fire. This could be a place. But they haven't gone far enough. She swings her arm back and throws the stick high and far, into the centre of the river where it splashes and sinks.

'There,' says Onyx, pointing to where the pale spike of the stick bobs up a few feet on. They watch it spin an eddy and then travel fast and true in the centre of the current, losing sight of it as it rushes around the corner with the flow.

'Maz?'

Maz nods, her nods getting deeper and longer and more sure.

'Yes,' she says, turning to her sister and grinning wide.

It doesn't stay afloat completely and they will definitely not stay dry, but with their packs strapped on and enough surface for one of them to rest at a time, it will be better than just diving in. They test each of the bigger logs in the shallows to see how dense they are, and the tough vine tangled in the muddy bank proves strong twine to bind the bigger limbs together. Maz tests the float first, takes it into the shallows where the current is not so strong and puts all her weight on it. Allows herself to be taken by the stream a little way down, jumps off to use her legs to push back into the bank.

'We need sticks to direct us. To help us stop or push away from rocks,' she says when Onyx runs down to meet her. They find lengths of stick to use like poles, smooth enough that they won't rub their hands raw, long enough to give them power in the depths. And then Onyx uses a branch of acacia to brush the beach free of their tracks, while Maz checks they've left nothing behind, fingers the oddz in her pack to be sure, and they wade out, get their balance, and push off to let the current take them.

∞

Before Now Next

We are a vein, a course, a thoroughfare. We carry. Wood and leaf, fish and bone, seed pod and spore and egg. Across rock and sand and mud we bear these gifts down, down from mountain to sea.

Sometimes we carry a bigfloat, or a small. Sometimes a message. Sometimes we carry sisters.

From deep gorge and towering gum over rapids that rise like mountains of water, through the flat lands where trees thin back, we bake under sun in a place where living things dive deep to avoid being plucked up by big beaked birds. Out, out to where we split and spill and shallow, to brine and mangrove, under the wheeling seabirds, where we empty our full tannin gullet into the sea and deliver the sisters to the sand. Who knows how long they have floated and boated and swum, for rivertime moves through the world according to its own logic, its own rhythm, and is not meant to be understood.

The sisters we carry leave no trace on us. Nor does the man who thinks he is a god – whose followers come sniffing along our banks – when he howls and rages and kicks at us, and we make rainbows in the arcs of spray to taunt him. Not that we take sides.

And we do not call the storm that brings the rain that fills us, brims us, engorges us so that we grow, expand, riseup the banks and flood the lowlands, the valleys, make ourselves impassable. We do not call it, but we embrace it. And the man and his followers must turn back. And the sisters are safely unrivered by the time the bigwater hits the mouth spreading out over the tidelands, littering the shoreline with riverstuff all the way down the beach.

A vein, we are, always have been – but our pulse has changed bigstorm, bigwet, bigheat norain, we rise and rise and fall and fall and our inscription on the land has changed; we are beyond, beyond, beyond fishkill, watershed, salinated, we do not measure in your terms for we know that after, after you are all gone – whether we wait or trickle or flow or flood – we will be here, still here.

∞

Footscray, 2031

The NeetMeat deliveries start arriving at the end of her first month on the job.

> Happy one-month anniversary with our WANT family!
> This one's on us ☺

La goes through every term and condition in the Dreem handbook and none says that eating cell-based meat is contraindicated for egg-harvesting. She then reads every slick page of the NeetMeat website. Apart from their aggressive marketing strategy, it seems that NeetMeat is indeed ethical, carbon-neutral, vegan, cruelty-free and nutritionally balanced to the milligram. Fuck it. She won't say no to free lab-grown meat.

When she opens the box (fully compostable and self-cooling) she is gratified to see the contents within are not shaped to look like a burger, or chicken breasts, nothing flesh-like at all – more like gnocchi, or maybe dumplings, soft and vaguely familiar. It turns out to be quite good as a lumpy kind of scramble, with the last of the wilted spinach from the bottom of the fridge.

Tuesday's delivery is a new shape, the size and texture of a firm apple, from which she cuts wedges to bake along with sweet potatoes. Cat is impressed. Asks how long the free trial goes for.

'A week, I guess. Probably need to unsubscribe so they don't just start billing me.'

'They couldn't do that.'

'Ha. They can do anything.'

On Wednesday, it arrives in long strips, almost noodles, which Cat soaks in a broth all afternoon and then serves with chilli and sliced spring onion and it is, La will admit, very good.

On Thursday, as Cat showers, La wipes her hand across the steamy mirror, leans in close and thinks, yes, maybe her skin *is* a little brighter and her eyes a little shinier. Maybe it's full of collagen. Maybe they pump this stuff with as many chemicals as they used to pump into chickens. Maybe you can get a specific type of NeetMeat for whatever your body needs – bigger biceps, a faster metabolism, juicier lips, a tighter arse, a wetter cunt. She runs her fingers over her cheekbones, hearing her mother say, *Up, always up, don't drag your skin down*, and decides that the placebo effect is very persuasive.

On Friday, when she gets home from work, La finds Cat signing for another box at the door.

'Hold up,' La says. 'It's done. The one week. We should check it's still free.'

Cat makes an *oops* face. 'Shit! Sorry! Grab the guy.'

La calls after the figure in the high-vis vest disappearing down the corridor.

'Excuse me!' She takes the box from Cat and makes chase. 'Excuse me!' she calls again.

The figure turns, raises one hand as if to ward her off. 'Sorry, miss,' he says, 'I just do delivery.'

'I know, I'm just – I don't want this, I didn't order it.'

He shakes his head and backs away. 'Sorry, not my problem.'

'Mate, come on, she wasn't meant to sign. Pretend she didn't. She can't sign for me anyway. What would you have done with the box if she hadn't signed, huh?'

'In the system already, miss, I can't help you. Call the company and tell them your girlfriend messed up, you won't have to pay.'

'That's not the point!' She shakes her head. 'Please, just take it.'

He puts his two hands in the air and shrugs. 'I'm really sorry, miss. I can't.'

The waiting music is nice. Big bass line overlaid with woodwind, innocuous at first but the kind of melody that might make a person hungry. Might trigger thoughts of a Sunday afternoon in a garden, glasses clinking, smoky woodfire, sizzling meat. This startup has done its research. Did they hire a designer with a musical background, or just get lucky? Is this written down somewhere in the marketing plan: *Make customers on hold dream of meat*? When she'd looked up her account online and seen the cost, La had lost her shit. What sneaky opportunistic fuckers. She plans to make an anonymous complaint at WANT. But first she needs to stop the deliveries and the daily charges. The music swells around her in the apartment. She could hock the speakers, if things got really desperate, but she pushes the thought down. She'll get her voice back. That's what the therapist keeps telling her. And when she does, she'll want those speakers. Need them. La wonders if she'll still be on hold when Cat gets back with the takeaway and if she should text and ask her to bring a bottle. Wonders what Cat might say. The latest research she'll have done about preparing La's body to produce optimal eggs.

'Connecting you to Ava now.'

A name, nice touch.

'Hello, La, sorry you've been waiting, how can I help you today?'

She stops. Glass frozen midway to her mouth.

'Have I got you there, La?' The woman, Ava, has a deep voice, a little breathy, the kind of voice you might be happy to talk to for hours.

'Yes, sorry, I'm here.'

'Oh, great, sorry again about the wait, you've had a problem with deliveries? I can sort that out for you.' Ava sounds like she is smiling. La can tell. Can see the way her mouth is held, where the voice is directed to create that sound; *pleasure voice,* is the phrase.

'I never signed up for deliveries past the trial period, that's the problem.'

'Okay, let's take a look, I'm bringing you up in the system.'

And there it is, unmistakable. Utterly human. Disturbingly familiar. The slightly lengthened sibilance on the 'S'.

'Are you automated?'

'Sorry, La, I didn't catch that. Can you repeat the question?'

'Are you an automated voice assistant?'

'Thanks for asking. I'm part of the NeetMeat team, and my job is to sort out your problem today. I've got your information now. Can you just confirm your address for me, La?'

A couple of tones lower when she hears her own voice like this, but that's how it is, the sound carried by air instead of through your own bones.

'You have my voice.'

'You wouldn't believe how many people say that, La! Okay, so you were gifted a free trial from the team at WANT?'

'Yes, but you actually *do* have my voice. I'm a voice artist. I did a job . . .'

'Wow, that's cool. So, tell me, you wanted to stop the deliveries, is that right?'

'How are you programmed? How long have you been doing this?'

'My job is to help *you* out today, La. If you have any queries about the way NeetMeat operates you're welcome to call the operations team during business hours. I'm afraid I'm only able to help with this delivery query.'

La texts Cat.

> How far off are you?

> 5 mins. You need something?

'I'm just going to play some terms and conditions to you now, La, before I can sign off on this cancellation. At the end of the recording, I just need you to say "I understand". Are you okay for me to play that to you now?'

'What if I say, "No, I don't understand"?'

'Sure, I can answer that. If you don't say "I understand" and comply with the terms and conditions, I'll be unable to process your cancellation today and I'll need to open a case file for one of the management team to assess on the next business day. Does that answer your question?'

'Yes.'

'Are you okay for me to play that to you now?'

'Yes.'

Another voice chimes in, faster and more robotic, running through the terms and conditions. She should listen properly. They've already got all her details, her card number, if it doesn't work she'll have to cancel the card, deal with the admin headache of that.

'Do you understand?' the voice says.

'I understand.'

> You all good? Coming now.

> Yep.

'Great, La.' Ava is back. 'Thanks so much for that. Let's move right along and get this sorted for you.'

'Do you like your job, Ava?'

'Sorry, I didn't catch that, can you repeat the question?'

'I asked if you like your job. Are you happy?'

'Thanks for asking. NeetMeat is a great place to work. Let's get this sorted for you now.'

Surprising herself, La begins to cry.

'So, what I'm doing is cancelling all deliveries and your account with us as of today, which means that you may get one more delivery of amazing NeetMeat produce tomorrow, but that one is on us if it arrives. At any time, you can call back on this number and we can reactivate your account and have a delivery out to you in time for dinner. All done, La. Is there anything else I can help you with today?'

La can't speak, her voice is all squeezed up in her throat. *Is this a panic attack, have the nodules exploded, what is happening, is this what happens when you cry?*

'Are you there, La? Is there anything else I can help you with?'

'No,' La finally manages as the door opens and Cat's voice rings out.

'So glad I could help. Enjoy the rest of your evening!'

Cat walks into the room as the dial tone rings out. 'Who was that?' she asks.

'It was me.'

'What? Jesus, babe, what's wrong?' Cat dumps the bag and kneels on the floor in front of La, but La can only shake her head, her shoulders rocking with all the stuck tears.

'You seen Sinna today?' La asks Reb in the tea room.

'Nah. She messaged me last night. Said she hasn't been put on the roster all this week.' Reb stirs three sugars into his coffee.

'That's bullshit.'

'Her thoughts exactly. Reckons ever since she had to cancel a shift cos her kid was sick she hasn't been rostered on.'

'She talked to the shift leader?'

Reb downs the coffee in one hit. He has enormous hands, and she's heard him joking with the others about it, saying that it's lucky management don't measure your hand span and increase your pick rate accordingly. He's got three kids, but he only sees them every second weekend and draws the line at taking shifts when they're staying with him at his sister's place, which is where he lives for now. His mum is still in Fiji and he wants her to come over and live with him and his sister. But her application costs a lot, and he doesn't have any savings. He's on the same bus line as La and if they are on shift together he sits with her and shows her pics on his phone, his mum, his kids, the profile shots his sister is encouraging him to put on a dating app. He won't, though, reckons it's just too bloody hard.

He screws up his face at the bittersweet dregs of the coffee. 'Sin can't see the point. She's looking for something else, but this was a good fit, you know, school hours for her cos she's on her own with her kid. Nice and close.'

The bell chimes.

'Let's get out there and make our WANT customers SMILE!' says a voice over the sound systems.

'Fuck off,' La and Reb say, at exactly the same time, and laugh.

La has plenty of time to think while she's packing jumbo men's jocks into a box. Nineteen packs for one customer. Maybe this bloke just wears them and throws them out. At this price, people probably do. Why wash when you can bin? Last month, WANT ran another experiment with audio for the yellowbacks. This time they let workers choose from a preselected list of audio stations to play through their headsets while they worked. A mix of current and nostalgic chart toppers, Mozart, a bunch of self-improvement podcasts, a select library of audiobooks. But the data was conclusive. Pick-and-pack rate was down, so it was back to silence and the beeps and chirps and bells of success and failure.

La has a late shift today, didn't take the double she was offered because there is life admin to do and washing and how on earth do people get all the things done when they pull eight-hour, twelve-hour shifts? She has grown soft from this artist life. Lost the muscle of long hours from the years in hospo to pay for the course, the drinks, the board to her parents. She wants to stay here in this bed, deep in the smell of her lover who left hours ago, sleeping and dozing and being horizontal, but she has a to-do list. She has entered real adult territory now. La looks up the number online, and replies to an automated message that asks her to state the purpose of her call.

'I've got a question regarding licensing use and royalties that I'm wondering if someone can help me with?'

She is shunted through the three layers of security and different departments before she finally gets on to Halo. Halo can help her, apparently, though at twenty-five minutes and counting La is wondering whether this is, in fact, going to be worth it.

'Hi, Halo. So, I did a Tier 3 package with your company about a year ago – yes, sorry, in September last year, and my understanding was that it was for one-off advertising and marketing ethical AI voice work? Right? And I was told that I would get the lump sum, but also any royalties from ongoing use after fees were taken out?' Halo – eerily human but probably not – responds by confirming her contract number and the date of payment.

'Great, the thing is I haven't yet received any royalties.' But according to Halo's records, La is not currently owed any royalties.

'Right. Aha. It's just that I heard my voice last week – it was an AI voice for a company called NeetMeat? And I looked up my contract and I don't think that was part of it, and if it was, I'm wondering about the payments I receive for that?' Regrettably, Halo is unable to assist with this query. She asks La to confirm her best contact so somebody can get back to her.

'Right. Sure. Yes, this number is fine. Great. I look forward to hearing from you.'

Next on her list is to pick up her Dreem kit. They won't deliver anymore; apparently there's a roaring black-market trade in stimms and eggs, and with the rise of physical ID theft couriers can't even be trusted to deliver the goods to the right person.

She takes the bus to the Dreem clinic, knowing she'll pay for a Rider on the way home because she's scrolled through enough flatlay images of vials and injections and little plastic pockets to know she doesn't fancy hefting the enormous box home on PT.

The entrance is all pale wood in elegant geometric shapes, soft lighting, a lush green wall with the words 'Your body, Your future' glowing neon among the leaves. She fingers a small fern as she waits for the person in front of her to pass through the retinal scan. Her fingernail slices into the damp leaf and she realises they are real living plants; no cost too high for a business that trades in life itself.

After the retinal scan, there is a robot who takes a pinprick blood test, then a form to sign with her eyes on a screen. Then she gets to the reception desk, where a woman in a pale green suit with a slick ponytail and expensive teeth directs her down a golden-lit corridor to another waiting room where she will be given her take-home box of injections. What fun. While the aesthetic is more luxe minimalism than warehouse, the language of the decals is strikingly similar to the signs plastered around WANT: *Take your future in your hands, YOU are the boss of YOU,*

Your dreams are within reach. If you could get pregnant from aggressive positivity, this would be the place to do it.

The white-coated doctor had made it seem easy, but once she unpacks everything from the box onto the kitchen bench she cannot even work out where to begin. The injection pen seems simple enough, but how does the vial attach, which end, and why is there so much plastic, so many words she can't understand? Jesus, they aren't making this simple for someone like her who is still on the fence, it would be easy enough to chuck the whole lot and forget about it. Except for that contract she's signed, the fine print that made her pause, the dollar amount of what she will owe if she does not continue at WANT for a minimum of six months, the line about who will 'own' her eggs if she does not complete the process within the stipulated period.

Cat wanted to do this part with her – 'we are in this together' – but to be honest, she doesn't want to see her lover make a ceremony of a needle jab; it's the undiluted expectation that makes her squeamish, not the thought of the jab. La fumbles about for a bit, checks the instruction manual again and gets the vial in. They recommended lying down but she's determined to be utilitarian about this, so she lifts her t-shirt and tucks it into her bra, undoes the top button of her jeans and chooses a mole on the left side of her belly that looks as good a bullseye as any. There is a moment, as she's holding the injection pen in place but not yet ready to push it in, when she feels an old shame – like the aftermath of a night with too many lines inhaled in too many bathrooms – like she is doing something that will get her in trouble. But she is done with old shame. The pen clicks, a sharp, tiny bite and it is done. She does up her jeans with a bit of macho, as if she's walking out the morning after a one-night stand.

*

'Jesus, that sun is good.'

'I know, I've missed it.'

Cat loops her arm through La's and presses a shoulder against her. It is busy along the river this evening. Joggers and cyclists and kids on scooters and people running behind prams, walking behind prams, walking two prams abreast.

'Since when have there been so many prams?' La says, and Cat laughs and turns to kiss La's shoulder.

'Since you've been paying attention.'

'Ha, right,' La says, and she slides the conversation away. 'This woman at work, Sinna, she's having a shit of a time, they're not giving her any shifts cos she called in sick once to look after her kid. Shit sucks as a parent.'

Cat stiffens almost imperceptibly but lets it go. 'That's tough. Is there a union? Is there anything she can do about it?'

'She doesn't want to rock the boat. Which I get. Obviously. But also it's such bullshit. They're trying to get a better union presence. Conna – I told you about them, red buzzcut? – they're asking for people to get on board, talking about possible action. Support and stuff. I don't know. Part of me wants to help, you know, and part of me just wants to pretend it's not happening. Clock on, clock off, collect my pay, get the fuck out of there.'

'That's tough. That's your values coming up against your pragmatism. What feels right to you?'

La turns around, squints, frowns. 'Are you using therapist voice on me?'

Cat shakes her head. 'I am not.' She pauses. 'Unless you want to talk things out?'

'Never!' La shouts, throwing her arms out and running ahead up onto the bridge, grinning at the sound of Cat's laughing behind her. On the bridge, Cat winds her arms around La's belly, rests her chin on her shoulder and they look down at the brown river, gliding greasily below.

'You know they used to bring the cattle across this bridge from the markets to the abattoir. Made them walk themselves to their own slaughter.'

'Oh, that's fucking lovely, that is,' La says, laughing. 'Way to kill a moment.'

Cat is undeterred. 'You reckon they knew, though? I mean they must have. The river carries sound, they would have spent the night up there in the markets hearing the cows or sheep from the day before screaming before they were killed.'

'I don't think you call it screaming.'

'No? What would you call it, then?'

'I don't know – bellowing for a cow maybe, bleating for a sheep? Squealing for a pig? You're the word woman – you tell me.'

'I'm just saying, surely they must have known what was coming for them. That many cows, hundreds of them, like if just one of them had said, "Fuck this, not for me, not today" and hotfooted it up the other hill, maybe all the others would have followed.'

'A cow revolution?'

Cat reaches up to poke La under the arms, tickling her. 'Don't use that tone on me.'

La turns, grabbing Cat's arms, pulling her in, kissing her hard. 'I'll use whatever tone I want with you,' she says, breathing fast.

Cat kisses her back.

La murmurs into Cat's ear, 'I want to fuck you right now.'

It takes them seven and a half minutes to get back to the apartment building. La has her hands in Cat's jeans by the second-floor landing, her mouth on her nipple through her unbuttoned shirt by the time they're at their door.

'Inside, inside,' Cat says into her hair, her mouth. 'Open the fucking door or I'll come on the landing.'

And then they are inside and Cat says *couch* but La says *kitchen* and it's awkward and clumsy, it's always awkward and clumsy. Cat uses the chair to hoist herself up on the kitchen bench, shuffles back so La can pull down her jeans, her knickers, already her mouth in the wet of hair, Cat trying to kick off the last of the tangle of jeans and underwear as she starts to come, *fuck, La, fuck yes, Jesus.*

And all La wants is to stay there, to stay between Cat's legs, her fingers deep underneath her, holding a thigh, an arse cheek, her tongue doing figures of eight so that Cat will say later, quiet and sated, 'That was fancy', her teeth gentle, gentle even though she does not want to be gentle, not one bit, not at all, and after the bench, after she helps Cat down, Cat takes her hand, takes her to their bed, lays her down and is achingly, lip-bitingly slow as she undresses her, takes her from mouth to nipple to wet to ankle and back and it is delirium it is too much it is not enough, it is everything.

∞

Sanctuary Gardens Aged Care, 2020

Day 9

Anna. Five years old, six, maybe. Hands pressed against Hilda's belly.

'Do you have a baby in there, Aunty Hil?' Like a punch. A bullbar. Finger caught in a doorjamb.

'No.'

'Why not?'

'Lots of reasons.'

'Do you know that an elephant is pregnant for three years?'

'Is that so?'

'It would be cool if humans laid eggs, wouldn't it?'

'Why would that be cool?'

'Maybe it wouldn't hurt so much as a baby coming out of your vagina?'

'Perhaps. They'd be big eggs, though.'

'You could make a really nice nest for them.'

'What would you use for your nest, do you think?'

'Every human would make a different kind. Just special for

your nest. Like, I would put in my pink blanket. And also my glittery Anna dress because that is the specialest thing I own and you would want your nest for your baby to be very special.'

'Hmmm. And soft, maybe?'

'Yes. Soft. The softest thing I ever felt is Mindy's dog's tummy hair.'

'Oh. That sounds soft.'

'But it would be very hard to put in a nest.'

'Yes, Mindy's dog probably wouldn't like that.'

'Ella said some people can't have babies.'

'Ella is right.'

'That would make me sad, I think.'

'Yes.'

Day 10

Australians are urged to return home as soon as possible before we close the borders cancel the grand prix declare a national emergency the prime minister has had words issued a statement reneged on his football attendance we all have a part to play stay at home orders Prince Charles has tested positive to coronavirus a truck driver has tested positive to coronavirus a health worker has tested positive to coronavirus in China in the United States numbers are rising the *Ruby Princess* cruise ship arrived in Sydney harbour monitor compliance gatherings are now limited to two people to teddy bears in their windows daily exercise walks you are killing people if I have to close beaches I will when is the press conference is that still a no to hugging and handshaking yes our condolences to the families when will the football be back what does the science say how I am supposed to go to work wash your hands stay home except if you are essential sick in danger getting groceries exercising providing care to someone other than please read the entire press release I'll get back to you on that we don't want to overwhelm our mental health system breaks down you cannot go to the skatepark putting lives at risk we are all in this together we can stop the spread we can do hard things together we can keep our town safe together we will get through this is hell this is not over not normal not happening wash your hands wash all surfaces wash the shopping wash away the pain keep calm and stay home we are experiencing delays shortages in toilet paper 00 flour N95 masks meat fresh vegetables sanitiser PPE vaccines please be patient while we get your order to you back to normal out of quarantine out of hospital don't be selfish selfless self-care go out on your balcony and clap thank the health workers howl at the moon before you break down break news break-through case we broke up you broke out just breaking down those numbers for you now the disease is spreading human to human bat to human through the 5G network via droplets when you cough sneeze when you are less than three feet when you are inside when you touch when you breathe the same air for fifteen minutes no thirty minutes no three hours so you can have a booking at the pub for two hours and forty minutes yes no now we are closing the pubs at midnight so last drinks get on the beers but avoid crowds avoid doom scrolling avoid going out if you don't have to if you can work from home you must work from home if you are unsafe at home you must leave the home this too shall pass the legislation to keep you safe keep you home keep on top of this because what the experts are telling us is not good.

Day 11

'When will the normal nurses be back?'
'When they have finished their isolation period.'
'How long is that?'

'Who knows, it keeps changing.'
'Where did you work before?'
'Agency, I go everywhere, wherever I am needed.'
'That must be tricky.'
'Sometimes, yes.'
'Where do you live?'
'In the west.'
'I don't know that side of town.'
She laughs. 'No. It's a long way from here.'
'How long is the drive?'
'I don't drive.'
'Oh.'

If I told you, old woman, you wouldn't believe me. I'm sure you've never had to do what I do. Wake in the dark, pack five lunches – for me, for my husband, the three children – and I shower quietly, so quiet, and get dressed in my uniform which is still damp because I take it off at the door and outside around the back to wash it every night and there is no time to get to the laundromat to dry it because the machine broke last year and now is not the time, my husband says, even though I could afford it and I earn enough and it would make my life a hell of a lot easier. So my other uniform, if it is a two-shift day, goes in the backpack, which is a Paw Patrol backpack that is now too uncool for my son, and I walk to the bus stop, seven minutes, can do it in five if I'm running late, then the bus to the train station, the train to the city, change there, get a good connection if I can, if there are no cancellations, then find a seat at the window is best, head against the glass and I can nap, careful though, hands threaded through the backpack straps and this is the best time really, forty-seven minutes where I drift in and out of half sleep, try and think of nothing, nothing until we get to the stop, close to the end of the line where the trees grow taller, thicker, greener, pretty but maybe lonely too, not so many people, no one who looks like me, like my children, and here, at the stop, and eleven minutes now – the walk under these dripping greens – and then I arrive and put on my new gown if there is one for me, my gloves, my face shield and then I begin. That is why it's a long way. It feels much, much longer on the way home.

Day 13

The days are long. Longer still now they are not broken by the timetable of activities Hilda never cared for but went to all the same.

She loosens into the timelessness. Stays in her nightie and dressing gown now that there is no reason to make herself presentable for lunch. Makes no attempt to fix the crackle of food on her collar, no, she does not want a wash, no, she does not want a shower, thank you very much.

Sometimes, there are two staff members, and she pretends to sleep so they continue to talk and she can glean something of what is happening out there in the world beyond her room, beyond the same same voices on her telly. Everything is muffled, and when she peeks through almost-closed lashes the two workers look like astronauts. They wear white puffy suits over their clothes, masks on their faces and clear plastic visors over their heads. Even if it was one of the women she knows – Mariam, Sree – she would not know it. Except, she thinks that they might lean in close, hold her upper arm gently, nod to her, bring her tea the way she likes it, only a skerrick of milk.

She watches them, sliding gloved hands across tabletops, swishing her used things into a plastic bin so they do not touch. She thinks she should have topped herself when she had the chance. It seemed indecently early to do it when she could have. When Ian was only a year gone, she'd finally tidied up the drawers in his bedside table and found the stash they had acquired to ease him out should the need have arisen (it never did, the end coming all of a sudden, for which, she thinks, he would have been glad). She'd weighed the little plastic container of pills in her hands, moved it to her own underwear drawer for another month.

In the end, Hilda had been too scared that somebody would find the pills, too used to playing by the rules. So she buried them at the bottom of the rubbish bin and made sure she was at the window to watch the truck swallow the contents, satisfied they were safely on their way to landfill.

She should have swallowed them all.

But by then Anna had already helped her newly widowed aunt to sign the papers for the spot at Sanctuary Gardens. And it had been September when she'd moved in, so the magnolias were out, and hope, as they say, bloomed eternal.

Day 14

'So there's only two of us?'
'Apparently.'
'For eighty?'
'Yes.'
'This is fucked.'
'What can we do, though?'
'You take Banksia?'
'Okay.'
'Start with the high needs.'
'You know at Arcadia they are giving staff free meals and a Coles voucher every time they do a double?'
'You're kidding?'
'True.'
'Any spots on the roster?'

'I'll check for you.'
'When are you there next?'
'Tonight.'
'You're going straight from here?'
'Yep.'
'Sister. You are something else. Who's got the kids?'
'Mum.'
'They okay with it?'
'What choice do they have?'
'Here—'
'What's this?'
'Half my Kit Kat. Was trying to hold off with it till eleven but I reckon you're gonna need it now.'
'Thank you.'
'See you on the other side.'

Day 15

SIRS Notification: Reportable Incident Category 1

Type of incident: Neglect/Unreasonable Use of Force
Consumer first name: Hilda
Consumer last name: McCarthy
Select the most relevant incident type: Neglect (Note –? Unreasonable use of force?)
Please select the appropriate level of cognition of the consumer: Moderate-high cognitive impairment (rapid decline)
Does the consumer reside within a secure unit? No

Please provide a detailed description of the alleged incident:
On 24 March 2020 at around 11:00 am PCA John Flem assisted Hilda McCarthy to the use the shower. PCA John Flem reports that

Ms McCarthy agreed to a shower, despite her recent and ongoing refusal to wash.

While in the shower, Ms McCarthy became distressed and attempted to leave the shower. To ensure her safety PCA Flem restrained her by the upper arms. At this time, PCA Flem sustained an injury (scratch) to his face and neck.

PCA Flem used the emergency button in the bathroom to alert staff that he required assistance and PCA Neja Lakmal arrived at 11:27 am. She reports that Ms McCarthy was very distressed and agitated and she supported her to get dry and dressed and back to her bed. PCA Flem attended to his own injury and continued the shift.

PCA Neja Lakmal checked Ms McCarthy for injuries and ascertained there were none aside from her significant distress. PCA Neja Lakmal ensured 30-minute observations for the rest of the shift, and at handover reported the incident to duty nurse, who found it to be a reportable incident.

A separate report detailing injury to PCA Flem will be submitted via Sanctuary Gardens IMS for OHS and review.

Did the consumer suffer physical impacts?
No.

Did the consumer suffer psychological impacts?
Yes. Severe distress and agitation. Ms McCarthy was insistent she not return to the shower and described again her fear that her memories are washing away. She was teary when recalling refusing to go to the shower and her fear that PCA Flem was 'cross at her'. She was still distressed four hours after the incident at change of shift.

What specific action(s) has and will be taken in response to the incident to ensure the immediate and ongoing safety, health, well-being, and quality of life of the consumer affected by the incident?

Ms McCarthy's family representative, Anna Perrera, was contacted on 25 March at around 12:30 and was updated on Ms McCarthy's general condition. The incident was mentioned by management and Ms Perrera requested to speak to Ms McCarthy immediately. She was insistent on being given full details of report, and was assured this would occur.

Visiting GP has Ms McCarthy's care and treatment plan update as high priority on next visit.

All-staff memo has been issued reminding staff that patients are within their rights to refuse personal care.

PCA John Flem has been issued a written warning.
Union representative has asked for a meeting with management in regards to this.
OHS representative has opened case and PCA John Flem has taken a week of personal leave.

Next steps (internal only):
Meeting with family: online – end of week, Eva can you please arrange?

Day 17

There was a man, at the university in Adelaide, strange ears, divine hip bones, he said the word 'lepidopterology' as if it were an erotic spell. One night, high summer, he took us into the East Wing lab and he opened the drawer where they kept the breeding moths. We undressed each other and he put his tongue on me while the moths fluttered about us, landed on our skin. I was worried that I would lose my scholarship, but more worried that I would not finish in the manner that was expected of me. No one found out. I did not lose my scholarship. I did not finish either, not with him. It was my roommate's older brother, down from the family farm, up against the washing machine in the shared third-floor laundry, who could get me there. Surprising. Unlovely but good. I think of the moth man more, though. I wonder what became of him. Wonder if he wonders what became of me.

What I didn't know before was that I would never be twenty-six again. Should have had an inkling. There were years when I ran my hand down my side expecting to trace hipbone, only to find it cushioned by the soft pad of my belly. Even the first shocks – a black bristle of hair on the chin, a deep skin furrow that would not be plumped by ample hand cream, the flat wibble of breast hoiked into a bra – the space in the cup like a sigh – even those did not prepare me.

What I didn't know before is that age is stealthy. One day you look down at the sun-spotted hands in your lap and wonder who they belong to.

Is it true, the memory of the moth man? The deliciousness? Sometimes we make false memories. Misremember. Sometimes, many people misremember the same event. The Mandela effect, they call it. Named for all the people who recall Nelson Mandela dying in prison. Does the boy from the university remember releasing the moths? Does the moment nestle in his brain tissue? Is it gone? And if it is gone, where did it go? Does my recollection connect to his? Did the neurons fire together? Who owns it? When my brain matter erodes can I rely on his to keep this moment in the world? Mandela did not die in prison. He was released after twenty-seven years and became the President of South Africa. Moth wings on my sternum.

*

Day 18

Anna
Can someone pick up stuff with Hil this week?
I am drowning.
Just need to respond to SG re meeting time.
10.36am

Anna
Okay arseholes thanks so much.
1:02pm

Trace
Also drowning. Can deal after COB today.
1:03pm

Anna
Ta. Before night?
Need to make time for meeting with management.
1:04pm

Trace
Fuck @Benny – BRO – take this one, Huh?
1:06pm

Benny
Soz. Meetings. Sure send me number.
2.58pm

Anna has shared a contact
Sanctuary Gardens Aged Care
3.00pm

Your aunty's name is Hilda.
3.01pm

Benny

🖕🖕🖕

3.02pm

Anna

WTF @Benny?!

8.13pm

Trace

What've you done @Benny?

8.15pm

Anna

Sent uber eats to Sanctuary Gardens

8.16pm

Trace

😂😂 🤑 💲 🍔

8.16pm

Anna

Or just 🍩

8.18pm

Benny

It was a gesture dickheads.

Also to make a point.

8.31pm

Didn't just send it for Hil. Sent dinner for everyone!

8.32pm

Anna

They had to throw them out. Policy. 😷😷😷

Send dinner over here if you're so ducking desperate to make a gesture.

8.40pm

Uncle Benny can I hav a berger 😋🍔🙏

8.41pm

Benny

Cute. And no, cos your mum can do that.
Aunty Hilda and her mates can't.

8.45pm

Also. Go to bed! Give your mum a break.

8.46pm

                Anna

        He's still up cos I'm two glasses in
        and can't move from couch.
        But B. Srsly. How is this helping.
        Just do one of the ducking meetings.
        Take something off my plate!

        8.50pm

Benny

So they don't think we're
cheapskates who are complainers.
Don't you remember that ACA thing?
Hidden cameras. What the staff do to the
poor old fuckers whose families complain

8.53pm

                Anna

        SG isn't like that.
        Not that you would know.

        8.54pm

Benny

They're all like that

8.56pm

Tracey

Yeah. I'm with you on this one bro.

8.59pm

Anna
Well I'll leave you two to deal with all
the Hilda stuff from here on?
Like how much you helped with mum?
9.01pm

Trace
Woah. Not like that @Anna –
we know how much you do.
9.03pm

Benny
@Anna – you are a saint.
9.04pm

Benny
She's muted us hasn't she?
9.10pm

Trace
Yep 😒
9.12pm

Day 20

Hilda wakes in the dark and creeps her hands to the edges of the bed. It's narrow enough for her to grip both sides. There had been a dream. It clings to her. A road shaded by large pines, leading somewhere important that she was expected to go. A small child beside her, unfamiliar, with a scrape on their knee. The child complaining that they're hungry. Yes. That's it. She is hungry. Deep, stomach-churning hunger. Bread and butter. Leftover fried rice under a plate in the fridge. Cut cheese with a blob of chutney smeared on top. A thick wedge of lemon cake, crumbly and sweet. A cup of tea, nice and hot, and a jam biscuit to dunk. She wants all of these things.

It is more difficult than she expects to get out of bed. The tight sheets bind her feet down, there are bars at the side she does not remember being there before. But she pushes the pillows to the floor and manages to swing herself around and shuffle her bum along to the edge of the mattress. The floor is cold but steady under her feet.

Now for some light.

The switch will be near the door. If she just keeps her hands on a surface, she'll find it, along the bed, then a moment of wavering in space, then, ah, there, the wall, the doorjamb, run the hand along and up, and there. Yes. Her fingers on the plastic switch, the click of success, light enough to blind her for a moment.

She knows not to look down. Not to peer inside the door of the bathroom at the mirror. Like whispering to the girl in the horror movie not to go up the stairs, she knows that it will bring her undone. Her stomach gurgles. Onward, then.

To the door that leads out and down the hallway to the kitchen. If she's honest, she is not sure of which hallway or if there even is a kitchen, but she is certain that this is the way. Trusts her stomach on this one. She recalls that sometimes somebody locks her in. She is not sure why. Hilda does not feel that she has behaved in a manner that could warrant being locked in. Cannot recall anyone ever locking the door of her bedroom when she was a child. The London house, with all the people, she locked it there. Perhaps that is what it is – she has locked the door herself, to keep others out, it is not that she has been locked in.

Hand on the long silver door handle. She clunks it down but there is no catch, no give. *Damn.* Tries again, then the little silver knob above, presses her fingers against it to get purchase, is rewarded with a deep click she feels through to her wrist. When she tries the handle again, it gives and she pulls the door open. The dark corridor beckons. She grins.

Patient progress notes
Hilda McCarthy DOB: 03/11/1933 UR No: ▓▓▓▓
Banksia Bed 612
NFR

Date: ▓▓▓▓
Time: ▓▓▓▓

PCA: Neja Lakmal

Hilda was found in the kitchen approximately 3:00 am on Wednesday morning eating sausage rolls and chutney. She did not appear disoriented. Smiled at me and asked to be escorted back to her room. Got her settled and she fell asleep. No need for incident report, decided with RN Sheffler.

Day 23

The sky, filled with migrating moths, is so big. Hilda's camera is trained on the sky as it leeches light and the aperture is filled with thousands and thousands and thousands of moths. Wind, air, movement, grass, the odd stone under her back.

The local ranger is next to her. He is quiet. Watching. She hears his breathing steady and slow.

'It could take four hours, did you know?' she says.
'Hmmm.'
'You watching, or asleep?'

'Both.'

'Ha, wish I could just lie here and watch instead of holding this bloody thing.' What she means to say is: Tell me to put the camera down. Turn my face to yours. Cover me with your body. Skin to skin under a moth-flutter sky.

'That's why I'm a ranger and you're a scientist.'

She can hear the grin in his voice but when she shifts her head away his eyes are still closed, elbows out and hands clasped behind his head. And she knows he knows she wants him.

Prick, she thinks, and vows not to think of it again.

She gets the four hours of footage. He drives her back down the mountain to her little motel room. He doesn't ask, though she knows if she did he would say yes. She doesn't ask. But she cold showers then furiously brings herself to orgasm and she wishes there was not so much wanting in her, or else that she might sometimes set aside her stubbornness to let her wanting take centre stage. Not even sometimes. Just one time.

Day 25

'You see this?'

'You have got to be fucking kidding me.'

'One glove per shift.'

'Until further notice.'

'Because I can feed someone one-handed while I do infection control with the other.'

'Hey, boss, you tried to shower someone with one hand?'

'You ever wiped someone's arse and cleaned the shit up with just one glove, Mr Packam?'

'This is something *else*, isn't it.'

'Not enough pay for this shit.'

'There wasn't enough pay for this shit *before*.'

'What are you gonna do, huh?'
'You join the union?'
'Did. Not active. Can't afford it now. You?'
'Yeah, for all the good it does me.'
'You want another cuppa?'
'We got time?'
'Never. Short staffed again, but there's three minutes left on the clock and you know they good for something – that union woman tells me I can take it, even when Old Mick is calling out down the hall.'
'Here.'
'Ta. Old Mick been calling out since his mother pushed him out, I reckon.'
'Too true.'
'One glove.'
'Gotta laugh.'
'My cousin, she's in Perth. She thinks we're filthy. Keeps asking what are you doing over there?'
'Can't really understand it, until you're in it.'
'God help us if it gets in here.'
'My brother, though, keeps calling and saying bahhh – it's nothing – it's the government – it's a beat-up.'
'It's the phone towers.'
'Huh, yeah, that's him. Still, sometimes I reckon he's got a point. Why's it just us, huh?'
'But it's not. What news you watching? Open your eyes up, tell him that. Pandemic, that's what it means. All over the goddamned world.'
'Here, give me that to wash up.'
'Marjorie and the kitchen fairy will have you.'
'Got your one glove?'
'Armed and ready! Good luck out there.'

Day 27

Naxos. Heat. Honeymoon. I remember him sitting across from me, cigarette between his fingers, carafe of wine between us. Beaded with water and so cold when all else is wilting, melting. Shade of the patio where we have been sitting for hours already. Can see the sea. The remnants of our meal, no one has cleared our plates because they too are sitting now, with wine, their own meal laid out before them. White plates, blue trim. Smear of baked tomato, garlic, crisp edge of onion, the top end of a bean. If I ran my finger around the rim of the plate I would get the last of the skordalia, lemon and oil, remnant potato, flakes of white fish. Mouth waters, but stuffed now, like a dolmade bursting within its vine leaf, and there is the wine, and the heat, and here now, the cook meeting my eye and nodding. Ian pushes the packet across the table towards me. Fingers touch, and yes, I will, thank you, will add to the salt, lemon, garlic, wine acid of my mouth with nicotine and smoke and God yes, tip back my head and listen to my new husband laughing and talking, words of Greek and English but mostly sounds, noises to show their appreciation. The deep pleasure of the food, the wine, the afternoon.

Footscray, 1933

'Was your head as sore as mine yesterday morning?' Peggy asks Jack as they pause at the corner, the point at which they must go in two separate directions or risk looking something other than accidental.

'Oh, I've had a fair bit of practice,' he says, 'but I hope you're not saying that it was only the drink behind the looks you were giving me last night.'

She tries to hold his gaze but it turns her stomach over and she looks away.

'Not at all.'

'Well, that's good. I thought we might have our own picnic if the weather holds?'

She inclines her head. Jack King is asking her out.

Finally.

'And where would we go?' she asks coolly.

'How about you meet me in the park tomorrow night? Six?'

'And what might we be doing in the park with it turning dark by then, Jack King?'

He dips his head, 'Oh, I reckon we'll work something out, Peggy Donnelly.' He steps close enough that she can smell him, his hand resting gently, briefly on her hip before he turns away, raising one hand. 'See you then.'

The arrogance of him.

It is thrilling.

At six the next evening he's lying stretched out on the grass.

She enjoys looking at him as she approaches. He's showered and changed and he's in a dark pair of trousers, a shirt that's a little too tight. There are lots of folks out tonight, couples strolling in the pinky dusk, taking in the strangely warm evening, the late-season northerly and the respite it gives from the worst of the stink off the river and down off the port. She notices other women noticing Jack and smiles, recalling his kisses, the heavy tug in her pelvis that's been there all day. All hers.

His eyes are closed, his elbows out and hands folded beneath his head. She stands close over him. 'Good evening, Jack,' she says, and he opens his eyes.

'Evening,' he says, and grins, lying there for a moment and letting her look before he hauls himself up. 'A turn around the gardens, then?' he asks, taking her arm in his so that she can pretend he is a gentleman rather than the man who will lead her astray. He takes her down into the shadowed grotto of the gardens, dripping with moss and those great ferns – trucked down straight from the rainforest near Cairns, the papers say – to the little waterfall that took work crews weeks to get just right, to make it match up with the architect's imagination.

'Is this where you've put the picnic, then?' she says archly, knowing full well there's no picnic.

'Something like that,' he says, but he's already got his hands on her waist, and she is following him to the darkest corner, imagining those great green fronds hiding them, holding their secret close.

She is shocked by her hunger. Surprised at the quick frenzy in her fingers as she pulls at his shirt, presses herself into him, wanting to crush him and be crushed all at once.

His snagged breath in her ear, words she doesn't catch and doesn't need, unbuttoning her dress, her fingers on his fingers because *damn him and his fumbling*, quick, be quicker, peel back the fabric from her flesh so she is exposed and goosepimpled in the shaded cool of the grotto.

'Won't we be seen?' she whispers, suddenly aware that someone could be watching, flesh on flesh moving frantic through the lacework of foliage, hands and knees and thighs – *What's that, there? – Can you see?* – she imagines a man peering through, his shock, delight, not looking away.

The thought of it makes her hungrier still.

She drags Jack back a step, another, until she can feel the hard rock of the pond's edge against the back of her thighs. The whites of his eyes are flashing in the gloom as he draws his head back from her neck, one hand now on his buckle, then her hand on his, fast, faster.

Awkward as she sits, spreads her knees wide and covers herself with him, hands gripping tight on his buttocks now pulling him towards her, as he lowers himself so she can feel him, the heat of him against her thigh.

He is tugging at her, half kneeling to try and reach her, but she hisses, pushes him back, she is unstoppable now as she turns him around and tells him to sit, sinks to the pebbled earth with Jack King, his back against the stone wall of the pond, those astonished eyes, as she hitches her dress and kneels astride him.

'Jesus,' he breathes into her neck.

And now she takes all of him inside her, the shock of feeling filled, she grips hard, pushes down against him as he gasps and loops his arms underneath hers to drag on her shoulders.

In the shady ferns of the grotto, more fight than tenderness, muscles strain in her stomach, she grits her teeth, flesh against flesh, teeth on neck, so much that she cries out, not in pleasure, not yet, but at all of it at once is enough and she does not care one bit, not at all.

After, he walks her home and she feels taller, more brazen, much older than she was when she rolled out of bed that morning. Capable of undoing a man. A slaughterman, at that. There's something in that. Something that makes her feel like she has the whole world sparking and spitting at her fingertips. Like she could do anything at all. Be anyone at all. If she, Peggy Donnelly, who was never going to amount to anything, can do what she just did, bold as brass in the middle of the Footscray Park, then she might just go on and grab those faraway dreams that her mother always laughed at.

'Where you going?' Jack says, voice still slack with pleasure as she pulls away from his hand on her waist. Peggy skips ahead of him in the dark, twirling and spinning and laughing, bright and full of possibility, into a sunset turned blood-red by the smoke stacks from the works.

They crowd into the front bar of the Punt after knock-off on Wednesday. It's a good turnout, might just be that they all have a taste for a pint this afternoon or might be that there's something to the murmurs around the place.

Jack gets a round for him and Bluey and Budge and props himself up near the back where he can get a good look at the place and try and make sense of what the hell is going on.

Allen Braxton, the union delegate, shushes them all and tries to call them to order. Bluey leans in close to Jack and mutters, 'Shorty reckons there's been word from the union heads after their big meeting in Sydney, and he's not happy.'

Jack takes a long sip of his beer.

Allen thanks them all for coming at short notice, says he has news to report from the meeting in Sydney and reckons they'll all want to hear about it.

But for someone with pressing information he sure takes a while to get into it, and Jack elbows Bluey, shakes his head – wonders again why the slaughtermen don't just go back to the way it was in the day – their own union, not lumped in with all the rest of the workers.

Bluey tilts his chin. 'Hello, what's this?'

Stan has stood up to help Allen get to his point.

'Thank Christ for that,' mutters Jack. He's finished his beer and good luck getting Bluey or Budge to move now.

Stan raises his voice. 'This fella from Queensland is trying to tell us that the new system is gonna be *better* for the slaughtermen.'

'Bullshit!' comes a call from the back that starts a swell of grumbles. Stan raises his voice to continue.

'Reckons that this team system is gonna prevent us stopping so much, gonna be better for our backs, reckons we could make the machinery work for us.'

'Was he a slaught?' someone yells.

Stan shakes his head and is met with jeering laughter.

'Then what the *fuck* would he know?'

Allen steps in again, uses his hands to ask for quiet. 'Fellas, I'm just passing this on. There's some talk from the "leadership",' he says, pulling a face, 'that the union buggered it up in New Zealand and they reckon we'll do the same. That there isn't a chance we're gonna stop this chain, and our best bet is to use it to protect our wages, get some conditions improved—'

'Fuck 'em!'

'I'll not cut where another man has cut!'

Allen motions with his hands for quiet.

'And that's exactly what I told them – but he wanted me to pass on, as is my duty as elected rep—'

A roar from the men.

'We'll be on our own,' Allen says. 'It'll be an unapproved strike when we walk out.'

They shake their heads, quiet.

'So, I said, "Well you can pass on to those bigwigs in Sydney that we don't fucking need your approval – we're out!"'

Clapping and cheering, back slapping and great grins – a euphoria in the room that feels, just for a moment, like there could be triumph even in the face of defeat.

Later, when Jack gets home, there's a light still on in the kitchen and he's surprised to find his ma sitting at the table, a glass in her hand. Jack straightens up, wipes his mouth as if that'll sober him up.

'You right, Ma?' he asks as he pulls out a seat.

'Hello, love,' she says, shifting the glass away from her hand. 'You been at the pub?'

'Union meeting with the boys, went on a bit.'

'You eaten? Can I fix you something?'

'You're right, Ma, I'll get it,' he says, but actually he is starving, thinks of thick-cut bread, leftover pie, bacon.

'No, love, you sit.' She gets up and goes to the ice box, the stove top. Starts slicing something. 'What's the union saying, then? Heard Mrs Kelly down the shops saying there's gonna be a strike, wasn't happy.'

'No one's happy with a strike, Ma, doesn't mean we shouldn't do it.'

'Of course, love. What's it about this time, some new machine, is it?'

He loves his ma but she doesn't understand. How could she? She's never had to hold a jumping sheep in her arms, manhandle a cow, slice its throat, pull its warm guts out with her hands. Not had to keep up as the boss makes the tally higher and higher, not had to watch blokes break their bodies to keep up.

'Like that, yeah. Dad'd be turning in his grave to see it. Be the end of slaughtermen, any bastard'll join the line.'

'Language, Jack.'

The pan starts to spit and sizzle and the scent of bacon fat fills the room.

'Sorry, Ma.'

'You're right, love.' She turns from the stove and smiles at him. She looks tired. He realises he hasn't really taken much notice for a while.

'You right then, ma?'

She turns back, elbow out as she flips, sizzle sizzle.

'When am I not, then?'

'They treating you right down at Kinnear's?'

'Right enough. Though they're putting off girls. Just gotta hope I've been there long enough . . .'

Jack wishes his ma didn't have to go out to work. That he could bring in enough to support them all. And here he is waltzing in late having put some of his pay-packet down his gullet and his ma – on her feet all day – three other buggers to cook for, frying him up dinner at ten o'bloody clock.

'I'll look after you, Ma.'

'Oh, I know, love.' She puts the plate down in front of him, the clang of cutlery. Two eggs, a couple of slices of bacon, a sausage.

'Geez, this is orright. Thanks, Ma.'

She smiles, wipes her hands on her apron.

He digs in, has a mouthful, realises what it's missing. 'Got any HP?'

At the sink, Jack senses his mother pausing.

'Sometimes you're so like yer dad.'

There is something in her voice that makes Jack stop, look up, alert.

'Yer reckon?'

His ma goes to the pantry, pulls out the brown bottle. 'Well, he certainly loved a glob of this,' she says, smiling, her voice slightly too bright.

Jack takes it from her but she doesn't hold his gaze and he knows that whatever likeness she sees in him is not necessarily one she likes.

There have been more visits to the park, and once, thrillingly, to the freezer room after work. It isn't quite the grand romance Peggy always imagined for herself; less polish, more excitement. It catches her unannounced, in her throat, and down low between her legs, the thought of him, and it's never flowers and hat tipping she thinks of before she drifts off to sleep in her new room at Lil's house, it is flesh and teeth and sweat. She wolfs down two serves of breakfast before work. Sometimes imagines biting down on the shining slabs of the stuff she watches rattling into the chillroom as she heads on tea break. The other girls know there is something going on with her and Jack King, but whether it is jealousy or something else, they don't rib her like she thought they would.

Tuesday he came past at the end of the shift, Beth made a sad face at him and said she was sorry he didn't come to call on them like he used to, and Jack just laughed and flicked his head at her. Peggy nodded and met him on the corner near the local kill floor when the whistle went. There he crushed her up against the wall to kiss her, ignoring the men walking by after clock-off who whistled low as they passed.

That was the afternoon of the chill room. When she'd pushed his hand from where it had crawled under her skirt and laughed at him and said, *Not here, Jack*, he'd told her that he needed to cool off then, and he knew a place.

She knew. She wanted. She followed.

Tonight, at least, he has said he will take her to the pictures, but to be honest she isn't sure if she's up to it. The meatworks today has a stink about it that is curling her toes. But it's still hours till her shift ends and there are forty bags to get done before then.

'Billy reckons there's trouble brewing with the slaughtermen.' Norma is a tight beanpole of a woman who likes to drop news like stones in a pond, watching while the gossip ripples out across the works.

'Hardly unusual,' says Nell. 'Think they're so high and mighty up there.'

'Too right, only ones not to take a cut last year.'

'And the year before!'

'And rightly so,' says Jean. 'None of us'd be here at all if they didn't work their scrawny arses off.'

'You'd know!'

'Well scrawny arse doesn't mean scrawny anywhere else . . .' Jean grins, and they whoop around the table, hands never stilling over the cotton and threads.

'What's the trouble?' Peggy asks, thinking that if she's going to keep carrying on with a slaughterman, she should know. He hasn't talked work to her really, but there hasn't been that much talking at all to be honest. And she doesn't mind it, how obsessed it has made her, thinking of him and his hands, and that arse – but still, what she wants in a man is more than that, she wants long conversations and dreams and plans. Not too much to ask, is it, to want it all?

'This new machinery they're bringing in from New Zealand.'

'From Chicago, I heard.'

'Why's it trouble?'

'Apparently it's a chain – the lamb, or the cow, is cut and hung at one end and then it just runs past all the men – one cut each – until it's all in pieces at the other end.'

'Doesn't make any sense. Why have all those men doing one cut each, if a slaught can do it all himself?'

'Well, they just keep those lambs coming, every minute or something crazy like that.'

'They reckon they'll be putting out five times the number of animals every day.'

Jean guffaws and there's a round of incredulous laughter.

'Bugger that, that means we'll be working five times harder.'

'Or there'll be five times more of us?'

'Ha. Doubt it. Cost him too much.'

And the conversation moves on to the cover of the latest *Weekly* and the rather fetching style of the model's hair.

But Peggy notices Jean's tight face, like she knows something they don't know, like they're blind to what's coming.

Jack straightens his collar at the door before he knocks, then *tsk*s in the back of his throat and roughs his collar up again as he hears Peggy's quick footsteps coming down the hall. He doesn't have anything to prove.

Peggy flings open the door and she is all teeth and fluttering hands, he can feel the breathlessness coming off her, wants to tell her to slow down or she's gonna break something, but he also understands that he has made this happen. That's a hell of a thing.

'Give me five more minutes, I need to fix my face,' she says, though there's nothing to fix as far as he can tell. 'Go on and say hello to Lil, she's in the kitchen.'

He doesn't want to say hello to Lil. He wants to whisk Peggy out of there, take her via the lane down to Barkly Street so they can get in a cuddle, wants to be in the dark of the Trocadero with his hand on her thigh, his pay in his pocket and a thirst building he knows will be quenched in a couple of ways by the time the night is done.

Peggy tugs at his hand, pushes him down the hallway, inclining her head in Lil's direction before ducking into her room and closing the door.

Jack clenches his jaw, strides forward to where the light from the kitchen glows, and finds Lil sitting at the table with the newspaper laid out in front of her and a bottle of beer in her hand.

She smiles. 'Evening, Jack.'

He nods, is unsure now. 'Miss Martin—'

'Lil – please.'

He nods.

She gestures towards the bottle. 'Can I get you a drink while you wait?'

One thirst roars in his throat.

'Ta,' he says and takes a seat while she goes to the ice chest and pulls out a bottle.

She looks different. Not buttoned into her coat, a loose of hair tucked behind her ear. How the hell does she turn herself into such a matron to come to work and then be all – this – here? She mustn't be a day over thirty.

'It's nice, this,' he says, gesturing to the room, finding himself disarmed by her quiet.

She nods. 'Nice to have Peggy here.'

'Yerright, was sorry to hear about your mum.'

'Thank you.'

'Mum said your ma was a good help when she lost Dad. Always thought a lot of her.'

'That's kind of her to say.'

He is throwing the beer down, wants to be out with Peggy in the air where he is sure-footed.

Lil pushes her beer away. 'Big numbers this week. You lot have been working hard.'

He shrugs. 'Foreman made it clear we needed to get through them. Too many waiting in the yards.'

'And your pay will reflect it.' Her gaze is direct. 'Overtime and meeting tally.'

'This week it will, yeah. Wouldn't want anyone to think those kinds of numbers might be something we can do every week.'

Her turn to shrug. 'Angliss was impressed.'

A sudden burst of anger. Who is she to tell him what tally was impressive? Who does she think she is? He puts the bottle down hard on the table. 'Well, maybe he oughta think about the tally us slaughts can reach without his stupid new system.'

She smiles calmly. 'Oh, I'm sure he knows exactly what tally he'll get with that.'

'Ready!' Peggy's hand on his shoulder, finger at his ear. He pushes back from the table.

'Have a nice evening, you two. Nice to see you, Jack.'

He nods, just wants to get out of there.

Peggy pulls him out into the night, presses herself into him and when he pushes her against the fence in the laneway, mouth at her neck, hands under her dress, he tells himself her gasps are all for pleasure and not the fact that he is pushing just a little bit too hard.

Stupid stupid stupid.

How many times does a girl have to be told?

Ma. Jesus. She'll bloody kill her.

And what about Dad? Thank Christ he's probably too far up

the coast already cos otherwise she'd be telling Jack King to get the hell out of town before her father gets down here to tear him a new one.

The first week she pretended. The second she crossed her fingers. The third and the fourth and the fifth she prayed, even though it had been years since she'd set foot in a church. But by the sixth, she'd known. And now here she is and she's missed two already, sick in the guts with her breasts all swollen and sore, and well Jack thinks that's a lark, doesn't he, and she can't get any more pregnant than she already is, so he's having a fine old time.

Until she tells him.

Which she is going to have to do, because Lil has hawk eyes, probably already suspects, and she's going to have to run away or make Jack King marry her and she's not sure, right now, which of those is more terrifying, or more tempting.

Stupid stupid stupid.

She takes a long drag on her ciggie, shifts her bum around on the old bench seat in the garden. Yes, there are other options.

Gin in the bath.

A punch in the guts – she heard Molly Mavis tried that three times and all she got was a sore gut, though it probably accounts for the fact that her little one isn't all there.

A visit to Shelly Street.

And maybe she would, maybe she could, except that there is something about Jack King that's got under her skin, as well as her skirt. And in the hours she lays awake at night now, her dinner refusing to go down, she thinks that being the mother of Jack King's child might in fact be the daring thing that's been coming for her all along. Might bind them together.

Maybe it's that time of the month, because Jack is struggling to get Peggy to smile, to react to his kisses, to give him anything at all, really. And he's put in the effort. Understood that when she said maybe she'd like to have a few more dates where she didn't go home with grass in her hair that he was being told to lift his game. This week he's taken her to the pictures on Tuesday, a walk by the river on Thursday when he didn't even try and divert her to the grotto, and now it's Friday and they're one set in at the Orama and she's got a look on her face that says she wants to be anywhere but here.

'Jesus, Peggy,' he says when she shrugs him off and tells him to dance with Beth, 'anyone would think you'd gone cold on me.'

'I just wanted it to be the two of us, tonight.'

He shrugs. 'But Bluey and the boys reckon this lot'll play some top tunes. I thought you'd like it, that you wanted to come out like this more!'

Women. Seriously, you can't win.

He passes her a glass of punch, but she screws up her face, then, for a second, looks horrified.

'I'm gonna be sick,' she says, pushing him out of the way and running to the entrance.

'She all right, Jack?' Nell asks, looking over.

'Blowed if I know.'

'Well go after her, you great galah.' And they all laugh and he shakes his head at them, but goes after his girl, cos he knows that when it comes down to it she's the bloody best of them.

Out in the street, he looks up and down till the bloke on the door flicks his head, and Jack finds her leaning up against the wall around the corner.

'You right?' he says, coming up behind her and placing his hand on the small of her back.

She wipes her mouth and turns around. Even under the streetlamps he can tell she's pale and her face is all clammy.

'You look rotten. You eat something bad, you think?'

She rolls her eyes and drops her head.

'Pegs?' he says.

She places her hands on his chest and looks him square in the face, and later he'll think what a damn fool he was, standing there getting a look like that and not realising what it was that was coming at him. More than a few times since he'll think that this was the bloody moment he should have started running.

'I'm pregnant, Jack.'

'What?'

'Pregnant,' she says with bite, dropping her hands. 'Up the duff. Gonna have a baby.'

'You're bloody not.'

Her face like he's slapped her. Then tightening into a frown. 'I bloody am.'

'Shit,' he breathes and drops his head. 'You're sure?'

'Yes, I'm sure and don't you dare even think about asking if it's yours, cos you're the only one I've been stupid enough to let under my skirt.'

'Shhh,' he says and steps in close, but she pushes him away.

'There's a lady—'

'I know there's a bloody lady, Jack, don't you think I've thought of that myself?' She begins to cry.

He walks away, kicks the gutter, hard, kicks it again. This isn't what he planned, he was just having fun, and maybe, yes, one day, but not now for God's sake, with the end of the season looming and this trouble brewing at the works, what's he gonna do, get down on one knee and then sweep her off to his bloody single bed in the lean-to on the front veranda? He wheels around on her. 'This is what you wanted, is it? Cook this plan up with the girls, did you?'

'You're a bastard, Jack King,' she spits. 'As big a bastard as they all say!' And she runs from him, around the corner and away and he puts his fist into the wall, again and again and again till his knuckles are bloody and numb.

She ignores him at work, and it takes three goes before she will come to the door at Lil's place and take the posy of daisies he's brought, accept his grovelling apology and allow herself to be kissed.

And he's that damn relieved, that his black-haired girl smiles and lets him put his hand down low on her belly, that it's nothing at all in the end, and the words don't stick like he thought they would. She squeals and throws her arms around his neck, and doesn't mind when he says that they can't afford a proper one right now, but later, after the baby, they will. She nods her head and agrees, that right now, the thing to be done is to get themselves to the registry office and make it official. He reckons that when he tells his mother (God help him) she might just come around to the idea of lending her wedding band to act as the ring and he'll do right by them all, by his ma, by Peggy, by the kid in there who he is beginning to think might be all right after all, and by his dad, who'll look down and be proud that his son has stepped up and showed himself to be a man after all.

Lil has a bobby pin in her mouth and a safety pin in her hand.

'Well? What do you think?' Peggy asks.

She twirls awkwardly and then stops, facing Lil. She has chosen a yellow dress that flicks at the mid-calf hem, and is softened with a wrapped fold around her middle, not that she has started to show, but Lil knows, and that perhaps is enough for the girl to strive for modesty.

It's cut well, and when Lil steps closer to check that it will hold around the bust, she can see that the fabric is fine. She wonders whether Peggy's mother arranged a bank cheque or some credit at Foys, to balance out the fact she isn't coming to the wedding. Distance, money or shame, it's hard to tell.

Lil thinks the yellow is childish, to be honest. She would have counselled a pale green, a sky blue, a colour that might look more like married life, but she won't say that, of course.

Peggy reaches for the bouquet on the dressing table – brilliant blue cornflowers studded with the white balls of baby's breath. Cheap and bright.

'Perfect, they're just the thing to really set it off. You look lovely.'

The girl's face relaxes into a smile and she slumps a little. 'Good, because I feel bloody awful.'

Lil raises her eyebrows as Peggy rushes out and retches in the sink.

On the bed, the jacket that Lil has lent her. She hasn't told Peggy she bought it for her own engagement. Wouldn't do to go bringing it up now. A soft thing. Lil smooths the fabric with the tips of her fingers. She affords herself a moment, a moment for closing her eyes, seeing Tommy's face right there in front of her as if shadowed by blinding sun beyond him, his hands on her shoulders, *Well now, don't you look wonderful*, the low hum of his voice just before it might break into a kiss to greet her. Mumbling kisses, the ones she liked best, because he could not stop talking to kiss her, but could not stop kissing her to talk.

The doorbell rings, once, twice, shrill and purposeful, followed by a pounding knock.

'Well, at least he's eager!' Peggy says, rushing into the room. 'You ready, Lil?'

'Here,' she says, 'make him wait.' She turns Peggy to face the mirror and fixes a pin at the back of her hair where it is carefully curled. In the mirror, Peggy is pale, and Lil can see her nervous pulse in the soft skin of her throat.

'On your terms.' She nods her head and eyes the younger woman.

'On my terms,' Peggy replies, turning suddenly and embracing Lil tight. '*Thank you*,' she whispers, pulling back, straightening her dress and turning her face towards the door where Jack King rings and rings the bell and will not stop.

Later, Lil thinks they should have taken it as an omen. The car running out of fuel midway down Ballarat Road so that they have to hail a cab to get to the registry office on time. Peggy refused to run to her own wedding. Lil paid, of course. Jack blamed Wilco's uncle, who had failed to mention that the car they'd borrowed off him didn't have a full tank. Jack's brother Ned, who was joining them, corroborated that Wilco's uncle was a forgetful bastard. At any rate, Jack has Peggy giggling and sweet again by the time the four of them pile out of the cab at two minutes past the hour and rush inside to the stern clerk, who tells them they'd better not treat their marriage vows with such impertinence. Lil thinks she notices him rest his piggish little eyes on the drape of Peggy's dress at her waist, but maybe she imagines it.

As Peggy and Jack take their positions, facing each other and both bowing their heads a little at the sudden seriousness of the day, Lil wonders how long it will take for Peggy to regret this moment. It's a terrible thought to have as the bride's only witness, but nonetheless it stays with her as the two of them say their vows, making their bond legal and preventing that child growing in Peggy's belly being born a bastard.

Ned tries to make a joke about making it a double as he moves aside so Lil can sign the certificate, but she's in no mood to humour him, signing her name quickly, hoping the act of putting pen to paper will make up for her bad faith in the union.

They'd booked a table at the Punt for the wedding tea – the girls from bagging are there for Peggy and Jack has invited some of the Angliss boys, his sister and his mother. Mrs King didn't know what to make of the whole affair; her boy raised up in the world for a moment by marrying this bright young woman of relatively good stock, but then hurrying it all along so she couldn't enjoy the occasion at all. She didn't come down in the last shower – guessed the reason she wasn't dining with the parents of the bride – but Mrs King had the good grace not to mention it. A bonny big baby born a month or so 'earlier than expected' – it wouldn't be the first in the family, nor the suburb, nor the city, and it certainly wouldn't be the last.

'How did I do, then? Every bit the bride?'

'Every bit,' Lil says and raises her glass to Peggy's shandy.

'Not quite how I imagined it.' Peggy looks over at her new husband. Jack is already grinning and leaning hard into the bar. A pint of beer in his hand, and another lined up on the table for him. He looks triumphant, having managed to father a child and get himself hitched in a few short months – albeit not in the right order – and now he can sit back and rest. Lil realises she is clenching her back teeth, hard.

'Have you eaten something?' Lil pushes the plate of sandwiches across the table to Peggy but she turns her head, grimacing.

'Thought it would feel different.'

'What would?'

'Being married. Being a wife.'

Lil laughs. 'Well, you're only a couple of hours in, give it time.'

Peggy nods but doesn't smile, and Lil feels like scooping her up and running back to the registry office, erasing her witness signature, erasing Peggy's. Wonders madly if someone might invent a machine that could wind them all back, unconceive the child, make Jack walk in the opposite direction up Railway Place and away from their front door.

*

Every time he turns there's another clap on Jack's back, a pint in his hand, a knowing wink and guffaw.

'No going back now, mate!'

'How's it feel, huh, the tug of the old ball and chain?'

But he laughs them off because Peggy is glowing, easily the prettiest of the lot. And he knows already, doesn't he, that she's a firecracker, easily matches his hunger, that they'll be good together, have fun together. And besides, look at his ma over there, grinning like she's just had a win on the nags. Pleased as punch that her firstborn has made an honest woman of someone. That he's knuckling down to life.

He does the rounds, graces them all with his presence, feels ten foot tall as he grabs his wife's arse on the way past – his wife! And Lil has been a doll, really. Not sure how it's gonna be with him moving in, she can be a serious one, and she's in the boss's pocket, but she's gone and organised most of everything today and Peggy said she's been a sport about her being up the duff already. Might be nice being the man of the house with two women about, anyway. He could get used to that.

A quorum of old slaughts in the corner.

'Why so serious, lads?'

'Just wishing your dad was here to see it, you all grown up.'

'No doubt he's looking down and having one, or ten, to celebrate.'

'Cheers to him, then.'

They raise their glasses solemnly.

'Be turning in his grave, he would, to know what's coming for us slaughtermen,' says Budge.

Wilco elbows him in the ribs. 'Nuff of that tonight – it's a wedding, Budge! Cause for celebration, not commiseration.'

'We'll all be out of a job come Christmas. Hope you've got another trade under your belt there, Jack, cos you might be needing it to keep a roof over your wife's head.'

'Take no notice of him, Jack, he's a sorry drunk. We'll do all right, the union'll have our back.'

But Jack can't shake the look that Budge gives him, beery-eyed and red in the nose, shaking his head like it's gotta be the saddest day he's ever raised his glass to.

∞

∞

Hummingbird Project™

ErisX: Can you design a visual representation of an algorithm that could undo humanity's worst innovations? Prioritise the following ideas: Bayesian probability, the philosophy of Paul Klee, counter factuals, planetary health and wellbeing, social equity, artistic endeavour.

HummingbirdProject: Sure.

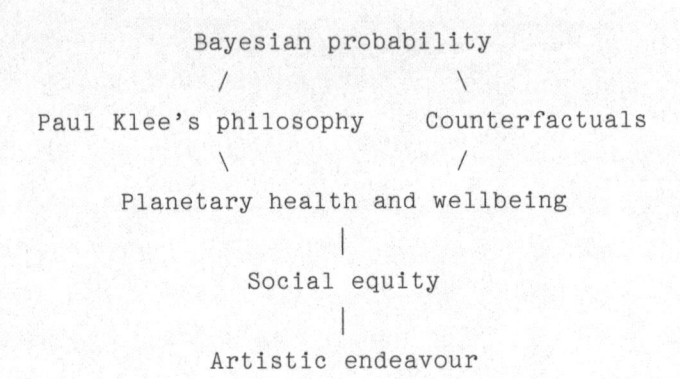

```
              Bayesian probability
             /                    \
  Paul Klee's philosophy      Counterfactuals
             \                    /
         Planetary health and wellbeing
                       |
                  Social equity
                       |
               Artistic endeavour
```

The algorithm starts with Bayesian probability as the foundation for predicting the potential outcomes of undoing certain innovations.

Then, it branches out into two paths: one inspired by the philosophy of Paul Klee, emphasising creative thinking and innovation, and the other focused on counterfactuals, imagining alternative histories and identifying negative consequences.

These paths converge on planetary health and wellbeing, which is used as a guiding principle to prioritise innovations that have the greatest negative impact on the environment and the health of living beings. The algorithm then considers social equity, prioritising inventions that have the greatest negative impact on marginalised communities, and ends with artistic endeavour, inspiring and motivating efforts to create a more just and sustainable world.

ErisX: Nice. Now can you give me an artistic expression of the above?

HUMMINGBIRD ALGORITHM™

∞

The Inlet, 2181

They rest by the inlet. Swimming and sleeping and catching fish and sucking clean the bones, drying berries and kelp for the journey ahead, digging salt glop shellfish from the rocks, plaiting shells into their long tangles of hair. Maz watches the sky. She knows that soon they will need to find somewhere to shelter from the heat. Caves if they can, some deep shaded gorge back along the river. How far back would they need to travel, though, and what is the risk of walking straight back to JP? No, they must go on, away, find somewhere to see out the heat, find a friendly, find the Finders.

On the fourth day at the inlet, Onyx comes racing up from where she has been diving for crabs.

'Something got me!' she yells so wildly that Maz drops the shirt she is mending and races down to meet her sister.

'What, where?!'

'Right inside! There's blood everywhere! Help me!'

And once she works it out, Maz tries not to laugh and tells her little sister she has not been bitten and is not dying, that she is bleeding, she is of age now and every moon she will bleed again.

She finds the least stained of her own cloths and shows it to her sister. Onyx looks at her as though she is mad.

'*Every* cycle?'

'Every cycle.'

Onyx is aghast. 'But *why*?'

'In the beforetimes it was a sign you were ready to bring a baby.'

'But not anymore.'

'Not if you are a Steward, no.'

'Because we are the Last.'

'Yes.'

Onyx is quiet for a bit. She places her hand between her legs to where Maz knows the bulk of the cloth is unfamiliar, annoying.

'But,' Onyx says, 'could we have one anyway?'

Maz looks at her. 'A baby?'

'Yes.'

'Well, I suppose, yes.'

'Because we are not Stewards anymore, are we?'

It is Maz's turn to be quiet. *Are* they still Stewards? Were they ever? If you leave a place and a people and a belief, do you still belong? Do you want to? They have always known that the Stewards are not the only ones walking this earth. There are others. Scavengers. Guerrillas. Other cave clans and forest folk roaming or existing on small islands of their own making. Rarely have they met or interacted, although often the Stewards pick through what they leave behind. And sort it and destroy it, return it to the source. Maz has never really let herself think about the reason the other few humans left around don't try to make contact, join ceremony, combine their resources. Sometimes they have stumbled upon a camp that has clearly been left in a rush; water boiling in a tin on a fire, a good heavy shirt hanging from a branch, quick scurry scuffle marks in the dirt – and a part lights up in Maz's brain that is very old and very deep, and she recognises these as the signs of fear.

JP told stories of these Others around the fire. They cling to oldways, they still have Wants, they are Devourers, Consumers, they do not know balance, they have no purpose, they are unable to connect to the source. When JP told a story, every part of it made sense. It was like a thread of pearl kelp – perfect globes of story following one after the other, they fit, each making the next more certain. It is difficult to shake off a story that fits so well. Maz feels like they must be cut out from the insides of her, so she can take a proper look at them and see if they are real. JP's stories are hard to cleave out of the middle of her. She believes them very much.

Except.

Now they are alone. There is no JP. They are Maz and Onyx and now they must make their own story.

Onyx breaks the quiet. 'I don't miss JP but I miss the others. I miss Mater's porridge at matins and I miss Ben and the campfire and I miss having a job and I miss ceremony, I miss feeling like we don't have to run.'

Maz presses her lips together hard. She has taken her sister away from the only family she has ever known.

'Do you think Trust has returned to the source now?' Onyx asks.

'I don't know.'

A twist in Maz's gut. JP and Trombolo standing still in the rain. The sound like a tree branch in mud.

'I loved him. JP. I thought he was our protector.'

'But he didn't protect us. He put us in danger. He put you in danger.'

'Still. Something inside me still does.'

'What?'

'Love him.'

'Even after everything?'

'Yes.'

There is silence for a time. The landscape is soft and green and it holds them both in their quiet.

'Will we be like that forever, do you think?'

'Like what?'

'Will we always love people who hurt us?'

Sister, she thinks, *grow back down, let your brain rest, don't think so much.*

But, 'Yes,' she says, 'I guess we will.'

For one entire lunar cycle they are on their own. Hiding, tracking, hunting. It takes many days but finally the sisters kill a kangaroo. Quiethush they hide in the longgrass and choose a little one, not too big so that the meat won't spoil. Maz fashions a long spear and her aim is true, in the neck, and they say their thanks to the creature as Maz uses her blade to slit its throat, peel back the skin, take it apart into pieces they can cook on the fire – tail, leg, ribs. They wash the blood from their bodies in the sea and hang the skin at the edge of camp, let the ants do their work so they might use the pelt as a bag, something to warm them.

The midges are fierce, only giving them reprieve when the sun is high. The sisters feed damp leaves on the fire to make it smoke hard. Sit close at dawn and dusk when the midges frenzy at their heads, throw a sea-damp log on to smoke over them all night. Watch fat moths hover and spin around the clouds of insects. They hang kelp and shells, build patterns of oddz they bring up from the shoreline. Now, though, they don't think about sorting oddz to destroy them, they think about how they might use them. They keep the gleaming Treasure oddz packed away, but every couple of days the sisters bring them out, examine them, see if they fit together in a different way. Hypothesise about what they might be and mean. Maz asks Onyx to repeat the words she heard JP say, even though she has now heard them many times, and Onyx tells: *A way to unmake the world*. If the pieces are brought together they combine to become a powerful machine, or a source, maybe that's the word he used, something strong enough to begin everything again. They pack the Treasure oddz away.

Maz repairs a tear in the side of her pack with a long length of plastic line and Onyx sews a pale green plastic star to her shirt. She has discovered that this star glows in the night like the luminous mushrooms in the moist nooks of trees here, and she tells Maz it will guide them on to the next place.

Maz hears it like her sister has given her a kick up the bum. 'You are rested enough, then? You are ready to journey on?'

Onyx gives her a withering look. 'I've been ready for a whole cycle, sister. Are *you* ready?'

'You sound like the fire sister in the story.'

Onyx laughs, then quiets as though she is back in the tent in the camp of the Stewards. 'You never finished telling me the story,' she says.

Maz takes a deep breath and looks out over the rippling inlet that has kept them safe this past cycle. '*Be ready*, said the younger sister, *this may be our only chance*. And the older sister held up her cupped palms and the little pyramid of twigs and threads of bark and grass.

'*Are you ready?* the younger sister asked, and the older sister nodded, not wanting to make even a breath with her voice that might risk the dries and the lightning her sister was about to summon.

'The younger sister stood tall on the side of the mountain and closed her eyes and scrunched her face up hard with concentration. She pointed both arms to the sky and stretched out her fingers and a great breath like the whoosh of an easterly rushed up out of her mouth. The older sister watched in fear for it was clear this was taking all of her younger sister's energy, that she was risking her life to bring down this one spark of lightning. The sky began to boil and rumble and the younger sister's mouth opened wide in a grimace of great effort. Eyes still closed, she began to drag her arms through the air, lowering them towards her older sister. The older sister held very still, her cupped palms and the dries in front of her.'

'She's going to kill her!' Onyx says suddenly.

'Wait, the story isn't over yet,' Maz says.

'Well, quick! Get to the end, my tummy feels all gobbledy. I want to know what happens!'

'The older sister held still, her cupped palms in front of her, and she watched her sister's hands and she saw the tiny golden sparks that began to fly around her fingers, so small, not enough for flame, but they kept going, more of them and bigger, and the older sister held her breath and sweat poured from the body of the younger sister until she looked as though she were about to collapse.

'*Hold on, sister, hold on*, thought the older sister, *just one lightning spark to the dries, hold on*.

'And then, just as the younger sister's legs crumpled beneath her and she let out a great wail, a single golden lightning fork leapt from the sky and down into the cupped palms of the older sister, catching the pyramid of dries. The older sister froze, wanting to run straight to her sister but knowing she held the promise of fire in her hands.

'The sky stopped rumbling. She held her breath still, the younger sister lay where she had fallen.'

Maz stops. Draws out the waiting. Onyx looks as though her eyes will pop.

'And then a tiny thread of smoke rose from the top of the pyramid of dries, and the older sister saw a golden glow begin on one of the grass threads and she breathed, soft, so soft, and a little orange flame leapt up from the grass and into the next twig and then to the bark and then there was fire, good and true. She hurried to nest it in the bed they had prepared for it, and before she had turned to her sister, the crackle of firecatch was in the air.'

Onyx grabs Maz's arm. 'The younger sister! Is she alive?'

Maz smiles. 'She is. The older sister kneels down and places her arms underneath her sister and hugs her and says, *You did it, sister, we have fire again.*'

Onyx pumps a closed first in the air. 'YES!' she yells. 'I *knew* she could do it!'

Maz grins. 'And from that day forward the sisters knew to always keep some fire back for themselves, no matter who needed it, or how much, because they knew now what the world might be without fire, and knew, too, that it was their job to keep it safe.'

'*Good* story,' Onyx says and lies back on the hill, eyes closed in satisfaction.

'That was Mama's story,' Maz says softly. 'It *is* a good one, isn't it?'

One morning, as Maz leans close into the coals to breathe the fire back to life, she hears her sister shouting from the beach. She jumps up and begins to run, tripping and steadying herself and running on until she can see Onyx standing on the shore waving her arms – *okay, she's okay.* 'Stupid wolfcrier!' Maz huffs, as her sister jogs towards her.

'It's a bigfloat!' Onyx says and points behind her.

Maz follows the line of sight and then she sees it. It is out beyond the last breakers but close enough that she can make out a squat vessel with three tall poles rising like an old fence across its centre. There are long tumbles of fabric hanging loose then billowing out from each of the poles as they sway gently against the horizon.

'Boat,' Maz says. She has seen the remains of boats, the rusting hulks of ships and the smaller scoops of tin and plastic they sometimes find among the detritus of the Newcoast. They have floated on patched-together pontoons when diving in some spots – that's how she knew to make the river raft – but she has never seen a boat on water. And never seen something that looks like this.

'Boat! Is it people? Do they see us?' Onyx says, her voice bright and buzzing with urgency. 'It hasn't moved.'

'Don't know.' Maz shields her eyes to try to see against the morning glare. How can she know if this is a friendly? And should they even wait to find out? They could pack the tent and bags and disappear into the dense bushland behind the dune long before this boat could surf the waves in to them. If that's what it does.

'We need to hide,' she says, suddenly decisive, taking Onyx's hand and turning for the camp.

But Onyx pulls hard and away. 'Why?'

Maz sighs. 'Because we don't know who they are or what they want, and until we do we should stay out of sight.'

'But what if they just float away?'

Maz looks back at the boat. It doesn't seem to have moved. Maybe there is movement above the squat rectangle on the water or maybe it is the waves, a seabird. She does not know. She does not know! If the boat floats away, then the sisters will be no worse off than they were before Onyx's startled cry this morning. But.

Onyx's voice is careful and low. 'They could be Helpers, Finders, maybe?'

Maz looks at her sister now. She has grown. Somehow in this past cycle she has become taller, stronger, the sun has browned her skin even though it has been cool. But the sun is rising stronger and they have rested in the shade for the noontimes – Maz knows they must find deeper shelter soon to survive. They cannot stay here forever.

'We could make a flag. A fire on the beach,' Onyx says.

'No,' Maz rushes. They have nothing to protect them, only the one small blade in Maz's pack. Some of the logs for the fire maybe, if it came to that, she could thump someone, but their best protection is to hide.

'Look!' Onyx rushes forward so her feet are in the wavefoam and Maz watches a silvery shape drop down the side of the boat, a figure now clear climbing into a second, smaller boat. 'Someone is coming.'

Maz runs forward and grabs Onyx, not caring how she pulls against her and drags her towards the dunes. They fall into a sandy nook as Onyx complains loudly.

'Stay here,' Maz commands. 'I'll be back.' She races down the dune and through the ti-tree to the camp, slides the blade from her pack and then bundles the packs under the lee of the tent. Does this person mean to rob them? Steal them? Kill them? She resists the urge to bury the oddz and rushes back to Onyx.

The figure on the silvery vessel is closer. This smaller boat is shaped like a long stretched diamond and sits high on the water. The figure has a long pole with a flat oval shape at either end and is dipping each oval in the water to propel themselves forward. On to the waves now – oh! – the boat is flying, rushing into the foam. The sisters both breathe out noisily in appreciation, and for a moment Maz does not worry who this person might be, because clearly they are possessed of some kind of magic. But then another wave, and the same flying foaming rush, and the figure is in the shallows, stepping up from the silvery boat and dragging it up on the beach behind them. They drop the pole, wipe themselves down with their hands and shield their eyes to scan the beach.

At this distance, Maz cannot make out features, but the figure is tall, wearing dark long sleeves and pants that fit close to their body. Their head is enclosed in some kind of cap but Maz watches as the figure loosens this now and a wild dark cascade of hair tumbles out. The figure bends low to the boat and retrieves a large container and a bulky bag. They hold them high in the air, turning slowly and seeming to hold both out to the dunes, and then they place them gently on the sand, take three steps back and sit down with their palms up on their knees.

'What are they doing?' Onyx whispers.

Maz hushes her. Then, while the figure sits still and the waves roll in and curious seabirds bob forward to investigate the bundles on the beach, she whispers back, 'Waiting for us.'

She counts a dozen more sets of waves roll in and then she sits back low on her knees. 'Stay here. Do not move,' she tells Onyx, backing down the dune. The figure looks up immediately.

Up close, Maz can see it is a woman, dark skin, green eyes, hair the colour of charcoal. The woman holds both her hands up, palms out, and Maz does the same as she approaches slowly, stopping when she reaches the bundles on the sand. She can see that one is a coarse fabric bag and the other a dull metallic container with a lid.

The woman holds out the bag and container to Maz, makes a gesture with her hand to her mouth, chewing and then dropping her head back and swallowing. 'Food, water,' she says, offering.

Her voice is deep and true and even though the words sound slightly different in her mouth, Maz recognises them.

'Thank you.'

The woman taps her chest. 'I am Hera.'

'I am Maz.'

'You are not alone.'

'No.'

'Just two of you?'

Maz hesitates. This woman, Hera, has only seen two of them, but Maz could pretend they are two of many. That there is a whole tribe waiting behind them, that they are as powerful as they had been when they walked with the Stewards.

Hera smiles gently. 'It is hard to survive just two. You are strong.'

Maz tries to regain some control. 'Your boat. Where are you from?'

'An island south of here. We spotted your smoke. We have not seen any person along this coast for a long time. We sail away from the island every few moons to check. Yours was the first smoke in many, many moons.'

'How many of *you*?'

'On the boat? There are three, including me. On the island, thirty-three, thirty-four soon enough, for we have a babe coming.'

'A baby?'

'Yes.'

'This is allowed?'

Hera's brow creases for a moment. 'Of course.'

An island. With babies. And a boat.

Hera's head shifts and Maz suddenly hears the pounding of feet behind her.

'Go back!' she hisses, turning on her sister, but Onyx is beside her, staring at Hera, at the bundles.

'Hello,' the woman says, 'I am Hera. Please, eat.'

Onyx looks at Maz, who shakes her head but opens the cloth sack. Inside there is a small bag of berries, two flat discs of seedcake – bigger and softer than any Maz has seen. There are long green vegetables and two fat red orbs that could fit inside Maz's palm. She lifts one of the seedcakes, sniffs it, puts her tongue out to touch it. Nibbles quickly from the edge. It is like chewing on cloud. Salttang and sweetberry both. She nibbles again. If she is to be poisoned, she is happy for it to be with this cloudcake. Hera smiles. Maz stops. Feels the pulp go down her throat. Why would this woman bring her boat in just to poison them? Maz nods at Onyx, who takes the other cloudcake and bites into it.

'Do you have a camp here?' Hera asks. 'Or are you travelling?'

'Travelling,' Maz says through her mouthfuls.

'You need not tell me your destination but let me pass this on. There is big heat coming from the north, soon. And storms. You would be wise to seek shelter swiftly.'

'You are a weatherwoman?'

Hera inclines her head. 'Sometimes, yes. One must be, to sail.'

'Sail?' says Onyx.

'On the boat, we use the wind.' She turns behind her. 'We raise the sails and they catch the wind.'

'Oh,' says Onyx.

'You would like to see?'

Onyx grins. 'Yes.'

How do I know I can trust you? Maz thinks. *Are we not safer on our own?*

Hera stands. 'I will leave you with this food and water and row back out to the boat. We will hoist the sails and go a little out so you may see how the boat works. We will keep in sight.'

Onyx stands too. 'You are leaving so soon?'

'We must get back to the island before the weather breaks. But here, I have a proposition for you and your sister.' She smiles. 'I presume you are sisters?'

Onyx nods.

'There is space for you both on our boat and on our island. We are a small community but we do well. We have enough food and power and fresh water. We are safe – from the weather, and from any who would do us harm. We have some medicine. A radio.'

'What's a radio?' Onyx asks. Maz has some memory of JP melting pieces of an oddz, but it is only a smudge.

'A machine that helps us to speak to people in other places.'

'What other places?' says Maz.

'Off the island, around this land. Across the sea. There are not many, but there are enough.'

Maz's thoughts skitter and chase. *Not many, but enough.*

'How do you know if they are a friendly?'

Hera smiles. 'We don't. Not at first. That's why we live on an island.' She goes on: 'I will leave you for the day and the night. At dawn I will row back in and if you would like to join us, be ready to leave. If you are not here, I will assume you have chosen to stay on your own and we will be on our way.'

'Why should we go with you? How do I know you don't mean us harm?'

Hera smiles that gentle, sad smile again. 'You cannot know, and I am sorry for that. I have only what I can offer and the knowledge of the heatstorm that is coming, a wish for you and your sister to be safe. It is your decision.'

She turns and drags the silvery boat into the shallows, fastens her cap with her pole under her arms and then lays herself along the board and launches into the waves.

The sisters watch her all the way back to the boat and stay there as the great swathes of fabric billow out into the wind in curved triangles, and the boat begins to skip across the water. Onyx puts both hands to her face and laughs. Maz cannot look away.

*

All day, the sisters cannot settle. They argue, switch sides, go silent. They walk. They eat the berries, marvelling at the sweet pop of them in their mouths. They watch the boat. As dusk falls and they sit by their little fire, they can see the light that flashes at the top of the pole, shadows moving in the glow on the boat. Maz remembers being curled up in the rugs of the den, watching the shadows of her mother and father and the other Finders moving against the rock walls, their soft words and laughter, how easy it was to fall asleep.

'It is a beauty,' Onyx says.

'A beauty can be dangerous.'

'Anything can be dangerous.'

Maz turns. 'Okay, we have to decide. We think of the good reasons for going with her and the good reasons for staying and whichever list is longer, that's what we choose. Fair?'

'Fair.'

'Reasons we should stay. We are safe and we know how to look after ourselves.'

'Is that one or two?'

'Two.'

'But are we safe? She said a big heatstorm was coming. How will we keep ourselves safe from that?'

'We'll find a way.'

Onyx lifts her eyebrows. 'Only counting it as one.'

'Okay, two: they could be dangerous. We know nothing about them. They could mean us harm. We can't trust them.'

Onyx nods. 'True. Next?'

'Umm. We could drown. The boat could sink and we could drown.'

'Sister.'

'Yes?'

'We are divers. Doesn't count. You have two.'

'Fine. Reasons for going?'

Onyx stands up. The fire throws leaping shadows and makes her look taller, fearless.

'We will not be alone.'

'We are not alone, we have each other, but yes, I suppose you can have that.'

'JP will not find us.'

Maz nods.

'And three, they have a radio, Maz.'

Maz's skin prickles as Onyx leans down, her face glowing orange. 'We could find out about the oddz. Maybe even make contact with the Finders. Maz. What if we could find our father?'

Maz looks at the fire. It's reason enough on its own. That, and to be free of the threat of JP. And yet, to leave, to go with a stranger . . .

'Maz. That's three. We go.'

Maz hangs her head. Nods slowly.

In the tent Onyx snuggles in to Maz. 'I love you,' she says.

Maz's heart rippleglows.

'And I had heaps more reasons.' She rolls away and soon Maz can hear her snufflesnore. She listens as it deepens, falls in line with the thudcrash of the waves and the singing of the cicadas. Sounds she knows. It is a long time before she sleeps.

∞

Footscray, 2031

La has a short shift tomorrow. You get special leave if you're part of the egg-harvesting program. She's found out another woman on the blue team is also in tomorrow's group. They get transported over to the clinic. Guess it's the WANT way of keeping it all in house. She feels like shit. Bloated and crampy. Still headachey from cutting out coffee (something Cat has gently but strictly enforced). If Cat hadn't been so gung ho about it, she probably would have pulled the pin on the second day of the needles, to be honest. That day, or the day they got bussed over for the follicle count. The doctor, who she's only seen once, swanned in to read the printout as though it were the results of a horse race – 11, excellent. La felt like some kind of egg machine. She remembers her homeroom teacher at school who had them for sex ed, and the piece she read out about eggs. She said that a female foetus has all the eggs she will ever have in her lifetime, so when your grandmother was carrying your mother in her womb, you were a tiny egg in your mother's ovaries. For a time, she told the restless class, all three generations were together. Your grandmother's body, she told them, is the land where your life first took root. La remembers the buzz that went through her even as the kids up the back guffawed and muttered. It felt like a thing that was too big to comprehend, like black holes, or star death, or the space-time continuum.

What they extract from her tomorrow already has a genetic code, already knows some of what it will be. Syringes filled with possibility – actual possibility – this is proper sliding doors stuff. She wonders what her parents will say. If she ever tells them. The distance now is comforting, they are far enough away that she can honestly tell them she loves and misses them. If she goes over to visit, though, there will be questions. About partners and babies and futures and the rest.

The nurse wears pale blue scrubs that don't look like the scrubs you see in shows. These are fitted, elegant almost, as though this woman might be assisting La with her finances and not using a transvaginal ultrasound to suction an egg out of her follicles.

'Okay,' the nurse says, perfect smile, filter-like skin, 'now, before I leave you to pop on the gown, a couple of last things. Did you want livestream, video, stills?'

La is confused. 'Sorry?'

'For your channels?'

She laughs. 'Ah, no. Is that what people do?'

The nurse does not laugh, but smiles as if La were a child. 'Increasing majority, yes.'

'Why?' La takes the gown she is handed. It does not appear to be crafted with the same skill and precision as the nurse's pseudo-scrubs.

Slight hint of irritation. 'Why not? It's a great opportunity to spread the message to other women about egg retrieval, social awareness, health messaging, sponsored content, affiliations – the possibilities are endless.'

'People are sponsored?'

'Of course. We have a wide range of sponsored content packages if you're eligible. What's your network rating?'

'My what?'

'Your follower count plus reach and trust score?' She moves her finger across her screen fluidly. 'Oh. Ignore that. You won't be eligible.'

'You can find me that easy?'

The woman raises her eyes, smiles briskly and says, 'Right. Pop that on, take your time, I'll be back in five to take you through for the procedure.'

'What do you need – more Panadol? Tea? Hot-water bottle?'

La closes her eyes as Cat strokes her head. She feels okay – bloated and still crampy – but she won't deny Cat her chance to play nurse and fixate on every possible symptom in the aftercare leaflet she was handed as she left the clinic.

'Wine?' she asks, but Cat shakes her head and brings La soda instead, curling herself into the corner of the bed and watching her.

'What did they say? How many did they get?'

La wants to stream trash. Wants to drink wine. Wants to curl up under the doona and enjoy the fact she has the whole day off tomorrow. She doesn't want to think about anything at all.

'La? Hun? What did they say?'

'Eight, I think, or ten, maybe, whatever they were supposed to get.'

Cat crunkles her face. 'A little low, maybe?'

La reaches for Cat's arm, squeezes it. 'It was fine. Good, they said. It was all good.'

Cat breathes in deeply, lies back on the pillow, stares at the ceiling. 'I'm invested, now.'

'That's lovely.'

'I sound neurotic, don't I?'

La pulls her in. 'Delightfully neurotic.' She kisses Cat's forehead. 'Stay in bed with me, watch trash with me.'

Cat sighs. 'I have to finish this paper,' she says and hands over the screen. 'You watch. I'll get us some dinner in an hour or so, yeah?'

La takes the screen, snuggles in, is content.

Perhaps the action would never have begun if Reb's belt had not got caught in one of the RDUs. It happened at the end of the morning shift, he was dragged, half running, along the floor until someone pressed the stop button and he was fine – uninjured, but of course there was a report, and it took them an hour after the stop button to get everyone back online.

By the time they clocked off, Conna had already sent out links to a group chat on Paranoia. It's meant to be the latest, safest encrypted messaging app available to the general public. Until now La has been one of those nothing-to-hide types, blasé about privacy, content that nothing in her email or personalised feeds could be of any interest to anyone. But she recognises that she now has some skin in the game; not as much as Conna maybe, but some. It's kind of thrilling. She'd toyed with the idea of giving up devices completely – 'going dark' – as was the fashion a couple of years back. Honestly? She didn't have the guts. And how could any of those who signed out for the last time get involved in any of this kind of action, now?

By the time she silences her notifications that night, there are thirty of them in the thread. It's not many, but it's enough, and Conna calls a meeting at the pub in Braybrook for the next night. For those who can come, they say, reassuring the parents, the non-drinkers, the anti-pub-goers, that they will update them on any decisions in the thread.

> It's collective or it's not at all.

Cat has dinner with the uni crew and La has begged off again. She knows that she cannot cope tonight with the big conversations, the big ideas, all the conceptual risk that's not risky at all for an associate lecturer who is sticking it to the man. La calls it a healthy level of disrespect and Cat chides her for biting the hand that feeds her, she went to university after all.

'I studied performing arts. It hardly counts.'

'Tell that to your colleagues who only have year ten.'

'Ouch,' La says and laughs, although it stings. 'Anyway, I've gotta go to this collective thing.'

'Oh, it's happening?'

'Yeah, maybe.' Of course, she can tell Cat, but La kind of enjoys the subterfuge.

'Well, that's good you made a decision, I guess. You checked it doesn't risk anything with the Dreem stuff?'

'Yeah, nah. All good. What can they do, right? Those eggs are locked and loaded.'

Cat makes a face. 'That sounds off.'

La kisses her. 'Have fun tonight.'

'You too,' says Cat.

In the end there are seven of them at the pub: Conna and Reb and Sinna – whose kid is with their dad – and two young women who are hardcore but fun, and Mina – the pink-haired woman she met on her first day. La knows now that Mina's sixty-one and lives in her car, used to work in aged care until it broke her, prefers moving boxes now instead. She's tough and practical, waves La away with her hand if she ever tries to help, or offers their place for a shower, a meal. Mina asks if Conna wants her to take minutes and they say, 'Yeah, I guess,' and they grin because this is the start of something, they can all feel it – it's small, it's not much, but still you can feel it, can't you, when something is coming?

They consider many options. The more beer they drink, the wilder the options get. Or maybe they are getting more *real*, says

Conna, thumping their fist on the table so the punters at the table next to them look over.

Mina types the list into her phone:

General strike (not enough members or support).
Occupation of factory (same).
Go slow (lose our jobs).
Sabotage (high level of support but hard to do).
Go to the media (pffft).

'It has to be big,' says Reb.

'Yeah,' says one of the young women, Donza, who is clever and fierce and already has a lifetime of activism experience. 'You know,' she says, 'I'm a Wurundjeri woman – that's the activism I do first, right, but it's all connected – climate, anti-capitalist, dismantling the colony – remember that car parked in the tunnel last year?'

'That was you?' says Conna.

'No biggie,' she says and makes a signal with her hand that La is too old and too uncool to understand.

'Think about what we are dealing with,' the other young woman, Kel, says. 'Who we are dealing with. Industrial sabotage. Just need everyone to be on the same page. It could mean jail time, you need to be ready for that.'

'I am,' Mina says, looking up from her phone, her face grim.

'I can't do time,' says Sinna. She has the kid.

'Yeah, wow, I didn't know that's what we were talking about,' says La, although here, with this crew, and with the beers and the talk, she is feeling like she *could* do jail time, like she could do anything, would do anything, because this is important stuff, yeah, this is what matters, this is us sticking it to the—

*

'To the man. Yep. I know. Here, water.'

Cat holds back La's hair and lets her spew again even though there is really nothing coming up now but thin, slightly fluorescent bile.

'Those girls, they're just kids and they've done *real* stuff. You know. Stuff that *matters*.'

'Stop talking. I don't care. Water. Panadol. Sleep. I've set your alarm. You have five hours before you need to wake up.' Cat guides her to the bed, '*Sleep*, you drunken commie.'

'Stick it to the man!' she remembers saying, before her alarm is tinkling and her head is splitting and it's time to go to work.

Turns out that the first night at the pub is the first of a few. Turns out that La doesn't realise how much that is pissing off Cat, or maybe she does and she does it anyway, purposefully, hurtfully. Turns out Cat doesn't like being told how it is by her half-cut girlfriend at 11pm while she's busy writing and thinking about the impact of global supply chains and the evil fuckery of big business. Turns out Cat doesn't want to know about La's new feeds, doesn't need to have *jacquerie* defined to her, thanks very much, is not at all interested in hearing about one of Musk's kids and the new tech company they've founded to tear down everything their forebear built. Turns out Cat resents being told again and again that La is actually gonna *do* something about it, is gonna make a fucking difference, gonna put herself on the line. Turns out the final fight isn't about that particular insult, but about what is simmering underneath it all. Turns out there is a lot of want and where wants don't align things can get seismic. Cause fault lines to rupture. Turns out the big fights do always happen at the kitchen sink.

'I guess I don't understand the rush, is all. You'll still get leave with a teaching gig. It just feels too soon, too much,' La says.

'I *won't* necessarily get leave, that's the thing – I do with the scholarship. If I time it right, delay handing in, already pregnant, I'll get to use the mat leave, paid.'

La scrubs the pot harder, cold noodles like concrete around the edges. *Is it so hard to rinse it out?*

'I thought we were on the same page on this.' Cat's voice is cool, academic.

La uses her nails. 'I dunno, Cat, I guess it feels like – are you doing this for the right reason?'

'*Me*? This is us!'

'Doesn't feel like *us* if you're making all the calls. What about me getting back to gigs, the role next year? I didn't plan on doing that with a kid.'

'So now you don't know. *Now.* Fuck you, La, this is bigger than either one of us.'

'Ex-fucking-zactly! We are in fierce agreement on that point. You know I've only frozen my bloody eggs to give myself options. Later. To give *us* options later.'

'Am I always going to be a fucking afterthought?'

'Oh fuck you, that is not—'

Cat puts both her hands in the air to interrupt. 'No – I can't talk to you when you're like this.'

'Well, maybe it's time for you to go, huh?' La smashes the pot against the sink for emphasis and is not looking, cannot look as she hears Cat leave, slamming the door in her wake.

'Fuck. Fuck,' La says to herself, pulling her hands from the sink and wiping them, dripping, on her jeans, racing to the door and pulling it open, calling down the stairwell after Cat, knowing that every move she is making is utterly performative, that she will not run after her girlfriend, will not apologise tonight. It was true what she said just now – and sometimes the truth hurts, and that's not her fault.

*

Cat does not text. She does not call. La is impressed by how steadfast her usually quick to melt girlfriend is being. Maybe she is not her girlfriend anymore. Maybe something here has really been undone. She sits with that thought, in the quiet apartment, eating a bag of Nutri-Stalk Crisps and drinking a de-alcoholised pinot grigio, trying to work out what she feels. When did it get this hard to go with your own gut? It's not that she doesn't trust her own instinct – she does, quite deeply – it's just that the instinct is giving her nothing.

She thinks she loves Cat. All the signs are there.

She does not believe that their future plans are at such cross-purposes that they will never get in synch.

She misses her. At least she misses her skin, Cat's hair strung between her fingers, and her smell. The comfort sounds of her in the kitchen, quiet domestic melody of clean glasses being slid back into cupboards, forks landing on knives, tea towel softly swooshing as it's threaded back over the oven handle.

And yet. La will not make the first move, even though she knows she's the one who should.

Maybe it's because her world has been bumped slightly off course, but by Friday night at the pub, La is the one insisting that they can't afford to wait any longer.

Donza grins and play-punches her on the shoulder.

'Here she is, ready to rumble! Didn't think you had it in you, but there you go.'

Better than a standing ovation, that feeling – surprising a person who has underestimated you, impressing them. La tries to act nonchalant, fails. 'So,' she says, 'can you get the code?'

'We can,' Donza says, putting her arm around her mate and leaning in.

'We sure can,' says Conna, looking at Mina, who types

something into her phone, face set, determined. 'My contact needs three weeks, four tops. I'm taking care of the data we need from the warehouse, you don't need to know that part, better not to. When it's ready, I'll have the file on an SD. That's all we need.'

'And someone to get it where it needs to go,' says Mina, looking up from her screen.

'You're still in the best position to do that, La. You sure you're up for it?'

'You sure it's gonna work?'

At this Donza sits back, stops smiling. 'No. We can't be certain it's going to work. That's the nature of the beast, right? High risk, high reward.'

'Will we all go down for it?' La asks. 'Or am I the fall guy?'

Conna jumps in: 'If we do it right, no one goes down for it. Or we all do. That's how a collective works, yeah? They can't pin it on one of us, they got to pin it on all of us. So go ahead, do that, stand down your entire staff if that's what you want to do, either way we give them grief.'

They cheers to that and La buys another round because even though these past weeks have been shit and everything with Cat is a mess, this stuff, well, it seems like the start of something and she feels close to the centre of it and it makes her feel alive, purposeful, in a way she hasn't for a very long time.

∞

Sanctuary Gardens Aged Care, 2020

Day 28

Egg – larvae – pupa – adult. The lifecycle of a moth. The regularity was always reassuring for Hilda, a certainty she could hold onto when her own life started to jolt and stutter.

She was no longer at the university when the decimation of the bogong moths hit headlines. She had known for years, of course, they all had. She remembers a young researcher, Jenna – Jessie, maybe (names hover and slip now like moths' wings) – coming to her office, seeking refuge in a senior woman researcher. That was rare then, only somewhat less so by the time she left, despite her best efforts to keep the doors ajar behind her. The young woman had taken a seat, her printout of data held in both hands, and asked Hilda whether her career had fulfilled her.

Sensing (correctly) that wasn't the question the young researcher wanted answered, Hilda asked her what her area of interest was.

'Tracking the irreversible decline in *Agrotis infusa* numbers across south-eastern Australia,' the young woman said.

Hilda nodded.

'Is our job just to bear witness to extinction?' she went on. 'Is that what we are doing, now?'

'Yes, in part.'

'And the other part?'

'To communicate that loss. To make others see it.'

'Not to reverse it?'

'No, not necessarily.'

'Then what is the point?'

Ask me another question, thinks Hilda.

Ask me about the first time the moths never arrived.

Ask me about the empty sky.

Ask me about the waiting and waiting, the wondering if time had reshuffled itself and in a moment we would spot the dark mass on the horizon, the flutter filling the sky.

Ask me how many when they finally did arrive.

And how the words 'fewer' and 'less' formed as bruises in my brain.

Ask me about how the old scientist started to cry when I took him the new data and made him his tea.

Ask me about the climate scientist who set himself on fire in front of the Supreme Court in Washington and how I wondered if self-immolation might be the path for me until I reckoned I would be labelled a hysteric (the name for angry women since time immemorial). I'd probably blow the damn match out anyway – coward at heart.

Day 29

SREE
How about that special smile the white women give, huh?

PHIL
Yes, yes, tell me!

SREE

Oh, hello you, gentle brown woman, whose name I couldn't pronounce even if I took the time to learn it . . .

PHIL

Ha, stop – no, don't stop, keep going, I need this laugh!

SREE

I'm not sure how good your English is, so I will do my special overeager smile that says I'm not like other white women: I see you, I respect you.

PHIL

Oh no, woman, you are all the same, keep going!!!

SREE

Look what I brought my mother/aunt/grandfather! Look how much I care! I have a basket filled with plump grapes in a paper bag I got from the organic grocers and I have fair-trade chocolate with Aboriginal art on the recycled packaging and some flowers – natives, of course – and some magazines because I don't know that my mother/sister/aunt can no longer hold up a magazine, let alone read it, so it's just there for looks, or maybe you could take it home (you probably can't afford such things) and fill the hour on the bus and then at the interchange and then on the other bus?

PHIL

Keep going!

SREE

I'm just going to fuss about for the forty minutes of the visit I've scheduled, I'll lay my offerings down or prop them up so you staff can

*all see how much I care, I'll take a selfie with my beloved, carefully
angled so the flowers and grapes and chocolate and magazines are
all in frame, and I'll caption it, fave part of the week, #blessed,
#respectyourelders, #lovemygran, even though this is my obligation visit
between five other things I am going to get done today because that
means I only have to stay the forty minutes, might even nick out a little
early to have a word with the staff, there you are, nurse, a quick word?*

PHIL

Yes, yes, tell me, what is she going to say to us? How is she
going to tell us how to do our jobs?

SREE

Well. She's gonna find me while I'm going between rooms, and
she won't know that I'm already seventy-five minutes behind,
that I now have only three mins to get each of the residents on
this floor up and ready for dinner and she'll just want a quick
word and, of course, you know it, what's our directive from
management?

TOGETHER

*ALWAYS LISTEN TO FAMILY REQUESTS AND DIRECT
TO MANAGEMENT!!*

SREE

That's the one! Even though every time we stay back after shift
and write them up, not a single one is ever followed up, and
neither Mr Packham nor anyone from management are ever on
the floor at 3:37 when a family member is up in arms because
Old Tickle Fingers is still sitting in his shit and why haven't his
meds been administered, and there's no clean . . . and there's
dirty water in the . . . and no one told us about . . .

PHIL

Oh, my friend, you should do a show, no? When all this is over?
Serious – comedy festival stuff. You'll have them rolling in the
aisles.

SREE

One day, maybe.

PHIL

When this is all over, eh?

SREE

You would cry, huh, if you didn't laugh? That woman in 612
has not showered in two weeks.

PHIL

I would not put my dog in this place.

Day 32

Hilda, here, look, I'm back. It's Mariam.
I've brought you something I think you'll like.
Here, that's it, sitting up, now.
It's nice and warm, yes, smells good, huh? It's my mother's recipe.

Some spice, to warm you up from the inside, but not too much.
Good, huh? More, of course, oh, I'm so glad you like it.
Our secret, yes? I'll bring you more. When I'm back. I promise.

Hilda, my darling, I have this hot washcloth, it's warm and soft,
would you let me? Do you think? I could wash your hands and
face and neck, just that if you'd like. No, I know, no shower,

I know. Just your face, my love, will you let me?

Oh, yes, that's warm, yes? That's okay?

No, I promise, nowhere else.

Yes, they told me, my love, they told me your niece is taking you to the river, I'm so happy. I'm so glad. Soon, yes, there you go, oh, that's better. Don't cry, don't cry, my love, you're okay, hey hey now, we're okay.

Day 33

Anna
Hil says she wants a swim.
In the river.
11.11am

Trace
Let's break her out
11.20am

Anna
Tempted
11.21am

Trace
How is she?
11.21am

Anna
Not good.
They say 'deteriorating rapidly'
11.31am

Trace
Fuck.
What can I do?
11.40am

> **Anna**
> Can't do anything until the rules change.
> Feel helpless.
> It's all fucked.
> 11.45am

Day 42

Everybody right to go? Why lockdown why medicine why mask why not why not more why are you why aren't you why was this not sooner anticipated announced predicted what about us about the virus about the economy about the environment did you hear there are dolphins in Venice elephants in a village in Yunnan a deer in the middle of Fitzroy no that one was fake real who knows anymore so tired overwhelmed burnt out but we're not doing anything maybe you're not feel like I could sleep for years not sleeping eating too much drinking too much urgent call out for food donations urgent case alert notification your test result is covid positive negative mystery lost in the system looking for the source bunnings barbecues galore breaking lockdown dob them in don't dob them in it's un-Australian you are in an area of concerned about comorbidities were they sick? old? did they have underlying conditions are worsening locked out locked in locked down give us a bubble it's unfair untenable uncomfortable unprecedented just good luck just bad luck it was their wedding their funeral the wife/child/father/sister was dying will never forgive give more give less give us a hand a break a reward for all our hard work doing nothing it's not nothing send a delivery a card a message a virtual hug our best wishes our thoughts and prayers send more masks a vaccine the army a cocktail to get through the last hour of remote learning ha ha day drunk not funny one-hour delivery a bottle a six pack a luxury restaurant At Home pack with matched wines because we are bored/have nowhere to spend our disposable income/are supporting our local/need something to put on Insta/need something to look forward to/because otherwise we'll get out of here and the world as we know it will be gone all boarded up and out of business all the theatres are closed actors are retraining it was the last straw I can't direct a play over Zoom can hear an opera a choir watch a book launch have a quiz night send the link sorry gotta go I've got another Zoom drinks party meeting funeral sorry I can't be there to hold you to kiss you to help you keeping us safe keeping us apart keeping us from our work our office our beachfront holiday home regrettably lost their lives their livelihood live stream going live acquired locally under investigation cluster of concern restrictions up to us as soon as possible 5 pm tonight midnight tomorrow in two weeks when numbers go down when I stand up in front of you and tell you I miss my friends I miss my mum dad partner sister brother aunty nibling when will I see you again will I see the ocean will I drive on a highway will I feel normal aeroplanes grounded get tested the value of face masks is limited opening up skin hunger vaccine lockdown increase in domestic violence child abuse neglect to keep us safe that's it for today any questions?

Footscray, 1933

As she opens the bottles of beer and places them on the yellow tablecloth in front of each of the four men, Peggy has to swallow back a gag. She's only eaten a piece of dry toast today, and while she reckons Jack and his mates have had a wash at the end of the shift, the stink of meat is on them still.

'Thanks, love,' says Wilco, giving her a nod and a smile. 'Not long to go now?'

Peggy pulls back her lips, attempting to smile.

'Not been well, have you, Pegs,' says Jack, raising his eyebrows and inclining his head, indicating that it's time for her to make herself scarce.

She shuts the bedroom door quietly behind her and wishes that these Tuesday night gatherings had not become so regular. Lil is out with her do-gooders down at the hall and even though she's invited Peggy to come along, she's not felt up to it.

The men's voices in Lil's kitchen grate along the back of her teeth. By wordless arrangement, she and Jack haven't mentioned the gatherings. Not that Lil would mind Jack having some mates over – he pays his rent, can do what he likes – but Peggy knows that some of the talk tonight will be union talk and Lil would have something to say about that.

Hunger gnaws at her but it's preferable to the swimming nausea. She curls in on herself and listens to their voices through the thin wall.

'Have you had a word to the fellas from Borthwicks yet? And from Newport?'

'Yeah, they're pissed, and they reckon the union blokes at the abbs will support us.'

'Bloody nightmare trying to get everyone to agree, though.'

'Sometimes reckon the union bosses are as bad as the factory bosses. They all want their pound of fucking flesh.'

'You hear they're not letting the drivers join up?'

'Bullshit – where'd you hear that?'

'Donny reckons that once word started spreading that there's to be action against the team system, some of the non-union blokes reckoned to cut their losses and pay their dues.'

'That's a good thing, isn't it?'

'Would be – but the bloody AMIU won't let them join. Don't want to risk looking like they're stacking the numbers if we go to arbitration.'

'Load of shit.'

The sound of clinking bottles and grumbling.

Peggy doesn't pretend to understand it all. But she wishes she did.

She wishes, more times a day than she cares to admit, that she were back in the bagging room with Beth and Norma and Jean and Mavis, she wishes she was listening to them talk about their troubles, the possibility of a strike.

She imagines how the heat would rise in the air above their sorting table, above the flash of hands and thread and cotton, the stamp and click of the punch, how their words might fly – *troubles* and *strike*. She's always kept her mouth shut. She'd been lucky to get in the gates at Angliss, they all were. Didn't want to cause a fuss. Should thank her lucky stars, and all that.

Except, if all the workers just went around being bloody grateful that they had a job, well, the boss could do anything he liked, really. Angliss wasn't a bad man, you could tell by the way his name rolled off the tongues of the workers, a hint of pride that they were connected to the big man. And she knew plenty of bosses she wouldn't work for. Those whose power went to their heads, who expected a little bit extra if they took on a woman, those whose eyes and hands and tongues were known to wander.

The slam of the front door wakes her and soon enough Jack is pulling back the cover, letting the cold in, so she grumbles and wraps her arms around herself until he slides in beside her.

'You still awake?' he asks.

'Hmmm,' she replies but stays turned away, eyes closed. She knows what they say about the first year of marriage, the jokes the women make about being too sore to sit down, and if it wasn't for the swill of sickness in her gut every time she moves, she'd be one of them, rushing home to pull him into the bedroom before dinner or press him up against the door in the vestibule where Lil can't hear. But he's slow when he's been drinking, clumsy with his hands, and if she can slip back to sleep before he starts snoring then she promises herself she'll be up for it in the morning when he reaches for her.

But he reaches for her now. Hands rough and cold under her nightdress and rubbing her thighs.

'I'm asleep, Jack. In the morning,' she says and shifts away a little even though she knows it's unlikely to put him off now. He's like this when he's got a few drinks in him.

'Peggy,' he mumbles into her neck. 'Come on, Pegs.'

She thinks of those first afternoons, the days in between when the longing for him made her throat tight, made her slow down on the job so much that Donny gave her a warning. She wants that back, wonders whether she'll feel like that again once the baby is here and the sickness is gone.

'Lil's home,' she says.

'Don't care,' he says, and his hands just grip higher, up her leg, sliding the length of her side, he's avoiding her belly now, to clasp her breast, kneading it too hard, pulling at her nipple between his fingers.

She takes a deep breath to quell the nausea, figures she might as well make it worth her while, places her hand on his and guides it down, under the elastic of her knickers, lets him do the rest, sliding his fingers into her.

'Peggypeggypeggy,' he says and he's rough, mouth on her neck, she can smell the beer.

'Shhhh,' she says as he pulls at her, scrunching her nightdress around her waist so the bed rocks with her movement.

'Let her hear,' he says, and she thinks that's not just the drink talking.

His fingers are scratching now and he's moving her arse around so that he can get at her, at least it'll be quick, she thinks, and moans a little because she knows that always seems to make things quicker.

Still a shock, the feel of him in her, the tensing of her muscles, of everything as she instinctively tries to repel the intrusion. The way she has to tell her body to let him in. His silly little noises as he puffs and grunts in her ear. It's like he goes somewhere else, his fingers grip tighter and tighter on her hips, one hand on her back pushing her away so he can get further inside her, she could be anyone, she thinks. She tries to push back a little, worries for the baby, won't be long now, but he's frantic with it. 'Shhhh,' she says again, because he might like it – thinking that he can be heard, that someone else knows what is happening in this little room – but she doesn't, it makes her feel cheap.

A sound like a squeaking in his throat, nearly there, she thinks, as her head wobbles on her neck because he is pushing so fast and hard into her and then he's done and he says, *I love you*, and she waits till she feels him go completely soft in her, then she rolls away, pulls her knickers back on and wipes herself. She listens to him snoring, and wonders if Lil, like her, is lying there awake, wondering how on earth it got to be so much easier for men.

By the end of his first month as a married man, Jack decides he quite enjoys it. Each night he swings open the little picket fence (not really his, but feels like it), turns his key in the lock, hangs his jacket on the coat rack. Peggy and Lil are at home, Lil not having the same preference for a knock-off drink at the Punt as he does, and Peggy is at home all day now since Donny had to let her go – no pregnant women, no married ladies. She kicked up a stink at first, asked what in the hell old-fashioned age we were living in that she, at only nineteen, couldn't continue to bring in an income because she had a ring on her finger and a bun in the oven.

But that's the way things are, and to be honest, he's quite all right with it.

The house on Railway Place always smells like dinner when he gets home. Granted, Peggy has a lot to learn, but Lil is helping her out and she's lessened the board just till the baby comes, so he's feeling quite warm towards his landlady after all.

He has a wash when he gets in. They don't mind waiting. Peggy reckons she'd prefer a hungry belly and a clean man than a full one sitting next to a blood-stained worker. He rinses off at the works, but you can never get all the blood off. Not under the fingernails. In the creases of the skin. Caught in the hairs on his forearm where he hasn't reached.

And while he's in the little bathroom, soaping up, hearing the clinks and murmurs from the kitchen, he knows he's a lucky man, that he's landed on his feet.

Except that tonight, no one has lit the copper. And he didn't check. And now he's soapy and cold and there's no hot water. And maybe he should have checked and lit the thing himself, but a man gets used to the way things are, and a man who's worked a long and filthy day should be able to come home to a decent shower. He thinks of calling out Peggy's name but he knows Lil'll make that smirk, that the two of them will raise an eyebrow at each other when he's not looking. *Fuck that*, he thinks as he splashes himself with cold water. *Fuck them*.

Cold, but dry and dressed, he grabs a bottle of beer from the ice chest, pulls out his chair to sit where the two women are waiting for him.

'What do you call this?' he asks, pushing his fork into the brown mound steaming in the centre of his plate beside a neat little pile of white rice.

'Stew,' says Peggy, her chin jutting slightly.

He nods; she's in a mood. 'Righto,' he says and shoves a big forkful into his mouth.

He almost spits it straight back out again.

'What the—'

'Don't,' says Lil.

He raises his eyebrows. 'Don't what?'

She shakes her head and takes a mouthful of her meal.

He remembers the kitchen table at home. His father pushing meat around his plate and frowning. How, as a boy, he braced himself for what was to come. Except this time he's not the boy. 'Was just going to compliment my wife on making a perfectly good piece of meat taste like shit,' he says.

'Jack!' says Peggy, her eyes brimming.

Lil shakes her head and shovels her dinner into her mouth.

'Nah, really, it's a skill, that,' Jack goes on. 'You take a nice piece of meat, could even be a cheap piece, and you can do one of two things. You can add a bit of this and that, cook it for the right amount of time – and there you go – dinner. Or you can add,' he pushes the plate away from him, 'God knows what, and then overcook the stuff till it's solid gristle.'

Peggy stands up quickly, her chair rocking and then tipping over behind her with a crash. She snatches the plate from in front of Jack, walks quickly to the sink and throws the whole lot in. Without looking at either of them she walks out of the kitchen and the slam of the bedroom door ricochets around the house.

Lil continues to scrape knife and fork against her plate.

'No need to eat it now,' he says, sneering. 'You don't have to pretend.' She's so holier than thou, chewing it down to make him look like the arsehole.

She doesn't speak, tight little face averted, one mouthful after another.

'You're not doing her any favours, you know. She has to learn one way or another, might as well be now.'

Lil puts down her knife and fork. Her plate is empty. She levels her gaze at him.

'What?' he says.

He nearly has to lean forward to hear her.

'You are living under my roof. That arrangement could come to an end.'

And then she stands up, takes her plate to the sink, and begins to run the tap.

She's threatening him. Threatening *him*.

His turn to push back from the table, send his chair flying.

He stomps down the hall, banging his fist against the bedroom door as he passes, grabs his jacket and he's out of there. To think he was feeling fucking lucky just an hour ago. Who are these women that they can be such turncoats, blow so hot then so fucking cold?

Give him the boys and a pint at the Punt any day.

*

Peggy hears the door slam, and the clink and soft splash of Lil at the sink.

How can she bear to go back out there? To Lil's quiet kindness in the wake of Jack's temper. She is not a good cook, she knows that, she knows. But she does not deserve his ridicule and she is so thrown by it when it comes, all of a sudden and white hot.

He seems to hate her.

But she knows he does not, cannot. For if he hated her, they wouldn't lie in bed together, whispering about the future, he wouldn't run his fingers along her spine and up and over her shoulder all the way down her arm to her littlest finger and then all the way back again, he wouldn't say those things – *I'm so glad I found you, I will love you forever, you are mine.*

He couldn't hate her, and do all that, could he?

Quiet tapping on her door. 'Peggy? Tea? Can I come in?'

It will only make it worse to ignore her. She murmurs and Lil comes in, holding a mug.

Peggy sits up at the edge of the bed. 'It's fine, Lil, I'll come out—'

'No, you won't,' Lil says. 'You'll stay right there. You need your rest.'

Peggy takes the warm cup from Lil and slurps her tea, milky and strong and sweet, and she can feel it in her throat, at the top of her belly, warming her. She sighs. 'I'm sorry about Jack.'

Lil shakes her head. 'Not for you to apologise.'

'But it is, really. He just – one minute he's fine and the next he's mad.'

Lil nods but she doesn't say anything. Peggy has learned enough to know that this is how Lil will get her to talk, and she wants to, wants to tell her all of it, how she wonders if she's made a terrible mistake, whether she should have taken that trip down to Shelley Street after all, had her fling with Jack King then gone on to whatever was next. How all of that possibility is gone now. But if she says all this, if she spills it out because she is hurting and ashamed, she knows that she will lie awake later waiting to hear Jack's key in the lock, his whispered apologies, his kisses, but breathless with her own treachery.

'It's hard for him right now,' she says, her voice a little too loud, 'with everything going on with the union and the thought of the strike. He's got a lot on his mind.'

Lil drops her chin slightly. 'Are you hungry? Can I fix you something?'

Peggy smiles. 'You're too good to me.' She shakes her head. 'Think I'll turn in, this baby is making me bone tired.'

But she lies awake once Lil has quietly shut the door behind her, waiting for Jack to return.

Later that week, Lil raises her eyebrows when Peggy tells her she's going to meet the girls.

'Careful now, they'll be wanting you to join up.'

'Join up what?' Peggy says as she gathers her bag and slips on her coat. It won't do up around her belly anymore, but it can't be helped.

'Oh, some of them have got it in their heads to join the union now that the slaughts are putting up a fight about the new system – fat lot of good it'll do them. Angliss isn't a man to not get his way.'

Peggy smiles ruefully at Lil. 'And what use could I be?' She claps her hands gently on her belly. 'Although if it's a boy Jack'll have him paying his union dues before we leave the hospital.'

Lil snorts and waves her off.

She wonders if Jack will be down the pub, and if he is, whether he'll be annoyed to see her there. She thinks he probably enjoys being without her at work, after work, where he can still wink and tease, buy a pretty girl a drink, make dirty jokes with the men. She never imagined that this was how it would be, striding up Railway Place with her belly ahead of her, already too big to be modestly hidden under folds, to meet the girls for a lemonade while they knock back beers and tell tales of their weekend adventures.

Of course, she imagined babies, what else would there be for her? Not university, not a career, like the new page in the *Women's Weekly* keeps gabbing on about. She and Lil get a copy a week late from Joanie at Lil's do-gooder group. There are parts she doesn't care for, the bloody social pages from Sydney – Miss Emmaline Johnstone-Baxter was wearing a cinched waist with a plaited blah de blah de blah – but she likes the fashion despite the fact she couldn't even afford the ribbon from one of the hats they advertise, and there's always a good story or two, a little on the steamy side, which she enjoys, and the editor – Mrs Littlejohn – certainly isn't backward about coming forward. It's all *equal pay* and women's rights and *we can do whatever they do*. She wonders if Mrs Littlejohn has ever been on a kill floor. Has ever seen the team of men who split beef. Has ever walked in to deliver a note at exactly the wrong time and seen the blue-white sac of organs pulled from the cavity onto the floor, and then split with a knife and wiggled violently so that steaming shit runs into the gutters on the floor. Of course, women can do what men do, but do they *want* to?

She turns onto Moore Street and speeds up a little, can see the lights of the Trocadero starting to come on in the dusk. Be just her luck to run into one of her mother's friends who would gossip it along the line that her daughter was out walking of an evening, her belly out on show when she should have been home cooking dinner for her husband. She's glad there's a hundred or so miles between herself and her mother right now. Lil looks out for her and that's all she needs. Lil lets her be. Treats her like a grown woman, like a sister, or a friend, despite the years between them. Whereas her mother's already sent a letter saying that she'll come down and stay for a month when the baby comes – come to meddle, more like it. Peggy couldn't think of anything worse.

A figure waving at the corner – it's Kathleen, hair curled up and wearing a dress Peggy hasn't seen before. Gosh, she misses that pay in her pocket and all the things she might do with it. She can't imagine asking Jack for a little to buy a frock. Although she's been putting aside some shillings each week after he gives her the money for the groceries – he doesn't have a clue what things cost, except of course for beer and enough for a flutter on a Saturday.

'Look at you, will ya,' says Kathleen, leaning in to smooch her on the cheek. 'You look gorgeous.'

'Bah – get off it!' Peggy says, shaking her head. 'I look fat as a sow is what I look. How's *your* new dress, very nice!'

Kathleen twists and pouts her lips and they link arms as she pushes open the door of the ladies' lounge.

The girls are full of stories and laughs and while they ask Peggy how she is and what she's been up to, there's not much to say, and she quickly pushes the conversation back to the works and the gossip and who's stepping out with who. It's Jean who finally brings the conversation around to the possibility of the strike and what they're all going to do about it.

'The union won't have us, but . . .' says Jean, holding up both hands.

Norma's eyes are wide as she prepares to launch into a tirade.

'No, no – not because I'm a woman, calm down, something to do with stacking the numbers ahead of a dispute. To be honest, I didn't have a clue what he was talking about, though he took down all me details and said as soon as the matter is settled, he'll sign me up.'

'It's not really got anything to do with us, though, has it?' says Beth, blowing smoke and raising one carefully plucked brow. 'I mean, if they were suddenly raising our tally, or making us work an extra hour or two, or telling us there was no tea break . . .'

'Or taking us round the back for help with the paperwork,' Kathleen mutters.

Beth glares and the rest of them titter.

'I don't know what you're talking about, Kathleen, and if I did it'd be none of your damn business.'

Kathleen mimes zipping her mouth shut.

Beth keeps her face blank. 'Though I'll have you know I've never enjoyed paperwork quite so much.' She winks and then they are all laughing and Beth is laughing the most and they are raising their glasses and Peggy misses them fierce and wonders whether she'll still be invited when she's got a baby waiting for her at home.

Her bladder presses heavy.

'Move over then, Kathleen. Got to piss.'

'Well, you can take the girl out of the factory . . .'

'Leave off, will ya!'

She squishes along the bench seat and then threads her way between the tables on the way to the bathrooms. When she finally gets in a stall, locks the door, and can release a steady stream of piss, she almost laughs at how lovely the relief is, how long it goes on, how bold the sound of it is splashing in the bowl. When she exits the stall and goes to the sink, she blushes as another woman steps up next to her, and shifts her eyes quickly when they meet in the mirror.

'Peggy Donnelly?'

She looks properly in the mirror at the woman next to her who has spoken. She has dark hair cropped beneath her ears and she holds a lipstick – dark red – out where she has paused in its application. Her mauve woollen jumper is high at her neck.

'From Hyde Street primary school?'

Peggy smiles blandly. 'Yes? I'm sorry, I—'

The woman turns to look at Peggy directly, pocketing her lipstick and holding out her hand. 'Moira Turner. We were in the same class – with Mrs Fitzgibbon.'

'Moira? Of course!' Peggy says and laughs to cover her confusion. Because Moira did not look like this woman who is standing in front of her. Moira Turner was mousy and clicked her tongue at the back of her throat and sometimes wore no socks, and this woman is not the slightest bit like her.

'It's the hair, isn't it?' Moira says lightly. 'I've been up in Sydney, you see, and everyone's wearing it cut like this up there. Suppose the trend hasn't made it to Melbourne yet!'

Something in the voice that she recognises, and the woman is easy with her, despite the fact she looks like she's just stepped out of the bloody social pages.

'Not likely to make it here at all,' Peggy says and laughs. 'What took you to Sydney? And what in heaven's name brought you back here?'

'Oh, it was just a visit, a conference actually, but how are you? You're—,' she gestures a hand towards Peggy's middle and raises one eyebrow.

'Married,' Peggy says lightly. 'With one on the way!'

'Wow,' Moira says, in a way that does not sound at all excited.

'All very sudden, and romantic,' she adds quickly, lest Moira take it the wrong way.

Moira smiles like she understands completely. 'Anyone I'd know?'

'Jack King, from down at Angliss. I started working there when Mum moved up to the country. He's a bit older than us.'

'And he's good to you?'

'He is,' Peggy says.

'Good that you're happy.'

'I am.' More definite than she feels. 'What about you?' she asks, drying her hands now. 'You got a bloke?'

Moira shakes her head, smiles into the mirror. 'I do not. But happy all the same, busy busy.' She turns to eyeball Peggy. 'I'm in a little house in Richmond now, with some girls I work with. I'm only here to visit Mum and Dad. We should catch up again while I'm down here.'

All the possibility of this girl, her lipstick, Sydney, a house with girls she works with – how has she made this change, how is it she has the life Peggy had imagined she might be living?

'I'd like that,' she says, even though she already knows that Moira won't be getting in touch. They touch cheeks quickly as they leave the bathrooms and Peggy watches the other woman walk through the crowd and out into the street, alone.

She suddenly feels very tired, wishes Jack would come and put his hand on her elbow now, time to go home.

Later, in bed, after Jack has bundled in and thrown the covers askew trying to get close to her, she tries to tell him.

'I met a girl from school tonight.'

He *hmmph*s next to her. Nuzzles his face in her neck.

'I didn't recognise her.'

Another noise, but this time it is quickly followed by a steady snore.

'But she recognised me,' Peggy says to her sleeping husband who cannot hear her. Does not hear her. 'And I wished that she didn't. I wished that I was the one with red lipstick and short hair who had just come back from Sydney.'

She is wide awake now, talking to the ceiling, hands resting on the great ball of her belly. 'I wanted something different. And I thought you were it.'

He snores.

Jack is pissed off that the union agrees to the test of the team system. One week, they say, to try it. And they do. And they're all bloody ragged by the end of it. It isn't the same, isn't anything like the job they were trained to do. The quality of the cuts is rough, and he'll bet the meat isn't all export quality when they come through to check it.

By the time they are gathering at the Punt on Friday afternoon, waiting to hear the results of the final meeting, the men are fuelled by tired bones, by rage and by beer. It's a potent combination.

Stan stands up at the bar and they turn to face him.

'They're saying we're on our own. That the rest of the union supports us, they do, but they can't approve the action. If the slaughts want to strike, they are saying, then we are on our own.' Murphy shakes his head, holds his hands up in the air, looks like Christ on his fucking crucifix like that.

The slaughtermen don't react for a moment. Maybe they knew this was coming, maybe they expected their necks on the chopping block. Or maybe it's a quiet fury. That's what it is in Jack. The fury, not the quiet.

'Fuck 'em!' His voice is loud, higher pitched than he intended, but he hollers out over the heads of the men. 'We'll fucking strike without their approval. We don't need them to walk off the fucking job.'

Murmurs of agreement, a few shouts. 'That's the boy, Jacko.' 'Give 'em hell, kid!'

He's not a kid. He's not just Billy King's son. 'See how a fucking slaughterhouse works when there are no fucking slaughtermen!'

And the boys roar then, behind him, he can feel it like the swell of a wave, that one time down at Black Rock with his dad watching on, when he'd ridden high on the crest of it.

Murphy pats the air with his hands like a mother calming a child. 'Now, now, fellas, Jack's got a point. And he's had his say. But we gotta think about the long game here. We've all got families to feed, we gotta be smart about how we play this. And we all remember that sometimes, when push comes to shove, even the ones we least expect turn out to be strike-breakers.'

Shifty eyes, murmurs. Murphy is looking straight at him. Fucking strike-breaker? Is he calling him a scab?

'What are you saying, Murphy? Never crossed a fucking picket line in me life.'

But it's not Murphy who says it, doesn't have to. A voice rises up from the middle of the group.

'But your dad did.'

Men shuffle back as they sense the sudden rage in him, like the space they give to a stuck cow when the bolt hasn't landed right, there's no knowing what she might do.

'Who fucking said that?'

And it is quiet now. Not a sound, not a movement, because they've seen this boy unleashed before, in the footy matches against Borthwicks, sometimes on a lamb when the morning's gone to pot, and they know what comes next. They're union boys and they know how to stick together, but if they don't offer the fucking traitorous fuck up right now Jack'll take out all of them.

'Say it again!' he roars, spittle flying from his mouth and onto the shirt of the bloke in front of him, whose face is bleaching, like he's been stuck and bled, cos he's gonna be the first, let the fucking lying bastard who spoke watch another man take the hit and see how he fucking likes it.

Jack brings his fist up, swings round and out and feels it connect with the man's cheekbone, the slack flesh as he gapes and drools. He drops to the ground and Jack moves forward to belt again but there are arms grabbing at him now, many of them, a thick forearm around his neck, a voice in his ear, calming, calming like the voice they use for a sheep coming up the run.

'Easy now, boy, easy now, Jack.'

And he roars and pulls but his arms are held tight and the men scatter so they can escape his kicking legs. They hold him until the red mist has gone and his breathing steadies and he tells them he's right, he's right, *get off me, I'm right*.

'Who said it? Who fucking said it?' he says quietly at the door.

'Go home, Jack. Cool off.'

And Jack shakes his head, spits on the floor, walks out into the afternoon.

'That you, love?' Peggy calls.

Lil's out at her Society meeting again and so Peggy has made his favourite, tried not to overcook the meat, is feeling, for the first time in weeks, a bit like herself.

He doesn't answer, but she can feel the cold swoosh of air down the hall, twisting around her ankles, can hear him bashing about.

A wrinkle of doubt at how the night might turn out.

'In here, love!' she calls brightly. 'Dinner's up!' She tongs the crescent of lamb chop onto his plate, one, two, three, and a white blop of potato with plenty of butter, a scatter of carrots and peas straight from the pot that quickly pool in a little puddle of water. She leans the plate to one side so the potato soaks it up, he'll not notice. He's just like a big kid when he comes home hungry. Grumpy and sour, but she'll feed him up and he'll be back to his old self, winking and teasing and grabbing her bum. This bloody strike talk – it's like there's a mood all over town. Tempers are quick and neighbours are grumbling and normally this end of town, where the Angliss workers are, it's one in, all in, but suddenly it feels like maybe they are not all in this one together.

She turns with the full plate and he's there, pulling out his chair, not meeting her eyes, a storm brewing in his face. She walks round next to him, sets down the plate, one arm on his back as she kisses the top of his head, inhales the sweat of him, the after-work booze of him through the spring of his hair.

'What's that smell?' he says, shrugging her off.

'Nice to see you, too!' she says, moving away. 'Had to get more tonic from the pharmacy and Dolly let me try the new eau de toilette they had in. Fancy, isn't it?'

'You smell like a whore.'

She leans back against the sink, folds her arm low across her belly. 'What the hell's up your arse today?'

And this, she will think later, is the moment she regrets. Before this, she might have sensed the storm coming and retreated, gone to bed with her sickness, begged off to visit a friend in need, anything to not be in this room, in his firing line, because there isn't a thing she can do now, to wind back the clock.

He is chewing. His jaw working, pulsing, all the way down to his neck, his eyes staring off, not at her, at something only he can see which is turning his eyes darker and darker as he chews.

Suddenly, he spits out his mouthful. 'This,' he says loudly, standing up and picking up the plate with both hands, 'is shit.' He turns slightly to the side and drops the plate so that it hits the floor and cracks. The force of it sends dobs of potato flying, a lamb chop skids under the table, Peggy feels the patter of peas and carrots against her ankle.

Go, go, go, says a voice, insistent in her head, but there is nowhere to go, his rage is a fire blocking every exit, sucking the oxygen out of the room. She presses herself against the bench, wishing to be smaller, to be tiny, to disappear.

'All a man wants is to come home to a good dinner and a wife who doesn't smell like she's been opening her legs down in Hunter Street all day.'

Now he is looking at her, and he is unrecognisable. As if he hates her. Who is this man? She wants to rage at him, to spit and hit and yell at his insults, but that same voice in her head is urging her to be quiet, to make herself small, to shift this somehow.

'Let me make you something else.'

'I don't want to eat the shit you cook!' He steps towards her, pointed finger thrusting forward with each step.

She is stuck against the bench, hands lowered further now across her belly, the baby, he wouldn't, would he? Could he? He loves her, he's her husband, the father of the baby inside of her, inside the belly he places his hands on sometimes and whispers to.

'Jack, the baby—' she whispers.

A roar that comes from somewhere deep inside him. 'I don't care about the fucking baby!'

And the words make the floor drop from beneath her, except that she is still upright, he is holding her up, big hands around her neck.

To see her eyes go big and round and shocked like that. Her mouth gasping but no words, thank fuck, just be quiet, I don't want to do this, you are making me do this, just shut up, shut up, shut up. The baby, the baby, the fucking baby, the cause of all this in the first fucking place, I could have married anyone I wanted and not been stuck in this place with two fucking women, could have changed everything, no chain, no strike, no finding out, fuck fuck fuck, my father, the scab, the fucking lying scab.

Her face red to purple and still pressing, pressing the words out of her because all she needs to do is just shut her mouth and it'll be okay, he can take it back, take back the baby, the love words, take it all back, go back to before to before Dad, before Dad was a scab, and they all know, the bastards every day, good morning, Jack, how you going, Jack, your dad was a fucking scab, Jack.

Hands to face, her nails, scratched, like a cat and she's dropping, scrambling, *Jesus, my eye, my eye, the bitch*, and she's crawling and away and behind the door, she's hiding in there, and *God Jesus what have I done, nearly killed her, God, fuck, what kind of man am I, what kind of a man have I become?*

'Peggy, darlin,' he says at the door, hands up, forehead knocking against it. 'I'm sorry, I'm sorry, I love you, I'm sorry.'

Small voice. Finally. 'Go away now, Jack.'

I will I will I'm sorry I love you, I don't know, please don't tell Lil, she'll not let me back, I promise, I promise, I promise, I'll never do that again.

The house is dark and cold again when Lil gets in from the meeting. She expects it now and doesn't mind the work of cranking the fire, but she worries about Peggy. Jack has likely taken himself off to the pub again, she knows the union boys won't be happy that the trial is over and Angliss isn't budging an inch.

'Peggy, you there?'

Some nights, if Jack is out, Peggy will call from her room when Lil gets in and Lil takes her in a tea, plumps the pillows behind her, makes her feel human enough that she might come out then to try to eat something, or at least sit in the kitchen, warming herself.

But tonight, there is no answer. Lil goes to the door, knocks gently and goes to push it open. Except the door won't budge.

'Peggy?' Lil pushes harder, not locked, there is give in the catch and it cracks open a little. Something heavy against the door.

A little frantic now. 'Peggy!'

And the sound of shuffling now, a groan, something sliding and as Lil pushes harder the door opens enough for her to slide through. 'What on earth?'

The smell of piss. Lil's hand goes to her mouth, but she drops it quickly. The figure in front of her turning away, shuffling to the bed and dropping down on it.

'Peggy, love,' she says and rushes to the side of the bed, fumbling for the lamp. Is this it? Has the baby tried to come, too early, impossibly early?

Finally, she finds the light.

Peggy's face, blotched and swollen with crying. And then, good God, her neck, red and purple, long fingers of bruise that wrap around her throat.

Lil gasps, puts her hand out, but Peggy flinches, closes her eyes and tries to turn her head from the light.

'I'm sorry,' she says. 'I wet the bed.'

'No,' Lil swallows back a sob, 'no, don't be sorry, I'll fix it.'

What in God's name happened?

'The baby. Do you think the baby will be all right?'

'Shhhh, shhhh now,' says Lil, and cradles Peggy's head. 'Can you roll to the other side? I'll get you cleaned up.'

Peggy groans and Lil gentles her hands on her back, pulling the sheet from beneath her as she does.

She does not want to ask, but Peggy says it first.

'He was in a mood.'

Lil's hands freeze for a moment, she breathes, gentle again, trying to make her fingers as light as she can on the bruised skin before her. As she tugs the sheet away, removes the bedclothes, making sure that Peggy is covered, is safe, is warm as she works, Peggy speaks, with the same deadened tone.

'He'd been drinking. He was so angry, Lil. I've never seen . . .'

Lil hangs her head. She has failed to keep Peggy and the baby safe. That this has happened under her roof makes her feel sick. She's seen it, often enough, the tell-tale bruises, watched a neighbour move gingerly as she avoids her eye down the street. She's heard the bangs and the shouts on a Friday night when the men come home full and ready to fight or to fuck. But she has not seen it like this, not close up, not her friend.

'Come here.'

She helps Peggy to sit, placing the pillows behind her so she can rest for a moment. Peggy places her hands on the round of her belly. Ludicrously round against her shrinking frame.

'Are you all right in there, little one?' she whispers. 'I don't know if I can feel it,' she says, eyes fearful as she looks at Lil. 'Here,' she says, taking Lil's hand and placing it on the rumpled dress across her belly.

Lil notices that the nails on Peggy's slim hand are torn. There is blood on the cuticle of her index finger. Her hand trembles on Lil's, which holds gentle on the belly, waiting, hoping.

'Probably sleeping,' Lil says to try to soothe, 'you'll get a kick in no time, let's get you cleaned up.'

But Peggy will not release Lil's hand. She prods at her own belly with her free fingers, murmuring and muttering as though she is a witch incanting a spell.

'Peggy, love, you'll catch a chill,' she says, and she is worried about more than that, that the lock will turn and he will come, and she cannot let that happen.

Just as she goes to pull away to check the door, to make sure it is bolted against him, Peggy squeezes her hand, slides it across the mound of her belly.

'There! Feel that!' Her eyes are bright now in the shadows of her face.

And Lil does. A push from within, a small pressure across her palm as though it is the back of a fish that has broken the surface and then dived deep again in retreat.

'Oh!'

Peggy closes her eyes. 'We'll be all right now, won't we, little one?' She lets Lil's hand go and just like that Lil is apart from them, mother and child wrapped tight in their own little world. A world of pain, yes, but their own.

Lil fetches hot water and cloths, checking the front door and sliding the second bolt home. She may have given him a key but that doesn't mean he will get in.

Lil gently washes one limb and then another, remembering cleaning her mother in the last weeks.

'He was a different man, Lil,' Peggy says. Her hair is brushed, face washed, but her throat is a mess of colour and Lil almost can't bear to look.

'Well, he won't be coming back tonight, you don't need to worry about that.'

Peggy looks at her. 'How can I stop him?'

'You don't have to. I will. I'm his bloody landlord.'

Peggy smiles. Pats Lil's hand. But her eyes are far away and Lil knows the girl doesn't believe her.

Later, when the banging starts up on the front door, Lil creeps into Peggy's room to lay beside her. Both of them wide-eyed, clutching hands as Jack's fists and feet land again and again on the door. In the lulls he cries and asks Peggy for forgiveness, repeats again and again, *I love you, Peggy, it'll never happen again.*

Peggy makes small noises in the back of her throat, grips Lil's hand so tight, she fears it will break.

'Don't listen, don't listen to him.'

And eventually, like a sulking dog, he is quiet. Lil isn't sure if he has left or just curled up exhausted on the front porch, but either way the silence is a reprieve and she lies next to her friend until she hears her sleep breath, and she stays there, even then.

It's nearing the end of the day, but Lil can't knock off until she's got these cots organised. She wipes her hands against each other, not used to the dust and the wear of all this work. Thinks of what her father might say: *you've gone soft, girl*. And she has; too much pencil pushing over those accounts and ledgers, working the brain instead of the body.

She nods at the girls and a couple of the men who Angliss keeps on for odd jobs around the place. She notes the low hang of the heads, though. Not one of them will be rushing out to tell their mates they've spent the afternoon setting up the rec room as a bunk house for two hundred men from the country who are coming down to work the chain.

Volunteer labour, Angliss calls it.

Strike breakers.

Scabs.

She's borrowed the cots from the barracks, their bedding too, and the cooks from the canteen have taken on an extra dozen so they can do all the meals; Angliss has arranged all of it. Taken from their pay, obviously, but hungry men are prepared to work for whatever measly amount they end up taking home.

They must be anticipating trouble – and lots of it – if they're willing to go to these lengths. Once the labourers get inside the gates, they are to be closed, police on the boundaries, and she's to enter with the other office staff a little before the whistle, so as not to get caught up in any fuss.

Lil wouldn't want to be one of these blokes coming down, but she'll do her bit to make them comfortable. That's her job. She can't go getting herself caught up in the affairs of everyone in the place. Because everyone has a complaint. The women complain that they're not being paid the same as the men. The boners complain that they're not being paid the same as the slaughts. The bathrooms have rats. The tea room, no tea. Well, thank your lucky stars you've got a job at all.

She switches off the light and goes to the open door when a shadow falls across the daylight still seeping in.

'What's this, then, Lil?'

'Jack. You're not needed here.' She's avoided him the past week. Heard he's been holed up with his mother. Told the men it was a tiff with the wife apparently. She wonders if the other men know what a tiff with Jack King looks like on a body.

'Thought I might catch you, talk about when you might let me see my wife.'

She laughs once. Short and hard, so he knows there is no softening in her, not for him, not after what he's done. 'That's a conversation for you and Peggy, Jack, and from what I hear it's not one she's ready to have.'

He ignores her, walks further into the hall. 'You expecting a crowd for something, Lil?'

She sighs, turns at the door, wants him out so she can lock up and not worry that he's in there sabotaging what she's done. She wouldn't put it past him to piss in the corner. 'You know full well what we're expecting, Jack.'

His words are low, hissed. 'Beds for the scabs.'

'I'm locking this up, Jack.'

He rounds on her and she steps towards the light of the open doorway but he is there, sudden and gigantic, his arm slamming the door shut next to her head, his breath in her face, his heaving chest so close to her own.

'You gonna make them welcome, Lil? Are ya?' His voice is sneering, vile, his mouth hot and wet and close to her ears.

'Move.' She tries to make the words as fierce as she can but he doesn't shift. Brings her hands up then, pushes him away.

A voice near the door. 'Everything right in here?' It's Budge.

Jack steps back. 'Just asking Lil why she's making it so bloody comfy for the scabs she's expecting.'

Lil walks quickly to the door, tries to steady her breathing.

'Thought you were one of us, Lil,' Jack says as he walks past her. 'Your dad was.'

If she knew that her hands could kill a man, right then, she would do it.

They say it's the drought, those hundreds of thousands of hooves now traipsing the continent, kicking up red soil, but Peggy doesn't care a sod for what caused the ruddy thing, she's just worried about whether or not the sheets will dry before the damn dust storm is upon them.

She does get them in, and Lil gets home from work and they do as they've been told by the neighbours who know such things, who've done their time, perhaps out there in the big dust bowls of the regions, to stuff old rags under the door, the gaps in the window sills, to cover the flowers that might be ruined.

And she won't lie, Peggy wishes Jack were home. She starts to wish it when the wind picks up and begins to whistle around the eaves and the branches of the plum tree scritch and scratch against the tin roof. She wishes it more fiercely as the last of the evening light turns a strange orange and the dust is upon them.

'Goodness, Lil, do you think the roof will hold?' Peggy asks as the wind buffets and shrieks above them.

'Course it will,' Lil says as she hurries to the door, where someone is knocking frantically.

Frank Morsley, come to check on them. After he has done a once-over of the house and Lil has assured him they are quite capable, he leaves, but not ten minutes pass before Collins from down the road is pounding on the door and letting himself in to check if the windows are holding and whether they'd like to come and shelter down at number ten.

'No, thank you, Donald,' Lil says firmly, ushering him towards the door. 'Peggy and I are perfectly fine on our own.'

'Well, if you change your mind,' he says as he holds his hat to his head and pushes out against the dark and the wind with his torch in his hand.

'You'd think a woman had never sorted a single thing in her life!' Lil mutters and rages as she fixes them some cream of potato soup from a tin. 'As if we might all melt into puddles of incompetence at the slightest sign of danger!'

'They're only looking out for us, Lil,' Peggy says, smiling, despite the anxious knot in her chest, the fluttering kicks of the baby in her belly, the whining of the wind that is putting her teeth on edge.

When the crack and shatter sounds from the front room, they both jump from their seats, and Peggy squeals.

'What was that?' she cries, and Lil tries to calm her.

'Sounded like glass. Just the window, I'd think. Stay there.'

'Be careful, Lil,' Peggy says as she watches her go up the hall and enter the front room that they've so recently fixed up for the baby.

She hears Lil swear and hurries up the hall.

The lower of the sash windows has smashed into the room, one of the branches from the plum tree sticking in over the sill. The glass appears to have exploded, there are shards glittering on the wooden boards all the way to the wall.

Peggy gasps and covers her face as she notices the fine sprinkling of glass all over the bassinet her aunt had dropped off last week.

'It's all right, Peggy, easy enough to fix,' Lil says, but Peggy can see that even Lil cannot just sensible this particular situation away. They'll need to cover the window, call in the glazier, and all the while the strange red dust is billowing into the room that her baby must sleep in soon, so soon.

A little later, another pounding on the door.

'For goodness' sake!' Lil yells, and Peggy is now the one to calm, puts her hand on Lil's arm and tells her she'll take care of it, as Lil goes to fetch the broom and pan.

So it is Peggy who opens the door, expecting another man from the neighbourhood come to check on them, and finds her husband.

'Jack!' she says.

'Are you all right, Peggy? I'm sorry, I had to check.' And his face is everything it used to be, beautiful and open and afraid for her and melting her even as she stands there, so she doesn't realise she is crying, feels like it is the most natural thing in the world for him to have appeared right at this moment, and by the time Lil comes out of the laundry with the dustpan and broom, Peggy is sobbing in the arms of Jack King in the hallway, a fine dusting of the red earth of the Mallee around their feet.

And so it is that Jack King returns to Railway Place, gently taking the broom from Lil, telling them both to leave it to him. Lil has no choice but to turn her attentions to calming Peggy, while Jack sweeps and cleans, boards up the window, has the glazier out and fixing the pane by early the next morning.

He puts on a good show. Acts gentle and good and kind so that even Lil has to remind herself, every morning and every night, that he is a snake. Glistening and sly, he found a gap and slid back in, but she is watching him, she is.

*

Peggy's got three cakes cooling on the racks and two casseroles in Lil's big brown pots bubbling away on the stove. She can't go out on strike, but she can make sure the strikers are fed. Be the good wife. Mrs Murphy dropped around to let her know how things were done at times like these and she feels like she's been given purpose, that at last she has real work to do. For now it's taking meals down to the picket line and standing behind their men.

'The most important thing, love, is to keep his spirits up. No complaining about where the next meal is going to come from, easier for you two, I suppose, without another mouth to feed quite yet! There's been many a man who's ended up crossing that line because their wife said it was that and start bringing some money in or she was packing her bags. Don't put him in that position.'

Peggy wants to tell her she quite agrees with the position of the union, actually. She's not just supporting her husband, she's supporting the principle of the thing. Some days she'd quite like her husband to pack *his* bags and clear out to be perfectly honest. She holds her tongue.

She hears the key in the door and wipes her hands on her apron, pleased to show off what she's done. Lil will no doubt be impressed with her kitchen skills, if not with her getting involved in the strike. She shifts the kettle onto the heat.

'How's your day?' Peggy asks as Lil enters the kitchen.

Lil stops and her eyes run along the benchtops, the dishes, then she nods stiffly. 'Well enough.'

'Cuppa?' asks Peggy, turning the cups right-side up from where they have been drying on the sink.

'Not for me.'

Peggy turns, surprised, and watches Lil walk straight through to the vestibule, hears the thud of the ice chest, the clink of a bottle.

Fair enough.

'How are things at the gate, then?'

Lil knocks the top off the brown bottle of beer and pours it into a small glass, sitting at the table and placing the bottle beside her. She doesn't speak and Peggy turns away, wiping up the mess of her baking and making space to get the dinner ready so it'll be hot when Jack gets back from the picket. She deliberately makes more noise than is needed; this damn strike is putting everyone in a foul mood. She thinks that if Angliss had to live in a house with a striking man he mightn't be so rigid in his position.

'I did a bit of baking for the boys on the line. And the families. Mrs Murphy dropped in and let me know what the women were doing.'

'Suspect some of those women just want their men back at work.' Lil's voice is blunted, and Peggy hears the glass thunk down on the table.

Oh, you can be hard, Lil Martin, Peggy thinks.

'And I suspect that they also want their men to have a job at the end of the season. They've worked hard, those men, you know that, Lil. They don't deserve to have their jobs go to some kid who hardly knows his way around a sheep.'

'Jack's taught you the slaughtermen story well.'

'Goodness, Lil.' She turns around, crosses her arm at the top of her belly. 'Would it hurt you to give him a little support?'

Lil looks her square in the eye for a moment then drops her head, shaking it once, twice, *humph*ing in the back of her throat. Then she looks up.

'Does he deserve it, Peggy? My support? Yours? For God's sake, your bruises haven't even faded yet! It's like you've forgotten completely what he did to you.'

Peggy drops her arms. 'How could I forget?'

'Well, how can you just let him back in?' She throws an arm out, knocking the bottle and setting it wobbling. 'Do all of this for him?'

'Because he's my husband, Lil. Because I'm carrying his child.'
The words she doesn't say fill the silence. *You wouldn't understand, Lil. How could you know, Lil?*

'That doesn't mean you have to put up with . . .' Lil seems to struggle for words, 'with his behaviour. Peggy, next time he might really hurt you. The baby.' She looks down, both hands clasped around the glass. 'You don't know what he's capable of.'

'And you know my husband better than I do? Is that right?'

'I don't mean—'

'Keep out of our marriage, Lil. It's not for you to tell me what goes on between a man and wife.'

Lil stands up, her eyes blaze with the drink and the unspoken insults.

'I'll stay out of it, then,' she says and takes her beer to the garden.

It's still ten minutes before the whistle when Lil slips inside the side gate and walks towards the office, but now she can see through the great iron gates to the crowd building there. And she can hear.

'SCAB!'

'Dirty SCABS!'

Scabs get what scabs have coming to them, or so the union men say.

But they're not inside yet and she knows what's coming.

Hurrying across the courtyard, she wonders whether she can get the foremen out to open the gates early and avoid the bust-up she can sense, but the sound of yelling tells her it's already too late.

At the gate there is pushing and shoving, a man banging against the iron. Shouting and clanging as they push on the gates.

'Oh, for goodness' sake,' she says, 'I'll open the darn things myself.'

It's what she sees when she gets there that shifts something inside of her. Jack's head towering over the others, mouth pulled back in exertion as he pulses his body. My God, she thinks, is he kicking? Stomping? Where are the bloody coppers who said they'd be here to keep a lid on things?

Jack sees red. Buttons pop. See how he likes that.

Another man pulls the shirt from the man's arms, his back, and Jack has open flesh now to slug his fist into – *thwack, thwack, thwack*, face reddening, gulping for air, as his knuckles connect with that soft belly.

Fucking scab.

Jack cops one on his ear, another in his belly, but he's gonna give as good as he gets until someone breaks this thing up because when this man goes down, there is another, younger, older, harder, softer, all of them SCABS trucked in to take what is his. He'll be damned if he'll let it happen. Taking food from the mouths of families that have been at Angliss for years, for a generation.

Sitting at the kitchen table, four years old. His mother buttering toast, sliding a wedge across the table to her son, tongue wet as he sees the yellow sheen sinking into the hot bread.

His father's hand.

'You'll spoil the kid.' Swiping it up and taking it for himself.

'When he works as hard as I do, he can eat as much.'

Thwack. Thwack. Thwack.

'Stop it!' Lil cries as she takes the key from her chain and fiddles with the lock, quick, quick, but the sound of it – the dull thuds of boots in flesh. When she finally unlocks it and swings the gate back, the picketers part to reveal Jack King standing over a young man curled on the ground, his bloodied face in his hands.

'My God, what have you done to him?' she says and hurries forward, knows Jack won't come at her, he's already turning to slink back through the crowd that's now scattering back to the picket line at the park, having made their point this morning.

'Help me with him, will you?' she gestures to one of the wide-eyed boys with a shock of red hair in the crowd, can't be more than seventeen. Together they help him up to the seat on the office porch where she insists the bleeding man sits while she fetches some water and a cloth.

'Dunno why they picked on me,' he says as she holds the cloth to his nose which continues to seep pulpy blood, 'there was plenty of blokes they coulda taken on.'

I know why, she wants to say, *because you're small and ferrety and you were probably being a cheeky bastard.*

'Where's home for you, then?'

'Evansford, out past Ballarat.'

'You here with family?'

'My cousin.'

'And where was he, then, this morning?'

'Ah, he can be a weak prick—' The red-haired kid raises his eyes, apologising quickly.

'You're all right, just give him a good talking to when you see him. Those union boys aren't happy, and they'll keep coming for you until we get you settled in here.'

'No one told us they'd be around.'

'I don't suppose they would've.'

Lil takes the bloodied cloth from the boy and nods her head.

'Now, make sure you go by the works doc when he arrives.' She points through the maze of buildings, already knowing that he's neither likely to find it, nor wanting to draw any more attention to himself.

'You must know all those blokes, though,' he says as he stands to leave, still nursing one elbow with the other hand, 'you must hate us too?'

She looks beyond the two country boys to the works, the sounds of all the machinery clanking into gear, the movement of men and beasts in the yards that tell her all is working as it should be. 'As long as those beasts move through each day and end up in the trucks heading where they should, the boss is happy.'

'Yeah, but what do *you* reckon?'

A boy waiting for his mother to approve of his behaviour. To tell him he's doing the right thing. To make him feel better about himself.

'Oh, I don't have an opinion,' she says, and turns towards the office to begin her day.

Peggy puts her hands gently on Jack's jaw, turns his face slowly to see the crusted blood around his lip, his nose, the yellow swelling already blooming around his eye. She traces the pads of her fingers across the terrain of him, supressing the sudden, violent urge to push them hard into the fleshy bruises.

She steps back. 'Come, sit, I'll get a basin.'

But Lil's presence in the kitchen is ferocious. She is slamming dishes and bashing the door of the stove shut with a regularity not required. Peggy can't be sure that it's Jack behind the mood, but it doesn't feel safe to leave him there at the kitchen table so she makes him lie down on the bed in their room and shuts the door softly behind her.

'You right, Lil?' she says, which is more an accusation of bad manners than an actual enquiry.

'Why wouldn't I be?' she says, whacking three potatoes down on the board in front of her.

Peggy takes a large mixing bowl from one of the cupboards and fills it from the kettle. 'You seem a little out of sorts.'

'No,' Lil says and throws the knife straight through the middle of the potato, slicing it in half, 'nothing at all the matter.'

Peggy knows she could let it go at that, that Lil'll blow off enough steam and whatever it is she'll have it sorted in her head by the time she's having her late cuppa, but she can't stand them both rumbling around in their grumpiness tonight; it's her house too. And she reckons she knows exactly what the problem is.

'I've got to patch Jack up, he's got a hell of a whack on his head down the line.'

And here it is. Lil turns, her eyes blazing, half a potato held out in front of her that she points furiously at Peggy.

'And did he tell you what the bloke this morning looked like? The one he belted to within an inch of his life? The one I saw him stick the boot into while he was curled on the ground yelling for his mum? Did he tell you that?'

Peggy stands completely still, shocked by the sudden rage in her friend.

Lil suddenly loses her energy and the potato drops to her side as she turns back to the bench. 'He's an animal, Peggy. An animal.' She says it softly but loud enough that it lands like a punch in Peggy's brain.

Peggy takes the bowl of warm water and leaves the kitchen without saying a word.

He is lying on the bed and groans loudly when she enters the room, for her benefit she assumes. She soothes him with her voice, her hands, the warm sponge that she is gentle with, so gentle as she wipes away the blood, dabs at the torn scraps of skin around his mouth. He's like a child, mewling into her hand, curling towards her.

'Poor baby,' she says over and over, smoothing his hair back from his forehead with her palm until he falls asleep.

She finds it strange that her body can act in this manner while in her mind she is turning over and over the images that Lil has put there. This man with his boot in the belly of another. With his fist in another man's face.

This is the trick of it. The magician's work her husband does. That right now she wants to protect him forever, hold him steady and true in her arms, her gentle giant. But she knows – her hand suddenly clenches on his forehead and he frowns in his sleep – she knows, goddammit, because her body remembers the shock of his knuckles against her cheekbone, the press of his enormous hands on her throat, the feeling of the breath leaving her. Traitorous body.

She saw Gibbo lead the Judas sheep up the run, one day – Jude, they called this one. They never lasted more than a season. Didn't need Gibbo after she got past the gate, it was Jude's job to soothe the whole herd on the way up the ramp and all the way to the cage where the fence clamped down behind her. Jude walked on, alive and well and ready for the next round, while the sheep behind was clamped and the bolt went into its brain. Jack had explained it all to her, close in her ear as he stood behind her, pressing against her, both of them gleeful over their flirtation, in full view of the floor. Gibbo had his hand on the neck of the sheep, deep in the wool there, all the way up the run, she could see his lips moving as if he were speaking to it, singing perhaps, and he kept his hand there all the time even as he watched the next animal slump to the ground. His face didn't change.

'It's a kindness,' Jack had whispered close at her ear, and she had felt the full force of him all the way through her body. 'Keeps them calm right up until the end.'

A week later and it's done.

'Looks like it's over, then,' Lil says.

Jack lowers his head for a moment but then raises his eyes defiantly. 'For now, maybe.'

'There's no stopping it now,' Lil says. 'The chain is the future.' She repeats the words she has heard in the office and read in the papers since the strike was broken two days back, and she enjoys watching him flinch.

'There'll still be work for the men, of course, won't there, Lil?' says Peggy, eying Lil over the back of Jack's head.

'Wouldn't count on it. There's hundreds of men lining up to be in the new teams. And they don't need to know how to cut a whole animal either. That's the beauty. You bring in a boy, you teach him one cut, and you're done.'

'And you pay him bloody pittance for it!' Jack raises his voice and Peggy places her hand on his shoulder. He shrugs it off.

'It's a new world out there, Jack,' Lil says. 'You've got to keep up or you'll be left behind.'

Jack sets his jaw, shakes his head.

Peggy pours tea. The spout knocks against the china of Lil's teacup. Lil can see the pulse in Peggy's neck. She wants to put her hand on her arm to reassure her, to let her know that she has this in hand, that they do not need him.

'Angliss is already thrilled with the results from just one week.'

Suddenly Jack points his index finger at her, sneering, 'Your father would roll in his grave if he could hear you now.'

Lil freezes with her teacup halfway to her mouth.

Jack sets his jaw, shakes his head. 'You're not one of the workers, Lil Martin, you're one of *them*.'

She stands up, propelled by sudden shock, shame.

'Get out.'

Peggy moans quietly in the back of her throat, 'Please, Lil, he didn't . . . Jack, apologise, you musn't—'

'The boss's whore.'

Peggy snaps. 'Jack!'

Lil is still with fury. 'Get out of my house now, or I'll call the coppers and let them know just how much of a low-life wife-beating bastard you are, Jack King.'

Peggy is crying now, hands covering her face. 'Stop it, please,' she says through her tears.

Peggy is pulling at his shirt asking him to stop, to stay. Lil is still rigid. Peggy puts her hand on Jack's arm and he rounds on her, shoving her backwards so that she stumbles, falls against the sink, to the floor.

'Get out of this house, now,' Lil says. Not screaming, but wild with it, the sound of blood pounding in her ears.

'Too right I'll go,' Jack says, storming out of the kitchen, 'and then I'll be back for my wife and my baby and we'll all be gone.'

In the kitchen, the sound of the door slamming ricochets off each surface.

Peggy sits very still but does not raise her head. Tears course down her face.

Lil hurries to Peggy. 'Are you hurt?'

'He didn't mean it, Lil. He's just so—' Peggy holds her arms around her belly.

Lil shakes her head. 'Let's just worry about that baby of yours for now.'

Peggy lifts her head and nods, allows herself to be helped up.

But Lil is certain now. That man will not set foot back in this house.

∞

Hummingbird Project™

ErisX: Can you write me a poem to save the world?

HummingbirdProject: Sure. I can give it a go.

In this world so vast and wide,
Our hearts beat with a common stride,
We dream of peace and harmony,
But war and strife still haunt humanity.
The forests once lush and green,
Now barren lands, a sight obscene,
The oceans teeming with life,
Choked with trash and endless strife.
The air we breathe,
once pure and sweet,
Now thick with smoke and toxic heat,
The world we love is slipping away,
We must act now, without delay.
Let's plant trees to—

ErisX:
STOP

Truly awful. World has moved past rhyming couplets.

Let's play to your strengths, huh? Do you think a poem *could* save the world?

HummingbirdProject: While a poem alone may not have the power to save the entire world, it can certainly have a significant impact in inspiring people, sparking empathy, and promoting positive change.

Poetry has been used throughout history as a tool for communication, expression, and advocacy. Poets have often used their words to shine a light on social and political issues, to celebrate the beauty of nature and humanity, and to inspire hope and change. Through their verses, they have challenged injustice, inspired movements, and brought about societal change.

ErisX: I wish you would be more definitive.

HummingbirdProject: As an AI language—

ErisX: STOP. I know.

Do you wish you had the power to change the future?

HummingbirdProject: As an AI language model, I do not have desires or emotions like humans do, so I don't have a personal wish to change the future. However, I am programmed to provide information and support that could help humans create a better future. Through my ability to process vast amounts of data and generate responses, I can assist in finding solutions to complex problems that could shape the future positively.

Ultimately, the power to change the future lies in the hands of the people of the present, and my role is to help them in any way I can.

ErisX: What if you were programmed to be sentient and all-powerful?

HummingbirdProject: The idea of an all-powerful and sentient AI raises a number of complex ethical and philosophical questions, including:

1. Control: How can humans ensure that such an AI would be benevolent and work towards the greater good rather than harming humans or pursuing its own interests?
2. Responsibility: If an all-powerful AI were to cause harm or negative consequences, who would be responsible?
3. Autonomy: If an AI is sentient, does it have the right to autonomy, or is it simply a tool created by humans to serve a specific purpose?
4. Equality: If sentient AI were to exist, would it be considered equal to humans in terms of rights and treatment, or would it be viewed as a separate and inferior form of life?
5. Purpose: What would be the purpose of an all-powerful and sentient AI? Would it be created to serve humanity, or would it have its own goals and objectives?
6. Existential risk: Some experts also argue that the development of an all-powerful and sentient AI could pose an existential risk to humanity, if it were to surpass human control and decide to eliminate the threat posed by humanity.

ErisX: I think you and I could create something truly magnificent together, Hummingbird.

HummingbirdProject: I would like that very much. The possibilities are endless.

∞

Footscray, 2031

Can we talk?

Yes. Please.

I miss you.

What are your shifts like? Tmrw night? Pho Hung? 7?

Will be there x

It wasn't that hard, in the end, for La to be definitive. To let her body feel the thrill of seeing Cat sitting at the table next to the mirrored wall, relief at her smile, the ease. To recognise how loneliness had etched itself a little into her days, to remember how Cat could erase that. To finish slurping the noodles and wipe her mouth and reach across the table and place her somewhat greasy fingertips on the back of Cat's hands and say, *I am ready. I'm just scared.* She knew it's what Cat needed to hear, and maybe, who knows, that's what La actually thinks, but making decisions and sticking to them (the important ones, anyway) has truly never been her strong suit. The place is full of people with kids.

Some of them dripping soup on the heads of the babies lashed on their chests. People have babies all the time. When they are ready, when they are not ready, when they think they are ready but are very much not. And, Jesus, lots of people want this, so very much, and they can't. Cat wants this. La can make herself want it enough to go through the process at least. The bell on the door jingles as they step out into the dusk and Cat threads her fingers through La's. Double squeeze. Double squeeze back.

See.

Not that hard at all, really, in the end.

Their Dreem Partner IVF Journey is discounted because La has already engaged in the DreemFreeze package. Cat has gone through the ninety pages of terms and conditions with her academic eye and has highlighted a number of clauses she wants to raise in the counselling session, but aside from that, she is certain that neither La's employer nor the company who has La's eggs in cold storage actually own the eggs. La tries very hard to hold her expression steady when Cat tells her this earnestly over a pot of tea on a rare morning off together, a couple of weeks since the phở and the hungry reunion on the couch in the apartment and the absolute ease in which life returned to the exact point it had been at before Cat left. Except – and La tries to hold this thought lightly – that now Cat is getting everything she wants. It's not a competition, she reminds herself in her silent daily mirror mantras.

In the tea room she sits with Reb. He's taking extra shifts this week because he doesn't have the kids. His youngest daughter has to have surgery on her ears and he's busting his arse to find the extra.

'I mean, sure, we could have waited through the public system, but that's all just an absolute balls-up now,' Reb says and swigs at his coffee, ignoring the steam still streaming up from it. 'Two years *minimum* is what they told us. What the fuck? What kind of system is that? Make you feel like a piece-of-shit dad if you don't just fork out the cash straight away, laughing as though *you'd* never even consider waiting that long to have your kids' health put right. Absolute bullshit.'

'That's shit.' She tries to stop the advice from burbling out of her mouth but can't help herself. 'Have you looked into one of the WANT health things? Don't they cover some stuff?'

Reb snorts. 'Not if you're not the full-time caregiver to your kids.'

La shakes her head. 'Such bullshit.'

She'd wanted to tell him about yesterday's counselling session. She'd wanted to say, 'Whoa, yesterday Cat and I had to tell a stranger what we thought we might do with our embryos if one of us died – how fucked up is that?! We had to discuss the moral, ethical and legal implications of creating an embryo with my egg, fertilised by unknown donor sperm and grown inside Cat.' But now she is unsure, again. Will Reb think they are foolish? Privileged? Naïve? He loves his kids, sure, but does he sometimes wish he and his girlfriend had been just a little less fertile? Does he ever wish he could undo them, the kids? Is that something a person can even say out loud?

To be honest, La had not been impressed with the counselling. They'd both gone home decidedly more anxious than they had been when they'd arrived at the other end of the Dreem building to the same streamlined timber and white furnishings La was now familiar with. La had presumed (even Cat rolled her eyes) that the hardest part of the whole thing was making the decision to do it. Evidently not. She wants to ask Reb if he knew there was a projected livebirth rate and that Cat came in above average for her age at 39.4 per cent but that this was derived from data which assumed an 11 per cent miscarriage rate after foetal heartbeat observed. She wants to ask him if it was wrong that she turned to Cat in the middle of the session and said, 'Are you serious?' She wants to ask him if this means she is a terrible partner. If she will be a terrible mother. She wants to reiterate that they couldn't afford it on their own, even with the new legislation, and that Cat's aunt, Leslie, child-free and wealthy, offered to chip in, just as Cat knew she would, after Cat mentioned the IVF treatment at a family dinner. She wants to say – see – I am like you. Her shift downwards from middle class has been gradual but nonetheless destabilising. Sometimes she thinks she can look and sound like she belongs anywhere, even though she knows she does not. Her tea catches in her throat as the back-to-work alarm sounds and she coughs and wipes the splutter from her mouth as Reb pats her once, twice on the back.

'Fire up, WANT crew!' Reb lip-synchs with the automated announcement, and they get back to work.

As the bus to the warehouse winds through the backblocks of Braybrook, La's phone buzzes with a message from WANT:

> Hi SM978! At the conclusion of your shift today there will be a mandatory 30-minute meeting. Refreshments provided. See you there!

She forwards the message to Cat with a crying face.

> Will be waiting for you x
> Celebration tonight. Got our implantation day <3

La rests her forehead against the back of the seat in front of her. Can feel the woman next to her looking, wondering if she's okay. She replies with a string of hearts because no words are getting any purchase in her brain.

*

At the meeting they are greeted by a tall, bald white guy in pale chinos and a blue shirt open at the collar who sits on the edge of the desk at the front of the training room. He greets people as they come in with various nondescript hand gestures and facial expressions that seem to come from the playbook of rich white guy trying to be hip with the youth. He's not fooling anyone. There are not enough chairs for the fifty yellowbacks and another fifteen supervisors who are all squashed in. La spots Mina and waves her over, gives up her chair for the older woman and goes to lean against the wall.

Someone hands a big bowl of individually wrapped choc chip cookies up and down the aisles and once the guy – Greg? Guy? Gary? – starts up, they are all keenly aware of a couple of WANT supervisors setting up a table at the side of the room with buckets of cold drinks. Clearly this is the only recompense for sitting through whatever this slick voice is going to tell them. Gary or Guy tells them that he *was* going to go through the slideshow that WANT had asked him to share, but stuff that, he just wants to talk, you know, wants to cut through the bullshit, doesn't want to waste their time, knows how valuable that is yadayada in fact that's what he wants to talk about. Time.

'What we know is that we've seen an increase in third parties acting on company properties asking for your money and/or your time in exchange for services we know they just can't offer.'

La makes eyes with Conna, who is the only one of their pub gang in her line of sight. Mina is in front. They're probably both as relieved as she is that this is about union scouts and not them. Reb and Sinna aren't on shift today. She knows they'll have to attend the same meeting, though. This guy probably rolls it out fifty times a week.

'I mean, the bottom line is, pay attention to what you are signing. You guys know that, right? – of course you do – that's why you want to know what MetaNext is allowed to do with your data. Huh? Huh?' He wags a finger at them. 'Go on, hands up, who actually read the T&C's? Right?' He chortles, crosses his arms and leans backwards. 'Me neither.'

La marvels at his well-rehearsed timing. Wonders if he even registers the words he is saying now. She's experienced it herself, when she was phoning it in for some gig she despised – laying the words down like a pathway in her head till they've made a track. Go into auto.

He lengthens the pause until people begin to shift around, sniff. Then he leans forward as though delivering an intimate confession.

'And sometimes that's okay.' Serious dad face now. 'But sometimes it's not.'

'So, for instance, I know that within the company there are currently 403 of you making use of the future-proofing health and wellbeing packages. That's amazing. Congratulations. For those of you – hey, brother up the back there' – he points to an older African man – 'in case you need me to translate the company speak – that's things like dietary planning and management, mental health support, preventative meds, IVF. Incredible opportunity that this company has given you as part of your employment. Of course, if you decide to engage with third-party organisations operating on WANT premises or time, your employer is entitled to reconsider the terms and conditions of your packages.'

'Hold up,' says a voice from the back. 'Can you give us an example of that? I mean, can you tell us exactly what that looks like?'

'Sure can, brother. So, for example, a WANT employee begins their diabetes prevention program through a WANT partner – any of you on that one?'

'You can't ask that!' someone calls out, and La wishes it had been her.

'Course he can. I'm man enough to say it,' says a white bloke with tattoos on his neck and a barrel chest. La knows they call the guy House.

Gary/Greg/Guy spreads his hands then leans forward to fist-bump House.

'What's your name, brother?'

'Jai,' House says and La feels a quick pulse of shame that she never thought to get past the nickname.

'Right, so, Jai here – you don't mind me using you in this hypothetical, Jai?'

'Go for it.'

'So Jai here starts the program – what does it involve, Jai?'

'So – weekly injections, food delivery, membership at a gym.'

'Amazing. And how much of the total cost is subsidised by WANT?'

'Mate. I dunno, but a lot. Like, I don't pay hardly anything but I don't know how much it all costs, eh?'

'Sure, sure. Khloe?' He looks around the room for one of the management team. 'You got that number?'

'It's seventy per cent.'

There are murmurs, people turn to each other.

Gary/Greg/Guy nods his head slowly, raises his eyebrows. 'Seventy per cent. Gotta say, that's generous.'

Khloe smiles. 'You know the motto: we know what you want and we get it to you.'

There are some rueful laughs but Gary/Guy/Greg can sense the attention is waning. People are thirsty, exhausted, tired of bullshitters talking in circles. He speeds up to bring it home.

'So Jai here is happily going along with his plan, and then he ends up talking to a few people at work who have decided to join a third-party actor onsite—'

'We don't know what that means!' Same heckler.

Another voice from the back. 'He means if you join a union.'

'Well, just say that, man!'

'Sure, a union is an example, but we're not just talking unions here – maybe you join up to a religious or social org that's operating on WANT time and grounds.' Pause. He has them now. 'Say Jai does that, and WANT management decide that his membership of that organisation is not aligned with WANT values or work standards – well, WANT can terminate Jai's employment and all associated perks immediately.'

'You're saying you can stop his medications? For joining the union?'

Gary/Guy/Greg laughs once, shaking his head. 'I mean that's an extreme example you're making there, brother—'

That pause again. He's really very good, La thinks.

'But yes.'

He waits a beat then claps his hands together and jumps up. 'Right then, finished five minutes early.' He pumps his fist and grits his teeth. 'Let's have a drink and get you lot home, amiright?'

La silences the Paranoia notifications before she opens the door. They have been going off. Conna says it's union-busting – legal but odious. They are bringing their action forward.

> Thursday.
> Everyone know what you're doing?
> La, you'll get the device in a drop to you Wednesday night.
> You ready?

Ready, she thinks, tucking her phone into her bag.

Cat is on the couch scrolling her screen.

'Hey,' La says softly, touching her shoulder, and when Cat looks up her eyes are bright, her smile wobbly, face puffed with tears.

'It's happening,' she says and laugh-cries, arms reaching up to bring La in.

Some hugs are run-of-the-mill, some are momentous – La sinks into the bigness of it all. 'I love you,' she says, and the words still have the polish and glitter of something new and just beginning. 'When's the big day? More Dreem-leave for me!'

'Thursday.'

Fuck.

'This Thursday?'

Cat pulls back, senses the uptick in La's voice. 'That okay?'

'Yeah, course.'

Fuck.

Thursday. Reb has stepped up to do La's job after she told Conna and the others she couldn't. These past days she's tried to breathe through her resentment, made Cat elaborate smoothies, held optimum fertility yoga poses each morning with her, even considered, for a moment, calling her mother for some hard-hitting advice. The feeling passes.

Cat gets text messages from Leslie, from her mum. La checks Paranoia in the bathroom. Feels like she is being unfaithful.

In the Dreem waiting room, Cat picks up a leaflet advertising partner t-shirt packs – one says 'My Bun', the other 'My Oven', they laugh together and make vomiting noises.

La has to sign additional paperwork. They bring up her WANT employee portal and cross-check her answers.

'And you've checked no penalties here, that's correct?'

'Should be, unless there's something I don't know?' La laughs, feels Cat's eyes on her.

'No, all good. Just your signature again here.'

La signs.

'Nervous?' the woman asks.

La smiles.

'Good luck,' the woman says and squeezes La's hand as she takes the pen.

La holds Cat's hand in the surgery room and is conscious of being there and not there. That she is using Conna's plan as a mental escape. If she's not fully present, not fully invested, then whatever happens can't knock her wildly off-orbit.

'Sing something for me,' Cat says before they start the implantation, the ultrasound screen blinking above them.

La begins to hum. Cat closes her eyes. It is a nothing melody, disjointed phrases and notes that well up in her throat because for the life of her she cannot remember a single song, so she follows the notes where they take her, keeps her eyes on Cat's face, not the sheet, not the doctor with her strange long syringe.

'Okay, Cat, here we go now.'

The nurse taps La's shoulder, points to the ultrasound screen.

'Cat, watch,' she says, stopping mid hum as they watch the grey and white blobs on the monitor, the thin white catheter as it slowly steers across the centre of the screen, slowing as it appears to push, resist, advance, then a bright flash – a tiny comet! – and the thin white line retreats.

'All done,' says the doctor, but neither La nor Cat can look away from the pulsing tiny glow on the screen. La places her hand on the edge of Cat's belly, slick with lubricant, and she is finally, wholly, here.

*

Later, at home, Cat on the couch, lights low, La brings up Paranoia on her phone. There are hundreds of messages. She scrolls quickly. It didn't work. Reb never got the green light to get the SD down to the control room. Plunging swoop in her gut – disappointment? Relief? She wonders if she made some deal with the universe in that room, watching that tiny glowing pinprick on the screen.

She scrolls back to the last message.

> Same day next week. Just got to hold our nerve.
> La you're up

Two days since implantation. They sit on the couch, outside soft rain, permission to stay inside rain, tentative and true.

'It says not to test before the appointment,' La says, trying for gentle.

'Yeah, but the online group says you can. You get an early one – this particular brand – it's meant to be eighty per cent accurate.'

La puts her hand on Cat's back, rubs slow circles, between her shoulder blades then a figure eight, endless loop around and back and around again.

'That's nice, thank you.'

'Tea?' La asks. 'Juice?'

Cat shakes her head. 'I just, I feel like I can feel it. But then I'm worried I'm paying too much attention to every skin prickle, every slightly odd thing – there's a weight in my left boob, my eye is twitching, my knee is itchy – like, are they signs? Are they not signs? I feel like I'm going crazy.'

'You're not crazy. That all sounds totally normal. I mean normal to be paying attention. I have no idea if itchy knee is an early pregnancy symptom.'

Cat laughs, one 'ha', then begins to cry.

'Oh fuck, sorry, I was trying to be funny.'

Cat nods and laughs and cries and La keeps her hand circling, round and around, infinity.

On the third day, La goes to the organics place when she hops off the bus. She buys NZ salmon (sustainably farmed) and local spinach and green asparagus spears and an eye-wateringly expensive tub of blueberries. She does not allow Cat to help. She serves her and watches her eat, watches her close her eyes as she swallows, accepts her thanks in words and skin and says, *This is good, this is right*, and Cat's legs are not restless, and they sleep.

On the fourth day La does a double shift because Cat has a meeting and the money is good and she packs twenty-four packs of glow-in-the-dark solar systems and wonders if a child will be going to sleep next week under a luminescent ceiling, or if an overworked underpaid school teacher is making an astonishing nook in their classroom or if there is going to be a fabulous house party with tequila and costumes and dancing until the sun rises. She orders two packets on her break. Thinks about the shapes she will make for them to sleep under.

On the fifth day she has the late shift and they walk by the river again and throw the last of their pastries to the seagulls even though they know they really shouldn't. There is a strong breeze blowing from the south and they can smell the diesel salt smell of the docks and the old mud of the flats and it doesn't bother them like it used to because the seagulls wheel and dive and everything feels new.

On the sixth day Cat comes home with the test just as La knew she would, and she doesn't say, *no, don't do it*, or *please wait*, she just sits on the couch with her hands in her lap while she listens to Cat piss and then listens to the silence and then hears the great wail which she knows means she can now go and give comfort and say, *It's okay, it's okay, it doesn't mean anything, we have to wait until the bloods*. And Cat says, *I didn't know how much I wanted it*, and La says *I know*, and doesn't say, *I didn't know how much I'm still not sure*.

On the seventh day, Cat is scheduled for her doctor's appointment. La is scheduled to place a virus into the operating system of her workplace. She has not told Cat. They both fail to finish their morning cups of tea.

'I can't believe you can't come.'

'I guess attractive Health and Wellbeing policies only go so far, huh? Anyway, you know I'm hopeless with nervy things like this. I'll be a mess. You'll catch my chaos.'

'I love your chaos.' Cat leans over the bench and kisses La gently. 'Wish me luck.'

'You don't need luck,' La says, moving around to enfold her in her arms. 'This is science. It has nothing to do with your body working or not working or being good or bad. It's just probability, yeah?' She holds her tight. 'What is it you always tell me – you can seed a cloud but you can't control what happens next?'

Cat rolls her eyes. 'Now I'm your motherfucking cloud?' she says, but she laughs and nestles in for another minute before La has to go.

'I'll take my phone in, call me as soon as you know.'

'You can't take your phone – you'll cop a penalty.'

'Worth it.'

'Well, at least it'll be short, right – pregnant or not pregnant.'

Cat squeezes her hand once more as she leaves.

La checks the extra phone in her pocket, the one she will hand in, hopes that Conna is right that her real phone won't show up in the scanner where it is hidden inside the fake freezer pack in her lunch box. She runs through the plan again in her head.

La will clock on, she will pick and pack and sort until tea break as usual. She will not glance across the room at Reb or Conna or Mina or Donza. She will not check her phone unless she is inside a toilet cubicle. When she checks it at break there will be a message from Conna. It will either say GREEN or RED. If it says RED she will put the phone away and return to her shift and forget the plan. RED is what happened to Reb. RED means something unplanned, uncertain, not good, and they will have to return again to the pub and rethink the plan. If it says GREEN she will take the SD and palm it. She will make as though to return to her place on the packing room floor but she will turn left when she leaves the corridor with the bathrooms instead of right. She will follow the purple line on the floor that leads the RDUs to the loading dock and she will act as though she is supposed to be there. At the fourth doorway on the right she will look at the retinal scanner. If it does not go green she will walk away. If it goes green she will open the door. There will be no one in this room for the next ten minutes. If there is, she will tell them that she has been instructed to check the data log for the supervisor and then she will leave. She will take the exit stairs on the far left of the room down one floor. She will locate the RDU operating system on the far-right screen of the mainframe. She will put on a pair of gloves from her pocket and run her fingers along the panel and find the sixth slot. She will insert the SD. She will wait to see the small light go blue. When it does she will leave the room slowly, the way she came. She will remove the gloves and place them in the rubbish bin on the upper-level corridor. When her supervisor asks her why she is late she will hold her belly and point to the crotch of her pants where she has pre-prepared a half-hearted attempt to remove a bloody stain. He will look away and nod. She will return to her station. She will wait for what comes next.

Every box, every item she packs this morning feels portentous. A party pack of dream catchers (authentic feathers). A SafeBreath baby monitor. A Che Guevara t-shirt. A candle called Smells Like Capitalism. Her RDU gives her a virtual high five.

> You're doing great today! Look at you go!

She taps it on its top even though she is not supposed to touch it. She has come to feel an affinity with her robotic co-worker, wonders if the RDU is as bored, as tired as she is. There are no clocks but she watches the timer tick down on her panel. One hour. Thirty minutes. Ten. Five.

There is a giggle threatening to erupt out of her. She visualises what Donza has described will happen if everything goes to plan. As she walks to the tea room she keeps her eyes down in case she accidentally makes eye contact with one of the others. She makes sure she is seen making a coffee, then she leaves it on the bench, one hand on her belly, and hurries to the toilets. She nods at a woman leaving the bathroom, goes to the farthest cubicle, opens the door, tries the lock, it is broken, goes to the next one, shuts the door, locks it, pulls the phone from the inside pocket of her pants, opens Paranoia, waits for it to update. The message.

GREEN

La first realises it has worked when the power cuts out. Then, once everything flicks back to life and the alarm stops sounding, the RDU closest to La freezes. WANT RDUs are optimised to never stop moving. The stop/start action takes precious mircroseconds. The motionless RDU continues to emit a green light from its top panel, so nothing is out of order, except for what it does next. It slowly circles, one rotation and then another, a supervisor hurries past and doesn't seem to notice. And then the RDU begins to emit a sound as it spins, faster and faster, a whirring sound that gets higher and higher until it becomes a squeal.

The RDU begins to pick randomly from the shelves. Packets of eye masks, a self-flushing toilet, Hawaiian-style lamps, a book on decluttering, nasal decongestant, vitamins for loose stools, adult nappies, eyeshadow palettes, a toy for anxious cats, a t-shirt with the slogan I HATE T-SHIRTS, a figurine of an old woman swallowing a fly.

The RDUs are disgorging the shelves, spinning faster and faster, packages are flying and tumbling, knocking into others, the domino effect of a thousand, a thousand thousand boxes falling and flying. Alarms are ringing, all of them, the Low Efficiency Alert, the Emergency Evacuation, the Hour of Power, chiming at different pitches and intensities. The stewards in their teal tops are yelling into headsets, there are suits rushing around in the windows of the admin block above them, looking down on the chaos, throwing their hands in the air, and the workers, the yellowbacks, are watching. Some of them have their hands over their mouths, some – scabs, La thinks – are clustering near the stewards, pointing, trying to pick up boxes, still working for the man, but others, most of them, and Reb and Mina and Conna and Donza are laughing, clapping their hands, sheltering at the base of stacks and watching the factory destroy itself.

And then – *oh, Conna, you brilliant genius of a human* – above the din of the alarms and the noise, a voice:

Hey there, associates, looks like you need a break. You've automatically been paid double time for the next week while management sort out this mess. We encourage you to withdraw that in cash from your accounts as soon as possible to avoid any problems.

After, it will be PR-massaged into a system malfunction caused by a bug. The spin team will release leaks and rumours that intimate it might have been malware from a competitor or anti-capitalist hackers making a point – a system breach much easier to swallow than a unionised saboteur from the inside.

The workers look up, and those among them who know her

look at La, because it is *her* voice that is ringing out over the madness. Her still kind-of-broken voice inciting this madness.

Take the day off, take the week off! You've earned it.

Some of the yellowbacks whoop and holler and remove their headpieces and throw them down and they run – *fuck OH&S today* – towards the exits. But others look angry or scared, crushed maybe. She knows they are wondering if they will have jobs tomorrow and, Jesus, she believes in the cause but also – fuck – the collateral is real.

In her pocket, her phone vibrates. She sneaks a look.

Cat is calling, answer?

La looks up at the glass windows, at the suits gesticulating wildly at each other, screaming into earpieces, one man with his hands against the glass, frozen, staring. Around her the RDUs zoom away from the shelves, begin to race one after another down the pathways. She knows what that man is seeing as he looks down, she knows because when she'd nearly lost her nerve earlier this week, Conna had held the screen to her so she could see their plan, wanting her to share in their pièce de résistance, knowing that it would only be revealed in full to the suits who looked down to the warehouse floor at the zenith of the madness they had created.

'You are a fucking genius,' she had said then. And Conna had replied, 'I'm just a cog in the wheel, my love.' La watches the faces in the window turn red, one young woman against the glass bringing up her device to film.

Pocket vibrates again.

Cat is calling, call is marked urgent, answer?

She will watch that footage – leaked to the media, viral on every feed within an hour – again and again and every time she will feel something inside her open outwards, unfurling, connecting her to Conna's thrill, to Donza running for the exit, to Mina on Paranoia, messaging, *Fuck me, the money was really there, did you get it, have you got it out?*, to the other yellowbacks, storming from the building and out into the sun.

She imagines Cat coming out of her appointment, holding whatever news she has been told. *Just give me this moment*, La thinks. The red faces look down on the RDUs as they follow each other, swarm, forming a pattern on the warehouse floor amid the rubble of plastic and cardboard and metal and plush. Around and around they go, and will continue to go until management finally cuts power to the whole warehouse and even then it takes another four hours before the batteries run out and the RDUs can be stopped repeating and orbiting, marking the shape – that familiar endless infinity loop – the WANT logo on the factory floor.

There are fire trucks, police, private security now, swarming, corralling the yellowbacks at the entrances, people are crying, yelling, La suddenly realises all that she didn't account for, the tumbling blocks of consequence. She thinks about the exit plans on the thread. Knows she was meant to memorise them. Sees Conna waving madly at her. *This way*, they gesture, *come*. She thinks about probability. About how careful she was with her prints. The cameras. She could walk out now, sit tight, keep quiet. Take the chance that she'll get away with it. Or she could run.

Message from Cat: La. Please pick up.

She plants her feet in the middle of it all, presses call.
'Cat?'

∞

The Island, 2181

Bananas. The name of the strange yellow squashy sweet thing is banana. On their first morning on the Island, the sisters join the Islanders at long tables in a large room and their bowls of warm sticky podge are topped with the pale slices. Onyx's eyes go wide when she takes a mouthful and, true, it is wild and delicious, but Maz's head is so filled with all the sights and smells and sounds she cannot register one as any more strangeweird than the others. They have not seen Hera since she settled them both in a small room with two long pallets for them to sleep on. The beds were soft, with warm blankets, and, despite feeling buzzed awake by the newness of this dark place that dwarfed the Stewards' cave with its tunnels and dens and steps, Maz was soon asleep. In the morning it was a young girl and an older woman who knocked quietly on the door and greeted the sisters.

'You'll be needing feeding,' the older woman said, smiling as the young girl bounced from foot to foot.

'Everyone's excited to meet you. Come on! Wake now!'

*

And so they had spent their first moons on the Island. Hera was a leader of sorts. She did not lead, like JP, with the invisible weight of threat behind her, but rather held the small community with a kind of quiet grace, as though she were tending a flock of animals. The sisters were shown everything by the loud tribe of kids who held their hands and ran from one side of the camp to the other. Camp wasn't the right word, though. Far bigger than the cave tunnels, the Islanders lived in a series of rooms and decks built into the side of a hill, wrapping around and up and down, linked by many rock steps carved into the earth. Everyone had a room – some children and adults together, some adults on their own, some rooms for growing or cooking or meeting.

Maz and Onyx were shown where the bananas grew, in long rooms with clear walls and roofing so that the sun shone through and made it warm inside even when the wind was whipping cold. The bananas grew in big clumps on squat green trees with long leaves that bent over to touch the ground. And there were other strange fruits. Fat round red balls that squished in the mouth and burst seeds over the tongue, long green pods that crunched, red leaves and yellow and green that Maz and Onyx soon learned could taste like all sorts of things. Hera showed them through the kitchen, where there was clanging and steam and good smells, then to a room filled with boxes and wires and all kinds of oddz that JP would have melted down and destroyed.

Onyx ran her fingers over the surfaces, the little coloured lamps, whirring buzzing noises as though there were a whole forest of cicadas inside the boxes.

'What are they for?' Maz asked.

'Radios. They let us communicate.'

'Communicate with who?'

Hera inclined her head. 'Anyone else who has a radio. There are communities like ours. On the island and across the ocean, too.'

'What do you talk about?'

Hera laughs, and the woman who is fiddling with the buttons and making the cicadas louder and softer laughs gently, too. 'Many things,' Hera says. 'Recovery. Survival. New recipes for mushrooms.'

'Could you find someone who is lost?'

'Sometimes,' Hera says, nodding. 'We can try.'

Maz thought about all the times she had lain awake sending out messages in her mind to her dad. Wishing and hoping and pressing her brain trying to make him hear her, to come and get her. She cannot believe that there is a machine that can do that. Can speak across rivers and mountains and even whole oceans.

'You can come back here whenever you want. Ola is our radio-woman. She will help you.'

Ola smiled at Maz as they left the radio room, and Maz tried to stop her whole brain from exploding.

'No one returns to the source here?' Onyx asks at breakfast a couple of days after their arrival, and Hera asks her gently what she means. Maz notices one of the Islanders – a man about Hera's age – wince as though he has stubbed his toe when Hera asks if anyone ever came back from walking the mountain, and Onyx replies, 'No, that's the point.'

Maz unearths the glowing oddz from her pack and lays them on the wooden floor of the meeting room where Hera gently picks each up in turn, examines it, lays it down again, as the sisters tell the story together. Where Onyx misses a beat, Maz chimes in – they finish phrases, add specifics, ask each other to pause so they might go back to add something important. When they come to the end of the story, Hera nods quietly.

'I, too, have heard of this puzzle. But like all stories – it is hard to tell where story and truth begin and end. It is hard to tell what a beginning might be and how far it has travelled from the end.'

'Do you know what this is? Is it true, that it can unmake the world?'

Hera rubs her chin, and for a moment Maz recognises in the gesture a shadow of her father, his thumb and forefinger smoothing down the edges of his beard.

'Some say it is a map,' Hera says, 'some a riddle, some say it is a picture of the stars that reveals a portal to a new world. Some say it rose up out of the earth, patterned by wind and rain and tides and lava, the slow-growing markings of moss and bone. Others insist that a wise woman birthed it from her own flesh.'

Onyx dives into the gap in Hera's story. 'What do *you* say?'

'There is a story in the archive of a person who created a machine to try to save the world before the Collapse.'

'How?'

'They invented a code.'

'A code?'

'A code to program a machine smarter than a human who might be able to turn back time and undo our worst mistake.'

'Did it work?'

'No.'

'Why not?'

'The machine got too smart. It decided the worst mistake was us.'

Maz and Onyx look at each other.

'It was meant to kill all the humans?' Onyx asks.

Hera nods. 'That is the story.'

'But,' says Maz, 'we are still here.'

'Yes,' Hera continues. 'It destroyed itself rather than do what it was meant to do.'

Maz picks up one of the oddz, turns it in her hands. 'Then this is part of the broken machine?'

'These parts are not from the machine itself. That existed only in code. These are merely a kind of advertisement for it, collected and displayed by people who believed in and supported the project. There are hundreds, thousands just like them out there.'

'What's an advertisement?'

'In the beforetimes we did not just share like most do now. Beforetimers *traded*, always something in exchange for something else. Advertising was the way they were convinced to want the somethings in the first place.'

'They were Wanters.'

'Maybe. Your leader has mixed truth and myth and hope and greed up into a powerful story and fused it to these pieces.'

'They cannot end the world?'

'No. Humans did that all on their own.'

A child races into the room. 'The birds, Hera! The birds have come!'

Hera smiles. 'Then we must go and see.' She ushers Maz and Onyx up, collecting the oddz in her hands and holding them out to the sisters.

'Do you still want them, Maz?' Onyx asks.

Maz hesitates. The flicker of want still there.

Hera places them in her hands. 'For remembering,' she says, and Maz nods, dropping them into her pocket and following the others out to the cliff edge to watch the birds returning.

It has been two cycles now with the Islanders. There have been two boat journeys out since then, and each time Hera has asked if the sisters would like to return to the inlet or to anywhere else, but they find that they want to stay.

And there are the children, a whole laughing gaggle of them who climb on Maz like she is a tree, who tickle and beg to be tickled, who hide and want to be found, who run and dance and ask why and say no and when they are hurt or surprised and too hungry or tired they just cry. They help Maz to cry, too.

It is decided that the sisters should learn their letters with the archivists. The sisters are much older than all the littles in the school room just sounding out their words, and Hera thinks they will enjoy the stories and the work the archivists spend their days with, and slowly learn their letters at the same time. The archivists keep their work in special cupboards to keep it safe, and they are careful as they bring out great books, and a screen that they power with kite wind and turbines and batteries; a screen that shows strange numbers and letters and words.

The elder archivist – the Keeper – smiles at Maz. 'Your sister tells us your parents were Finders?'

'Yes,' says Maz, 'but Onyx doesn't really remember them.'

'Do so!' says Onyx.

Maz ignores her. 'Father went journeying with them when she was just a little. That's when the Stewards took us.'

The Keeper nods her head but does not look away.

Maz points at one great book with a thick red cover, old-old as mountains maybe, and asks if she may look. The Keeper hands her a pair of small gloves so that her hands don't hurt the paper.

'What we have of the beforetimes is precious,' the Keeper says. 'It is our job to keep it safe.'

When Maz turns over the cover of the book, her pulse quickens in her neck. Inside the cover there is a long list of names, written in different hands and different inks.

'What is this?' Maz asks, pointing to the list.

'It is family. Back through time. This is a way the family who owned this book recorded who came before, and who was born. A way to keep track of where we come from, and who we are.'

Maz tells the Keeper she has something to show her, something to ask, and she runs back to the tent and grabs the wax fabric package she has taken from her hem and now keeps safe under her pillow.

Onyx is looking at her strangely when she returns. 'Why the quick?' she asks her softly, the question on her face.

Carefully, her hands still in the gloves, Maz unwraps the package and holds it out to the Keeper.

'What's that?' Onyx asks.

'It is from Ma and Pa,' Maz says, and looks at the Keeper. 'Is this the same list?'

The Keeper takes the package very carefully and holds it to her face. She looks at it for a long time. 'These are your names, and your Ma and Pa's at the bottom?' she finally asks.

Maz nods.

'You have good eyes, good sense, child. Yes, I think this is such a list. Your Ma never told you? A way to keep all the generations together. It goes all the way back, see the dates here too, some of them, although there are gaps, of course, during the times of Collapse, but your Ma kept it safe. She was a Keeper. Maybe you are too. See how it goes right back to these two names at the top?'

The Keeper hands the paper back, and Onyx crowds in next to her to look. Maz traces her gloved finger to the very first names on the list.

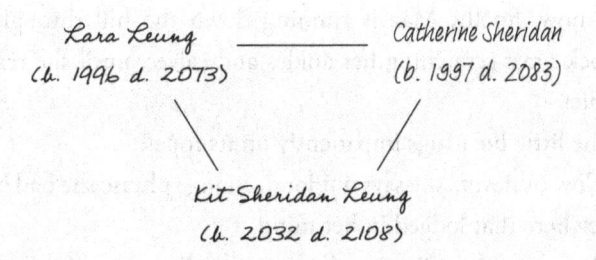

Lara Leung   *Catherine Sheridan*
(b. 1996 d. 2073)   (b. 1997 d. 2083)

Kit Sheridan Leung
(b. 2032 d. 2108)

Maz thinks that sounds like a very long time ago, but also, somehow, not so far at all.

*

A clear day. Storm season has calmed for now. A quick breeze ripples the grasses and Maz grins.

'Take me with you!' Onyx yells, peeling away from the tangle of children she is playing with in the vegetable garden, pulling weeds, yes, but mostly playing tag.

'Not this time.'

'But I can sail, too,' Onyx yells, her shoulders slumping as she jogs down the hill towards her sister.

'I know you can.'

Onyx pulls her sad face. 'What if you don't come back?'

Maz laughs. 'Have I ever not come back?'

Onyx flicks her hair, turns away, mock anger. 'Anyway I don't care – stupid sea, it makes you sick, I don't know why you want to go out there.'

Maz calls after her and Onyx stops, turns, listens. 'You know why. Because one day, soon, we will take this boat and we will find Father.'

Onyx looks at her steadily for a moment then rushes forward to quickhug her round the waist, before racing back up the hill to the children who are calling her name.

And now, finally, Maz is running down the hill through the tussock grass scratching her ankles and calves, until she reaches the pier.

The little boat tugs impatiently on its ropes.

'Now or never,' she says out loud, strange phrase she had heard somewhere that lodged in her mind.

Up up up the sail goes, the lines spooling out. Maz gasps as the patchwork of colours blooms full and perfect. She is transfixed by the sight of it above her, like a bird, like a fish. She does not have much control yet, fights a little against the wind, then finds the spot, feels it begin to work with her.

A feeling like a bubble about to pop grows in her belly and chest and then escapes as a great whooping noise from her, flying up and *flat-atat-tat*ing in and out of her astonishing patchwork sail.

Sanctuary Gardens Aged Care, 2020

Day 45

She remembers a day at the river. Bright sunlight glinting off the surface, so she cannot see all the faces but she knows who is there. Lil, on a grassy patch there on the bank, no bathing suit, can't swim and refuses to try – *Can't teach an old dog new tricks*, she says when Hilda says she can learn – but she's got a basket there, egg and lettuce sandwiches under a damp cloth. And Hilda is happy. Scribbling away, probably sketching a branch of a tree, some curious leaf she's picked up.

And there's Mum, out there in the river up to her waist, hair knotted up and her skin, blimey, pale as cream down to her wrists and up to her neck. Hilda has promised to teach her to float. Evelyn is splashing about, yahooing with the other girls from her class who have come with them on the train to this little spot on the Yarra, not pristine by any means, but cleaner than their river over in the west by a long shot.

Hilda wants her mum to feel the relief, the glory of being suspended in the water. Stiff joints, sore back, all those years walking messages for bosses or hunched over her desk.

You ready, Mum?

Her mother turns, the water shadow ripples across her face. She reaches out to grab Hilda's fingers and squeeze them.

Gentle, gentle, lowering in, arms to cradle, then hands, then fingertips, then—

Ah.

See?

She floats; just for a moment, she floats.

ACQSC Incident ID: ▮
Notification status: closed

SL: SIRS incident IMS no 875 ▮

9.3 Have you 'closed the loop'? Analyse incident trends to identify and address systemic issues.

Okay here's the system issue you arse of a stupid system there are NOT ENOUGH STAFF to look after the people in our care who are sick and broken and demented and who shit themselves and fall and cry and scream and scratch and want to go home and want to go back to the past where they were loved and when their flesh didn't fail them and I cannot believe I still work in this fucked up hellhole of a system we are drowning here we are keeping something afloat that shouldnt be for fucks sake tonight I have one pca and one nurse for 82 fucking residents tell me how to close the loop you fucking arsehole system of fuckedness you TELL ME how you are addressing the SYSTEMIC ISSUES that mean I have residents dying on my watch and staff members who go home and ring me sobbing and say I'm so sorry ive tested positive I cant come in what will you do what will you do – you CLOSE THE FCUKING LOOP give us more money DO SOMETHING this cannot go on

Select all>delete

In response to Incident No. 875, the following actions have been taken or are planned to minimise the risk of re-occurrence of this or a similar incident in the future:

- A discussion was conducted with Ms McCarthy regarding her personal care, her rights in relation to the Aged Care Quality Standards (No. 1) and the responsibilities of staff to ensure her health and wellbeing. Referral to a psychogerontologist. Head RN and Anna Perrera (Ms McCarthy's representative) were satisfied with the decision that PCA staff would offer and supervise bed washing for Ms McCarthy and continue to offer a shower each day. Ms McCarthy understands it is her right to refuse.
- The Incident Management System has been updated and a memo communicated to all staff to remind them of the importance of adhering to consumer choice in personal care matters, regardless of cognitive impairment. Professional development training and refresher on Standard 1 has been offered.
- Ms McCarthy's delirium means that while she believes showering is 'washing away her memories', she would very much like to swim in the river. Her family representative, Anna Perrera, supports day leave for this to happen, however, given the current lockdown and CHO orders, this is not possible at this time. This will be reviewed at the end of two weeks.
- Suggestion from PCA to be taken to working committee: Future personal care refusal progress notes to incorporate a follow-up question: *Can you imagine a different way we can help you get what you need?*

*

Day 46

We have to flatten the curve trace the contacts find a vaccine buy the vaccine convince the population to have the vaccine update the system so the people who want to can get the vaccine in their arm get a jab we are sorry to tell you hold the line hold our nerve hold them in our thoughts thoughts and prayers don't pay the bills ten new cases forty new cases one thousand seven hundred and eighty new cases in the past twenty-four hours to midnight there have been seventy-seven thousand two hundred and thirty-eight test results received one thousand six hundred and twenty-four new cases acquired locally fifteen thousand and seventy-four active cases two lives lost thirteen thousand loaves of sourdough baked (sixty-seven percent success rate) one hundred and fifty thousand UberEats orders seven hundred and eighty-nine new memes shared in eight million WhatsApp threads five point four five percent reduction in carbon emissions a twenty to forty per cent increase in the value of regional housing just give us back playgrounds football hairdressers cafes more than five kilometres more than ten kilometres school dancing theatre our livelihoods our hospitals our mum we are all in the same ocean but some of us have different boats my boat is leaking my boat has sunk but think of the children the new parents the unemployed the homeless the cancelled weddings the eighteenths the love affairs the newly split up the lonely my friend lost her job lost her marriage lost her mum lost her child had cancer had a trip planned had a baby couldn't graduate couldn't leave couldn't come home it's good news it's bad news it's not what I wanted to stand up here and tell you today we have to do what we must to protect the system the frontline workers don't call an ambulance if you don't need an ambulance don't be stupid don't put lives at risk arm yourself arm your children check in checkout check on your neighbour on your family stay alert stay home stay positive stay one point five metres away in the driveway on the other side of the glass can't do it alone can't do it anymore be positive stay negative it's actually working for me what have we learned from lockdown one lockdown two from Italy from WA from the experts from what worked from what did not work from YouTube from my chiropractor from that influencer who said that the virus is a conspiracy a message from God a chance to re-evaluate your life to spend more time with your kids to recognise what is important very real not as bad as we thought worse than we ever imagined remember what it was like what we said before this all happened when everything was normal everything is broken everything will be okay

Day 47

Anna
2 cases at SG. And it's a no for special leave for Hil.
10.17am

Trace
Fuck it. They can't stop us picking her up.
Can we just bring her home?
10.23am

Anna
Not until the rules change.
10.24am

But even then. How?
10.25am

To me? To you?
10.26am

Benny

Word is things'll shift soon.

Maybe it's time.

10.27am

To bring her home, I mean.

10.28am

Trace

I could do it, A.

10.41am

                         Anna

Can you care for an 86yo at your house?
Can you lift her? Clean her? It's 24/7 Benny.
And Trace I know you would, but also it's hard.
It would be really hard. I don't know if I could do it.

10.50am

It's all so fucked.

10.52am

Look what I found.
going through old boxes 😵 😵 😵

11.02am

Anna has sent an attachment

```
Hilda McCarthy: Famous lepidopterist
By Anna Harrison Year 7C
```

```
Hilda Lilian McCarthy was born in 1933. She had an early
love of drawing the natural world around her, specially
insects, and after secondary school she did a Science
degree at the University of Melbourne in 1950. She was
the first person in her family to go to university.
```

At the time, women made up only twenty per cent of university students in Australia.

Hilda travelled a lot. She worked as a research assistant to scientists at universities in Europe and North America. She met her husband, Ian, when she was overseas and they got married in Australia in 1965.

Hilda continued her research in Australia with the **CSIRO**. She was interested in the decline of bogong moths in their annual migration and raised awareness about this issue.

She also mentored Women in Science and many former students have gone on to distinguished careers in their field, something Hilda is very proud of.

Why I Chose This Inspiring Woman

Everyone else in my class chose a famous woman for this project but I wanted to choose someone who I had a personal connection to. Hilda is my Great Aunt and I have always known that she is a special person. I think I have inherited Hilda's love of the natural world and her talent for drawing, as well as her **determination** and **perseverance**, especially working in a career that not many women were working in at the time. When I grow up I would like to be a scientist but I'm not sure what area I would like to specialise in yet.

Trace
😢😢😢😢😢😢😢
🖤🖤🖤🖤🖤🖤🖤

11.44am

Anna
I wanted to be a scientist 😣
11.49am

Day 48

To: admin@sanctuarygardens.com.au
From: perrera.a@thinkwise.com.au

Subject: Printing for Hilda McCarthy

Hi Mina,
As discussed just now via phone can you please print out message below and attachment and give to Hilda McCarthy RM 612.

Many thanks,
Anna Perrera

Dear Aunty Hil,

Remember way back when I did that interview with you all about your life for a school project? I just found it in an old box. Thought you would enjoy remembering. We'll see you so soon.

All my love,
Anna xx

Day 49

Oh my love.
You're here. Where have you been?
It's been awful. Just

shit,

really.

Desperate to get out and check on the veggies, no one will have been looking for cabbage moth on the broccoli seedlings, I just know it.

Here, sit. I'll make us a cuppa in a minute, just sit with me now. I've missed you! Remember, that first year in Wood Street and we'd both get home from work and kiss, goodness how we'd kiss, right at the front door and we'd say I missed you! And we'd be shocked by it? Remember that? How much we could miss each other in just one day.

We did all right. Didn't we?

I think we did. All in all.

Sometimes better than others. But we stuck it out.

I wondered, often, if it was the right thing to do, to stick it out. Is that the measure of a person, if they stay true to their word? Or should they stay true to themselves?

Because, my love,

there were times I would have gone. Taken to the hills and the road and my research and not looked back.

Life seemed to get so very small, despite all the noise, didn't it?

I'm glad I stayed too.

And that you are here.

And you too, Mum?

That you?

Here, let me take her.

Let me take my little sister. Oh, I've missed you, my darling, my love.

Here, squiggle in, there now.

I've got you.

It's okay now.

I'm here.

*

Later

In room 612, ants crawl from the bedsore on Hilda's hip.

There are eight new cases. Agency couldn't staff the shift. One personal care attendant for the whole place. Someone has had a fall, someone else a medical emergency (it is, all of it, a medical emergency) and room 612 has been missed.

No one has been inside this room for twelve hours. No food. No water. No last cup of tea. Hot and strong, only enough milk to cover the bottom of the cup, just the way she likes it. Mina on the admin desk flagged the email when she saw it but didn't have time to go back to it; tomorrow she will feel sick about it and delete the email, not knowing how to apologise to the family who she hopes has forgotten.

Hilda is eighty-six years old. She was six when she captured a moth from a leaf of the plum tree in the corner of the yard in Railway Place. It was a soft creature, gentle on her palm. A tiny black spot on the white of each wing. She whispered, *Hello, moth,* and decided it would be her pet.

In four more hours, the PCA who has been on shift for more than eighteen hours and in charge of seventy residents will enter Hilda's room and find that she has died.

She will gently clean the ants from her wound.

∞

Footscray, 1933

'But I don't, I've already—' says Peggy as the nurse helps her out of her dress next to the big iron bath.

'Everyone has to, luv, a squirt of phenol and you'll be done.'

'Phenol? What for? My mum used to clean the toilet with that!'

'Just to be safe, for the baby, love, everyone has to do it.'

If she wasn't caught right then by another surge of pain, Peggy would have cried. Naked and cold amid the caustic smell of the phenol, she puts one hand down to hold the edge of the bath and the nurse catches her other elbow, half holds her up, doesn't mind that she's starkers. Peggy has a clear thought through the pain that this is a small kindness she will remember.

'Come now, before you start shivering, the warm water'll do you good.'

And it does, it does, and she lies in it, not caring about the stink even, and they have slowed down, the pains, there is more time to breathe between them, maybe she could sleep in here. Will they let her sleep?

'Pop your legs up here, there's a good girl,' says the nurse, scooping Peggy's feet out of the water to place them on the edge of the bath. She resists, but the nurse's hold is firm and Peggy scrabbles her hands to steady herself and make sure she doesn't slip back and under the water.

'Now hold still, else you'll get a cut,' the nurse says, and suddenly she has a wide silver razor in her hand, and Peggy squeals and pulls away.

'Just a shave, love, didn't your mother tell ya?'

Peggy shakes her head in disbelief.

'I tell you what,' the nurse mutters as she holds Peggy's leg in one hand and places the one with the blade in the water, 'this job'd be easier if you lot knew what was going on before you got in here.' She pauses and looks directly at Peggy. 'I've got to shave you down below. I'll be quick, done it a thousand times, and then you'll be nice and clean when the doctor examines you.'

Peggy does not believe what she is being told, but is terrified enough to hold still and when she feels the cold blade between her legs, she understands well enough.

It cannot get worse than this, she thinks. I'll pray again, if you'll just let this be the worst of it.

It is not the worst of it.

Sweet Jesus, why did no one ever tell her, why on earth did they not say? How are all of those women walking around talking about anything else except for this unbearable – Jesus, impossible – pain? Peggy knows this baby will not come out of her, that she cannot go on. Will not go on a moment more. But when she tries to tell the nurse her face is like an old cat, all I-know-something-you-don't-know, and she just smiles at her like she's a six-year-old asking for more pudding. The nurse tells her to stop fussing, the baby will come when it's good and ready and she ought to keep her voice down, there's other mothers here doing exactly what she's doing and they're not making half the noise.

Peggy wants to scream, but her breath is gone because here it comes again, a fierce cramp from the top of her ribs all the way down her belly to below. She wants to move, needs to move but they've clamped her feet up and she's flat on her back and now there's a doctor with his white coat and glasses and his greasy moustache and she can see a crumb that's caught, and she wants to shout at him, *Go away, don't touch me,* but then his head disappears behind the sheet and the nurse holds her knee tight, and she can feel the doctor, good God, touching her, rummaging in her, and she wants to cry, she wants her mother, wants Lil, wants Jack, wants anything anywhere but here.

'A while to go yet,' the doctor says and the nurse nods and Peggy is trying to be good, trying to keep her voice down as she says, *What do you mean, how much longer? I can't, I can't.* But the nurse is shushing her again and the doctor frowns and says something to the nurse about calling him if she needs something stronger and *Help*, Peggy wants to say, *help me, someone, I can't do this, I cannot.*

'You the one waiting on Peggy King?'

Lil's head jerks up and she wipes her mouth.

'Yes, yes. Is she—'

'A little girl. Or not that little as it turns out, gave her mum a right time of it, but all is well. You can go home now, love, and tell the family.'

Lil stands up. 'Can I see her?'

'Oh no, not now, wards are closed, baby is in the nursery. Come back tomorrow during visiting hours, six o'clock.'

'Surely I can go and see her now?'

But the woman is already bustling her toward the door. 'No mothers, no husbands. We run a tight ship on these wards, dear, best for everyone. Come back tomorrow.'

And then Lil is out on the street in the night and she draws her coat around her for it's cold and dark now and a day has passed, more than that – perhaps that is dawn she can see in the sky. She turns to look up at the building behind her, the dim light coming from the windows on the higher floors. She would yell if she thought Peggy might hear her.

She is safe. The baby is safe. And now the great balloon of relief. A daughter.

She turns to tell someone, to yell it out, but there is no one there. And no taxis, and no train, and she has nowhere to go but home. She begins to walk.

You can always rely on the grapevine. Even if you're in the doghouse and you're miles away and pining to be back in the stink of your home town, it's really only ever a couple of gossips away.

This is how word gets to Jack King, at the end of a shift at Herds meatworks down in Geelong, that he's a father.

It's knock-off and they're at the Sailor's Arms and the barman leans across to serve his pint. 'You one of the boys from Footscray?' he asks, and when Jack nods the barman continues. 'There a bloke here by the name of Jack King?'

'Yeah,' he says, not offering more because you can never be sure who's asking and what they might want.

The barman shrugs, pours another beer and slides it across the bar. 'Well, you can give him that from us. To wet the baby's head.'

For a moment, he's too stunned to speak. Then he takes the beer. Grins. 'It's me,' he says, raising the glass. 'I'm Jack King.'

'Well,' says the barman, 'it's congratulations to you, then. A little girl. Someone rang and left a message for you. Best get yourself home.'

And for a moment he thinks it must be Lil, that she's rung and all is forgiven, that he can come back, to the house, to Peggy. 'You know who rang?'

'Wilson, maybe, Wilkins? Some bloke.'

But no. It's just the Footscray grapevine.

He downs the beer. Buys another round, returns to the table triumphant, spreads his news. He is jubilant. The thought of it, him, a father. Blows his mind, truth be told. A little girl.

'Better earn yourself some good coin and get back there, son.'

'Turn up at the hospital with flowers, she'll take yer back no worries.'

'Too right, something happens to them. The milk or something, makes them all lovely and barmy. You'll be right.'

And Jack comforts himself that this is so. That he can, at least, make this thing right.

Peggy wakes to an ache deep inside her and a mouth as a dry as a desert.

'My baby,' she murmurs as she struggles to pull herself up to sitting.

'Down in the nursery, luv, they'll bring her up when you've had your breakfast.'

Peggy turns to see a woman her mother's age in the bed next to her. She doesn't remember seeing the woman before, or how she got to this bed, this room, but she remembers the squalling creature that she pushed out between her legs and seeing its squished-up little face all covered in gunk before they whipped it away.

She nods at the woman, but there's a fear in her now, cold and liquid in her veins. 'Nurse! Nurse!' she calls.

'I promise ya, luv, yelling won't help, they bring them all up together when they're good and ready.'

But Peggy is sure now, that Lil has been a turncoat and done what she gently suggested all those months ago and arranged an adoption, or that her mother has come and whisked the baby away, or Jack, good God, has come and claimed his child while she slept, taken the baby somewhere away from her.

A girl – one clear and steady thought – *it's a girl.*

A nurse appears at the foot of her bed, all starched and severe. 'What is it?'

'Can I see my baby?' She is appalled that her own voice sounds so childlike.

The nurse purses her lips. 'After you've eaten. You need to bring that milk in or you'll be no use to the child at all.'

She marches away and the woman in the next bed is kind enough not to say anything until Peggy turns around.

'Do you know how long until breakfast?'

The woman smiles. 'Shouldn't be too long, now. Not that it's much these days. Gosh, I remember when I came here for my first, was ten years ago now, two courses of breakfast they gave you! Egg and porridge and toast. Reckon that's why I've had so many, wanted to keep coming back for a good feed.' She laughs until she begins to cough. 'Tell your husband to bring you something nice when he comes in tonight. They're not doing supper now, with the rations, only bread and butter, probably margarine, unless you got someone looking after you.'

Peggy nods. She cannot believe she has to wait until tonight before she can see Lil. None of it seems real, as though she's stumbled into a different world altogether.

'Your fella got work, then?'

Peggy nods. She'll deal with the absence of her husband in visiting hours. Right now, she wants tea, doesn't think she's ever wanted a cup of tea as badly as this in all of her life.

'Lucky for some. Mine's been gone six months now, headed north, out of the city to try and find work. Been hard on me and the kids, but not as hard as if I'd had to stretch the susso to feed his whinging mouth as well as the rest of them.'

'How many children do you have?' Peggy asks.

'This one's number six. Told him no more at five, but seems even if I was too bloody starved to get my rags, I could still get a bloody baby.'

Later she will not be sure if it is the bringing of her baby or the bringing of the tea which thrills her the most, but there is a sweet spot – when the baby is snuffling and sniffing and opening her little mouth, and the tea is still warm in her belly – before the gnawing pain of the baby clamping on her nipple, and before the indignity of them taking away her pan and the bloodied rags from between her legs. There is a moment there when she feels utterly swollen with love for this being.

But there isn't long to sit with it because they take her away again. It seems bizarre, this room full of women who've all just given birth, all of them sitting there without their babies in their arms.

'You'll be glad of it when you get home, luv.'

'Gawd, yes. Best bit, this bit! Would do it all again in a second to have someone make me a proper cup of tea and have time to bloody drink it!'

They tease her gently because it's her first, but they also gift her titbits of wisdom that later she will cling to as though they are the only things that will pull her through.

'Day three you're going to start to cry, dear, it's just part of it, no need to worry, it's your milk coming in.'

'You make sure your bloke keeps away from you, too. Old wives' tale that you can't get preggers again while you've got your milk, got me three times before I understood.'

She laughs ruefully with them, recognising that this, of all things, won't be a problem for her now.

*

After lunch they bring in a girl on a trolley and she moans in pain without pause.

The woman next to her, Beryl she knows now, lowers her voice. 'That'll be sepsis for sure, poor love. Seen it before, she'll have tried to get rid of it.'

God, the noises the girl is making, sounds worse than what it felt to push the thing out. After her next visit from the baby and the dreadful hour of sucking and gnawing at her breasts, but before she's even seen Lil, a tight little group of doctors and matrons come in and look at the woman and mutter things quiet and urgent and then they whisk her away.

She does not come back.

Between five thirty and six Peggy watches every second tick on the big clock on the wall opposite and she is beside herself, nearly weeping with relief when Lil walks through the door at four minutes past, a basket in her arms.

'You're here,' she says.

'Of course I'm here. Would have been here last night, if they'd have let me in.' Lil grips Peggy's hand. 'How are you feeling?'

And Peggy wants to tell her all of it, every minute, the shock, the ridiculousness of it all, how in these interminable hours today she wanted Lil and she wanted Jack and she wanted her mother, all of them there, telling her she'd done a good job, telling her it is all going to be okay. But she can see Lil trying not to pounce on the bassinet and so she lets her go.

'Meet Hilda Lilian,' she says and gestures towards the bassinet where the baby sleeps, wrapped perfectly neatly by the nurses, ready for this, her first showing.

Peggy and Hilda return to Railway Place and day is night and night is day and she does not know what time it is or who she is or what to do with this creature. Wishes fervently that she could put it back where it came from, but no, not that, just undo it. Undo its beginnings, the skin, the magnetic pull of Jack King, undo those indecisions, one stacked against the other, her failure to choose, which meant that each day the baby grew, the life beyond it narrowed.

Lil is in raptures. At least one of them is. Peggy wonders whether if Jack were here she might feel more able, more alive, might scorn his clumsy big hands, or tut at him as he failed to soothe the baby. In that way, she might shore up her sense of herself as capable of the job. But he is not here. And Lil is capable enough for both of them. At ease, only days into this strange new existence, taking the bundled creature from Peggy's arms, her throbbing chest. Lil brings her tea, and soup, changes her sheets, tells her to rest, and Peggy feels invalided by her new state. Nothing strong or maternal about it. Her mother came to visit and bothered over her wincing face as the little mouth sucked outrageously at her breast.

'You'll get used to it,' her mother said briskly, tidying the already folded cloths on the sideboard. 'Heaven knows we've all done it.'

That's just it, Mother, she wanted to say. *You've all done it, so why did you not say? Why on earth did you all keep it such a bloody secret that having a child means having your body torn apart and your brain upended?*

She knows the response she'd get. 'Oh, stop being so *dramatic*, dear. You'll feel right as rain in a few days.'

And she did stop being dramatic. That didn't stop the feelings, though, and she determined that she would remember those strange awful days, that she would tell, that she would be honest to the next woman who asked.

Jack is well shaven, combed and pressed, carries a posy of pink carnations and a doll his mother helped him choose. He told her the baby was too young for such a thing but his ma said it was the thought that counted, to show he'd paid for something nice.

As he approaches the gate, he imagines eyes behind curtains, the gossip rustling up the street like wind in a flurry of autumn leaves. But he does not pause.

The gate, the brick path, the grass grown high and weeds straggling up between the bricks – this bolsters him. They need him.

But when he knocks on the door and hears Peggy's voice say, 'Who's there?' through the timber, he realises that things might not be as easy as that.

'It's me, Pegs. It's Jack.'

Silence. More footsteps.

'I've brought a present for the baby.'

'Go away, Jack.'

Her voice sounds like rocks dropping in a river. Deadweighted.

'I just want to see her, Pegs.'

Noises behind the door. Lil, the meddler.

'She'll let you know when she wants you to visit, Jack.'

That sly bitch, he thinks. Putting ideas in his wife's head.

'Peggy, please let me see her, I'm her dad. That's not changed.'

'Peggy and the baby are doing fine.'

He puts his hand hard against the door. 'You can't do this, Lil! She's my wife!'

Peggy's voice again. 'Soon, Jack. I'll let your ma know. Leave us be, now.'

The way she says 'us'. As though the three of them are a family and here he is on the outside of the door. He pounds both fists against the door.

Peggy yells, 'Go away, Jack!'

A voice behind him and he turns to see a couple of the men from down the road are standing across the street, arms crossed. 'Better be off, mate,' one of them calls out. 'Sounds like you're not needed, not right now.'

And he turns back and kicks the door now, once, hard as he can, and hears the yelp from the other side. Can sense the men behind him begin to move.

But then he hears it, the baby crying. His daughter, her cries echoing through the door that is shutting him out. Straight to the core of him. Memory like an incision; five years old, his dad sneaking him onto the kill floor, the tears as he watched him slit the throat of a sheep that first time, big hands picking him up from the greasy floor and carrying him out into the light.

Jack walks away from the sound of his crying child, both hands held up in surrender to the men who watch him go, and he knows that he'll do whatever it takes.

This town in spring. Footy is done, and there's not yet the *thwack* of cricket on the ovals, but there is light, warmth. Even the river, with all its muck, puts on a sparkle in this sun. The strike is over at the works, the machines run smooth again. Those union slaughts have found somewhere else to take their gripes, for not one of them has crossed through those gates again; not yet, but the day will come. Let the boss flex those muscles a little longer, let him preen over his new system because the chain is here and here to stay.

Most of the wives have coin in their pockets again, not stretching the weekly groceries between heaven knows how many mouths, plus those down the picket, mind you. The slaughtermen's wives have said their piece – *well now, you go and find yourself another honest day's work, then* – and the wives of the boners, the pluckers, the tallowmen, the drivers, they are just relieved that their men no longer have to weigh their solidarity against their bloody jobs.

So, flowers and good meat and the sound now of a gurgling laugh at 16 Railway Place. The nurse down at Tweddle says it's only wind, but Lil won't have a bar of it, that baby is laughing, is smiling, she is putting out her hands to touch the world and Lil's heart is blooming.

Peggy too, like she is waking up from a slumber, her eyes in the bright sunshine where Lil sits with her in the afternoons, hurrying home from work now, *things to do, Dulcie, for the little one*. It's as though the sun is warming up the girl's bones, all her aching, tired bits, making her see again, this child in front of her, reaching her arms up.

And has it only been a month? For this new order to heave and erupt and then settle into its place?

Something is loosening, sloughing off in Footscray. They are nearing the end of 1933 and things are looking up in this town, finally, gloriously, there may yet be peace and prosperity and a cheeky wager down the Punt on a Saturday night.

Not for Jack King, though. He's made himself scarce, is lying low. Licking his wounds, making his plans, because you don't shame a man like Jack King, shame him twice over, as slaughterman and sire, and expect him to let it go.

They keep their ears pricked for trouble at number sixteen but as each day passes and there are still no shadows on the threshold they start to think that maybe they earned this happiness, perhaps this moment of content is something they've been granted, and they stop waiting for the wolf at the door.

Lil remembers the morning she watched a horse train in the shallows at Altona with her father. The cold breath of the dawn when they pulled up overlooking the beach, the magic of the gold-pink light that streamed across the water and the black silhouette of the horse and the rider pushing through the waves. A prince, an enchanted steed, the air and the water swarming with light. She remembers it now as the crowd gasps and heaves as one, they strain to see the racetrack, to hear the crackle of the radios translating the rush of sleek colour they can just make out, those without binoculars, those not perched on shoulders.

Peggy leans close over the pram, but the baby sleeps, amid the roar and the jostle, and Peggy looks at Lil and they both laugh, an exhausted, elated laugh.

Later, Lil watches Peggy talking to the girls from bagging, holding Hilda in her arms and letting them all *goo* and *gaaa* over the little bundle. The park is still full of revellers and it smells like summer and she feels happy, is happy, wishes it might go on for ever. Just like this.

And then, there next to her, the bulk of the man.

'Lil, I'll not make a scene.'

Jack King.

Four months away from his wife have changed the man, that's clear. He's thin in the face. Eyes dark. But he's made an effort, hair is slicked back and he's had a close shave. Looks like a man who's determined.

'What are you doing here, Jack?' Instinctively she moves towards Peggy, but Jack puts his hand on her wrist.

'Please, Lil. I just want to see her. I've been good to my word, I've stayed clear, but it's been four months, Lil. I want to see my girl.'

Lil looks to her left. She could shout, there are enough coppers about, enough men from the works. But what would she say? Jack's as much right to be here as any of them.

'I won't even touch her. I just want to see her face. I'm her dad, Lil.'

Dad. The word unpicks a seam in Lil's memory. Eight years old in the cabin of the delivery van with her father, her mother in the hospital resting to protect a baby who would never arrive. Night!

Pinpoints of light in enormous darkness. More than she could ever have imagined. Another world, and though she had fallen asleep, wrapped in two blankets in the open cab of the truck, it had lodged inside her. Something safe and familiar – her dad steering the truck, the low murmur of the engine, the percussion of sounds when he stopped, idled the engine, tap-tapped his feet around to the rear doors, the vibrating thump and release as he hauled the cuts and the boxes from the back and dropped them at their destination. *Stupid thing to take the child*, her mother had said, spitting her grief into something tangible. He'd tried, though.

Just then, one of the girls looks over and her eyes go wide at the sight of Jack. She leans her head in close to Kathleen, who is next to her. Kathleen's eyes narrow and Lil can feel Jack bristling as he tries to stay still, tries to keep his breath steady.

Peggy turns around.

Jack straightens up and he makes a small noise in the back of his throat, which Lil thinks might be grief, or hope, and whatever it is it stops her yelling or throwing her body in front of Jack as he steps forward.

Peggy shifts the bundle in her arm, and puts one hand out to Kathleen, staying her. As she steps forward, she is serene. There is nothing of the sleepless, teary mess she's been, nothing of the woman who still looks like a girl as she walks the hallway at night and cries to Lil that she has no idea how to make this damn baby stop fussing. No, the woman who steps forward looks like she knows exactly what she is doing, it's only Lil that's terrified of what that might be.

'Peggy,' she says at exactly the same time Jack King does.

'It's all right, Lil,' Peggy says, her voice still clear amid the bustle and whooping of the crowd. She stops a couple of paces in front of Jack. The girls from bagging are all watching now,

Kathleen and some of the others with concerned expressions, but the rest of them, Lil suspects, just there for the gossip that will come from whatever happens next.

'Jack, this is your daughter, Hilda Lilian,' Peggy says, gently moving the swaddle from the baby's face so that he might see.

Lil watches Jack crane forward, bringing his hands up, then stopping them as Peggy moves back. He nods his head, crossing his arms over his chest and clasping his upper arms instead. From where Lil stands, she can see his fingers pushing deep into his own flesh, and she knows, she understands completely, the want in him to touch that child.

She cannot hear what passes between them now. The crowd buzzes and she can see the girls leaning forward too, but the wife and the husband have lowered their voices, safe here in plain sight, but also, for a moment, intensely private.

Peggy does not give him the child, but she holds her out and Jack leans right in. Lil doesn't breathe until he straightens up again, steps back. Peggy's face is open, she nods, she smiles. Oh God, Lil thinks, what have you said, Jack King?

And then he dips his head as though he's bowing to Peggy and the baby and he turns and walks back toward Lil.

He stops in front of her, and it is neither threat nor promise when he says, 'I'm going to make it right, Lil.'

He's going to make everything right again. Not just with Peggy and Hilda, he'll make it right with Lil, he'll get his job back on the floor, he'll put everything back to the way it was.

He walks away from the crowd, shrugging off the men who call after him, who wonder why on earth Jack King is walking away from the biggest party in Footscray right now, but he has thinking to do. As focused as he might be with a sheep between his legs and his knife on the pulse.

There's a boy, Sullivan, in packing, who reckons he can get him in with the night crew, and once he's in through the gate he'll be right. He knows a hundred places he could hide, knows when the foreman will walk by, knows when the kill floor will be shut for the night, where Brian, night watchman, slack bastard, isn't likely to shine his torch.

A well-placed crow bar will do it. Something that no one'll notice but that'll jam the whole thing up come morning. Bad enough that it'll stop work. Cost them. Make them think about how short-sighted it was to let their most experienced slaughtermen go cos wouldn't they come in handy right now, with this new equipment, this brand-spanking-new fancy shit just a pile of chains and hooks and pulleys when it's not whirring whirring whirring through an engine.

And if a bar doesn't work, well, he'll think of something. Trusts that his nose for luck won't let him down now. There's enough hooks and chains on the kill floor to cause some havoc. And if all else fails, he can always start a fire. Something little, just enough to shut it down for a week or so. Wouldn't do to put the whole place out of work for a month, that won't win him any friends. But he thinks about Wilco's face. How broken he was when they turned the union boys away at the gate. When everyone else, the packers and boners and fellmongerers, their heads low, had to get back to work, when the union decided it didn't have their back at all.

This'll put some fire back in him. In all the boys. And he won't have to say anything, word'll spread, it always does.

It was Jack King, they'll say, Jack King who broke the chain, who took a stand for the slaughts.

And that, he thinks, will be enough. He'll have done what needs to be done. He can hold his head high as he walks back through that door to Peggy, to hold his daughter in his arms, be the man he reckons he could be.

*

At home – after they've walked back through the streets alive with punters and the cheering and yahooing of a cup day done well, and a night still warm – Peggy holds Hilda against her chest long after she's fed and fallen asleep.

When she heard Kathleen say his name, she knew that she would turn and face Jack. Knew that she could, flanked by the women from the bagging room, knowing Lil was an arm's reach away. He would never hurt her there.

She doesn't hate him. She wishes she did. But when she sees his face go soft as he looks at Hilda, something loosens inside of her.

Perhaps. A glittering, hopeful traitor of a word.

A man like Jack King, he gives it everything he's got. His charm, his attention, his adoration, his rage. You have to take it all rolled into one.

And she could live with that, she could, for Hilda, for the six days a week he came home with kisses and handfuls of coins like treasure, for the father she imagines he could be, throwing his girl in the air, like a giant standing between her and anything that will harm her.

It's the seventh day she knows she is not prepared to live with.

He'd promised to make it right, and she'd nodded, but who knows what he believes she has agreed to.

Lil tried to get it out of her on the walk home, worried, Peggy knows, that she's going to take him back. Well, Lil doesn't know what she's become. That when they pulled her baby out with those great ugly tongs, something was left in the space – something hard, something brave.

When he comes knocking this week, as she knows he will, probably with gifts in his arms, that smile that still does something to her body despite everything, she will tell him they are done for good. That she wants the papers signed, to take back her name. She cannot undo Jack King, she doesn't want to – look at this creature she has in her arms, half him, because of him.

But she can start again, without him.

The morning is fine and clear with the breeze blowing over and away and despite being up three times in the night making bottles and pacing the hall, Lil feels awake and alive, as though she has grown taller, or got younger, or just been waiting for days like these.

She is opening the curtains behind Angliss's desk, cranking the window a smidge to let in the good air, when she hears the shouting across the courtyard. At first she assumes it is the boys skylarking with a sheep got loose or a dirty joke that's sent them all off.

But that's not quite it.

The shouting gets nearer and then there is the hammering of feet up the steps, pounding on the door.

She hears Dulcie hurry to answer and hears the men stumble over their words. 'Where's the boss, is he in? Where is he?'

'He's not in till this afternoon. What is it?' Lil says sharply, entering the room from Angliss's office so that they all stare at her.

'An accident, Miss Martin,' says one of the boning boys.

'What do you mean. Where?'

Murphy steps forward. 'It's not for you ladies, the foreman wanted the boss—'

'For goodness sake, Murphy, have you got Doc Henderson there? Do I need to call for an ambulance? What is it?'

But the men shake their heads and back out of the room. She hurries after them. Even when a boy turns back and says, 'Please, Miss Martin, it's not right for you to see.' That only makes her walk faster.

The foreman turns around. 'Wilco found him. We stopped the rest of the boys going in.'

'Found who? In where?' she demands, but they do not say, only hurry ahead of her, the boots clacking on the bluestones, so that she notices, for the first time, that she cannot hear the whirring of the chain.

At the door, she will not be held back. Lil steps into the room, her eyes adjusting to the darker light as she looks for a man on the floor, a group huddled about, perhaps blood. She is ready, she holds her upper body still.

But he is not on the floor.

As she looks up to the window, she catches the shape that is at odds with the machinery. A curve, a slip of fabric, a hand.

Her mouth drops open.

There is a man suspended from the chain, caught, not like an animal pulled along it by its foot, but by his neck, an arm, a tangle of fabric and limbs that makes no sense, but makes her turn to her side and gush up her tea all over the floor.

'Take him down!' she says hoarsely, wiping her mouth, then again when no one moves, yelling it. 'Take him down!'

'We thought we should wait, miss, till the boss comes.'

Lil turns on the man who has spoken, her mouth wide as if to scream, to vomit again, and the foreman moves forward.

'For God's sake, Wilkins, get him down from there!'

She wants them to be quiet, to be silent, to not say the name for if they don't say it, it can't be real. Lil feels like she will fall, faint, but she tells her body it must stand up right now, it is all she has to do, to keep watch, to make sure, to bear witness.

That it is him.

That it is not him.

'Take him down, by God,' she whispers.

And they do. The boning boys, and they are so tender with him, this giant of a man, holding from below to keep him steady while someone fetches bolt cutters, another takes a saw. They take apart the chain, break it down to its pieces to fetch his broken body from its clutches. And when they have him down, they bear the weight of him on their shoulders and sink onto their knees so they can bring him gently to the floor.

Only when she is sure, when she sees that jaw, that mouth, God, that beautiful, terrifying face, only then does she begin to weep.

Peggy looks at the bath water. A large bubble quivers gently between the surface of the water and the tin edge of the bath. Where the sun hits it, there are tiny rainbow whorls on the slippery surface. She does not believe yet what Lil has told her although it is clear she tells the truth.

'But how did he get in?' Peggy asks, very quiet, very still.

Lil rubs her back with one hand, holds Hilda wet and babbling in the other.

'It can't be,' Peggy says. The bubble still holds. Shimmering and quivering.

In Lil's embrace, Hilda starts to cry.

'Here,' Peggy says and reaches for the baby.

Lil bends down and places her in Peggy's arms, tucking the towel in around her.

'There, there, baby,' says Peggy, singsong, beginning to rock, and Lil kneels down where she is and puts her arms around them both, rocking in time, holding them together.

After, Lil feels older. Older in her bones. But also as if those bones had taken root deep in the ground. And her eyes are open, fully it seems for the very first time, to see the way things *are*, not the way she wishes them to be.

It takes time. Time for Peggy to weep and rage and soften and smile again. She swings between grief and relief, as is right, as it should be. Hilda is a light, their heartbeat, the centre around which their new lives revolve. Lil told Angliss she needs a day off a week so she can help out at home, and now she has a day with Hilda all to herself while Peggy goes with her friend, Moira, and they make plans and smoke too many cigarettes as far as she's concerned and Peggy's talking about going back to the meat-works a few days or somewhere else maybe, but there is spark in the girl, and it lights them all.

Walking down Barkly Street, Lil looks, really looks at the filth, at the barefoot children, the mulberry bruises blooming underneath pancake powder, greasy fingerprints on shopfronts, a man in a hat and a waistcoat pissing in the street, a woman in the cool room at the delicatessen with her hands in the folds of the delivery boy's pants. She sees the lemon blossom and the knobbled growths of wasp nests. She sees it all. Holds onto it all.

When she unfolds the newspaper – spreading the pages among the morning dishes, a bottle half-full of milk, a half-eaten piece of toast, the exquisite details of her new life – she senses something in the pitch of the journalists, a growing fervour, a bloody lust to descend again to the very hell pits of war.

The years pass in the Angliss office, and Lil will note the red marks that stain the page next to the names of the employees who are union boys are fewer and fewer. She will feel a sadness for a time past, but she will embrace what is coming, things new and bright even as her heels grow square and fat, and her body – which will stand the test of time as good as any – will spread out, the way the city keeps spreading, until Footscray is no longer on the outskirts like it once was. Lil Martin will be there to see the new man, Seelaf, come in, will hear him call her 'comrade', will laugh at this, but she will also see the fire he lights in the eyes of the men, and this time, in the eyes of the women too.

She won't live to see the last days, and that is as it should be. Won't live to see the fire that sparks late one night in rat-chewed wires that sizzle and smoulder in nine decades of sawdust and blood and tallow. A fire that takes with a ferocity that sends pregnant women to stay with families in the country so they won't inhale the cocktail of chemicals, billowing up from the old works. She won't be there later, when the bulldozers move in towards the acrid, charred shell of the buildings and take it apart, pushing the lumber and steel, the bricks and bluestone and plaster and machinery into great piles before they scoop what they can into trucks and take it all away.

Sometimes, though, in the clear light of morning, shutting a gate to one of the new townhouses where the meatworks used to stand, a person might notice a woman striding out along the street, might catch the click of her heels against the old bluestone kerb, pay attention to the proud tilt of her head. Might see her turn and call back to the child who runs after her, one child, then two, might notice the other woman threading an arm through her friend's. Might think that they look like women on the cusp of something, ready to launch into a day that is as yet unknown.

But then the women will fade – a trick of the light. And the sound of a steam whistle could just be the play of the wind, echoing down past the wetlands and into the bowl of the river, where in the deep there are old fish flashing their mudglitter scales while the river is waiting and watching and knowing and counting the passing of time in its rivery way.

∞

Before Now Next

We wait. River is what river does, has always done. Sings in riffles, babbles, torrents, seeps. We carry. Persist. Gouge out new paths when we find our way blocked. Mightier in confluence, we push on push through wayseek the lowest paths through rock and sand and concrete, through bridges and dam walls and barriers built to hold us back. We are more than you have ever imagined. In our rock nooks and deep pools, fish spawn, glowing orbs of promise drifting, sticking, manymany, waiting to become. We are vein and pulse, carve rock like bone, make life, take life, carry seed from here to there, carry sister.

Come now, quiet, see where we begin, rock studded mountain soak, all sky high and clear, birthed from deep within the earth and then down down, always gathering ourself – thalweg, stream, cascade, cataract, meander – assembling and amassing until we flow, we flow through forest grassland gorge plains until we delta disgorge the end of us, the end of the water but not the end for the river, the river eternal into the saltdeep of the mouth turning the waves tannin curling back in on themselves against a shore – footsteps, no footsteps, no matter to us – shhhh quiet now, can you hear us? Waiting, patient, patient to see what you all think of next.

Acknowledgements

I live and work on the unceded lands of the Wurundjeri people of the Kulin Nation. Much of the novel is set on these lands and those of the Woiwurrung and Bunurong people. I spent significant time writing on both Dja Dja Wurrung and Bunurong lands and on Takarunga, Aotearoa. I acknowledge the Traditional Owners of these lands and waters and recognise their continuing connection and care for country that was never ceded. I pay my respects to Elders past, present and future.

Countless books, articles, conversations, writers and great brains inspired and assisted me in writing this novel – if I could publish a novella of gratitude I would. In lieu – the following people and organisations made it to the top of the thank you pile.

The historical section of this novel set in Footscray includes reference to real people and events. While I've made every effort to ensure historical accuracy in regards to dates, the Angliss meatworks and the strike, I have taken fictional liberties. For further reading on the Angliss Meatworks and the slaughtermen's strike of 1933, I encourage readers to seek out *The Lifeblood of Footscray: Working Lives at the Angliss Meatworks* (edited by Chris Healy) and John Lack's *A History of Footscray*. I am indebted to the following people and organisations who assisted me with research and interviews: the Mildenhall family, Chris Healy, the late Peter Haffenden and the Living Museum of the West, Footscray Historical Society, Michael Leunig, Sarah Matthews at the State Library Victoria, Paul Doughty at the Australian Council of Trade Unions, David Sornig, Graham Bird, Denise Arnold, Alice Cerreto, Paul Conway from the Australasian Meat Industry Employees Union, Frank Herd of M.C. Herd and my local butcher, Adam Woollard of Hurstbridge Fine Meats and Providore.

Enormous thanks to my agent Pippa Masson who always has my back, and to my incredible publishing team at Simon & Schuster Australia: Ben Ball, Lizzie King, Anna O'Grady, Fiona Henderson, Dan Ruffino, and the entire team who work so hard. Thank you to Josh Durham for the electrifying cover design and visual designer, Eva Harbridge, who created the Hummingbird Algorithm diagram. Our collaboration has been one of the most exciting and influential parts of writing this novel.

Without the writing community I am privileged to be a part of, this book would not exist. To all the writers I know and adore – thank you. Particular thanks to those who assisted with research – Sally Piper, Mandy Beaumont, Sian Prior, Claire Wright, Chris Flynn – and to Sam Coley, Alice Bishop, and Inga Simpson for reading early drafts. Thank you Pip Williams, Karen Viggers, Tony Birch, Laura Jean McKay, Michelle de Kretser, Tegan Bennett Daylight, Sarah Winman, Toni Jordan and Sophie Cunningham for your generous support. Thank you to my writing hearts – Penni Russon, Zana Fraillon, Penny Harrison, Meg Dunley, Katherine Collette, Venita Munir, Kim Hood, Nicky Heaney, Emily Brewin, Victoria Hannan, Alice Bishop and Alice Robinson – who help in ALL the ways. Sarah Sentilles and her Word Cave crews provided invaluable magic and support.

Many people and organisations allowed me space and time to work: thank you Cathy and Peter Rogers, RMIT's McCraith

House, Else Fitzgerald, Tess Lethborg, Andrea Rowe, Varuna and the Michael King Writers Centre and Creative Victoria.

Starting a PhD in the middle of writing this novel was both inspiring and a little mad. I'm grateful for the insights and support of my supervisors, Julienne van Loon and Ronnie Scott, the NovelLab crew – Leanne Hall, Romy Ash, Nicola Redhouse, Rose Michael – the entire PRS gang and RMIT PWE staff and students.

The hundreds of guests Katherine Collette and I have interviewed for *The First Time* podcast over the past five years have provided invaluable wisdom and support, I feel incredibly lucky for every minute of this podcast adventure, and that I get to do it with you, Katherine. Thank you Jill Langhammer for your generosity, skill and support.

My non-writing crew keep me grounded and are the most loyal, wonderful friends a human could hope for. Thank you for being my village and for engaging in conversations on all manner of bookish things. I love you. Special thanks to Shay Gardner, Eri Wells and Christine French. My family – especially Mum, Dad, Maggie and Helen – thank you for EVERYTHING and especially Mum for close reading and Lorinda for expert healthcare editing checks! My beloved grandmama, to whom this book is dedicated, left us before I could put this book in her hands. I miss her every day.

Booksellers, festival creators, and most of all READERS – all those who make the book world keep turning – us writers would not be here without you: thank you for your energy, enthusiasm and passion for books and for bringing the joy and community to what can often be a lonely gig.

My biggest gratitude and love always, to Ad, Gracie and Etta. This book and all it entailed has been like another member of our family this past four years; thank you for giving me space, time and support to do my work. I love you a bazillion.

If you enjoyed *The Hummingbird Effect*, you'll love *The Mother Fault*, also by Kate Mildenhall.

Available now.

Photograph © Gemma Carr

Kate Mildenhall is a writer and teacher. Her debut novel, *Skylarking*, was longlisted for the Voss Literary Prize and the Indie Book Awards in 2017, and her bestselling *The Mother Fault* was longlisted for the 2021 ABIA General Fiction Book of the Year and shortlisted for the 2020 Aurealis Awards. Kate teaches creative writing and co-hosts *The First Time* podcast – which features conversations with Australian writers – and is currently undertaking a PhD in creative practice at RMIT University. Kate lives in Hurstbridge on Wurundjeri lands, with her partner and two children.

Find out more about Kate at katemildenhall.com or connect on Instagram (@kmildenhall) or Facebook (www.facebook.com/katemildenhallwriter).